Bart Ridgeley: A Story of Northern Ohio

A. G. Riddle

ESPRIOS DIGITAL PUBLISHING

BART RIDGELEY;

A STORY OF NORTHERN OHIO.

BY

A. G. RIDDLE

1873.

CONTENTS.

CHAPTER I.

A FAILURE.

He could see from the top of the hill, down which the road wound to the river, that the bridge was gone, and he paused for a moment with an involuntary feeling that it was useless to go forward; but remembering that his way led across, at all events, he walked down to the bank. There it ran, broad, rapid, and in places apparently deep. He looked up and down in vain: no lodged drift-wood; no fallen trees; no raft or wreck; a recent freshet had swept all clear to high-water mark, and the stream rolled, and foamed, and boiled, and gurgled, and murmured in the afternoon August sun as gleefully and mockingly as if its very purpose was to baffle the wearied youth who looked into and over its changing tide.

In coming from Cleveland that morning he had taken a wrong road, and now, at mid-afternoon, he found his progress stayed with half his day's journey still before him. It would have been but a moment's task to remove his clothes and swim over, but the region was open and clear on that side for a considerable distance, and notwithstanding his solitude, he hesitated to make the transit in that manner. It was apparent, from the little-travelled road, that the stream had been forded by an indirect course, and one not easily determined from the shore. It occurred to him that possibly some team from Cleveland might pass along and take him over; and, wearied, he sat down by his light valise to wait, and at least rest; and as he gazed into the rapid current a half-remembered line of a forgotten poet ran and ran through his mind thus:

"Which running runs, and will run forever on. "

His reflections were not cheerful. Three months before he had gone over to Hudson with a very young man's scheme of maintaining himself at school, and finally in college; and finding it impracticable, had strayed off to the lower part of the State with a vague idea of going down the Mississippi, and, perhaps, to Texas. He spent some time with relatives near Cincinnati, and under a sudden impulse — all his plans, as he was pleased to call them, were impulses — he had returned, adding, as he was conscious, another to a long-growing list

1

of failures, which, in the estimation of many acquaintances, also included himself.

His meditations were interrupted by the sound of an approaching carriage coming over the hill. He knew the horses. They were Judge Markham's, and driven by the Judge himself, alone, in a light vehicle. The young man sprang up at the sight. Here was the man whom of all men he most respected, and feared as much as he could fear any man, whose good opinion he most cared to have, and yet who he was conscious had a dislike for him.

The Judge would certainly take him over the river, and so home, but in his frank and ingenuous nature how could he face him on his almost ignominious return? He stood still, a little away from the carriage-track, half wishing he might not be seen. He was seen, however, and a close observer might have discovered the half sneer on the otherwise handsome and manly face of the Judge, who had taken in the situation. The horses were held in a walk as they came down near where the young man stood, with a half ashamed, yet eager, expression of countenance, and turned partly away, as if he expected—in fact, wished for nothing.

"What are you doing here? " called out the Judge.

It was not a wholly courteous inquiry, and scarcely necessary, though not purposely offensive; but the tone and manner struck like an insult on the young man's sensitive spirit, and his answer went back a little sharply:

"I am waiting for the river to run by, "

"Ah! I see. Well, I am glad you have found something that suits you."

There was no mistaking the sarcasm of this remark, and perhaps its sting was deeper than was meant. The Judge was not an unkind man, though he did not relish the reply to his question; he held up his horses on the margin of the water, and perhaps he wanted to be asked by this pert youth for the favor of a passage over. Of course the petition was not, and never would have been made. He lingered a moment, and without another word entered the river, and, turning his horses' heads up stream for a short distance, drove out on the other side; as he turned into the regular track again, he caught a view of the young man standing impassive on the same spot where he first saw him.

It is possible that Judge Markham, the most wealthy and popular man of his region, did not feel wholly at ease as, with his fine team and empty carriage, he drove away, leaving the weary, travel-stained youth standing on the other side of the river; and it is possible that the form of the deserted one may be brought to his memory in the hereafter.

"'Something that suits me'—'something that suits me! ' All right, Judge Markham! " and as the carriage was hidden in the woods, the waters that rolled on between them were as nothing to the bitter, swelling tide that, for a moment, swept through the young man's bosom. He was undecided no longer.

Removing his boots and stockings, he entered the river at the point, and, following the course taken by the Judge, he passed out, and resumed his journey homeward.

As he walked rapidly onward, the momentary bitterness subsided. He was not one to hate, or cherish animosities, but he was capable of deep impressions, and of forming strong resolutions. There was a chord of melancholy running through his nature, which, under excitement, often vibrated the longest; and almost any strong emotion left behind a tone of sadness that lingered for hours, and sometimes for days, although his mind was normally buoyant and hopeful.

As he went on over the hills, in the rude pioneer country of Northern Ohio, thirty-six or seven years ago, he thought sad-colored thoughts of the past, or, rather, he recalled sombre memories of the, to him, far-off time, when, with his mother and brothers, he formed one of a sobbing group around a bed whereon a gasping, dying man was vainly trying to say some last words; of afterwards awakening in the deep nights, and listening to the unutterably sweet and mournful singing of his mother, unable to sleep in her loneliness; of the putting away of his baby brother, and the jubilee when he was brought back; of the final breaking up of the family, and of his own first goings away; of the unceasing homesickness and pining with which he always languished for home in his young boy years; of the joy with which he always hurried home, the means by which he would prolong his stay, and the anguish with which he went away again. His mother was to him the chief good. For him, like Providence, she always was, and he could imagine no possible good, or even existence, without her—it would be the end of the world when she ceased to be. And he remembered all the places where he had lived, and the many times he had run away. And then came the memory of Julia Markham, as she was years ago, when he lived in her neighborhood, and her sweet and beautiful mother used to intrust her to his care, in the walks to and from school, down on the State road—Julia, with her great wonderful eyes, and world of wavy hair, and red lips; and then, as she grew into beautiful and ever more beautiful girlhood, he used to be more and more at Judge Markham's house, and used to read to Julia's mother and herself. It was there that he discovered Shakespeare, and learned to like him, and Milton, whom he didn't like and wouldn't read, and the Sketch Book, and Knickerbocker's History, and Cooper's novels, and Scott, and, more than all, Byron, whom Mrs. Markham did not want him to read, recommending, instead, Young's Night Thoughts, and Pollock's Course of Time, and Southey—the dear good woman!

And then came a time when he was in the store of Markham & Co., and finally was taken from the counter, because of his sharp words to customers, and set at the books, and sent away from that post because he illustrated them with caricatures on the margins, and smart personal rhymes. Julia was sixteen, and as sweet a romping, hoydenish, laughing, brave, strong girl as ever bewitched the heart of dreaming youth; and he had taught her to ride on horseback; and then she was sent off, away "down country, " to the centre of the world, to Boston, where were uncles and aunts, and was gone, oh, ever and ever so long! —half a lifetime—nearly two years—and came back; and then his thoughts became confused. Then he thought of Judge Markham, and now he was sure that the Judge did not like him; and he remembered that Julia's mother, as he came towards manhood, was kind and patronizing, and that when he went to say good-by to Julia, three months ago, although she knew he was coming, she was not at home, and he only saw her mother and Nell Roberts. Then he thought of all the things he had tried to do within the last two years, and how he had done none of them. People had not liked him, and he had not suspected why, and had not cared. People liked his elder brothers, and he was glad and proud of it; and a jumble of odds and ends and fragments became tangled and snarled in his mind. What would people say of his return? Did he care? He asked nobody's leave to go, and came back on his own account. But his mother—she would look sad; but she would be glad. It certainly was a mistake, his going; could it be a blunder, his returning?

He was thinking shallowly; but deeper thoughts came to him. He began to believe that easy places did not exist; and he scorned to seek them for himself, if they did. The world was as much to be struggled with in one place as another; and, after all, was not the struggle mainly with one's own self, and could that be avoided? Then what in himself was wrong? what should be fought against? Who would tell him? Men spoke roughly to him, and he answered back sharply. He couldn't help doing that. How could he be blamed? He suspected he might be.

He knew there were better things than to chop and clear land, and make black salts, or tend a saw-mill, or drive oxen, or sell tape and calico; but, in these woods, poor and unfriended, how could he find them? Was not his brother Henry studying law at Jefferson, and were they not all proud of him, and did not everybody expect great things of him? But Henry was different from him. Dr. Lyman believed in him; Judge Markham spoke with respect of him. Julia Markham—how inexpressibly lovely and radiant and distant and inaccessible she appeared! And then he felt sore, as if her father had dealt him a blow, and he thought of his sending him away the year before, and wished he had explained. No matter. How he writhed again and again under the sting of his contemptuous sarcasm! "He wouldn't even pick me up; would leave me to lie by the wayside. "

Towards sundown, weary and saddened, he reached the centre, "Jugville, " as he had named it, years before, in derision. He was a mile and a half from home, and paused a moment to sit on the platform in front of "Marlow's Hotel, " and rest. The loungers were present in more than usual force, —Jo and Biather Alexander, old Neaze Savage, old Cal Chase, Tinker, —any number of old and not highly-esteemed acquaintances.

"Hullo, Bart Ridgeley! is that you? "

Bart did not seem to think it necessary to affirm or deny.

"Ben away, hain't ye? Must a-gone purty much all over all creation, these last three months. How's all the folks where you ben? "

No reply. A nod to one or two of the dozen attracted towards him was the only notice he took of them, seeming not to hear the question and comments of Tinker. His silence tempted old Cal, the small joker of the place, to open:

"You's gone an everlastin' while. S'pose you hardly know the place, it's changed so. "

"It has changed some, " he answered to this; "its bar-room loafers are a good deal more unendurable, and its fools, always large, have increased in size. "

A good-natured laugh welcomed this reply.

"There, uncle Cal, it 'pears to me you've got it, " said one.

"'Pears to me we've all got it, " was the response of that worthy.

"Come in, Bart, " said the landlord, "and take something on the strength o' that. "

"Thank you, I will be excused; I have a horror of a sudden death; " and, taking up his valise, he started across the fields to the near woods.

"Bully! " "Good! " "You've got that! " cried several to the discomfited seller of drinks. "It is your treat; we'll risk the stuff! " and the party turned in to the bar to realize their expectations.

"There is one thing 'bout it, " said Bi, "Bart hain't changed much, anyway. "

"And there's another thing 'bout it, " said uncle Bill, "a chap that carries such a sassy tongue should be sassy able. He'll answer some chap, some day, that wun't stan' it. "

"The man that picks him up'll find an ugly customer; he'd be licked afore he begun. I tell you what, them Ridgeley boys is no fighters, but the stuff's in 'em, and Bart's filled jest full. I'd as liv tackle a young painter. " This was Neaze's view.

"That's so, " said Jo. "Do you remember the time he had here last fall, with that braggin' hunter chap, Mc-Something, who came along with his rifle, darin' all hands about here to shute with him? He had one of them new peck-lock rifles, and nobody dared shute with him; and Bart came along, and asked to look at the feller's gun, and said something 'bout it, and Mc-Somebody dared him to shute, and Bart sent over to Haw's and got 'old Potleg, ' that Steve Patterson shot himself with, and loaded 'er up, and then the hunter feller wouldn't shute except on a bet, and Bart hadn't but fifty cents, and they shot twenty rods off-hand, and Bart beat him; and they doubled the bet, and Bart beat agin, and they went on till Bart won more'n sixty dollars. Sometimes the feller shot wild, and Bart told him he'd have to get a dog to hunt where he hit, and he got mad, and Bart picked up his first half-dollar and pitched it to Jotham, who put up the mark, and left the rest on the ground. "

"There come mighty near bein' trouble then, an' there would ha' ben ef the Major hadn't took Bart off, " said Bi.

And while these rough, good-natured men talked him over, Barton walked off southerly, across the newly-shorn meadow, to the woods. Twilight was in their depths, and shadows were stealing mysteriously out, and already the faint and subtle aroma which the gathering dew releases from foliage, came out like an incense to bathe the quick and healthy senses of the wearied youth. He removed his hat, opened his bosom, expanded his nostrils and lungs, and drank it as the bee takes nectar from the flowers. What an exquisite sense of relief and quiet came to him, as he found himself lost in the shadows of the young night! Not a tree in these woods that he did not know, and they all seemed to reach out their mossy arms with their myriad of little, cool, green hands, to welcome him back. They knew nothing of his failures and disappointments, and were more sympathizing than the coarse and ribald men whose rude taunts he had just heard, and to whose admiration he was as indifferent as to their sarcasm. These were grand and beautiful maple woods, free from tangling underbrush, and standing thick and stately on wide, gentle slopes; and to-night the lisping breath of the summer evening came to this young but sad and burdened heart, with whispers soothing and restful.

He had never been so long from home before; the nearer he approached it, the more intense his longings grew, and he passed rapidly through the open glades, disappearing momentarily in the obscurity of the thickets, past the deserted sugar camp, until finally the woods grew lighter, the trees more scattered, and he reached the open pasture lands in sight of the low farm-house, which held his mother and home. How strange, and yet familiar, even an absence of only three months made everything! The distance of his journey seemed to have expanded the months into years.

He entered by a back way, and found his mother in the little front sitting-room. She arose with—"Oh, Barton, have you come? " and received from his lips and eyes the testimonials of his heart. She was slight, lithe, and well made, with good Puritan blood, brain, and resolution; and as she stood holding her child by both his hands, and looking eagerly into his face, a stranger would have noticed their striking resemblance. Her face, though womanly, was too marked and strong for beauty. Both had the square decisive brow, and wide, deep eyes—hers a lustrous black, and his dark gray or blue, as the light was. Her hair was abundant, and very dark; his a light brown, thick, wavy, and long. Both had the same aquiline nose, short upper-lip, bland, firm, but soft mouth, and well-formed chin. Her complexion was dark, and his fair—too fair for a man.

"Yes, mother, I have come; are you glad to see me? "

"Glad—very glad, but sorry. " She had a good deal of the Spartan in her nature, and received her son with a sense of another failure, and failures were not popular with her. "I did not hear from you—was anxious about you; but now, when you come back to the nothing for you here, I know you found less elsewhere. "

"Well, mother, I know I am a dreadful drag even on your patience, and I fear a burden besides, instead of a help. I need not say much to you; you, at least, understand me. It was a mistake to go away as I did, and I bring back all I carried away, with the result of some reflection. I can do as much here as anywhere. I hoped I could do something for you, and I, poor unweaned baby and booby, can do better for myself near you than elsewhere. "

Not much was said. She was thoughtful, deep natured, tender, and highly strung, though not demonstrative, and these qualities in him were modified by the soft, sensuous, imaginative elements that came to him—all that he inherited, except his complexion, from his father.

His mother gave him supper, and he sat and inquired about home events, and gave her a pleasant account of their relatives in the lower part of the State. He said nothing of the discovery he had made among them—her own family relatives—that she had married beneath her, and had never been forgiven; and he fancied that he discovered some opening of old, old sorrows, dating back to her girlhood days, as he talked of her relatives. The two younger brothers came rattling in—George, a handsome, eager young threshing-machine, a bright, broad-browed boy, and Edward, older, with drooping head and thoughtful face, and with something of Bart's readiness at reply. George ran to him—

"Oh, Bart, I am so glad! and there is so much—a flock of turkeys—and a wolverine, and oh! so many pigeons and everything—more than you can shoot in all the fall! "

"Well, captain, we will let them all live, I guess, unless that wolverine comes around! "

"There is a real, true wolverine; several have seen him, and he screeches, and yells, and climbs trees, and everything! "

"There *is* something around, " said Edward. "Theodore and Bill Johnson heard him, over in the woods, not a week ago. "

"Likely enough, " replied Bart; "but wolverines don't climb. There may be a panther. Now, Ed, what has been going on on the farm? Is the haying done? "

"Yes; and the wheat is all in, and most all the oats. The corn is splendid in the old elm lot, and then the Major has been chopping down your old sugar camp, where we worked when you came home from old Hewitt's. "

"Oh, dear, that was the loveliest bit of woodland, in the bend of the creek, in all the magnificent woods; well? "

"He has nearly finished the Jenks house, " resumed Edward, "and is now at Snow's, in Auburn. He said you would be home before now."

9

"What about his colts? "

"Oh, Arab runs about wild as ever, and he has Dolf with him. "

"How many hands has he with him? "

"Four or five. "

"Dr. Lyman asked about you, " said George, "and wondered where you were. He said you would be back in three weeks, and that something must have happened. "

"It would be lucky for the Doctor's patients, " replied Bart, "if something should keep him away three days. "

"I guess he wants you to go a-fishing with him. They had a great time down there the other day—he, and Mr. Young, and Sol Johnson. They undertook to put up a sail as Henry and you do, and it didn't work, and they came near upsetting; and' Sol and old man Young were scart, and old Young thought he would get drownded. Oh, it must have been fun! "

And so the boys chippered, chirped, and laughed on to a late bed-time, and then went to bed perfectly happy.

Then came inquiries about Henry, who had written not long before, and had wondered why he had not heard from Barton; and, at last, wearied and worn with his three hundred miles' walk, Bart bade his mother good-night, and went to his old room, to rest and sleep as the young, and healthful, and hopeful, without deep sorrows or the stings of conscience, may do. In the strange freaks of a half-sleeping fancy, in his dreams, he remembered to have heard the screech of a wild animal, and to have seen the face of Julia Markham, pale with the mingled expression of courage and fear.

CHAPTER II.

THE BLUE CHAMBER.

In the morning he found the front yard had a wild and tangled, and the garden a neglected look, and busied himself, with the boys, in improving their appearance.

In the afternoon he overhauled a small desk, the contents of which soon lay about on the floor. There were papers of all colors and sizes—scraps, single sheets, and collections of several pages—all covered with verses in many hands, from that of the young boy to elegant clerkly manuscript. They seemed to represent every style of poetic composition. It would have been amusing to watch the manner and expression with which the youth dealt with these children of his fancy, and to listen to his exclamations of condensed criticism. He evidently found little to commend. As he opened or unrolled one after another, and caught the heading, or a line of the text, he dashed it to the floor, with a single word of contempt, disgust, or derision. "Faugh! " "Oh! " "Pshaw! " "Blank verse? Blank enough! " Some he lingered over for a moment, but his brow never cleared or relented, and each and all were condemned with equal justice and impartiality. When the last was thrown down, and he was certain that none remained, he rose and contemplated their crumpled and creased forms with calm disdain.

"Oh, dear! you thought, some of you, that you might possibly be poetry, you miserable weaklings and beguilers! You are not even verses—are hardly rhymes. You are, one and all, without sense or sound. " His brow grew severe in its condemnation. "There! take that! and that! and that! "—stamping them with his foot; "poor broken-backed, halting, limping, club-footed, no-going, unbodied, unsouled, nameless things. How do you like it? What business had you to be? You had no right to be born—never were born; had no capacity for birth; you don't even amount to failures! Words are wasted on you: let me see if you'll burn. " Lighting one, he threw it upon the hearth. "It does! I am surprised at that. I rather like it. How blue and faint the flame is—it hardly produces smoke, and"— watching until it was consumed—"no ashes. Too ethereal for smoke and ashes. Let me try the rest; " and he did.

11

He then opened a small drawer and took out a portfolio, in which were various bits of bristol-board and paper, covered with crayon and pen sketches, and some things in water-colors—all giving evidence of a ready hand which showed some untaught practice. Whether his sense of justice was somewhat appeased, or because he regarded them with more favor, or reserved them for another occasion, was, perhaps, uncertain. Singularly enough, on each of them, no matter what was the subject, appeared one or more young girl's heads—some full-faced, some three-fourths, and more in profile—all spirited, all looking alike, and each having a strong resemblance to Julia Markham. Two or three were studied and deliberate attempts. He contemplated these long and earnestly, and laid them away with a sigh. They undoubtedly saved the collection.

That night he wrote to Henry:

"DEAR BROTHER, —I am back, of course. It is an unpleasant way of mine—this coming back. It was visionary for me to try a fall with the sciences at Hudson. You would have been too many for them; I ran away. I found Colton sick at Cincinnati. The Texan Rangers had left. I looked into the waters of the Ohio, running and hurrying away returnlessly to the south-west. Lord, how they called to me in their liquid offers to carry me away! They seemed to draw me to linger, and gurgle, and murmur in little staying, coaxing eddies at my feet, to persuade me to go.

"How near one seems to that far-off region of fever and swamp, of sun and sea, of adventure and blood, and old buccaneering, standing by those swift waters, already on their way thither! Should I go? Was I not too good to go, and be lost? Think of the high moral considerations involved? No matter, I didn't go—I came! Well!

"On reflection—and I thus assume that I do reflect—I think men don't find opportunities, or, if they do, they don't know them. One must make an opportunity for himself, and then he will know what to do with it. The other day I stood on the other side of the Chagrin waiting for an opportunity, and it didn't come, and I made one. I waded through, and liked it, and that was not the only lesson I learned at the same time. But that other was for my personal improvement. A man can as well find the material for his opportunity in one place as another. See how I excuse myself!

"Just now, I am a reformed young Blue Beard. Fatima and her sister may go—have gone. I have just overhauled my 'Blue Chamber, ' taken down all my suspended wives, and burned them. They ended in smoke. Lord! there wasn't flesh and blood enough in them all to decompose, and they gave out no odor even while burning. I burned them all, cleaned off all the blood-spots, ventilated the room, opened the windows, and will turn it to a workshop. No more sighing for the unattainable, no more grasping at the intangible, no more clutching at the impalpable. I am no poet, and we don't want poetry. Our civilization isn't old enough. Poets, like other maggots, will be produced when fermentation comes. I am going about the humdrum and the useful. I am about as low in the public estimation as I can well go; at any rate I am down on hard land, which will be a good starting-point. Now don't go off and become sanguine over me, nor trouble yourself much about me.

"'The world will find me after many a day, ' as Southey says of one of his books. I doubt if it ever did. The Doctor contends that Southey was a poet; but then he thinks I am, also!

"What a deuce of a clamor is made about this new comet or planet! What a useful thing to us poor, mud-stranded mortals to find out that there is another little fragment of a world, away some hundreds of millions of miles, outside of no particular where—for I believe this astronomical detective is only on its track! The Doctor is in ecstacies over it, takes it as a special personal favor, and declaims luminously and constellationally about writing one's name among the stars, like that frisky cow who, in jumping over the moon, upon a time, made the milky way. I've always had some doubts about that exploit; but then there is the mark she left. Your friend Roberts is uneasy about this new star business; he is afraid that it will unsettle the cheese market, and he don't know about it, nor do I.

"There! I got home only last night, and haven't heard any news to write you. Some time I will tell of two or three things I saw and heard, and about some of our cousins, who regard us as belonging to the outer and lower skirts of the race. If I am to be one end of a family, let it be the beginning.

"Mother sends love. Edward and George speak of you constantly. I've not seen our Major since my return.

"Write me a good, sharp, cutting, criticising, deuced brotherly letter soon. As ever,

"BART.

"P. S. Have you read Pickwick?

"B. "

It was full of badinage, with only a dip or two into an absorbing purpose that he had fully formed, and which he evidenced to himself by the summary expulsion of the muses.

In the world of nature and humanity, is there such an embodiment of contradictions and absurdities as a youth in his transit from the dreamland of boyhood to the battle-field of manhood, through a region partaking of both, and abounding with strange products of its own? I am not speaking of the average boy, such boys as make up the male mass of the world—the undreaming, unthinking, plodding, drudging, sweating herd, whose few old commonplace, well-worn ideas don't possess the power of reproduction, and whose thoughts are thirteenth or thirteen hundredth-handed, and transmitted unimpregnated to other dullards, and whose life and spirit is that of the young animal merely—but a real young man, one of possibilities, intended for a man, and not merely for a male, one in whom the primitive forces of nature are planted, and who may develop into a new driving or forming power. What a mad, impulsive, freaky thing it is! You may see him bruising his still soft head a score of times against the impossible, and he will still contend that he can do it. He will spring frantically up the face of an unclimbable precipice, as the young salmon leaps up a cataract, and die in the faith that he can go up it.

Oh, sublime faith! Oh, sublime folly! What strides he is constantly taking to the ridiculous, and not always from the sublime! How strong! how weak! How wise! how foolish! Consistent only in folly, and steady in the purpose of being foolish. How beautiful, and how ugly! What a lovable, detestable, desirable, proud, wilful, arrogant, supercilious, laughing, passionate, tender, cruel, loving, hating, good sort of a good-for-nothing he is! He believes everything—he believes nothing; and, like Mary's Son, questions and mocks the doctors to their beards in the very temple. Patience! he must have his time, and room to grow in, develop, and shape out. Let him have coral for his teeth, and climbing, and running, and jumping for his muscle. No man may love him, and no woman but his mother, and she is to be tried to the extent of endurance. Wait for him; he will, with or without your help, turn out good or bad, and in either event people will say: "I always told you so, " "I always knew it was in him"; and cite a score of unhappened things in proof of their sagacity.

Barton was one of these; neither better nor worse, full of possibilities and capabilities, impulsive, rash, and unreasoning. He has just made a resolve, and will act upon it; proud and sensitive to a degree, he had heard a word of fault once at the store, which another word would have explained. He would not say it, and went. It was discovered that the fault was not his, in time for him to remain; but he left without that word. He is willing to take his chances, and must speak and act for himself.

He sealed and directed his letter, walked about with the plaintive airs of old melodies running and running through his head, and sang snatches and verses of sad old ballads, going over and over with some touching line, or complaining strain, till he was saturated with its tender melancholy, and so he came back to ordinary life.

CHAPTER III.

NEWBURY.

Newbury was one of the twenty-odd townships, five miles square, that then made up the county of Geauga, and a part of the Western Reserve, the Yankee-doodledom of Ohio, settled exclusively by emigrants from New England. It was so much of Massachusetts, Connecticut, Vermont, etc., translated into the broader and freer West. It has been said that the Yankee, like a certain vegetable, heads best when transplanted. It was the old thing over, under new and trying circumstances. The same old ideas and notions, habits of thought and life; poor, economical and thrifty folk, with the same reverence for religion and law, love of education, and restless desire for improvement, and to better the present condition. In the West the Yankee developed his best qualities in the second generation. He became a little straighter and less angular, and wider between the eyes. In the first generation he lived out his life scarcely refracted by the new atmosphere. This crop still stood firm and hardy on the Reserve, and they often turned homesick eyes, talked lovingly and lingeringly of "down country, " as they all called loved and cherished New England. Most of the first settlers were poor, but hardy and enterprising. The two last qualities were absolutely necessary to take them through the long, wearisome journey to Ohio, the then far West. They took up lands, built cabins, and forced a subsistence from the newly-cleared, stumpy virgin soil. This homogeneous people constituted a practical and thorough democracy. Their social relations were based on personal equality, varied only by the accident of superior talents, address or enterprise, and as yet but little modified by wealth or its adventitious circumstances.

Among the emigrants scattered here and there was occasionally found a branch of a "down country" family of some pretensions, dating back to services in the Revolution, to old wealth, or official position. Among these were one or two families at Painesville, near the lake, at Parkman, several at Warren, and more at Cleveland, who had made each other's acquaintance, and who, as the country improved and the means of communication were perfected, formed and kept up a sort of association over the heads, and hardly within the observation, of the people generally. Of these, as we may say, by right of his wife, was Judge Markham. He was a hardy, intelligent, and, for his day, a cultivated man, who came early into the woods as an agent for many large stockholders of the old Connecticut Land Company, and a liberal percentage of the sales placed in his hands the nucleus of a large fortune. Sagacity in investments and improvements, with thorough business capacity, had already made him one of the wealthiest men on the Reserve; while a handsome person, and frank, pleasant address, rendered him very popular. He had been for several years an associate judge of the court of common pleas for Geauga county, and had an extensive acquaintance and influence. Mrs. Markham, a genuine daughter of the old Puritan ancestry, dating back to the first landing, a true specimen of the best Yankee woman under favorable circumstances, was a most thoroughly accomplished lady, who had gone into the woods with her young husband, and who shed and exercised a wide and beneficent influence through her sphere. So simple, sweet, natural and judicious was she ever, that her neighbors felt her to be quite one of themselves, as she was. Everybody was drawn to her; and so approachable was she, that the lower and more common declared that she was no lady at all.

Their only child, Julia, just maturing into womanhood, was one of the best and highest specimens of the American girl, to whom refinement, grace, and a strong, rich, sweet nature, came by right of birth, while she inherited beauty from both parents; she seemed, however, unconscious of this last possession, as she was of the admiration which filled the atmosphere that surrounded her. She, too, must speak and act for herself.

At the time of the incidents to be narrated, the northern and eastern part of Newbury had a considerable population. It was traversed by a highway leading west through its centre to Cleveland, and by a stage-road leading from Painesville to the Ohio river, through its eastern part. This was called the "State road, " and on it stood Parker's Hotel, a stage-house much frequented, and constituting the centre of a little village, while further south was the extensive trading establishment of Markham & Co., using the name and some of the capital of the Judge, and managed mainly by Roberts and another junior. Judge Markham's spacious and elegant dwelling stood about half a mile south of the store.

The south-western part of the township, with much of two adjoining townships, remained an unbroken forest, belonging to an eccentric landholder who refused to sell it. This was spoken of as "the woods,

" and furnished cover and haunts for wild game and animals, hunting-ground for the pioneers, and also gave shelter to a few shiftless squatters, in various parts of its wide expanse. In the eastern border of the township was Punderson's pond, a beautiful, irregular-shaped body of limpid water, embosomed by deep wooded hills, and of considerable extent, well stocked with fish, and much frequented on that account.

In the afternoon of the second day after his return, Bart went down a highway leading east to the State road, to the post-office, kept at Markham's store, and this road took him down by the southern end of the pond, and thence southerly on the State road. He passed along by Dr. Lyman's, Jonah Johnson's, and so on, past houses, and clearings, and woodlands, looking almost wistfully, as if he expected pleasant greetings; but the few he saw merely nodded to him, or called out: "Are you back again? " He paused on the hill by the saw-mill, which overlooked the pond, and gazed long over its beautiful surface, sleeping in utter solitude amid the green hills, under the slanting summer sun, and seemed to recognize in it what he had observed, on the evening of his return, about the old homestead — the change that had taken place in himself — a change which often accounts for the strange appearance of the most familiar and cherished places. We find it reflected in the face of inanimate nature, and wonder at her altered guise, unconscious of the cause. He sauntered musingly on to the State road, and over by the old grist-mill, past several houses, up to Parker's. Here, by a beautiful spring under the shade of old apple and cherry-trees, near the carriage-way, was an indolent group of afternoon idlers. Conspicuous among them was the dark and striking face of Dr. Lyman, the rich mahogany of Uncle Josh, and the homely, shrewd, and fresh-colored countenance of Jonah Johnson. Bart could not avoid them if he would; and regretted that he had not gone across the woods to the post-office, and so escaped them.

"Well, young Scholasticus, " said the Doctor, after the slight greetings had been given to the new-comer, "you seem to have graduated with great rapidity. You went through college like—"

"One of your emetics, Doctor. I came out at the same door I went in at. Now, doctus, doctior, doctissimus, I am fair game on this point, so blaze away with everything but your saddle-bags, and I will laugh with the rest of you. "

A good-natured laugh welcomed this coming down.

"Well, " replied the doctor, "there can't be much more said. "

"I should like to know, young man, " remarked Uncle Josh, "whether you raly got into the college, I should. "

"Well, Mr. Burnett, I *raly* did not, I didn't, " mimicking Uncle Josh.

"What did you do, badinage apart? "

"I took a good outside look at the buildings, which was improving; called on your friends Dr. Nutting and Rev. Beriah Green, who asked me what church I belonged to, and who was my instructor in Latin. "

"What reply did you make? "

"What could I say? I didn't hear the first; and as to the second, I couldn't bring reproach upon you, and so I said I had never had one. You must own, Doctor, that I showed great tenderness for your reputation. "

"You certainly did me a kindness. "

"Thank you, Doctor. "

"I should raly like to know, " said Uncle Josh, "what you are thanking the Doctor for, I should. "

"Well, go on. "

"I went off, " continued Bart. "The fact is, I thought that that retreat of the sciences might hold that little learning, which is a dangerous thing—as you used to not quote exactly—and I thought it prudent to avoid that 'Pierian spring. '"

"What is the young man talking about now? " inquired Uncle Josh. "I would raly like to know, I would. "

"I must ask the Doctor to explain, " answered Bart. "I was referring to one of his old drinking-places, where, according to him, the more one drank the soberer he grew. You would not fancy that tipple, would you? "

"You see, Uncle Josh, " said the Doctor, laughing, "what comes of a young man's going a week to college. "

"The young man didn't know anything at all, before, " declared Uncle Josh, "and he seems to know less now, amazingly. "

This was Uncle Josh's sincere opinion, and was received with a shout of laughter, in which Bart heartily joined. Indeed, it was his first sincere laugh for many a day.

Johnson asked him "whether he went to the Ohio river, " and being answered in the affirmative, asked him "by what route he went, and what he saw. "

Uncle Jonah, as Bart usually called him, was one of his very few recognized friends, and asked in a way that induced him to make a serious answer.

"I walked the most of the way there, and all the way back. I went by way of Canton, Columbus, Dayton, and so to Cincinnati, and returned the same way. "

"What do you think of that part of the State which you saw? "

"Unquestionably we have the poorest part of it. As our ancestors landed on the most desolate part of the continent, so we took the worst part of Ohio. If you were to see the wheat-fields of Stark, or the corn on the Scioto, and the whole of the region about Xenia and Dayton, and on the Miami, you would want to emigrate. "

"What about the people? "

"Oh, dear! I didn't see much of them, and that little did not make me wish to see more. The moment you step across the south line of the Reserve you step into a foreign country, and among a foreign people, who speak a foreign language, and who know one of us as quick as they see us; and they seem to have a very prudent distrust of us.

20

After passing this black, Dutch region, you enter a population of emigrants from Virginia, Kentucky, Maryland, and some from North Carolina, and all unite in detesting and distrusting the Reserve Yankee.

"It is singular, the difference between the lake and river side of the State. At Cincinnati you seem to be within a step of New Orleans, and hear of no other place—not a word of New York, and less of Boston. There everything looks and goes south-west, while we all tend eastward. " In reply to questions, Bart told them of Columbus and Cincinnati, giving fresh and graphic descriptions, for he observed closely, and described with a racy, piquant exaggeration what he saw. Breaking off rather abruptly, he seemed vexed at the length of his monologue, and went on towards the post-office.

"That young man will not come to a single darn, " said Uncle Josh; "not one darn. He is not good for anything, and never will be. His father was a very likely man, and so is his mother, and his older brothers are very likely men, but he is not worth a cuss. "

"Uncle Josh is thinking about Bart's sketch of him, clawing old Nore Morton's face, " said Uncle Jonah.

"I did not like that; I did not like it at all. It made me look like hell amazingly, " said the old man, much moved.

"You had good reason for not liking it, " rejoined Uncle Jonah, "for it was exactly like you. "

"Dr. Lyman, what do you think of this young man? He was with you, wa'n't he, studyin' something or other? " asked Uncle Josh; "don't you agree with me? "

"I don't know, " answered the Doctor, "I am out of all patience with him. He is quick and ready, and wants to try his hand at every new thing; and the moment he finds he can do it, he quits it. There is no stability to him. He studied botany a week, and Latin a month, and Euclid ten days. "

"He hunts well, and fishes well—don't he? " asked another.

"They say he shoots well, " said Uncle Josh, "but he will wander in the woods all day, and let game run off from under his eyes, amazingly! They said at the big hunt, in the woods, he opened the lines and let all the deer out. He isn't good for a thing—not a cussed thing. "

"Isn't he as smart as his brother Henry? " asked Uncle Jonah.

"It is not a question of smartness, " replied the Doctor. "He is too smart; but Henry has steadiness, and bottom, and purpose, and power, and will, and industry. But Bart, if you start him on a thing, runs away out of sight of you in an hour. The next you see of him he is off loafing about, quizzing somebody; and if you call his attention back to what you set him at, he laughs at you. I have given him up, utterly; though I mean to ask him to go a-fishing one of these nights."

"Exactly, " said Uncle Jonah, "make him useful. But, Dr. Lyman and Joshua Burnett, the boy has got the stuff in him—the stuff in him. Why, he told you here, in fifteen minutes, more about the State of Ohio than you both ever knew. You will see—"

"You will see, too, that he will not come to a darn, " said Uncle Josh, regarding that as a sad doom indeed.

CHAPTER IV.

AT THE POST-OFFICE.

Barton found a more attractive group at the store. The post-office occupied a window and corner near the front of the large, old-fashioned, square store-room; and, as he entered the front door, he saw, in the back part of the room, a gay, laughing, warbling, giggling, chirping group of girls gathered about Julia Markham, as their natural centre. Barton was a little abashed; he might have moved up more cautiously, and reconnoitred, had he not been taken by surprise. There was no help for it. He deposited his letters and called for his mail, which gave him time to gather his forces in hand.

Now Barton was born to love and serve women in all places, and under all forms and circumstances. His was not a light, silly, vapid, complimentary devotion, but deep in his nature, through and through, he reverenced woman as something sacred and high, and above the vulgar nature of men; this reformed his mind, and inspired his manners; and, while he was generally disliked by men, he was favorably regarded by women. It was not in woman's nature to think ill of a youth who was always so modestly respectful, and anxious to please and oblige; and no man thus constituted was ever awkward or long embarrassed in woman's presence. She always gets from him, if not his best, what is proper. If he can lose self-consciousness, and receive the full inspiration of her presence, he will soon be at his ease, if not graceful.

The last thing absolutely that ever could occur to Barton, and it never had as yet, was the possibility of his being an object of interest personally to a woman, or to women. He was modest—almost to bashfulness; but as he never presumed, he was never snubbed; and now, on this summer afternoon, he had came upon a group of seven or eight of the most attractive girls of the neighborhood, accompanied by one or two strangers. There was Julia, never so lovely before, with a warm color on her cheek, and a liquid light in her dark eyes, in whose presence all other girls were commonplace; and her friends Nell Roberts and Kate Fisher, Lizzie Mun and Pearlie Burnett, and several others. The young man was seen and recognized, and had to advance. Think of walking thirty feet alone in the faces of seven or eight beautiful girls, and at the same time be easy and graceful! It is funny, what a hush the presence of one young man will bring over a laughing, romping cluster of young women. At his entrance, their girlish clamor sunk to a liquid murmur; and, when he approached, they were nearly silent, all but Julia and a stylish blonde, whom Barton had never seen before. They were gathered around a cloud and tangle of women's mysterious fabrics, whose names are as unknown to men as their uses. Most of the young girls suspended their examinations and rippling comments, and, with a little heightened color, awaited the approach of the enemy. He came on, and gracefully bowed to each, was permitted to take the hands of two or three, and greeted with a little chorus of—"You have come back! " "Where have you been? " "How do you do? " Julia greeted him with her eyes, as he entered, with a sweet woman's way, that thrilled him, and which enabled him to approach her so well. She had remained examining a bit of goods, as if unaware of his immediate presence for a moment, and he had been introduced to the strange lady by Kate Fisher as her cousin, Miss Walters, from Pittsburgh.

Then Julia turned to him, and, with a charming manner, asked: "Mr. Ridgeley"—she had not called him Bart, or Barton, since her return from Boston—"Mr. Ridgeley, what do the girls mean? Have you really been away? "

"Have I really been away? And if I really have, am I to be permitted to take your hand, and asked how I really do? as if you really cared?"

"Really, " was her answer, "you see we have just received our fall fashions, and it is not the fall style this year to give and take hands after an absence. "

"A-h! how popular that will be with poor masculines! Is that to be worn by all of you? "

"I don't know, " said Kate; "it is not fall with some of us yet. "

"Thank you! and may I ask Miss Markham if it was the spring and summer style not to say good-bye at a parting? "

The tone was gay, but there was something more in it, and the girl replied: "That depends upon the lady, I presume; both styles may be varied at her pleasure. "

"Ah, I think I understand! You are kind to explain. "

"Mr. Barton, " said Lizzie, "Flora and I here cannot determine about our colors"—holding up some gay ribbons—"and the rest can't help us out. What do you think of them? "

"That they are brilliant, " answered Barton, looking both steadily and innocently in the faces, in a way that deepened their hues.

"Oh, no! these ribbons? " exclaimed the blushing girl, thrusting them towards his eyes.

"Indeed I am color blind, though not wholly blind to color. " And a little ripple of laughter ran over the bright group, and then they all laughed again.

Can any one tell why a young girl laughs, save that she is happy and joyous? If she does or says anything, she laughs, and if she don't, she laughs, and her companions laugh because she does, and then they all laugh, and then laugh again because they laughed before, and then they look at each other and laugh again; thus they did now, and Barton could no more tell what they were laughing at than could they; he was not so foolishly jealous as to imagine that they were laughing at him.

Then Kate turned to him: "You won't go away again, I hope. We are going to have a little party before long, and you must come, and I want to see you waltz with my cousin. She waltzes beautifully, and I want to see her with a good partner. Will you come? "

"Indeed I would be most happy; but your compliment is ironical. You know we don't waltz, and none of us can, if we try. "

"Is that the awful dance where the gentleman takes the lady around the waist, and she leans on him, and they go swinging around? Oh, I think that is awful! "

"The Germans, and many of our best ladies, and gentlemen, waltz, " replied Miss Walters, "as they do in Baltimore and New York, and I suppose my cousin thought no harm could be said of it at her little party. "

"Oh, I am sure I did not mean that it was wrong, and I would like to see the dance! " was the eager disclaimer.

Barton had drawn away from this discussion, and lingered a moment near Julia, to ask after her mother. She replied that Mrs. Markham was very well, but did not ask him to call and see for himself, nor did she in any way encourage him to prolong the conversation. So, with a little badinage and *persiflage*, he took his leave.

I shall not attempt to set down what was said of him after he left, nor will I affirm that anything was said. Young ladies, for aught I know, occasionally talk up young men among themselves, and if they do it is nobody's business.

CHAPTER V.

MRS. MARKHAM'S VIEWS.

In the gathering twilight, in a parlor at the Markham mansion, sat Julia by the piano, resting her head on one hand, while with the other she brought little ripples of music from the keys; sometimes a medley, then single and prolonged notes, like heavy drops of water into a deep pool, and then a twinkling shower of melody. She was not sad, or pensive, or thoughtful; but in one of these quiet, sweet, and grave moods that come to deep natures—as a cloud passing over deep, still water enables one under its shadow to see into its depths. Her mother stood at an open window, inhaling the evening fragrance of flowers, and occasionally listening to the wild note of the mysterious whippoorwill, that came from a thicket of forest-trees in the distance.

The step of her father caught the ear of the young girl, who sprang up and ran towards him with eager face and sparkle of eye and voice.

"Oh, papa, the trunks came this afternoon, with the fashion-plates, and patterns, and everything, and all we girls—Nell, Kate Fisher, Miss Flora Walter, Pearlie, Ann, and all hands of us—have had a regular 'opening. ' We went through with them all. The cottage bonnet is a love of a thing, and I am going to have it trimmed for myself. Sleeves are bigger than ever, and there were lots of splendid things! "

"And so Roberts has suited you all, for once, has he? " said the Judge, passing an arm around her small waist.

"Roberts! Faugh, he had nothing to do with it. Aunt Mary selected them all herself. They are the latest and newest from Paris—almost direct. "

"Does that make them better? "

"Well, I don't know that there is anything in their coming from Paris, except that one likes to know that they come from the beginning-place of such things. Now if they had been made in Boston, New

York, or Baltimore, one would not be certain they were like the right thing; and now we know they are the real thing itself. Do you understand? "

"Oh, yes—as well as a man may; and it is quite well put, too, and I don't know that I ever had so clear an idea of the value of things from a distance before. "

"Well, you see, when a thing comes clear from the farthest off, we know there ain't anything beyond; and when it comes from the beginning, we don't take it second hand. "

"I see; but why do you care, you girls in this far-off, rude region? "

"Mamma, do you hear that? Here is my own especial father, and your husband, asking me, a woman, and a very young woman too, for a reason. "

"It is because you are a very young one that he expects you to give a reason. Perhaps he thinks you will not claim the privilege of our sex."

"Well, I won't. Now, then, Papa Judge, this is not a far-off, rude region, and you see that the French ladies want these styles and fashions, and all that; well, if they want them, we want them too. "

"Now I don't quite see. How do you know they want them? Perhaps they are sent here because they don't want them; and, besides, why should a backwoods girl in Ohio want what a high-born lady in the French capital wants? "

"Because the American girl is a woman; and, besides, the court must hear and decide, and not ask absurd questions. "

"And who is to see you in French millinery, here in the woods? "

"Oh, bless its foolish man's heart, that thinks a woman dresses to please its taste, when it hasn't any! We dress to please ourselves and plague each other—don't you know that? and we ain't pleased with poky home-made things. "

"Julia! Mother, " appealed the Judge, with uplifted hands, to Mrs. Markham, "where did this young lady get her notions? "

"From the common source of woman's notions, as you call them, I presume—her feelings and fancies; and she is merely letting you see the workings of a woman's mind. We should all betray our sex a hundred times a day, if our blessed husbands and fathers had the power to understand us, I fear. "

"And don't we understand you? "

"Of course you do, as well as you ever will. My dear husband, don't you also understand that if you fully comprehended us, or we you, we should lose interest in each other? that now we may be a perpetual revelation and study to each other, and so never become worn and common? "

"There, Papa Judge, are you satisfied—not with our arguments, but with us? "

"The man who was not would be unreasonable and—"

"Man-like, " put in Julia. "Let me sing you my new song. "

A piano was a novelty in Northern Ohio. Julia played with a real skill and expression, and her father, though no musician, loved to listen, and more to hear her sing, with her clear, strong, sweet voice, and so she played and sang her song.

When she had finished, "By the way, " remarked her father, "I understand that our travelled young townsman, who has just returned from foreign parts, was at the post-office this afternoon, and perhaps you met him. "

"Whom do you mean? " asked Julia.

"Your mother's pet, Bart Ridgeley. "

"Now, papa, that is hardly kind, after what you said of him the other day. He is not mother's pet at all. She is only kind to him, as to everybody. Indeed, he don't seem to me like anybody's pet, to be patted and kept in-doors when it rains, and eat jellies, and be nice. I saw him at the store a moment; he was very civil, and merely asked after mamma, and went out. "

"Did you ask him to call and see mamma? " asked her father a little gravely.

"Not at all. The truth is, papa, after what you said I could not ask him, and was hardly civil to him. "

"Was it unpleasant to be hardly civil to him? "

"No; though I like to be civil to everybody. You know I have seen little of him since I came home, and when I have, he was sometimes silent and distant, and not like what he was before I went away. "

"You find him improved in appearance and manners? " persisted the Judge.

"Well, he was always good-looking, and had the way of a gentleman. Miss Walters seemed quite taken with him, and was surprised that he had grown up here in the woods. "

Her father was silent a moment, and the subject was changed. Mrs. Markham was attentive to what was said of poor Bart, but made no comment at the time.

* * * * *

In their room, that night, in her sweet, serious way, she said to her husband, "Edward, I do not want to say a word in favor of Barton Ridgeley. I do not ask you to change your opinion of him or your course towards him; but I wish to ask if it is necessary to discuss him, especially with Julia? "

"Why? "

"Well, can it be productive of good? If you are mistaken in your estimate of him, you do him injustice, and in any event you will call her attention to him, and she may observe and study him; and almost any young woman who should do that might become interested in him. "

"Do you think so? Men don't like him. "

"Is that a reason why a woman would not? "

"Have you discovered any reason to think that Julia cares in the least for him? "

"Julia is young, and, like the women of our family, develops in these respects slowly; but, like the rest of us, she will have her own fancies some time, and you know" —with a still softer voice—"that one of them left a beautiful home, and a circle of love and luxury, to follow her heart into the woods. "

"Yes, and thank God that she did! Roses and blessings and grace came with you, " said the Judge, with emotion. "But this boy—what is he to us, or what can he ever be? He is so freaky, and unsteady, and passionate, and flies off at a word, and goes before he is touched. He will do nothing, and come to nothing. "

"What can he do? Would you really have him buy an axe and chop cord-wood, or work as a carpenter, or sell tape behind the counter? Are there not enough to do all that work as fast as it needs to be done? Is there not a clamorous need of brain-work, and who is there to do it? Who is to govern, and manage, and control twenty years hence? Look over all the young men whom you know, and who promises to be fit to lead? Think over those you know in Cleveland, or Painesville, or Warren. Is somebody to come from somewhere else? Think of your own plans and expectations. Who can help you? I see possibilities in this wayward, passionate, hasty, generous youth. He is a tender and devoted son, and I am glad he came back; and nobody knows how he may be pushed against us and others. "

"Well, " said the Judge, after a thoughtful pause, "what can I do? What would you have me do—change myself, or try to change him? "

"I don't know, " thoughtfully: "I think there is nothing you can do now. I would wish you to cultivate a manner towards him that would leave it in your power to serve him or make him useful, if occasion presents. He needs a better education, and perhaps a profession. He should study law. He has a capacity to become a very superior public speaker—one of the first. I don't think there is much danger of his forming bad habits or associations. He avoids and shuns everything of that kind. You know he deeded his share of his father's land to his brother, to provide a home for his mother, and I presume will remain, both from choice and necessity, with her for the present. "

The Judge mused over her words. He did not tell her of having met and left Barton the other side of the Chagrin; nor did he disclose fully the dislike he felt for him, or the fears he may have entertained at the idea of any intimacy between him and Julia. His wife mused also in her woman's way. She, too, would have hesitated to have Barton restored to the old relations of his boyhood. While she knew of much to admire and hope for in him, she knew also that there was much to cause anxiety, if not apprehension. In thinking further, she was inclined to call upon his mother, whom she much esteemed for her strong and decisive traits of character, soft and womanly though she was. Cares and anxieties had kept her from association with her neighbors, among whom, as she knew, she seldom appeared, except on occasions of sickness or suffering, or when some event seemed to demand the presence of a deciding woman's mind and will. She remembered one or two such times in their earlier forest life, when Mrs. Ridgeley had quietly assumed her natural place for a day, to go back to her round of widowed love, care and toil. She would make occasion to see her, and perhaps find some indirect way to be useful to both mother and son.

CHAPTER VI.

WHAT HE THOUGHT OF THINGS.

How grateful to the sensitive heart of the young man would have been the knowledge that he was an object of thoughtful interest to Julia's mother, who, next to his own, had his reverence and regard! He knew he was generally disliked; his intuitions assured him of this, and in his young arrogance he had not cared. Indeed, he had come to feel a morbid pleasure in avoiding and being avoided; but now, as he sat in the little silent room in the late night, he felt his isolation. He had been appalled at a discovery—or rather a revelation—made that afternoon. He knew that he loved Julia, and that this love would be the one passion of manhood, as it had been of his boyhood. He had given himself up to it as to a delicious onflowing stream, drifting him through enchanted lands, and had not thought or cared whither it might bear, or on what desolate shore it might finally strand him.

Now he felt its full strength and power, and he knew, too, that it was a force to be controlled, when perhaps that had become impossible. He had never asked himself if a return of his passion were even possible, until now, when his whole fervid nature had gone out in a great hungry longing for her love and sympathy. She had never stood so lovely and so inaccessible as he had seen her that day. How deeply through and through came the first greeting of her eyes! It was an electric flash never received before, and which as suddenly disappeared. How cool and indifferent was her manner and look as he approached, and stood near her! No inquiry, save that mocking one! Not a word; not a thought of where he had been, or why he had returned, or what he would do; the shortest answer as to his inquiry about her mother; no intimation that he might even call at the house. Thus he went over with it all—over and over again. What did he care? But he did, and could not deceive himself. He did care, and must not; and then he went back over all their intercourse since her return home, two or three months before he left, and it was all alike on her part—a cool, indifferent avoidance of him.

Oh, she was so glorious—so beautiful! The whole world lay in the span of her slender waist—a world not for him. Was it something to be adventured for, fought for, found anywhere? something that he could climb up to and take? something to plunge down to in fathomless ocean and carry back? No, it was her woman's heart. Like her father, she disliked him; and if, like her father, she would openly let him see and hear it—but doesn't she? What had he to offer her? How could he overcome her father's dislike? He felt in his soul what would come to him finally, but then, in the lapsing time? And she avoided him now!

He returned to his algebraic problem, with a desperate plunge at its solution. The unknown quantity remained unknown; and, a moment later, he was gratified to see how he had finally caught and expressed, with his pencil, a look of Julia, that had always eluded him before. But was he to be overcome by a girl? Was life and its ambitions to be crushed out and brought to nought by one small hand? He would see. It would be inexpressible luxury to tell her once—but just once—all his passion and worship, and then, of course, remain silent forever, and go out of her presence. He wished her to know it all, so that, as she would hear and know of him in the coming years, she would know that he was worthy, not of her love, but worthy to love her, whatever that may mean, or whatever of comfort it might bring to either. What precious logic the heart of a young man in his twenty-second year is capable of!

CHAPTER VII.

LOGIC OF THE GODS.

"Doctor, " said Barton, in the little office of the latter, "I've called to borrow your Euclid; may I have it? I have never tried Euclid, really. "

"Oh, yes, you can have it, and welcome. Do you want to try yourself on the *pons asinorum?* "

"What is that; another bridge of sighs? for I suppose they can be found out of Venice. "

"It is a place over which asses have to be carried. It is, indeed, a bridge of sighs, and a bridge of size. "

"Oh, Doctor, don't you do that! Well, let me try it! I want more work; and especially I want a wrestle with Euclid. "

"Work! what are you doing, that you call work? "

"Well, hoeing beans, pulling up weeds, harvesting oats, with recreations in Latin Grammar, Dabol, Algebra, Watts on the Mind, Butler's Analogy, and other trifles. "

"All at one time? "

"No, not more than three at the same time. Don't lecture me, Doctor, I am incorrigible. When I work, I don't play. "

"And when you don't play you work, occasionally; well, I think Euclid will do you good. "

"I won't take it as a prescription, Doctor! "

"A thorough course of mathematics would do more for one of your flighty mind, than anything else; you want chaining down to the severe logic of lines and angles. "

"To the solution of such profound problems as, that the whole of a thing is more than a fraction of it; and things that are exactly alike resemble each other, for instance, eh? "

"Pshaw! you will make fun of everything. Will you ever reach discretion, and deal with things seriously? "

"I was never more serious in my life, and could cry with mortification over my lost, idled-away hours, you never believed in me, and are not to blame for that, nor have I any promises to make. I am not thought to be at all promising, I believe. "

"Bart, " said the Doctor, seriously, "you don't lack capacity; but you are too quick and impulsive, and all imagination and fancy. "

"Well, Doctor, you flatter me; but really is not the imagination one of the highest elements of the human mind? In the wide world's history was it not a crowning, and one of the most useful qualities of many of the greatest men? "

"Great men have had imagination. I presume, and achieved great things in spite of it; but through it, never. "

"Why, Doctor! the mere mathematician is the most servile of mortals. He is useful, but cannot create, or even discover. He weighs and measures. Project one of his angles into space, and, though it may reach within ten feet of a blazing star that dazzles men with eyes, yet he will neither see nor know of its existence. His foot-rule won't reach it, and he has no eyes. Imagination! it was the logic of the gods—the power to create; and among men it abolishes the impossible. By its force and strength one may strike fire from hidden flints in darkened worlds, and beat new windows in the blind sides of the ages. Columbus imagined another continent, and sailed to it; and so of all great discoverers. "

The Doctor listened with some surprise. "Did it ever occur to you, Bart, that you might be an orator of some sort? "

"Such an orator as Brutus is—cold, formal, and dead? I'd rather not be an orator at all, 'but talk right on, ' like plain, blunt Mark Antony."

36

"And yet Brutus has been quoted and held up by poets and orators as a sublime example of virtue and patriotism, young man! "

"And yet he never made murder the fashion; " and—striking an attitude—"Caesar had his Brutus! Charles had his Cromwell! and George III. had—what the devil did George have? He was stupid enough to have been a mathematician, though I never heard that he was. "

"Oh dear, Bart! " said the Doctor, with a sigh, "for God's sake, and your own, do study Euclid if you can! Don't you see that your mind is always sky-rocketing and chasing thistle-down through the air? "

> "'The downy thistle-seed my fare,
>   My strain forever new,'"
> said Bart, laughing, and preparing to go.

"By the way, " asked the Doctor, "wouldn't you like to go fishing one of these nights? We haven't been but once or twice this summer. Jonah, and Theodore, and 'Brother Young' and I have been talking about it for some days. We will rig up a fire-jack, if you will go, and use the spear. "

"I am afraid I would be sky-rocketing, Doctor; but send me word when you are ready. "

* * * * *

Barton had now entered upon something like a regular course. He had one of those intense nervous temperaments that did not require or permit excessive sleep. He arose with the first light, and took up at once the severest study he had until breakfast, and then worked with the boys, or alone, the most of the forenoon, at whatever on the farm, or about the house, seemed most to want his hand; the afternoons and evenings were given to unremitting study or reading. His tone of mind and new habit of introspection induced him to take long walks in the woods and secluded places, and after his work for the day was done; he imposed upon himself a regular and systematic course, and compelled himself to adhere to it. He saw few, went nowhere; and among that busy people, after the little buzz occasioned by his return had subsided, he ceased to be an object of interest or comment.

It was remarked among them that they did not hear his rifle in the forests, and nobody had presents of wild turkeys and venison, as they sometimes had, and he was in his own silent way shaping out his own destiny.

He received a letter from Henry in reply to his own, full of kindness, with such hints as the elder could give as to his course of study. His observing mother saw at once a marked change in his manner and words. Thoughtful and forbearing, his arrogance disappeared, and his impetuous, dashing way evidently toned down, while he was more tender towards her, and seemed to fall naturally into the place of an elder brother—careful and gentle to the young boys.

CHAPTER VIII.

A RAMBLE IN THE WOODS, AND WHAT CAME OF IT.

Already the summer had deepened and ripened into autumn. The sky had a darker tint, and the breeze had a plaintive note in its voice; and here and there the footprints of change were in the tree-tops.

On one of those serene, deep afternoons, Barton, who had been importuned by the boys to go into the woods in pursuit of a flock of turkeys, that George had over and over declared "could be found just out south, and which were just as thick and fat as anything, " yielded, and, taking his rifle, started out, accompanied by them, in high glee. George's declaration about the turkeys was, without much difficulty, verified, and Bart, who was a practised hunter, and knew all the habits of the shy and difficult bird, managed in a short time to secure two. He felt an old longing for a good, long, lonely ramble, and directed the boys, who were in ecstacies at his skill and the result, to carry the game back to their mother, while he went out to the Slashing, adding that if he did not come back until into the night, they might know he had gone to the pond, to meet the Doctor and a fishing-party; and with a good-natured admonition from George, to look out for that wolverine that haunted the Slashing, they separated.

The "Slashing" was a large tract of fallen timber, all of which had been cut down years before, and left to decay as it fell. Near this, and to the east, an old roadway had been cut, leading south, which was often used by the neighbors to go from the Ridgeley neighborhood to settlements skirting the eastern border of "the woods" before mentioned. Still further east, and surrounded by forest, on a small stream, was Coe's carding machine and fulling mill, to which a by-way led from the State road, at a point near Parker's. The Coes, a shiftless, harmless set, lived much secluded, and were often the objects of charity, and as such somewhat under the patronage of Mrs. Markham and Julia; and some of her young friends were occasionally attracted there for a ramble among the rocks and springs, from which Coe's creek, a little stream, arose. From the old road a path led to the fields of Judge Markham, about a fourth of a mile distant, which was the shortest route from his house to Coe's.

* * * * *

On his return ramble, just as Bart was about to emerge from the woods into the opening made by the old road from the west, he was surprised to see Julia approaching him, going along that track towards home. She was alone, and walking with a quick step. Lifting his hat, he stepped forward towards the path in which she was walking. The meeting in the wild, still woods, under the deepening shades of approaching night, was a surprise to both; and, by the light in the eyes of the youth, and warmer color in the face of the maiden, seemed not unpleasant to either.

"This is a surprise, meeting you here alone, " said Barton, stepping to the side of the footway, a little in advance of her.

"It must be, " answered Julia. "Poor old lady Coe is quite ill, and I've been around there, and, as it was latish, I have taken this short way home, rather than go all the way around the road. "

"Indeed, if you are really going this way you must permit me to attend you, " said Bart, placing his gun against a stump. "It is a good half-mile to the path that leads out to your father's, and it is already darkening; " and he turned and walked by her side.

"It is really not necessary, " said the girl, quite decidedly. "I know the way, and am not in the least afraid. "

"Forgive me, Miss Markham, but I really fear that you must choose between my attendance out of these woods and turning back around the road, " replied Bart.

His manner, so frank and courteous, and his voice, so gentle, had nevertheless, to her woman's ear, a vibration of the man's nerve of force and will, to which the girl seemed unconsciously to yield. They walked along. The mystery of night was weaving its weird charm in the forest, and strange notes and sounds came from its depths, and these young, pure natures found an undefined sweetness in companionship. On they walked in silence, as if neither cared to break it. The young girl at length said:

"Mr. Ridgeley"—not Barton, or his first name, as in her childhood— what a heart-swoon smote the youth at the formal address! —"Mr. Ridgeley, there is something I must say to you. My father does not care to have me in your company, and I must not receive the most ordinary attention from you. He would not, I fear, like to know that you were at our house. "

Did it cost her anything to say this? Apparently not, though her voice and manner diminished its sting. A moment's pause, and Barton's voice, cold and steady, answered back:

"I know what your father's feelings towards me are, " and then, with warmth, "but I am sure that he would think less of me, if possible, were I to permit any woman to find her way, at this hour, out of this wilderness. "

It was not much to say, but it was well said, and he turned his face towards her as he said it, lit up with a clear expression of man's loyalty to woman—not unpleasant to the young girl. Why could not he leave it there and to the future? They walked on, and the shadows deepened.

"Miss Markham, I, too, must say a thing to you: from my boyhood to this hour, deeply, passionately, with my whole heart and soul, have I loved you. "

There was no mistaking; the intensity of his voice made his words thrill. She recoiled from them as if stunned, and turned her face, pale now, and marked, fully towards him.

"What! What did you say? "

"I love you! " with a deep, full voice.

"How dare you utter such words to me? "

Her eyes flashed and nostrils dilated.

"Because they are true; because I am a man and you are a woman, " steadily and proudly.

"A man! you a man! Is it manly to waylay me in this lonely place, and force yourself upon me, and insult me with this? You compel me to—to—"

41

"Scorn and despise you! " supplied the youth, in a bitter tone.

"Take the words, then, if you choose them. "

She was simply grand in her style, till this last expression, which had the angry snap of an enraged woman. Some high natures might have answered back her scorn; a lower one might have complained; and still another would have left her in the woods. Barton said nothing, but, with a cold, stony face, walked on by her side. If, in his desperation, he wanted this killing thrust, which must ever rankle and never heal, to enable him to overcome and subdue his great passion, he had got it. That little hand, that emphasized her words with a gesture of superb disdain, would never have to repeat the blow. It raised about her a barrier that he was never after to approach.

He was not a man to complain. He would have told her why he said these words; he could not now. Some men are like wolves in traps, and die without a moan. Barton could die, and smile back into the face of his slayer, and say no word.

Night was now deepening in the woods, with the haughty maiden, and high, proud and humiliated youth, walking still side by side through its shadows. They at length reached the path that led from the open way to the left, approaching Julia's home. There was a continuous thicket of thrifty second-growth young trees bordering the track along which the two were journeying, and the opening through it made by this narrow path was black with shadow, like the entrance to a cave.

"This is the way, " said Bart, turning into it.

These were the first words he had uttered, and came as if from a distance. Without a word of hesitation Julia turned into the path with him, yet with almost a shudder at the darkness. They had not taken a dozen steps when an appalling, shrieking yell, a brute yell, of ferocious animal rage—the rage for blood and lust to mangle and tear—burst from the thicket on their right. A wild plunge through tangled brush and limbs, another more appalling shriek, and a dark, shadowy form, with a fierce, hungry growl, crouched in the pathway just before them, with its yellow, tawny, cruel eyes flashing in their faces. The first sound seemed to heat every fiery particle of the blood of the youth into madness, and open an outlet to the burning elements of his nature. Here was something to encounter, and for her, and in her presence; and the brute had hardly crouched as if for its spring, when, with an answering cry, a man's shout, a challenge and a charge, he sprang forward, with his unarmed strength, to the encounter. As if cowed and overcome by the higher nature, the brute turned, and with a complaining whine like a kicked dog, ran into the depths of the woods. Barton had momentarily, in a half frenzy, wished for a grapple, and felt a pang of real disappointment.

"The brute is a coward, " he said, as he turned back, where the white robes of Julia were dimly visible in the darkness. She was a daughter of the Puritans, and had the blood and high courage of her race. The first cry of the animal had almost frozen her blood, but the eager, proud, manly shout of Barton affected her like a trumpet-call. She exulted in his dashing courage, and felt an irresistible impulse to rush forward to his aid. It all occurred in the fraction of a moment; and when she realized that the peril was over, she was well-nigh overcome.

"You were always brave, " said Barton, cheerily, with just a little strain in his voice; "you were in no danger, and it is all over. "

No answer.

"You are not overcome? " with an anxious voice. "Oh, " coming close to her, "if I might offer you support! "

He held out his hand, and she put hers in it. How cool and firm his touch was, and how her tremor subsided under it! He pulled her hand within his arm, and hers rested fully upon his, with but their light summer draperies between them.

"But a little way further, " he said, in his cheery voice, and they hurried forward.

Neither spoke. What did either think? The youth was sorry for the awful fright of the poor girl, and so glad of the little thing that eased his own humiliation. The girl—who can tell what a girl thinks?

As they reached the cleared land, a sense of relief came to Julia, who had started a dozen times, in her escape out of the woods, at imaginary sounds. Day was still in the heavens, and the sight of her father's house gladdened her.

"Will you mind the dew? " asked her companion.

"Not in the least, " she answered; and he led her across the pastures to the rear of an enclosure that surrounded the homestead. He seemed to know the way, and conducted her through a large open gate, and so to a lane that led directly to the rear of the house, but a few yards distant. He laid his hand upon the small gate that opened into it, and turning to her, said:

"I may not intrude further upon you. For your relief, I ought perhaps to say that the words of madness and folly which I uttered to you will neither be recalled nor repeated. Let them lie where they fell— under your feet. Your father's house, and your father's daughter, will be sacred from me. "

The voice was firm, low, and steady; and opening the gate, the young girl entered, paused a moment, and then, without a word, ran rapidly towards the house. As she turned an angle, she saw the youth still standing by the gate, as if to protect her. She flew past the corner, and called, in a distressed voice:

"Mamma! mamma! oh, mother! "

She was a Puritan girl, with the self-repression and control of her race, and the momentary apprehension that seized her as she left the side of Barton was overcome as she entered her father's house.

"Julia! " exclaimed her mother, coming forward, "is that you? Where have you come from? What is the matter? "

"I came through the woods, " said the girl, hurriedly. "I've been so awfully frightened! Such dreadful things have happened! " with a half hysterical laugh, which ended in a sob.

"Julia! Julia! my child! what under the heavens has happened? Are you hurt? "

"No, only dreadfully frightened. I was belated, and it came on dark, and just as we turned into the path from the old road, that awful beast, with a terrible shriek, sprang into the road before us, and was about to leap upon me, when Barton sprang at him and drove him off. If it had not been for him, I would have been torn in pieces. "

"Barton? —was he with you? Thank God! oh, bless and thank God for your escape! My child! my child! How awful it sounds! Come! come to my room, and let me hold you, and hear it all! "

"Oh, mamma! what a weak and cowardly thing a woman is! I thought I was so strong, and really courageous, and the thought of this thing makes me tremble now. "

They gained her mother's room, and Julia, seating herself at her mother's feet, and resting her arms on her mother's lap, undertook to tell her story.

"I cannot tell you how it all happened. Barton met me, and would come along with me, and then he said strange things to me; and I answered him back, and quarrelled with him, and —"

"What could he have said to you? Tell me all. "

Julia began and told with great minuteness, and with much feeling, her whole adventure. She explained that she really did not want Bart to come with her, for that it would displease her father; and that when he did, she thought he ought to know that he was not at liberty to be her escort or come to the house, and so she told him. She could not tell why she answered him just as she did, but she was surprised, and not quite herself, and she might have said it differently, and need not have said so much, and he certainly must know that she did not mean it all. Surely it was most his fault; if he really had such feelings, why should he tell her, and tell her as he did? It was dreadful, and she would never be happy again; and she laid her head in her mother's lap, in her great anguish.

When her burst of grief had subsided, and she was calm, her mother asked several questions, and learned all that was said, and was much excited at Julia's account of the encounter with the beast and Barton's intrepidity. She seemed to feel that they had both escaped a great danger, through his courage.

"My dear child, " she said, "I don't know what to think of these strange and trying events, mixed up as they are. There is one very, very unfortunate thing about it. "

"That I met Barton? Oh, mother! "

"No, no; not that. It was unfortunate that you came the way you did, or unfortunate that you went, perhaps; but it is not that. It was most providential that Barton was with you, but so unfortunate that he said to you what he did. "

"Is it a misfortune to be loved, mother? "

"Let us not talk of this to-night, my darling, " stooping and kissing her still pale cheek. "God only knows of these things. It may not be a misfortune, but it may bring unhappiness, dear, to somebody. "

"Perhaps, mother, if he had not had such feelings he would not have come with me. "

"My child! my child! don't say what might have happened. I am glad and grateful—so grateful that he was with you—that he was generous enough to come, after what you said to him; but now, how can we express our gratitude to him? "

"Oh, mamma! I am sure it is no matter. He won't care now what we think. "

"You are too much agitated, my daughter, to-night; let us not talk it over now. But what became of Barton? did he come in? "

"No, I left him at the back gate, without a word, only waiting for me to run in. Of course he went back to the woods and wild beasts. What other place was there for him? "

"Don't, don't, Julia! don't say such words. Harm will not come to him. "

"I know it won't, " said the young girl; "for when the whole world turns against a brave, true heart, God watches over it with the more care. "

"True, my child; and we can at least pray God to be near him, only don't think of this matter now. In a day or two you will be yourself, and look at it in a different light. Your father will return to-morrow, and it may not be best to tell him of all this at present. It would only disturb him. "

"Yes, mamma; I could not tell him everything as I have told you, and so I must not tell him anything, nor anybody else. How wretched it all is! "

CHAPTER IX.

A DARKENED SOUL.

As Julia left Bart, the full force of her scornful words seemed for the first time to reach him. The great restraint her presence imposed in some way suspended, or broke their effect, and he turned from the gate with a half-uttered moan of anguish. He did not then recall her words or manner; he only realized that, in a cruel and merciless way, she had crushed his heart and soul. It was not long; both recoiled with a sense of wrong and injustice, and utter helplessness, for the hurt came from a woman. Instinctively he returned to the point whence they had emerged when they left the woods, and the thought of the screaming brute came to him with a sense of relief. Here was an object upon which he could wreak himself, and in a half frenzy of madness he hurried towards a spot in the edge of the Slashing, towards which the cowardly thing had run when it fled from his onset. He paused to listen upon the margin of that tangled wilderness of young trees, briers, and decaying trunks. How solemn and quiet, wild and lonely it was, in the deep night and deeper woods! The solemn hush fell upon the bruised spirit of the youth with the quieting touch and awe of a palpable presence, rebukingly, yet tenderly and pityingly.

Quick to compassionate others, he had ever been relentless to himself, and refused to regard himself as an object of injustice, or as needing compassion. As he stood for a moment confronting himself, scorned, despised and humiliated, he felt for himself the measureless contempt to which he seemed to have fallen; yet, under it all, and against it all, he arose. "Oh, Bart! Bart! what a poor, abject, grovelling thing you really are, " he said bitterly, "when the word of a girl so overcomes you! when the slap of her little hand so benumbs and paralyzes you! If you can't put her haunting face from you now, God can hardly help you. How grand she was, in her rage and scorn! Let me always see her thus! " and he turned back into the old road. Along this he sauntered until his eye met the dull gleam of his rifle-barrel against the old stump where he left it. With a great start, he exclaimed, "Oh, if I could only go back to the moment when I stood here with power to choose, and dream! " It was a momentary weakness, a mere recoil from the wound still so fresh and ragged.

It was still in early evening, with time and life heavy on his hands, when he remembered that the Doctor had sent him word to come to the pond that night. Taking his rifle by the muzzle, and throwing it across his shoulder, he plunged into the woods in a right line for the west shore of the pond, at about its midway.

Through thick woods tangled with underbrush and laced with wild vines, down steep banks, over high hills and rocky precipices, across clearings and hairy brier patches, he took his way, and found relief in the physical exertions of which he was still capable. At last he stood on the margin of the forest and hill-embosomed waters of that lovely little lake. It was solitary and silent, but for the weird sounds of night birds and aquatic animals that frequented its reedy margin, and a soft, silvery mist was just rising from its unruffled surface, that gathered in a translucent veil against the dark forest of the opposite shore. Its simple, serene and quiet beauty, under the stars and rising moon, was not lost upon the poetic nature of Barton, still heaving with the recent storm.

He ran his eye along the surface of the water, and discerned in the shadow of the wood, near the island, a fourth of a mile distant, a light, and below it the dark form of a boat. Placing his closed hands to his lips, he blew a strong, clear, full whistle, with one or two notes, and was answered by Theodore. At the landing near him was a half-rotten canoe, partially filled with water, and near it was an old paddle. Without a moment's thought, Barton pushed it into deep water, springing into it as it glided away. He had not passed half the distance to the other boat, when he discovered that it was filling. With his usual rashness, he determined to reach his friends in it by his own exertions, and without calling to them for aid, and by an almost superhuman effort he drove on with his treacherous craft. The ultimate danger was not much to a light and powerful swimmer, and he plunged forward. The noise and commotion of forcing his waterlogged canoe through the water attracted the attention of the party he was approaching, but who had hardly appreciated his situation as he lightly sprang from his nearly filled boat into their midst.

"Hullo, Bart! Why under the heavens did you risk that old log? Why didn't you call to us to meet you? "

"Because, " said Bart, excited by his effort and danger, "because to myself I staked all my future on reaching you in that old hulk, and I won. Had it sunk, I had made up my mind to go with her, and, like Mr. Mantalini, in Dickens's last novel, 'become a body, a demnition moist unpleasant body. '"

"What old wreck is it? " inquired Young, looking at the scarcely perceptible craft that was sinking near them.

"It is the remains of the old canoe made by Thomas Ridgeley, in his day, I think, " said Jonah.

"Nothing of the sort, " said Bart; "it is the remains of old Bullock's 'gundalow, ' that has been sinking and swimming, like old John Adams in the Revolution, these five years past. Don't let me think to-night, Uncle Jonah, that anything from my father's hand came to take me into the depths of this pond. "

The craft occupied by the party was a broad, scow-like float, with low sides, steady, and of considerable capacity. At the bow was a raised platform, covered with gravel, on which stood a fire-jack. The crew were lying on the silent water, engaged with their lines, when Bart so unceremoniously joined them. He went forward to a vacant place and lay down in the bottom, declining to take a line.

"What is the matter, Bart? " asked the Doctor.

"I don't know. I've been wandering about in the woods, and I must have met something, or I have lost something, —I don't know which."

"I guess you saw the wolverine, " said Theodore.

"I guess I did; " and pretty soon, "Doctor, is this your robe? Let me cover myself with it; I am cold! " and there was something almost plaintive in his voice.

"Let me spread it over you, " said the Doctor, with tenderness. "What ails you, Bart? are you ill? "

"If you left your saddle-bags at home, I think I am; if they are here, I am very well. Doctor, " he went on, "can a man have half of his faculties shut off and retain the others clear and strong? "

"I don't know, —perhaps so; why? "

"Well, I feel as if one of your astringents had placed its claws on a full half of me and drawn it all into a pucker; and the other half is in some way set free, and I feel clairvoyant. "

"What do you think you can see? " asked the Doctor.

"A young man—quite a young man—blindfolded, groping backward in the chambers of his darkened soul, and trying to escape out of it, " said Bart.

"What a queer fancy! " said the Doctor.

"He must have an unusually large soul, " said Uncle Jonah.

"Every soul is big enough for the man to move in, small as it is, " said Bart.

"What is your youth doing in his, now? " asked the Doctor.

"He is sitting down, resigned, " answered Bart.

"If his soul was dark, why was he blindfolded? " asked the Doctor.

"Well, I don't know. For the same reason that men with eyes think that a blind man cannot see so well in the dark, perhaps, " was the answer. "And see here, " looking into the water, "away down here is a beautiful star. There, I can blot it out with my hand! and see, now, how I can shatter it into wavelets of stars, and now break it into a hundred, by merely disturbing the water where I see it, 'like sunshine broken in a rill. ' Who knows but it may be the just-arrived light of an old, old star which has just come to us? How easy to climb back on one of these filmy rays, myriads of millions of leagues, home to its source! I will take off the bandage and let the poor boy see it, and climb if he may. "

"You are fanciful and metaphysical, " said the Doctor. "Euclid has not operated, I fear. Why would you go up to the source of that ray? Would you expect to find God and heaven there? "

"I should but traverse the smallest portion of God, " said Bart, "and yet how far away He seems just now. Somebody's unshapen hand cuts His light off; and I cannot see Him by looking down, and I haven't the strength to look up. "

"How incoherently you talk; after all, suppose that there is no God, for do your best, it is but a sentiment, a belief without demonstrative proof. "

"Oh, Doctor, don't! You are material, and go by lines and angles; cannot you understand that a God whose existence you would have to prove is no God at all? that if His works and givings out don't declare and proclaim him, He is a sham? You cannot see and hear, Doctor, when you are in one of your material moods. Look up, if you can see no reflection in the waters below. "

"Well, when I look into the revealed heaven, for instance, Bart, I see it peopled with things of the earth, reflected into it from the earth; showing that the whole idea is of the earth—earthy. "

"Oh, Doctor! like the poor old Galilean; when he thought it was all up, he went out and dug bait, and started off a-fishing. You attend to your fishing, and let me dream. If God should attempt to reveal Himself to you to-night, which I wouldn't do, He would have to elevate and enlarge and change you to a celestial, so that you could understand Him; or shrink and shrivel Himself to your capacity, and address you on your level, as I do, using the language and imagery of this earth, and you would answer Him as you do me—'It is all of the earth—earthy. ' I want to sleep. "

The Doctor pondered as if there was a matter for thought in what he had heard, and a little ripple of under-talk ran on about the subjects, the everlasting old, old and eternally new problems that men have dreamed and stumbled over, and always will—which Bart had dreamily spoken of as if they were very familiar to his thoughts, and they spoke of him, and wondered if anything had happened, and pulled their boat to a new position, while the overtaxed youth subsided into fitful slumber. Theodore finally awoke him, and said that they proposed to light up the jack, if he would take the spear, and they would push out to deeper water, and try for bass. Bart stared about him uncomprehendingly for a moment. "Oh, Theodore, my fishing days are over! I will never 'wound the gentle bosom of this lake' with fish spear, or gig, or other instrument; and I've backed this old rifle around for the last time to-day. "

"Bart, think of all our splendid times in the woods! "

"What a funny dream I had: I dreamed I was a young Indian, not John Brown's 'little Indian, ' but a real red, strapping, painted young Indian, and our tribe was encamped over on the west side of this Indian lake, by Otter Point; and I was dreadfully in love with the chief's daughter. "

"Who didn't love you again, " said Theodore.

"Of course not, being a well-brought up young Indianess: and I went to the Indian spring, that runs into the pond, just above 'Barker's Landing, ' that you all know of. "

"I never knew that it was an Indian spring, " said Young.

"Well, it is, " replied Bart. "It has a sort of an earthen rim around it, or had a few minutes ago; and the water bubbles up from the bottom. Well, you drop a scarlet berry into it, and if it rises and runs over the rim, the sighed-for loves you, or she don't, and I have forgotten which. I found a scarlet head of ginseng, and dropped the seeds in one after another, and they all plumped straight to the bottom. "

"Well, what was the conclusion? "

"Logical. The berries were too heavy for the current, or the current was too weak for the berries. "

"And the Indianess? "

"She and all else faded out. "

"Oh, pshaw! how silly! " said Young. "Will you take the spear, or won't you? "

"Will you take the spear, or won't you? " replied Bart, mimicking him with great effect.

"Have you heard from Henry lately? " asked Uncle Jonah.

"A few days ago, " answered Bart, who turned moodily away like a peevish child angered with half sleep, and a pang from the thrust he had received.

"Henry is the most ambitious young man I ever knew, " said the Doctor; "I fear he may never realize his aspirations. "

"Why not? " demanded Bart, with sudden energy. "What is there that my brother Henry may not hope to win, I would like to know? He will win it or die in the effort. "

"He will not, if he lives a thousand years, " said Young, annoyed at Bart's mimicking him. "It ain't in him. "

"What ain't in him, Old Testament? " demanded Bart, with asperity.

"The stuff. I've sounded him; it ain't there! "

"You've sounded him! Just as you are now sounding this bottomless pond, with a tow string six feet long, having an angle worm at one end, and an old hairy curmudgeonly grub at the other. "

"There, Brother Young, " said Uncle Jonah, "stop before worse comes. "

"Mr. Young, " said Bart, a moment later, with softened voice, making way towards him, "forgive me if you can. I've done with coarse and vulgar speeches like that. You believe in Henry, and only spoke to annoy me. I take it all back. I will even spear you some bass, if Theodore will light up the jack. Give me the oars, and let me wake up a little, while we go to better ground below. "

For a few moments he handled the polished, slender-tined, long-handled spear with great dexterity and success, and told the story of old Leather Stocking spearing bass from the Pioneers. He soon ceased, however, and declared he would do no more, and his companions, disgusted with his freaky humor, prepared to return. Bart, casting down his spear, remained in moody silence until they landed. Theodore picked up his rifle, the fish were placed in baskets, the tackle stowed away, the boat secured, and the party proceeded homeward.

Bart lived further from the pond than any of the party, and Theodore, who loved him, and was kind to his moods, taking a few of the finest fish, accompanied him home. As they were about to separate from Uncle Jonah—the father of Theodore—he turned to Bart, and said: "Something has happened, no matter what; don't be discouraged, you stick to them old books; there's souls in 'em, and they will carry you out to your place, some time. "

"Thank you, thank you, Uncle Jonah! " said Bart, warmly; "these are the only encouraging words I've heard for two years. "

"Theodore, " said Bart, as they walked on, "what an uncomfortable bore I must have been to-night. "

"Oh, I don't know! we thought that something had happened, perhaps. "

"No, I'm trying to change, and be more civil and quiet, and have been thinking it all over, and don't feel quite comfortable; and we have both something to do besides run in the woods. You were very good to come with me, Theodore, " he said, as they parted at the gate.

CHAPTER X.

AFTER THE FLOOD.

The next morning Bart was not up as usual, and George rushed into the low-ceiled room, under the roof.

"Bart! breakfast is ready! Ma thinks it strange you ain't up. That was a splendid big bass. Where did you take him? Are you sick? " as he came in.

"No, Georgie; I am only languid and dull. I must have been wofully tired. "

"I should think you would be, running all day and up all night. I should think you'd be hungry, too, by this time. "

"Georgie, how handsome you look this morning! What a splendid young man you will be, and so bright, and joyous, and good! Everybody will love you; no woman will scorn you. There, tell mother not to wait! I will get up soon. "

Some time after, the light, quick step of his mother was heard approaching his door, where she paused as if to listen.

"I am up, mother, " called out Bart; and she found him partly dressed, and sitting listlessly on his bed, pale and dejected.

"It is nothing, mother; I'm only a little depressed and dull. I'll be all right in an hour. I ran in the woods a good deal, took cold, and am tired. "

She looked steadily and wistfully at him. The great change in his face could not escape her. Weary he looked, and worn, as from a heart-ill.

"What has happened, Barton? Did you go to anybody's house? Whom did you see? "

"No; I went to the pond, and met the Doctor and Uncle Jonah, and Theodore came home with me. "

"Did you meet Julia Markham anywhere? "

"I did; she was going home from Coe's by the old road, and I went out of the woods with her. "

A long, hard-drawn breath from his mother, who saw that he took her question like a stab.

"It is no matter, mother. It had to be over some time. "

"Barton! you don't mean, Barton—"

"I do, just that, mother, " steadily. "She was kinder in her scorn than she meant. It was what I needed. "

"Her scorn! her scorn, Barton! "

"Yes, her scorn, mother, " decidedly and firmly.

"You must have talked and acted foolishly, Barton. "

"I did talk and act foolishly, and I take the consequences. "

"You are both young, Barton, and you have all the world in which to overcome your faults and repair your mistakes, and Julia—"

"Not another word of her, mother dear! She has gone more utterly out of my life than as if she were buried. Then I might think of her; now I will not, " firmly.

"Oh, that this should come to you now, my poor, poor boy! "

"Don't pity me, mother! I am soft enough now, and don't you for a moment think that I have nothing else to do in this world but to be killed out of it by the scorn of a girl. Let us not think of these Markhams. The Judge is ambitious, and proud of his wealth and self, and his daughter is ambitious too. The world wants me; it has work for me. I can hear its voices calling me now, and I am not ready. Don't think I am to sit and languish and pine for any girl; " and his mouth was firm with will and purpose, and a great swell of pride and pain agitated the bosom of his mother, who recognized the high elements of a nature drawn from her own.

"You know, mother, " he continued, thoughtfully, "that I am not one to be loved. I am not handsome and popular, like Morris, whom all men like and many women love; nor thoughtful and accomplished and considerate, like Henry, whom everybody esteems and respects, and of whom so much is expected. "

"Do you envy them, Barton? "

"Envy them, mother? Don't I love the world for loving Morris? Don't I follow him about to feel the gladness that he brings? Don't I live on the praises of Henry? and don't I tear every man that utters a doubt of his infallibility? Poor old Dominie Young! I was savage on him last night, for an unnecessary remark about Henry; and I'll go and hear him preach, to show my contrition; and penitence can't go further. Now, mother dear, I probably wanted this, and I am now down on the flat, hard foundation of things. Don't blame this Julia, and don't think of her in connection with me. No girl will ever scorn one of your boys but once. "

She lingered, and would have said more; but he put her away with affected gayety, and said he was coming down immediately, —and he did. But the melancholy chords vibrated long.

There was another overhauling of the little desk, and innumerable sketches of various excellence, having a family resemblance, with faults in common, were sent to join the departed verses.

That night, in a letter to Henry, he said: "I've burned the last of my ships, not saving even a small boat. "

* * * * *

Mrs. Ridgeley pondered over the revelation which her woman's intuitions had drawn from Barton. No woman can understand why a son of hers should fail with any natural-born daughter of woman, and she suspected that poor Bart had, with his usual impetuosity, managed the affair badly. No matter if he had; she felt that he was not an object of any woman's scorn; and this particular Julia, she had every reason to know, would live to correct her impressions and mourn her folly. She, however, was incapable of injustice to even her own sex; and if Julia did not fancy Barton, she was not to blame, however faulty her taste. She remembered with satisfaction that she and hers were under no obligations to the Markhams, and she only hoped that her son would be equal to adhering to his purpose. She had little fear of this, although she knew nothing of the offensive manner of his rejection, and had no intimation of what followed it. To her, Julia was to be less than the average girl of her acquaintance.

In the afternoon the two mothers met by accident, at the store, whither Mrs. Ridgeley had gone to make a few small purchases, and Mrs. Markham to examine the newly-arrived goods. Mrs. Ridgeley had no special inducement to waste herself on Mrs. Markham, and none to exhibit any sensibility at the treatment of Barton; her manner was an admirable specimen of the cool, neighborly, indifferently polite. She was by nature a thorough-bred and high-spirited woman; and had Julia openly murdered poor Bart, the manner of his mother would not have betrayed her knowledge of the fact to Mrs. Markham. That lady busied herself with some goods until Mrs. Ridgeley had completed her purchases, when she approached her with her natural graciousness, which was so spontaneous that it was hardly a virtue, and was met with much of her own frank suavity. These ladies never discussed the weather, or their neighbors, or hired girls, —which latter one of them did not have; and with a moment's inquiry after each other's welfare, in which each omitted the family of the other, Mrs. Markham asked Mrs. Ridgeley's judgment as to the relative qualities of two or three pieces of ladies' fabrics, carelessly saying that she was choosing for Julia, who was quite undecided. Mrs. Ridgeley thought Miss Markham was quite right to defer the matter to her mother's judgment, and feared that her own ignorance of goods of that quality would not enable her to aid Mrs. Markham. Mrs. Markham casually remarked that there was much demand for the goods, and that Julia had had a long walk around to the Coes the day before, and home through the woods, and was a little wearied to-day, and had referred the matter to her. Mrs. Ridgeley understood that Miss Markham was accustomed to healthy out-door exercise, and yet young girls were sometimes, she presumed, nearly as imprudent as boys, etc. ; she trusted Miss Markham would soon be restored.

If either of the ladies looked the other in the face while speaking and spoken to, as is allowable, neither discovered anything by the scrutiny. Mrs. Markham thought Mrs. Ridgeley must suffer much on account of the rashness of so many spirited boys, though she believed that Mrs. Ridgeley was fortunate in the devotion of all her sons. Mrs. Ridgeley thanked her; as to her boys, she had become accustomed to their caring for themselves, and when they were out she seldom was anxious about them. Mrs. Markham thought that they must have some interesting adventures in their hunting excursions. Mrs. Ridgeley said that Morris always enjoyed telling of what he had done and met in the woods, while Barton never mentioned anything, unless he had found a rare flower, a splendid tree, or a striking view, or something of that sort.

The ladies gave each other much well-bred attention, and Mrs. Markham went on to remark that she had not seen Barton since his return, but that Julia had mentioned meeting him once or twice. Mrs. Ridgeley replied that soon after Barton came home, she remembered that he spoke of meeting Miss Markham at the store. The faces of the ladies told nothing to each other. Mrs. Markham gave an animated account of her call at the house being built by Major Ridgeley for Mr. Snow, in Auburn, and said that Mr. Snow was promising that Major Ridgeley might give a ball in it; and the Major undertook to have it ready about New Year's, and that the ball would be very select, she understood; the house was to contain a very fine ball-room, etc.

Had Mrs. Ridgeley received a letter recently from Henry? She had. Would Barton probably go and study with his brother? She thought that would be pleasant for both. Mrs. Markham was very kind to inquire about the boys. Would Mrs. Ridgeley permit Mrs. Markham to send her home in her new buggy? It stood at the door. Mrs. Ridgeley thanked her; she was going up by Coe's, and so out across the bit of woods, home. Did not Mrs. Ridgeley fear the animal that had been heard to scream in these woods? Mrs. Ridgeley did not in the least, and she doubted if there was one.

The ladies separated. Mrs. Markham decided that Barton had not told his mother of meeting Julia the day before, nor of their adventure afterwards, and she was relieved from the duty of explaining anything; and she thought well of the young man's discretion, or pride.

Mrs. Ridgeley thought that Mrs. Markham was talking at her for a purpose, perhaps to find out what Barton told her; and it was some little satisfaction, perhaps, to know that Julia did not feel like being out, —but then Julia was a noble girl, and would feel regret at inflicting pain. Poor Bart! Generous Mrs. Ridgeley! It also occurred to Mrs. Ridgeley that Mrs. Markham did not return to the subject of the goods, and she was really afraid that Julia might lose her dress.

CHAPTER XI.

UNCLE ALECK.

The marvellous power of Christianity to repeat itself in new forms apparently variant, and reveal itself under new aspects, or rather its wonderful fulness and completeness, that enables the different ages of men, under ever-varying conditions of culture and development, to find in it their greatest needs supplied, and their highest civilization advanced, may be an old observation. A change in the theological thought and speculation of New England was beginning to make its way to the surface at about the time of the migration of its sons and daughters to the far-off Ohio wilderness, and many minds carried with them into the woods a tinge of the new light. Theodore Parker had not announced the heresy that there was an important difference between theology and religion, and that life was of more consequence than creed. But Calvinism had come to mean less to some minds, and there was another turning back to the great source by strong new seekers, to whom the accepted formulas had become empty, dry shells, to be pulverized, and the dead dust kneaded anew with the sweet waters of the ever fresh fountain. Those who bore the germs of the new thought to the wild freedom of nature, in the woods, found little to restrain or direct it; and, as is usual upon the remoulding of religious thought, while the strong religious nature questions only as to the true, many of different temperament boldly question the truth of all. The seeds and sources of a religious revolution are remote, and its apparent results a generation of heretics and infidels. Heresy sometimes becomes orthodoxy in its turn, and in its career towards that, and in its days of zeal and warfare, the infidel often becomes its convert.

Those in the new colony, who turned to the somewhat softer and sweeter givings out of the Great Teacher, and to whom these qualities made the predominant elements of his doctrines, were few in numbers, scattered and weak, while the mass of the immigrants were staunch in the theology of their old home. The holders of the new ideas not only suffered from the odium of all new heresies, but their doctrines were especially odious, as tending to destroy the wholesome sanctions of fitting punishments, while, like the teachers of all ideas at variance with the old, they were surrounded by and confounded with the herd of old scoffers and unbelievers, who always try to ally themselves with those who, for any reason, doubt or question the dogmas always rejected by them.

And so it is that the apostles of a new dogma come to be weighted with whatever of odium may attach to the old rejectors of the old; and there is always this bond of sympathy between the new heretic and the old infidel; they are both opposed to the holders of the old faith, and hence so far are allies.

In Newbury, in that far-off time, a dozen families, perhaps, respectable for intelligence and morality, were zealous acceptors of the new ideas; and about these, to their great scandal, gathered the straggling, rude spirits and doubtful characters that lightly float on the wave of emigration, to be dropped wherever that subsides.

The organizing power of the new ideas in itself, was not great. Their spirit was not, and cannot, be aggressive. They consisted in part of a rejection of much that made Puritanism intolerant in doctrine, and that furnished it with its organizing and militant power.

Men organize to do, and not merely to not do. Among the most earnest in the support of these ideas were Thomas Ridgeley and his wife, who were also among the most prominent in their neighborhood. Their public religious exercises were not frequent, and were holden in a school-house in their vicinity, the most attractive feature of which was the excellent singing of the small congregation. Mrs. Ridgeley came from a family of much local celebrity for their vocal powers, while her husband was not only an accomplished singer, but master of several instruments, and in the new settlements he was often employed as a teacher of music.

The preacher of this small congregation was Mr. Alexander, "Uncle Aleck, " as everybody called him, who lived in the west part of the town, on the border of "the woods. " A man well in years, inferior in person, with a mild, sweet, benevolent face, and blameless, dreamy life, he spent much time in "sarching the Scripters, " as he expressed it, in constant conversations and mild disputations of Bible texts and doctrines, and sermonizing at the Sunday assemblies of his co-believers. He was a man without culture, without the advantage of much converse with cultivated people, of rather feeble and slender mental endowments, but of a wonderfully sweet, serene, cheerful temper, and a most abiding faith. His was a heart and soul whose love and compassion embraced the created universe. He believed that God created only to multiply the objects of His own love, and that the ultimate end of all Providence was to bless, and he did not doubt that He would manage to have His way. That He had ever generated forces and powers beyond His control, he did not believe. The gospels, to him, were luminous with love, mercy, and protecting providence; and while his sermons were faulty and confused, his language vicious, and his pronounciation depraved, so that he furnished occasional provocation to scoffers among the profane, and to critics among the orthodox, there was always such sweetness and tenderness, and love so broad, deep, rich and pure, that few earnest or thoughtful minds ever heard him without being moved and elevated by his benignant spirit.

He was always in converse with the Master in his early ministrations, in beautiful, far-off, peaceful Galilee. He was a contented and happy feeder upon the manna and wine of those early wanderings and preachings among a simple and primitive people; and was forever lingering away from Jerusalem, and avoiding the final catastrophe, which he could never contemplate without shuddering horror. No power on earth could ever convert his simple faith to the idea that this great sacrifice was an ill-devised scheme to end in final failure; and he preached accordingly. The elder Ridgeley had been dead many years; the simple faith had gained few proselytes; Uncle Aleck's sermons made little impression, and gained nothing in clearness of statement or doctrine, but ripened and deepened in tenderness and sweetness. His people remained unpopular, and nothing but the force of character of a few saved them from personal proscription.

The Ridgeley boys, the older ones, were steady in the faith of their parents. Morris openly acknowledged it and Henry had been destined by his father to its teachings; Barton stood by his mother, however he esteemed her faith, and occasionally said sharp and pungent things of its opponents, which confirmed the unpopular estimate in which he was undoubtedly held.

The Markhams were orthodox. Dr. Lyman was a nearly unbelieving materialist at this time, but had several times "wabbled, " as Bart expressed it, from orthodoxy to infidelity, without touching the proscribed ground of Uncle Aleck.

Mr. Young was an obsolete revival exhorter, whose life did little to illustrate and enforce his givings out. He had a weakness for the elder Scriptures; and hence the irreverent name applied to him in the boat by Bart.

CHAPTER XII.

A CONSECRATION.

Among the adherents of uncle Aleck were the Coes, a mild, moony race, and recently it was understood that Emeline, the only daughter in a family of eight or nine, a languid, dreamy, verse-making mystic, had expressed a wish to receive the rite of Christian baptism, at that time practised by Uncle Aleck and his associates in Northern Ohio.

The ceremony had been postponed on account of the illness of her mother, and was finally performed on the Sunday following the incidents last narrated. A meeting was to be holden in the primitive forest, near Coe's cabin, on the margin of a deep, crystal pool, formed naturally by the springs that supplied Coe's Creek. Few events happened in that quiet region, and this was an event. News of it had circulated widely, and hundreds attended.

The occasion was not without a certain touching interest. The beauty of the day, the wildness of the scenery under the grand old trees, with rude rocks, beautiful slopes, and running, pure water, and the deepening tints of autumn in sky, cloud and foliage, —the warm shafts of sunshine that here and there lit it all up, —the sincere gravity that fell as a Sabbath hush on the expectant multitude, who seemed to realize the presence of a solemn mystery, —carried back an imaginative mind to an earlier day and a more primitive people, when the early Christians, in the absence of schism, administered the same rite.

Uncle Aleck, imbued with the sweetest spirit of his Master, seemed inspired with a sense of the sacredness of the act he was to perform. Of its divine origin, and sweet and consecrating efficacy, he had not the slightest doubt. The simple services of his faith he performed in a way that harmonized entirely with the occasion and its surroundings. A grand hymn under the old trees was sung by the choir with fine effect; a short, fervent prayer, the reading of two or three portions of one of the gospels, and a few words of sweet and simple fervor, expressive of a great love and sacrifice, and the unutterable hope and rest of its grateful acknowledgment in the public act about to be performed, followed; and then the believing, trembling girl was led into the translucent waters, which for a single instant closed over her, and was returned, with a little cry of ecstasy, to her friends. Another hymn, a simple benediction, and the solemnly impressed crowd broke up into little knots, and left the spot vacant to the silence of approaching night.

Conspicuous in this gathering, as conspicuous everywhere where he appeared, was Major Ridgeley, an elder brother of Bart. Slightly taller, and absolutely straight in the shoulders, with an uppish turn to his head, the Major was universally pronounced a handsome man. His large, bright, hazel eye, pure red and white complexion just touched by the sun, with a world of black curling hair swept carelessly back from, an open white brow, with well-formed mouth and chin, and his frank, dashing, manly way, cheery voice, and gay manner, made him a universal favorite; and, farmer and carpenter though he was, he was welcomed as an equal by the best people in the community. He had little literary cultivation, but mixing freely among men, and received with universal kindness by all women, he had the ready manners of a man of the world, which, with a shrewd vigor of mind, qualified him for worldly success.

Bart came upon the ground with his mother, near whom he remained, and to whom he was very attentive. To him the whole thing was very impressive. His poetic fancy idealized it, and carried him back till he seemed to see and hear the dedication of a young, pure spirit to the sweet sacredness of a holy life, as in the days of the preachings of the apostles. When the final hymn was given out he stood by his brother, facing most of the crowd, and for the first time they recognized in him a nameless something that declared and asserted itself—something that vaguely hinted of the sheaf of the boy Joseph, that arose and stood upright, and to which their sheaves involuntarily did obeisance.

Still very young, and less handsome than his brother, he was yet more striking, pale and fair, with little color, and a face of boyish roundness, which began to develop lines of thought and strength. His brow, not so beautiful, was more ample; his features were regular, but lacked the light, bright, vivacious expression of Morris; while from his deep, unwinking eyes men saw calmly looking out a strong, deep nature, not observed before. He joined his mother and brother in the last hymn. Everybody knew the Ridgeleys could sing. They carried the burden of the grand and simple old tune nearly alone. The fine mezzo-soprano of the mother, the splendid tenor of Morris, and the rich baritone of Bart, in their united effect, had never been equalled in the hearing of that assembly. The melody was a sweet and fitting finale of the day, swelling out and dying away in the high arches of the forest.

* * * * *

The Coes were objects of the kindness of Mrs. Markham and Julia, obnoxious as was their religious faith; but Mrs. Markham was tolerant, and she and her husband and daughter, with most of the State road people, were present.

While they were waiting for the crowd to disperse, so that they could reach their carriage, the Ridgeleys, who began to move out, on their way home, approached, and were pleasantly recognized by the Markhams, with whom the Major was a great favorite. The two parties joined, shook hands, and interchanged a pleasant greeting — all but Bart. He moved a little away, and acknowledged their presence by holding his hat in his hand, as if unconscious that he was a spectacle for the eyes of some of them, and without betraying that he could by any possibility care. It was a sore trial for him.

Mrs. Markham looked at him several times as if she would go to him, and an expression once or twice came into the sweet and pensive face of Julia, that seemed to mean that she wished she could say to him, "I want so much to thank you for your courage and generosity! " Morris noticed the strange conduct of Barton, and felt an impulse to call to him, and on their way home he spoke to him about it.

"Why, Bart, what is the matter? I thought you and the Markhams were on the best of terms; especially you and Julia and Mrs. Markham. "

"Well, Major, you see a shrewd man can be mistaken, don't you? "

"What has happened? "

"That which renders it absolutely impossible that I should ever voluntarily go into the presence of these Markhams, and especially of Julia. "

The voice was low, and full of force, with a little bitterness. Morris looked at his brother with incredulous amazement.

"Morris, " said Bart, "don't ask more about it. Mother guessed something of it. Pray don't refer to it ever again. "

Morris walked forward, with their mother; and when he turned back to the stricken face of his young brother, there was a great tenderness in his eye; but his brow gathered and his face darkened into a momentary frown. He was by nature frank and brave, and could not long do any one injustice. His nature was hopeful, and bright, and manly. No girl could always scorn his brother Bart; nor did he believe that Bart would willingly remain scorned.

CHAPTER XIII.

BLACKSTONE.

The town of Burton was one of the oldest in the county. It was the residence of many wealthy men, the seat of Judge Hitchcock, Chief Justice of the State, as well as the home of Seabury Ford, a rising young politician, just commencing a most useful and honorable career, which was to conduct him to the Chief Magistracy of the State.

The young Whig party had failed to elect Gen. Harrison, but the result of the contest assured it of success in the campaign of 1840, for which a vast magazine was rapidly and silently accumulating. The monetary and credit disasters of '36-'37, occurring in the third term of uninterrupted party rule, would of themselves have overthrown a wiser and better administration than that of Mr. Van Buren, patriotic and enlightened as that was, contrasted with some which followed.

Men, too, were beginning to examine and analyze the nature and designs of slavery; and already Theodore Weld had traversed the northern and middle States, and with his marvellous eloquence and logic, second to none of those who followed him, had stirred to their profoundest depths the cool, strong, intellectual souls of the New Englanders of those regions.

One early October morning, as Gen. Ford, then commander of a brigade of militia, in which Major Ridgeley held a commission, was arranging some papers in his law office, a young man paused a moment in front of the open door, and upon being observed, lifted his hat and stepped frankly forward. Young men in Ohio then seldom removed their hats to men, and rarely to women; and the act, gracefully done as it was, was remarked by the lawyer.

"General Ford, I believe? " said the youth.

"Yes; will you walk in? "

"I am Barton Ridgeley, " said the young man, stepping in; "usually called Bart. "

"A brother of Major Ridgeley? "

"Yes; though I am thought not to be much like him. "

"The Major is a warm friend of mine, " said the General, "and I should be glad to serve you. "

"Thank you, General; I feel awkward over my errand here, " hesitating; "I wanted to see a lawyer in his office, with his books and papers, and be permitted to look, especially at his books. "

"You are entirely welcome. I am not much of a lawyer, and have but a few books, but nothing would give me more pleasure than to have you examine them. "

"I may annoy you. "

"Not at all. I've not much to do. Take a seat. "

Bart did so. He found the General, whom he had only seen at a distance on muster days, a man of the ordinary height, with heavy shoulders, with a little stoop in them, a very fine head and face, and a clear, strong, grayish, hazel eye; and, on the whole, striking in his appearance. There were files of leading newspapers, the *National Intelligencer, Ohio State Journal, Courier and Inquirer*, etc. These did not so much attract the young man's attention; but, approaching a large book-case, filled compactly with dull yellow books, uniform in their dingy, leathery appearance, he asked: "Are these law-books?"

"Yes, those are law-books. "

"And these, then, are the occult cabalistical books, full of darkness and quirks and queer terms, in which is hidden away, somewhere, a rule or twist or turn that will help the wrong side of every case? "

"So people seem to think, " said the General, smiling.

"Does a student have to read all of these? "

"Oh, no, not to exceed a dozen or fourteen. "

"A-h-h-h! not more than that? Will you show me some of them? "

"Certainly. There, this is Blackstone, four volumes, which covers the whole field of the law; all the other elementary writers are only amplifications of the various titles or heads of Blackstone. "

"Indeed! only four volumes! Can one be a lawyer by reading Blackstone? "

"A thorough mastery of it is an admirable foundation of a good lawyer. "

"How long is it expected that an ordinary dullard would require to master Blackstone? "

"Some students do it in four months. I have known one or two to do it in three. They oftener require six, and some a year. "

Bart could hardly repress his astonishment. "Four months! a month to one of these books! " running them over. "They have some notes, I see; but, General, a man should commit it to memory in that time! "

The General smiled.

"This is an English work; is there an American which answers to Blackstone? "

"Yes, Kent's Commentaries, four volumes, which many prefer. I have not got it. Also Swift's work, in two volumes, which does not stand so high. Judge Cowan, of New York, has also written a book of some merit. "

"Shall I annoy you if I sit down and read Blackstone a little? "

"Not at all. "

He read the title-page, glanced at the American preface, etc., and then plunged in promiscuously. "It has less Latin than I expected. Is it good classical Latin? "

A smile.

"It is law Latin, and most of it would have puzzled Cicero and Virgil, I fear. Are you a Latin scholar? "

"I'm not a scholar at all. I've been an idler, generally, and have picked up only a few phrases of Latin. I've a brother, a student with Giddings & Wade, at Jefferson, who would have told me all I want to know, but I had a fancy to find it out first hand. "

"Exactly; " and the General thought he looked like a youth who would not take things second-hand. "They are able lawyers, and it is said Giddings will retire from the bar and run for Congress. It is thought that Mr. Whittlesey will resign, and make an opening. "

Bart thought that the General spoke of this with interest, and he made another dab at Blackstone. He then wandered off to a small but select case of miscellaneous books. "Adam Smith! " he said, with animation; "I never saw that before. How interesting it must be to get back to the beginning of things. And here is Junius, whom I have only read about! and Hume! and Irving! and Scott's Novels! Oh dear, oh dear! General, what a happy man you must be, with all these about you, and these newspapers, to come and go between you and the outside world. "

"Oh! I don't know. I have but few books, compared with real libraries, and yet I must say I have more than I make useful. "

Bart plunged into Ivanhoe for a moment, and then laid it down with a sigh.

The General, who found much in the frank enthusiasm of Bart to attract him, asked him many questions about himself, surroundings, etc., all of which were answered with a modest frankness, that won much on the open, manly nature of Ford.

Bart said he most of all wanted to study law, but he did not know how to accomplish it. He was without means, and wanted to remain with his mother, and he wanted only to look at the books, and learn a little about what he would have to do, the time, etc. The General said "the laws of Ohio required two years' study, before admission, which would be upon examination before the Supreme Court, or by a committee of lawyers appointed for that purpose; lawyers who received students usually charged fifty or sixty dollars per year for use of books and instruction, the last of which often did not amount to much. "

Bart looked wistfully at the books, and arose to go. The General asked him to remain to dinner with such hearty cordiality, that Bart assented, and the General took him into the house and introduced him to Mrs. Ford, a tall, slender woman, of fine figure, with striking features, and really handsome; of very kindly manners, and full of genuine good womanly qualities, who believed in her husband, and was full of ambition for him.

The quiet, easy manners, and frank, sparkling conversation of Bart, won her good-will at once.

"Was he acquainted with Judge Markham's people? "

"A little. "

"Mrs. Markham is one of the most superior and accomplished women I ever met, " said Mrs. Ford. Of course he was acquainted with Julia, who was thought to be the belle of all that region?

Barton was slightly acquainted with her, and thought her very beautiful. His acquaintance with young ladies of her position was very limited, but he could believe that few superiors of hers could be found anywhere, etc.

Poor Bart!

Mrs. Ford presumed that a great many young men had their eyes on her, and it would be a matter of interest to see where her choice would fall.

It was some satisfaction to Bart to feel that he could hear this point referred to without any but the same pain and bruise of heart that any thought of her occasioned.

After dinner, General Ford said to Bart that if he really wished to enter upon the study of the law, he would do what he could for him; that he would permit him to take home such books as he could spare, and when he had read one he would examine him upon it, and give him another.

This was more than had entered Bart's mind; and so unaccustomed was he to receiving favors, that the sensations of gratitude were new to him, and he hardly expressed them satisfactorily to himself.

His new tutor had taken a real liking to him; he may have remembered that the Major was one of the rising young men in the south-west part of the county, whom he liked also. He called Barton's attention to the chapters of Blackstone that would demand his more careful reading, and they parted well pleased with each other.

Bart pushed off across the fields in a right line for home, with the priceless book in his hand; light came to him, and opportunity. Lord! how his heart and soul and brain arose and went out to meet them! As the branches of the young forest-tree that springs up by a river-side shoot out, rank, and strong, and full, to the beautiful light and air, and so, too, as the tree grows one-sided and disfigured, the danger is that this embodiment of young force and energy may develop one-sided. The poetic, upward tendency of his nature will help him, and his devotion to his mother will hold him unwarped, while the struggle with a great, pure, and utterly hopeless passion shall at least make a sacred desert of his heart, where no unhallowed thought shall take root. His was eminently a nature to be strengthened and purified by suffering.

But he had the law in his hands. No matter how gnarled, warped or obscure were the paths to its lurking-places, he would find them all out, and pluck out all its meanings, and make its soul his own. He had already learned from his brother the fallacy of the vulgar judgment of the law, and he knew enough of history to know that some of the wisest and greatest of men were eminent lawyers, and he thought nothing of the moral dangers of the law as a profession. He had never been even in a magistrate's court, but he had heard the legends and traditions of the advocates; had read that eminent fiction, Wirt's Life of Patrick Henry, and a volume of Charles Phillips's speeches, and had felt that strong inner going forth of the soul that yearned to find utterance in oversweeping speech.

Several times on his way home he stopped to read, and only suspended his studies at the approach of evening, which found him east of the pond, lying across his direct route, and which he found the means of passing.

Blackstone he took in earnest, and smiled to find nothing that he did not seem to comprehend, and often went back, fearing that the seeming might not be the real meaning.

At the end of a week he returned to his kind friend, the General, not without misgivings as to the result of his work. He found him at leisure in the afternoon, and was received with much kindness.

"Well, how goes Blackstone? "

"Indeed I don't know; and I am anxious, if you have leisure, to find out. "

The General took the book, and turning to the definition of law, and the statement of a few elementary principles, found that they were thoroughly understood. Turning on, he paused with his finger in the book.

"What do you think of the English Constitution? "

Bart looked a little puzzled.

"The English government seems to be an admirable structure—on paper; but as to the principles that lie below it, or around it, that govern and control its workings, and from which it can't depart, I am cloudy. "

"Yes, a good many are; but then there is, as you know, a great unwritten English Constitution—certain great fixed principles which from time to time have been observed, through many ages, until their observance has become a law, from which the government cannot depart, and they take the form of maxims and rules. "

"I think I understand what you mean; but to me everything is in cloud-land, vague and shifting, and the fact that nobody has ever attempted to put in writing these principles, or even to enumerate them, leads one to doubt whether really there are such things. When king, lords and commons are, in theory and practice, absolutely omnipotent, I can't comprehend how there can be any other constitution. When they enact a law, nobody can question it, nobody can be heard against it; no court can pronounce it unconstitutional. What may have been thought to be unconstitutional they can declare to be law, and that ends it. So they can annihilate any one of the so-called constitutional maxims. When a party in power wants to do a thing, it is constitutional; when a minister or great noble is to be got rid of, he is impeached for a violation of the constitution, and constitutionally beheaded. "

"Well, " said the General, smiling, "but this, for instance: the great palladium of British liberty, taxation, must be accompanied with representation. "

"Yes; that, if adhered to, would protect property and its owners; but then it never has been carried out, even in England, while the non-taxpayer is wholly out of its reach; and my recollection is, that the constitutional violation of this palladium of the Constitution by king, lords and commons, produced a lively commotion, some sixty-odd years ago. "

"Yes, I've heard of that; but the attempt to tax the colonies was clearly unconstitutional; they were without representation in the Parliament that enacted the law. "

"But then, General, you are to remember that, according to Blackstone, Parliament was and is, by the English Constitution, omnipotent. The fact is, we took one part of the constitution, and George the other; we kept our part, and all our land, and George maintained his, on his island, strong as ever; and yet there, property-owners always have been and always will be taxed, who do not vote. I fear that it will be found that all the other maxims have from time to time suffered in the same way. "

"You must admit, however, " said the General, "that the maxims in favor of personal freedom have usually been adhered to in England proper. "

"Yes, the sturdy elements of the natural constitution of the English people have vindicated their liberty against all constitutional violations of it; and while I cordially detest them, one and all, there isn't another nation in Europe that I am willing to be descended from. "

"I fear that is the common sentiment among our people, " said the General. "And so you think the world-famous British Constitution may be written in one condensed sentence—the old English formula—Parliament is omnipotent. "

"Yes, just that. Parliament is the constitution; everything else is ornamental. "

Without expressing any opinion, the General resumed, and turning at hop, skip and jump, he found that Bart happened to be at home wherever he alighted. He finally turned to the last page, and asked questions with the same result, closing the book with:

"Well, what else have you been doing this week? "

"Not much; I've worked a little, dabbled with geometry some, read Gibbon a little, newspapers less, run some in the woods, and fooled away some of my time, " answered Bart, with a self-condemning air.

"Have you slept any? "

"Oh, yes. "

"Oh, dear! " said the General, laughing good-humoredly, and then looking grave, "this will never do—never! "

"Well, General, " said Bart, crestfallen, "I've only had the book a week, and although I don't memorize easily, I believe I can commit the whole before a month is out, except the notes. "

"Oh, my dear boy, it isn't that! I don't know but there is a man in the world who, without having seen a law book before, has taken up and mastered the first volume of Blackstone in a week, but I never heard of him. What will never do is—it will not do for you to go on in this way; you would read up a library in a year, if you lived, but will die in six months, at this rate. "

With tears in his eyes, Bart said: "Do not fear me, General; I am strong and healthy; besides, there are a good many things worse than death. "

"I am serious, " said the General. "No mortal can stand such work long. "

"Well, General, I must work while the fit is on; I am thought to be incapable of keeping to any one thing long. "

"How old are you? "

"In my twenty-second year. "

"Have you ever practised speaking in public? "

"I am thought to make sharp and rough answers to folks, quite too much, I believe, " answered Bart, laughing; "but, save in a debating school, where I was ruled out for creating disorder, I've never tried speech-making. "

"You will grow more thoughtful as you grow older, " said the General.

"If I do, " said Bart, "I know those who think I can't grow old fast enough. "

The General gave him the second volume of Blackstone, with the injunction to be two weeks with it.

"Suppose I finish it in a week? "

"You must not; but if you do, bring it back, and take a scolding. "

"Certainly, " said Bart.

The General asked him to go in to tea. Bart thought that would not do, and excused himself.

* * * * *

The end of another week found Bart at the end of the second volume, and also at General Ford's office. The General was away; but he found an opportunity further to cultivate the acquaintance of Mrs. Ford, who introduced him to several of her circle of acquaintance, and permitted him to take the third volume of Blackstone.

The work was finished with the fourth week, to General Ford's satisfaction, and Bart was then set to try his teeth on Buller's "Nisi Prius, " made up of the most condensed of all possible abstracts of intricate cases, stated in the fewest possible words, and those of old legal significance, the whole case often not occupying more than four or five lines.

The cases, as there stated, convey no shadow of an idea to the unlearned mind. What a tussle poor Bart had with them! How often he turned them over, and bit at and hammered them, before they could be made to reveal themselves.

The General looked grim when he handed him the book, and said that he did so by the advice of Judge Hitchcock. He also loaned him Adam Smith and Junius, with permission to take any books from his library during the winter, and they parted—the General to go to his duties in the Legislature, and Barton to work his way on through the winter and into the law.

The devotion of Bart to his books took him wholly from association with others. He wrote occasionally to Henry, saying little of what he was doing, and going rarely to the post-office, and never elsewhere. He developed more his care of his mother, and a protecting tenderness to his younger brothers.

Kate Fisher's little party came and went, without Bart's attendance.

The Major was spreading himself out in building houses, clearing land, and unconsciously preparing the way to a smash-up; and the immediate care of the family devolved more and more upon the younger brother.

CHAPTER XIV.

THE YOUNG IDEA SHOOTS.

There was a region south, on the State road, partly in the townships of Auburn and Mantua, that, like "the woods, " long remained a wilderness, and was known as the "Mantua Woods. " Within the last year or two, the whole of it had been sold and settled, with the average of new settlers, strong, plain, simple people, with a sprinkling of the rough, and a little element of the dangerous.

They had built there a neat frame school-house, just on the banks of Bridge Creek, and were fully bent on availing themselves of the benefits of the Ohio Common School Fund and laws.

Here, on one bleak, late November Monday morning, in front of the new school-house, stood Bart Ridgeley, who appeared then and there pursuant to a stipulation made with him, to keep their first school. He undertook it with great doubt of his ability to instruct the pupils, but with none of his capacity to manage them. He stood surrounded by some forty young specimens of both sexes and all ages—from rough, stalwart young men, bold and fearless in eye and bearing, down to urchins of five. One-half were girls, and among them several well-grown lasses, rustic and sweet.

There had also come up seven or eight of the principal patrons, to see the young school-master and learn of the prospects. They were evidently disappointed, and wondered what "Morey" could be thinking of to hire that pale, green boy, with his neat dress and gloves, to come down there. Grid Bingham or John Craft would throw him out of the window in a week. Finally, Jo Keys did not hesitate to recommend him to go home; while Canfield, who knew his brother Morris, thought he had better try the school.

Bart was surprised and indignant. He cut the matter very short.

"Gentlemen, " he said quietly, but most decidedly, "I came down here to keep your school, and I shall certainly do it, " with a little nod of his head to Keys. "I shall be glad to see you at almost any other time, but just now I am engaged. " The decided way in which he put an end to the interview was not without its effect.

He called the scholars in, and began. They brought every sort of reading-book, from the Bible, English Reader, American Preceptor, Columbian Orator, Third Part, etc., to a New England Primer. But beyond reading, and spelling, and writing, he had only arithmetic, grammar and geography. On the whole, he got off well, and before the end of the first week was on good terms, apparently, with his whole school, with one or two exceptions; and so on through the second, which closed on Friday, and Bart turned gladly and eagerly toward home, to his mother and brothers.

The close of that week had been a little under a cloud, which left just a nameless shadow over the commencement of the third, and Bart began it with an uneasy feeling.

Bingham, a short, stout, compact young ruffian, of twenty-two or twenty-three, not quite as tall as Bart, but a third more in weight, and who had an ugly reputation as a quarrelsome fellow of many fights, had at first treated Bart with good-natured toleration, and said he would let him go on awhile. With him consorted John Craft, a chap of about his age, but of better reputation. Bingham had broken up a school the winter before, just below in Mantua, and was from the first an object of dread to parents in the new district. He was a dull scholar, and his blunders had exposed him to ridicule, which the teacher could not always repress. He left the school, on that Friday, moody and sullen, and came back on Monday full of mischief.

Not a word was said, that reached Bart's ears, but the young women had a scared look, and an ominous dread seemed to brood over the school-room. Monday and Tuesday came and went, as did the scholars, and also Wednesday forenoon.

The room was arranged with three rows of desks on two sides, and one on the third. Behind these sat the large scholars, with Grid, near the door. When he called the scholars in, after the recess, Bart quietly locked the outside door, and put the key in his pocket. He was cool, collected, and on the alert.

The first class began to read, each rising while reading, and then sitting down. Bart had observed that Bingham sat with his book closed, and wholly inattentive to the exercise, and quietly placed himself within a few feet of his desk.

As it came Bingham's turn, he sat with an assumed look of swaggering indifference. "Mr. Bingham, " said Bart very quietly, "will you read? "

"I'm not goin' to read for any God damned — —" the sentence was never finished, though Grid was; yet just how, nobody who saw it could quite tell. Something cracked, and Grid and his desk went sprawling into the middle of the floor. A hand came upon his collar as the last word was uttered. It was so sudden that he only seized his desk, which was taken from its fastening at the bottom as if it were pasteboard, and went in ruins with its occupant. As he struck, half stunned and surprised, he arose partly to his feet, and received on the side of his head a full blow from the fist of Bart.

Craft, who had been amazed at the suddenness of the catastrophe, and who was to have shared in the fight, if necessary, arose hesitatingly just as Grid received his *quietus*. Bart turned upon him with his white, galvanized face, and watery, flashing eyes, "Sit down, John Craft, " in a voice that tore him like a rasp on his spine, and John sat down. During this time, and until now, no other sound was heard in the room; now a half sob, with suppressed cries, broke from the terrified girls and children. "Hush! hush! not a word! " said the still excited master; "it is over, and nobody much hurt. " Bingham now began to rise, and Bart approached him: "Wait a moment, Mr. Bingham, " he said, and, unlocking the outside door: "There! now take your books and leave, and don't let me find you about this school-house so long as I remain — go! " and the humbled bully sullenly picked up his small property and went.

"Mr. Craft, " said Bart, approaching that cowed and trembling youth, "you and I can get along. I don't want to part with you if you will remain with me. I will excuse you from school this afternoon, and you can come back in the morning, and that may be the last of it. I will not humiliate you and myself with any punishment. " There was a tremor in Bart's voice, and a softness in his face. John arose: "Mr. Ridgeley, I don't know how I came to — I am very sorry — I want to stay with you. "

"All right, John, we will shake hands on it. " And they did.

"My poor, poor children! " said Bart, going up to the younger ones, who had huddled into the farthest corner and clambered on to the desks. "My poor scared little things, it is all over now, and we are all so glad and happy, aren't we? " and he took up some of the smallest in his arms and kissed them, and the still frightened, but glad and rejoicing young women, looked as if they would be willing to have that passed round. When they were pacified, and resumed their places, Charley Smith gathered up the boards and parts of the disabled desk, and Bart, with a few kind words to the older scholars, resumed the exercises of the school.

Scenes of violence were rare, even in that rude day, among that people; the sensibilities of the children were deeply wounded, and none of them were in a fitting condition to profit by their exercises, which were barely gone through with, and they were early dismissed to their homes, with the marvellous tale of the afternoon's events.

Bart was in the habit of remaining to write up the copies, and place everything in order before he left. The young men and older maidens lingered at the door, and then returned in a body, to say how glad they were that it had ended as it did. They knew something would happen, and they were so glad, and then they shook hands with him, and went hurrying home.

When they left, Bart locked the door, and, throwing himself into the chair by his table, laid his head down and burst into an uncontrollable flood of tears; —but he was a man now, and tears only choked and suffocated him. He was ashamed of himself for his weakness, and bathing his eyes, walked about the school-room to regain his composure. Every particle of anger left his bosom before Bingham left the house, and now he was fully under the influence of the melancholy part of his nature. Never before, even in childish anger, had he touched a human being with violence, and now he had exerted his strength, and had grappled with and struck a fellow-man in a brute struggle for animal mastery; he felt humiliated and abased. That the fellow's nature was low, and that he was compelled to act as he had done, was little comfort to him. He was glad that he decided not to punish or expel John. Darkness came, and he was aroused by a noise at the door. He unlocked it, and found Canfield and Morey and Smith.

"Hullo, Ridgeley! " exclaimed the former. "Good God! and so you had a pitched battle, and licked that bully before he had time to begin; give me your hand! Who would have thought it? "

"I did, " said Morey. "I knowed he'd do it. What will Jo Keys say now, I wonder? " And the party went inside, and wondered over the wrecked desk, and asked all about it. And then came in the stalwart Jo himself, celebrated for his strength.

"Wal, wal, wal! if this don't beat all natur, I give it up! What are you made of, young man, all spring and whalebone? I'd a bet he would 'a cleaned out a school-house full o' such dainty book chaps. I give it up. Let me feel o' you, " taking Bart good-naturedly by the shoulder. "You'll do, by — —. My Valdy said that when Grid gathered himself up the first time, he went heels over head, clear to the fire-place. "

And so the good-natured athlete went over with it all, with a huge relish for the smallest detail, and others came in, until nearly all the male patrons of the school had assembled; and Bart informally, but with hearty unanimity, was declared the greatest school-master of his day; they quoted all the similar instances within the range of memory or legend, and this achievement was pronounced the greatest. They were proud of him, and of the exploit, and of themselves that they had him. Morey, who had taken him because he could find no other, blazed up into a man of fine discernment; and Jo nearly killed him with approving slaps on his feeble back. Indeed, his apologies for what he had said were too striking.

Life in all new communities is run mainly on muscle, and whoever exhibits skill and bravery in its rough encounters, peaceful or warlike, always commands a premium. The people among whom Bart lived had not passed beyond the discipline of brute force, and he shared the usual fortune of heroes of this sort, of having his powers and achievements exaggerated, even by those under whose eyes he had acted.

A rumor reached Markham's and Parker's, from which it spread, that Bart's school had arisen against him, and the first version was that he was killed, or very dangerously wounded; that he defended himself with desperation, and killed one or two, but was finally overcome; that the neighborhood was divided and in arms, and the school-house had been burned. But the stage came in soon after, and the driver declared that he had seen Grid Bingham, whom he knew, brought out dead, that John Craft was badly hurt, and one or two more, and that Bart, who escaped without injury, would be arrested for murder. It was finally said that he would not be arrested, but that Grid was either dead or dying; that he headed four or five of the older boys, and they were whipped out by Bart single-handed, who locked the door, and pitched in, etc.

The rumor produced a deep sensation in Newbury; and, whilst it was thought that Bart had been rash, and undoubtedly in fault, yet he had behaved handsomely. When it was ascertained that he was victor, it was generally thought that he was a credit to the place, which was very natural and proper, considering that he had never before been thought to be a credit to anything anywhere.

CHAPTER XV.

SNOW'S PARTY.

It was called a house-warming, although the proprietor had not taken possession of the house with his family. The ball-room and most of the rooms were complete, and the building was, on the whole, in a good condition to receive a large company. The Major was the presiding genius of the festivities; and while the affair was in a way informal, and an assemblage of friends and neighbors of the owner, still he had made a judicious use of his authority, and had invited a good many rather prominent people from a distance. The evening of the occasion saw not only a numerous assemblage, but one in which the highest grades of society were fully represented.

As it was not strictly a ball, there was not the least impropriety in the straightest church-members—and they were strict, then—attending it; and they did. The sleighing was fine, and, as the usage was, the guests came early, and went early—the next morning. The barns, stables and neighboring houses were freely offered, and an efficient corps of attendants were on hand, while the absence of public-houses in the immediate neighborhood relieved the occasion of the presence of the unbidden rough element that would otherwise have volunteered an attendance.

The Markhams were there, with Julia, and the bevy of beautiful girls we saw with her at the store; Mrs. Ford from Burton, with some of her set; two or three from Chardon; the Harmons from Mantua; some of the Kings from Ravenna; two or three Perkinses from Warren, and many others. A rather showy young Mr. Greer, a gentleman of leisure, and who floated about quite extensively, knew everybody, and seemed on pleasant terms with them all, was among the guests.

The essential elements of pleasure and enjoyment—high and gay spirits, good-nature, with a desire to please and be pleased, where everybody was at their best, and where was a large infusion of good breeding—were present, and a general good time was the logical result.

There was a plenty of good music, and the younger part of the company put it to immediate and constant use. The style of dancing was that of the mediaeval time, between the stately and solemn of the older, and the easy, gliding, insipid of the present; and one which required, on the part of the gentlemen, lightness and activity, rather than grace, and allowed them great license in the matter of fancy steps. Two long ranks contra-faced, and hence contra dance—degenerated to country dance—was the prevailing figure; the leading couple commencing and dancing down with every other couple, until in turn each on the floor had thus gone through.

The cotillon, with its uniform step and more graceful style, had been already introduced by instructors, who had found short engagements under the severe reprobation of the Orthodox churches; but the waltz was unknown, except in name, and the polka, schottische, etc., had then never been mentioned on the Reserve.

The young people early took possession of the dancing-hall, where, surrounded by the elders, a quick succession of Money Musk, Opera Reel, Chorus Jig, etc., interspersed sparingly with cotillons, evidenced the relish with which young spirits and light hearts enjoy the exercises of the ball-room.

Julia Markham was the conceded belle, beautiful and elegant in form and style, faultless in dress and manner, brilliant with the vivacity of healthy girlhood. Next to her, undoubtedly, was Miss Walters, with whom ranked several elegant girls from abroad.

And of the young people here may be remarked what is usually true in all country places, that there were about three cultivated and refined girls to one young man of corresponding accomplishments.

As the ball went forward, the elders—and the elders did not dance in the young Ohio in those days, rarely or never—gathered into various groups, discussing the dancers and various kindred topics, and the little odds and ends of graceful "they says" that append themselves to the persons of those at all noticeable.

Mrs. Ford and Mrs. Markham were the centre of the principal of these. They were really good friends, and liked each other. Their husbands were friends, and possible rivals, and watched each other. Both were ambitious, and lived too near each other.

"Who is Miss Walters? " Mrs. Ford asked.

"She is from Pittsburgh. Her brother is in New Orleans, and she remains with the Fishers, relatives of hers, till he returns. "

"She is very elegant. "

"She is indeed, and she and Julia are great friends. "

"Who is that dancing with Julia? "

"A Mr. Thorndyke. He is of a Boston family, on a visit to his uncle in Thorndyke. Mr. Markham knew them, and he came up to call on us."

"He dances a little languidly, I think. "

"He feels a little out of place in this mixed company, I presume. His notions are high Boston. "

"How does that suit Julia? "

"It amuses her. He was telling her how this and that is done in Boston, and she in return told him how we do not do the same things here, and claimed that our way is the best. "

"Here comes Major Ridgeley. He seems much at home in a ball-room. "

"Yes, he is one of those ready men, who always appear best in a crowd. "

He saw and made his way to them; inquired about the General, spoke of his reply to Byington, complimented the dancing of Julia, inquired about her partner, and rattled on about several things.

"Will your brother Barton be here this evening? " asked Mrs. Ford.

"I don't know; he thought he would not, " was the reply. "He don't go out at all, lately. "

"What an awful time he had with that Bingham! " said Mrs. Ford. "They say he has broken up two or three schools, and was a powerful and dangerous man, twenty-five or six years old. I would really like to see Barton. He is quite a lion. "

"Bart is sensitive about it, " answered the Major, "and don't speak of it. Why, I was on my way up from Ravenna, the next day after it happened, and called at his school-house for half an hour; the desk had not been put up then, and I asked him what had happened to it, and he said the boys had torn it down in a scuffle. He never said a word of the fracas to me, and I only heard of it when I got up to Parker's. There I found young Johnson, who had just come from there. "

"Why, how you talk! What is the reason for that, do you suppose? "

"I don't know. He was at home a few days after, and seemed hurt and sad over it; and when I asked him how many innocents he had slaughtered since, he said one in two days, and at that rate they would just last him through. "

"It is funny, " said Mrs. Ford.

"As I have observed, Barton is not much inclined to talk about what he does, " said Mrs. Markham; "and, do you know, Major, he has not given me a chance to speak to him since his return. "

"He thinks, possibly, that he is under a cloud, " answered the Major.

"He chooses to think so, then, " said Mrs. Markham; and the music closed, and the dancers looked for seats, and the Major went away to meet an engagement for the next dance.

CHAPTER XVI.

WALTZ.

A little commotion about the door—a little mob of young men and boys—and a little spreading buzz and whisper—some hand-shakings—two or three introductions—then another buzz—and Bart made his way forward, with an air of being annoyed and bored and pushed forward as if to escape. He was under the inspiration of one of those sudden impulses upon which he acted, so sudden, often, as to seem not the result of mental process.

He discovered Mrs. Ford and Mrs. Markham, with Julia, Miss Walters, and several others, about them, whom he at once approached with the modest assurance of a thorough-bred gentleman, safe in the certainty of a gracious reception, and conscious of power to please. A happy word to the two or three who made way for him, and he stood bowing and smiling, and turning and bowing to each with the nice discriminating tact that rendered to all their due.

Mrs. Ford graciously extended her hand, which he took, and bowed very low over; she was nearest him. Mrs. Markham, in a pleased surprise, gave him hers, and its reception was, to her nice perception, even more profoundly acknowledged. To Miss Markham and Miss Walters precisely the same, with a little of the chivalrous devotion of a knight to acknowledged beauty.

"The fall and *winter* style prevails, I presume, " he said, in gay banter, as if anticipating that their gloved hands were not to be touched.

"Your memory is good, Mr. Ridgeley, " said Julia, with a little laugh and a little flush.

"Forgetfulness is not my weakness, " he replied.

"I was not aware you knew Mrs. Ford, " said Mrs. Markham, observing the little flutter in Julia's cheeks, and thinking there was a meaning in Bart's *persiflage.*

"Mrs. Ford and General Ford, " he answered with much warmth, "have been so very, very kind to me, that I have presumed to claim her acquaintance, even here; but then, they have only known me three months, " with affected despair.

"Well, " said Mrs. Ford, "what of that? "

"I find you with those who have known me all my life, " with a deprecating look towards Mrs. Markham.

"Well, Mr. Ridgeley, you are not deserving of forbearance at my hands, if I only knew of anything bad to say of you. "

"What exquisite irony! May I be permitted to know which of my thousand faults is now specially remembered against me? "

"You have not permitted me, until this moment, even to speak to you since your return last summer. "

"May I ask that you will permit that to stand with my other misdemeanors until some rare fortune enables me to atone for all at once? "

"And when will that be? "

"Oh!

> In that blissful never,
> When the Sundays come together,
> When the sun and glorious weather
> Wrap the earth in spring forever;
> As in that past time olden,
> Which poets call the golden."

Laughing.

"And so I have poetry, and inspire it myself—that is some compensation, certainly, " said Mrs. Markham, smiling.

"I fear my verses have deepened my offence, " said Bart, with affected gravity.

Kate Fisher intervened here: "Mr. Ridgeley, I have more cause for offence than even Mrs. Markham. Why didn't you come to my little party? I made it on your account. "

"The offence was great, " he answered, "but then staying away was ample punishment, as you must know. "

"No, I don't know it. I know you weren't there, and your excuse was merely a regret, which always means one don't want to go. "

"Oh, Mrs. Ford! " said Bart, "see what your coming here, or my coming here, exposes me to! "

"Have I heard the worst? "

"Well, you see, Mrs. Ford, " said Kate, "that Mr. Ridgeley can waltz, and so can Miss Walters, and I made a little party to see them waltz, and he didn't come. "

"That is grave. Will you leave it to me to pass judgment upon him? "

"I will. "

"And do you submit, Mr. Ridgeley? "

"She's so very kind to you, " remarked Mrs. Markham.

"I do, " said the young man, "and will religiously perform the sentence. "

"Well, it won't be a religious exercise—you are to waltz with Miss Walters, now and here. "

A little clapping of little hands marked the righteousness of the award.

"Mrs. Ford, " observed the culprit, "your judgment, as usual, falls heaviest on the innocent. Miss Walters, it remains for you to say whether this sentence shall be executed. If you will permit me the honor, I shall undergo execution with an edifying resignation. "

The smiling girl frankly placed her hand in his: "I should be sorry to prevent justice, " she said, which was also applauded.

Major Ridgeley was spoken to, and it was understood that the next dance would be a waltz, which had never before been more than named in a Yankee ball-room, on the Reserve; and it was anticipated with curiosity, not unmixed with horror, by many.

The floor was cleared, a simple waltz air came from the band, and the pleased Miss Walters, in the arms of Barton, was whirled out from her mob of curious friends, on to and over the nearly vacant floor, the centre of all eyes, few of which had witnessed such a spectacle before. The music went on with its measured rise and fall, sweet and simple, and youth and maiden possessed with it, seemed to abandon themselves utterly to it, and were controlled and informed by it; with one impulse, one motion, and one grace, each contributing an exact proportion, they glided, circling; and while the maiden thus yielded and was sustained, her attitude, so natural, graceful and womanly, had nothing languishing, voluptuous or sensuous; a sweet, unconscious girl, inspired by music and the poetry and grace of its controlling power, in the dance. Miss Walters dearly loved to dance, and above all to waltz. She had rarely met a partner who so exactly suited her step and style, and who so helped the inspiration she was apt to feel.

Bart had had little practice as a waltzer, but natural grace, and the presence of ladies, usually brought him to his best; and it was not in nature, perhaps, that he should not receive some inspiration from the beautiful girl, half given to his embrace, and wholly to his guidance.

So around and around through the hushed and admiring throng they went, whirling, turning, advancing, retreating, rising and falling, swaying and sinking, yet always in unison, and in rhythmic obedience to the music.

Sometimes the music rose loud and rapid, and then languished to almost dying away; but whatever its movement or time, it was embodied and realized by the beautiful pair, in their sweeping, graceful motions. The maiden's face was wrapt with a sweet, joyous light in her half-shut eyes; his, pale, but lit up and softened in the lamp-light, seemed fairly beautiful, like a poet's.

"How beautiful! " "How exquisite! " from the ladies.

"What a dance for lovers! " said Mrs. Ford.

"They are lovers, are they not? " asked a lady from Warren.

"I think not, " said Mrs. Markham, with a glance at Julia, who, never withdrawing her eyes, stood with lips slightly apart, and her face bright with unenvying admiration.

A little ripple—a murmur—and a decided clapping of hands around the room, with other sounds from the crowd at the entrance, marked the appreciation of the beautiful performance. The moment that this reached Barton, he led his delighted partner towards her group of friends, remarking: "Your admirers are sincere, Miss Walters, but too demonstrative, I fear. "

"Oh, I don't mind it, " said the straightforward girl.

"And I have to thank you for your courtesy to me, " he went on, "and only hope that all my punishments may come in the same form. "

"Mrs. Ford, is the judgment satisfied? "

"Satisfactory as far as you went, but then you did not serve out your time. "

"Have consideration, I pray, for the minister of justice, " bowing to Miss Walters.

"She seemed rather to like it, " said Mrs. Ford.

"Indeed I did! " and the young ladies gathered about to congratulate her, and cast admiring glances at her partner.

"Mr. Ridgeley, " said Mrs. Markham, "I was not aware that you were an accomplished waltzer. "

"You forget, " Bart answered mockingly, "that I am travelled; and you know my only aptitude is for the useless. "

"I did not say that. "

"You are too kind. I sometimes supply words to obvious thoughts. "

"And sometimes to those that have no existence. "

The floor filled again, and the music struck up. Standing, a moment later, at a window, Julia saw a figure pass out, pause at the roadway, turn and look up. The full glare of the lamps revealed the face of Bart, from which the light had faded, and its beauty and spirit of expression had departed. He gazed for an instant up at the brilliant and joyous scene, where a moment before he had been a central and applauded figure, and then, muffling his face in his cloak, he turned away.

He had not intended to go, and sat melancholy through the darkness of the early night; but somehow, a hungry, intense longing came to him to go and look for a moment upon the loveliness of Julia, as she would stand open to the eyes of all, just for one moment, and then to go away. He felt that he ought not to do it, but he went. He could not help it.

When he reached the place, three miles away, he was annoyed by being recognized and pointed at, and talked at, on account of his late encounter with Grid.

"He ain't a powerful-lookin' chap. " "I wouldn't be afeared o' him. " "He's a darned sight harder'n he looks, " etc.

When he escaped into the ball-room, the impulse to go into the immediate presence of Julia was followed, and ended by as sudden a retreat. He had not known how utterly weak and helpless he was, and felt angry with himself that he could ever wish for the presence of one who had so scorned him. He was ashamed, also, that the music, the dance, and gay joyance of the scene he had just left, had still such a seductive charm for him, and he recorded a mental resolution to avoid all similar allurements for the future. Having made this resolution, and strong in his faith of keeping it, he merely turned to take final leave, as he fell under the eyes of Julia, and without seeing her.

The night outside was cold, dark, and thick, with a pitiless snow, that was rapidly filling the track along the highway. Bart turned, without the remotest touch of self-pity, to face it, with a heart as cold and dark as the night that swallowed him up. He felt that there was not a heart left behind that would throb with a moment's pain for him—that would miss him, or wonder at his departure; and he was sure that he did not care.

Yet, with what a sweet, remonstrating, expostulating call the music came after him, with its plaining at his desertion! Fainter and sweeter it came, and died out with a wailing sob, as the night, with its storm and darkness, blotted him out!

Mrs. Ford, who may have anticipated his attendance at the supper-table, missed him. His late partner in the dance cast her eyes inquiringly through the thronged rooms. She remarked to Julia that she believed Mr. Ridgeley had left, and thought it very strange. Julia said she presumed he had, and did not say what she thought.

Most of the elders left early; the young people danced the music and themselves away, and the gray, belated dawn of the next day looked coldly into the windows of a sacked, soiled, and silent house.

CHAPTER XVII.

BART.

Bart devoted himself unselfishly and unsparingly to his school, to all its duties and to all his scholars, and especially to the children of the poor, and the backward pupils. He went early to the house, and remained late. He was the tender, considerate, elder brother of the scholars, and was astonished at his power to win regard, and maintain order. Order maintained itself after one memorable occasion—one to which he never referred, and of which he did not like to hear. It made his school famous, and drew to it many visitors, and to himself no little curiosity and attention.

He endeavored to carry on his law-reading; but beyond reviewing— and not very thoroughly—Blackstone, he could do little. As usual, he was homesick; and whenever a week was ended he left the school-house for his mother's, and never returned until the following Monday morning.

His kind patrons noticed with surprise that he seemed sad and depressed after the expulsion of Grid, and that this gloominess was deepened about the time of Snow's ball.

Barton came to take a real pleasure in his school. Formed to love everything, and without the power of hating, or of long retaining a resentment, he became attached to his little flock, especially the younger ones, and was loved in return by them, without reserve or doubt. He did much to improve, not alone the minds of the older pupils, but to soften and refine the manners of the young men under his charge; while the young women, always inclined to idealize, found how pleasant it was to receive little acts of gentlemanly attention from him.

In the afternoon of a long, bright, March day—one of those wondrous days, glorious above with sky and sun, and joyous with the first note of the blue-bird—the little red school-house by the margin of the maple-woods was filled with the pupils and their parents, assembled for the last time. Bart, in a low voice, tremulous with emotion, bade them all good-by, and most of them forever, and taking his little valise, walked with a saddened heart back to his mother. This time he had not failed, and he never was to fail again.

How many events and occurrences linked in an endless series unite to form the sum-total of ordinary human life! Incident to it, they are in fact all ordinary. If any appear extraordinary, it is because they occur in the life of an extraordinary individual, or remarkable consequences flow from them. Like all parts of human life, in and of themselves they are always fragmentary: springing from what precedes them, they have no beginning proper; causing and flowing into others, they have no ending, in effect; and as the dramatic in actual life is never framed with reference to the unities, so results are constantly being produced and worked out by accidents, and the prominent events often contribute nothing to any supposed final catastrophe. Strangers interlope for a moment, and change destinies, coming out for a day, from nothing, and going to nowhere, but marring and misshaping everything.

No plot is to develop as this sketch of old-time life continues, and incidents will be of value only as they tend to mould and develop the character and powers of one, and little will be noticed save that which concerns him. It is, perhaps, already apparent that he is very impressible, that slight forces which would produce little effect on different natures, are capable of changing his shape, will beat him flat, roll him round, or convert him into a cube or triangle, and yet, that certain strong, always acting forces will restore him, with more or less of the mark or impress of the disturbing cause upon him. He has a strong, tenacious nature, unstained with the semblance of a vice. He forms quick resolutions, but can adhere to them. He is tender to weakness, and fanciful to phantasy. His aptitude for sarcasm and ridicule, unsparingly as it had been turned upon everybody, brought upon him general dislike. His indecision and vacillation in adopting and pursuing a scheme in life, lost him the confidence of his acquaintances—ready to believe anything of one who had dealt them so many sharp thrusts. He was sensitive to a fault, and a slight word would have driven him forever from Julia Markham, and turned him back upon himself, as a dissolving and transforming fire. Mentally, he was quick as a flash, with a strong grasp, and a power of ready analysis; and so little did his mental achievements cost him, that his acquirements were doubted. He already paid the penalty of a nervous and brilliant intellect—that of being adjudged not profound. Men are always being deceived as to the real value of things, by their apparent cost.

We see this illustrated in the case of some grave and ponderous weakling, who has nothing really in him, and yet who creaks, and groans, and labors, and toils, to get under way, until our sympathy with his painful effort leads us so to rejoice over his final delivery that we have lost all power or disposition to weigh or estimate his half-strangled, commonplace bantling, when it is finally born, and we are rather inclined to wonder over it as a prodigy. No doubt the generation of men who witnessed the mountain in labor, regarded the sickly, hairy little mouse, finally brought forth, as a genuine wonder.

Great is mediocrity! It is the average world, and the majority conspires to do it reverence. Genius, if such a thing there is, may be appreciated by school-boys; the average grown world count it as of no value. If a man has a brilliant intellect, let him bewail it on the mountains, as the daughter of Jephtha did her virginity. If he has wit, let him become Brutus.

Readiness and genius are apt to be arrogant; and, when joined with a lively temper, with an ardent, impetuous nature, they render a young man an object of dread, dislike, or worse. Bart had grave doubts of his being a genius, but it had been abundantly manifest to his sensitive perceptions that he was disliked; and he had in part arrived at the probable cause, and was now very persistently endeavoring to correct it by holding his tongue and temper.

Like all young men bent upon a pursuit where his success must depend upon intellect, he was most anxious to ascertain the quality and extent of his brain-power—a matter of which a young man can form no proper idea. Later in life a man is informed by the estimate of others, and can judge somewhat by what he has done. The youth has done nothing. He has made no manifestation by which an observer can determine; when he looks at himself, he can examine his head and face; but the mind, turned in upon itself, with no mirror, weight, count or measure, feels the hopelessness of the effort.

If some one would only tell him of his capacity and power, of his mental weakness and deficiency, it would not, perhaps, change his course, but might teach him how best to pursue it.

CHAPTER XVIII.

SUGAR MAKING.

The long, cold winter was past; spring had come, and with it sugar making, the carnival season, in the open air, among the trees.

The boys had the preparations for sugar making in an advanced stage. A new camp had been selected on a dry slope, wood had been cut, the tubs distributed, and they were waiting for Bart and a good day. Both came together; and on the day following the close of his school, at an early hour they hurried off to tap the trees.

Spring and gladness were in the air. The trill of the blue-bird was a thrill; and the first song of the robin was full of lilac and apple blossoms. The softened winds fell to zephyrs, and whispered strange mysterious legends to the brown silent trees, and murmured lovingly over the warming beds of the slumbering flowers. Young juices were starting up under rough bark, and young blood and spirits throbbed in the veins of the boys, and loud and repeated bursts of joyous voices gushed with the fulness of the renewing power of the season.

The day, with its eager hope, strength and joyousness, filled Bart to the eyes, and his spirit in exultation breaking from the unnatural thrall that had for many months of darkness and anxious labor overshadowed it, went with a bound of old buoyancy, and he started with laughing, open brow, and springy step, over the spongy ground, to the poetry of life in the woods.

That one day they tapped all the trees. The next, the kettles were hung on the large crane, the immense logs were rolled up, the kettles filled with sap, and the blue smoke of the first fire went curling up gracefully through the tree-tops. What an event, the first fire! Not as in New England, sugar in the West is never made until the winter snow has disappeared, and the surface has become dry, and the woods pleasant, and the opening day at the boiling was as brilliant as its predecessor.

Bart and Edward, with a yoke of steers, gathered the sap towards evening, and George tended the kettles; many curious bright-eyed chickadees boldly ventured up about the works, peeping, flitting, and examining, with head first on one side and then on the other, the funny doings of these humans in their dominions, and searching for the store of raw pork, which, according to their recollection, ought to be hid away somewhere near by.

The boys had pulled down, removed and rebuilt their old snug cabin, with one end open to the broad and roaring fire; in the bottom of which, over its floor, were placed a large quantity of sweet bright straw, and two or three heavy blankets.

The "run" made it necessary to boil all night; and filling the kettles and adjusting the fires, Bart and the boys, hungry and tired, went up to supper and the chores; after which Bart and Edward, taking the former's rifle, and lighted by a hickory torch, returned to the camp for the night—Edward really to sleep, sweet and unbroken, in the cabin, and Bart to take care of the kettles and fires, to muse and dream, and think bright, strange thoughts, and watch the effects of the lights and shadows, listen to the dropping of the sap into the buckets, and the boding owls, whose melancholy notes harmonized with, rather than interrupted, the solemn effect of deepest night. Man easily reverts to savagery and nature; and this tendency was marked in Bart, whom this new recurrence to old habits of wood-life, so dear to him, filled with such pleasant sensations of joyous unrest, that until near the coming dawn he was disinclined to sleep, and when he did, the first note of an old robin from the topmost twig of a giant old maple awoke him fresh to the labor and enjoyment of another resplendent day. And so the days followed each other, and the spring deepened. Myriads of flower-beds shot up through the dead leaves, and opened out their frail and wondrously tinted petals for a single day, and faded. Not a new one opened—not a cloud or tint varied the sky—not a note of a bird or tap of a woodpecker, that was not marked by Bart, to whom Nature had at least given the power to appreciate and love her lighter works.

CHAPTER XIX.

HENRY.

The principal event of the spring among the Ridgeleys, was the return home of Henry. He had closed his novitiate, and was awaiting his examination for admission to the bar. He had already, on the recommendation of his friend and instructor, Wade, formed a favorable business connection with the younger Hitchcock, at Painesville; and now, after a year's absence, he came back to his mother and brothers, for a few days of relaxation and visiting. Less strong than the Major, of grave, thoughtful, but cheerful face and mien, heavy-browed and deep-eyed, with plain, marked face, and finished manners, he was well calculated to impress favorably, and win confidence and respect. His mind was solid, but lacked the sparkle and vivacity of Bart's, and compensatingly was believed to be deep. He was the pride and hope of the family: around him gathered all its expectations of distinction, and no one shared all these more intensely than Bart, who had awaited his coming with hope and fear. He was accompanied by a fellow-student named Ranney, of about his own age, and like him, above the usual height, broad and heavy-shouldered, with a massive head and strong face, a high narrow forehead; rather shy in manner, and taciturn.

They came one night while Bart was in the sugar-camp, where he spent many nights, and he met them the next morning at the breakfast-table. No one could be gladder than he to meet his brother, but, like his mother, he was struck by his emaciated form and languor of manner.

Bart had heard of Ranney as a man of strong, profound, ingenious mind, with much power of sarcasm, and who had formed a partnership with Wade, on the retirement of Mr. Giddings from the bar. He stood a little in awe of him, whose good opinion he would have gladly secured, but who, he had a presentiment, would not understand him. Indeed, he was quite certain he did not understand himself.

The young men had been fellow-students for two years, had many things in common, and were strong friends.

Bart soon found that they had a slender view of his law reading, and spoke slightingly of Ford as a lawyer. They had both diligently studied to the lower depths of the law, had a fair appreciation of their acquisitions, and would not overestimate the few months of solitary reading of a boy in the country.

Bart did not mention his studies, and only answered modestly his brother's inquiries, who closed the subject for the time by saying that if he was serious in his desire to study law, "he would either arrange to take him to Painesville in the Fall, or have his friend Ranney take him in hand. " Bart was pleased with the idea of being with either; and possibly he may have wondered whether whoever took him in hand would not have that hand full.

The young men strolled off to his sugar-camp during the forenoon, lounged learnedly about, evincing little interest in the camp and surroundings, although the deepening season had filled the woods with flowers and birds; and Bart wondered whether "Coke on Littleton, " and executory devises, and contingent remainders, had produced in them their natural consequences. He watched to see whether new maple sugar was sweet to them, and on full reflection doubted if it was.

They did not interfere with his work, and sauntered back to an early dinner, and Bart saw no more of them until night.

He closed out his work early for the day, and spent the evening with them and his mother.

Henry naturally inquired about his old acquaintances, and Bart answered graphically. He was in a mood of reckless gayety. He took them up, one after another, and in a few happy strokes presented them in ludicrous caricature, irresistible for its hits of humor, and sometimes for wit, and sometimes sarcasm—a stream of sparkle and glitter, with queer quotations of history, poetry, and Scripture, always apt, and the latter not always irreverent. Ranney had a capacity to enjoy a medley, and both of the young men abandoned themselves to uncontrollable laughter; and even the good mother, who tried in vain to stop her reckless son, surprised herself with tears streaming down her cheeks. Bart, for the most part, remained grave, and occasionally Edward helped him out with a suggestion, or contributed a dry and pungent word of his own.

As the fit subsided, Henry, half serious and half laughing, turned to him: "Oh, Bart, I thought you had reformed, and become considerate and thoughtful, and I find that you are worse than ever. "

"But, Henry, what's the use of having neighbors and acquaintances and friends, if one cannot serve them up to his guests; and only think, I've gone about for six months with the odds and ends of 'flat, stale and unprofitable' things accumulating in and about him—the said Bart—until, as a sanitary measure, I had to utter them. "

"How do you feel after it? " inquired Henry.

"Rather depressed, though I hope to tone up again. "

"Bart, " said Henry, gravely, "I haven't seen much of you for two or three years; I used to get queer glimpses of you in your letters, and I must look through your mental and moral make-up some time. "

"You will find me like the sterile, stony glebe, which, when the priest reached in his career of invocation and blessing—'Here, ' said the holy father, 'prayers and supplications are of no avail. This must have manure. ' Grace would, I fear, be wasted on me, and our good mother would willingly see me under your subsoiling and fertilizing hand. "

"Do you ever seriously think? "

"I? oh yes! such thoughts as I can think. I think of the wondrously beautiful in nature, and am glad. I think of the wretched race of men, and am sad. I think of my shallow self, and am mad. "

Henry, with unchanged gravity: "Do you believe in anything? "

"Yes, I believe fully in our mother; a good deal in you, though my faith is shaken a little just now; and am inclined to great faith in your friend Mr. Ranney. "

All smile but Henry. "Yes, all that of course, but abstract propositions. Have you faith, in anything? "

"Well, I believe in genius, I believe in poetry—though not much in poets—music—though that is not for men. I believe in love—for those who may have it. I believe in woman and in God. When I draw myself close to Him, I am overcome with a great awe, and dare not pray. It is only when I seem to push Him off, and coop Him up in a little crystal-domed palace beyond the stars, and out of hearing, that I dare tell Him how huge He is, and pipe little serenades of psalmody to Him. "

"Oh, Barton, you are profane! "

"No, mother, men are profane in their gorgeous egotism. We are the braggarts, and ascribe egotism to God Himself; while we are the sole objects of interest in the universe. God was and is on our account only; and when men fancy that they have found a way of running things without Him, they shove Him out entirely. I put it plainly, and it sounds bad. "

"This is a compendious confession of faith, " said Henry; and, pausing, "why do you put genius first? "

"As the most doubtful, and, at the same time, an interesting article. I am at the age when a young man queries anxiously about it. Has he any of it—the least bit? "

"Well, what is your conclusion? "

"Sometimes I fancy I feel faintly its stir and spur and inspiration. "

"When it may be only dyspepsia, " said Henry.

"It may be. I haven't ranked myself among geniuses. "

"Yet you believe in it. What is it? "

"I can't tell. Can you tell what is electricity or life? "

"That is not logical. You answer one question by asking another. "

"I am not sure but that is allowable, " interrupted Ranney. "You pose your opponent with an unanswerable question, and he in turn proposes several, thereby suggesting that there are things unknown, and that if you will push him to that realm you are equally involved. It may not be logical, but it usually silences. "

"Not quite, in this instance, " said Henry, "for we know by their manifestations that life and electricity are; they manifest themselves to us. "

"And by the same rule genius manifests itself to your brother, although it may not to you. "

"Thank you, Mr. Ranney, " said Bart.

"Now I do not suppose, " he went on, "that genius is a beneficent little imp, or genie, lodged in the brain of the fortunate or unfortunate, who is all-powerful, and always at hand to give strength, emit a flash of light, or pour inspiration into the faculties, nor does it consist in anything that answers to that idea. But there are men endowed with quick, strong intellects, with warm, ardent, intense temperaments, and with strong imaginations; where these, or their equivalents, are found happily blended, the result is genius. There is a working power that can do anything, and with apparent ease. If it plunges down, it need not remain long; if it mounts up, it alights again without effort or injury. "

"And such a 'working power, ' you suppose, would, of itself, be a constant self-supply, and always equal to emergencies, and of its own unaided spontaneous inspirations and energies, I suppose, " said Henry, "and has nothing to do but float and plunge about, diving and soaring, in the amplitude of nature? "

"Well, Henry, you can't get out of a man what isn't in him. You need not draw on a water-bottle for nectar, or hope to carve marble columns from empty air; genius can't do that. An unformed, undeveloped mind never threw out great things spontaneously, as the cloud throws out lightning. Men are not great without achievement, nor wise without study and reflection. Nor was there ever a genius, however strong and brilliant in the rough, that would not have been stronger and more brilliant by cutting, " said Bart, with vehemence. "All I contend for is, that genius, as I have supposed, can make the most and best of things, often doing with them what other and commoner minds cannot do at all. "

"This is not the school-boy's idea of genius, " said Ranney.

"And, " said Bart, a little assertively, "I am not a school-boy. "

"So I perceive, " said Ranney, coolly.

"The fault I find with you geniuses—"

"We geniuses!! —"

"Is, " said Henry, "you perpetually fly and caracol about, and just because you can, apparently, and for the fun of the thing. "

"Eagles fly, " said Bart.

"And so do butterflies, and other gilded insects. "

"Therefore, flying should be dispensed with, I suppose, " said Bart. "Because things of mere painted wings, all wing and nothing else, can float in the lower atmosphere, are all winged things to be despised? Birds of strong flight can light and build on or near the ground, but your barn-yard fowl can hardly soar to the top of the fence for his crow. "

"But your geniuses, Bart, will not work, will not strip to the long, patient, delving drudgery necessary to unravel, separate, analyze, weigh, measure, estimate and count, and come to like work for work's sake, and so grow to do the best and most work. They deal a few heavy blows, scatter things, pick up a few glittering pebbles, and—"

"Leave to dullards the riches of the mines they never would have found, " broke in Bart.

"And fly away into upper air, " pursued Henry.

"Oh, I know that some chaps rise for want of weight, as you would say; but mere weight will keep a man always at the surface. Your men who are always plunging into things, digging and turning up the earth—who believe with the ancients that truth is in a well— often lose themselves, and are smothered in their own dirt-holes, and call on men to see how deep they are. God coins with His image on the outside, as men mint money, and your deep lookers can't see it; they are for rushing into the bowels of things. "

"There is force in that, Bart. Men may see God in His works, if they will; but men don't so stamp their works. At his best, man is weak; unknowing truth, he puts false brands on his goods, mixes and mingles, snarls and confuses, covers up, hides and effaces, so far as he can, God's works, and palms off as His the works of the other. And it is with these that the lawyer has to do: a work in which your mere genius would make little headway. He would go to it without preparation; he would grow weary of the hopelessness of the task, and fly away to some pleasant perch, and plume his wing for another flight, I fear. "

"Might not his lamp of genius aid him somewhat? " put in Bart.

"It might, " said Ranney, "and he might be misled by its flare. He would do better to use the old lights of the law. Some are a little lurid, and some a little blue, but always the same in tempest or calm. The law, as you have doubtless discovered, is founded in a few principles of obvious right. Their application to cases is artificial. The law, for its own wise purposes, takes care of itself; of its own force, it embraces everything, investigates everything, construes itself, and enforces itself, as the sole power in the premises. Its rules in the text-books read plain enough, and are not difficult of apprehension. The uncertainty of the law arises in the doubt and uncertainty of the facts; and hence the doubt about which, of many rules, ought to govern. A man of genius, as you describe him, ought to become a good lawyer; he would excel in the investigation and presentation of facts; but none but a lawyer saturated with the spirit of the law until he comes to have a legal instinct, can with accuracy apply it. "

This was clear and strong to Barton, and profitable to him.

"Now Barton, " said Henry, turning to Ranney, as if Bart were absent, "went through with Blackstone in a month, and probably would go through it every month in the year, and then he might be profitably put to read Blackstone. If I were to shut him up with the 'Institutes, ' in four days there might be nothing of poor Coke left but covers and cords. "

"And what would become of Bart? " asked Ranney.

"Go mad—but not from much learning, " answered the youth for himself; "or you would find him like a dried geranium-leaf hid in the leaves of the year-books, —

'Where thy mates of the garden lie scentless and dead. '"

There was a touch of sarcasm in his mocking voice; and flashing out with his old sparkle, "Be patient with me, boys, the future works miracles. There

> Are mountains ungrown,
> And fountains unflown,
> And flowers unblown,
> And seed never strown,
> And meadows unmown,
> And maids all alone,
> And lots of things to you unknown,
> And every mother's son of us must
> Always blow his own—nose, you know."

And while the young men were a little astonished at the run of his lines, the practical and unexpected climax threw them into another laugh.

Soon Henry took a candle, and the two young men retired. They paused a moment in the little parlor.

"Was there ever such a singular and brilliant compound? " said Ranney. "What a power of expression he has! and I see that he generally knows where he is going to hit. If you can hold him till he masters the law, he will be a power before juries. "

"I think so too, " said Henry; "but he must be a good lawyer before he can be a good advocate, —though that isn't the popular idea. "

"Let him work, " said Ranney. "He will shed his flightier notions as a young bird moults its down. "

How kind to have said this to Bart! Oh, what a mistake, that just praise is injurious! How many weary, fainting, doubting young hearts have famished and died for a kind word of encouragement!

When Bart returned to the sitting-room, his mother and younger brothers had retired.

"I am scorned of women and misunderstood of men—even by my own brother, " he said bitterly to himself. "Let me live to change this, and then let me die. "

The old melancholy chords vibrated, and he went to his little attic, remembering with anguish the stream of nonsense and folly he had poured forth, and thought of the laughter he had provoked as so much deserved rebuke; and he determined never to utter another word that should provoke a smile. He would feed and sleep, and grow stupid and stolid, heavy and dull, and bring forth emptiness and nothings with solemn effort and dignified sweatings.

Early on the morrow he was away to the camp, to renew the fires under his sugar-kettles. The cool, fresh air of the woods refreshed and restored his spirits somewhat. He placed on the breakfast-table two bouquets of wood-flowers, and met his guests with the easy grace and courtesy of an accomplished host; and both felt for the first time the charm of his manner, and recognized that it sprung from a superior nature.

As they were about to rise from the breakfast-table, "Gentlemen, " said he, "Miss Kate Fisher gives, this afternoon, a little sugar party, out at her father's camp. Henry, she sent over an invitation specially for you two, with one to me, for courtesy. I cannot go; but you must. You will meet, Mr. Ranney, several young ladies, any one of whom will convert you to my creed of love and poetry, and two or three young, men stupid enough to master the law, "—with a bright smile. "I promised you would both go. The walk is not more than a mile, the day a marvel right out of Paradise, and you both need the exercise, and to feel that it is spring. "

"And why don't you go, Barton? " asked Henry.

"Well, you are not a stranger to any whom you will meet, and don't need me. In the first place, I must remain and gather the sap, and can't go; in the second, I don't want to go, and won't; and in the third, I have several good reasons for not going, "—all very bright, and in good humor.

"What do you say, Ranney? "

"Well, I would like to go, and I would like to have Barton go with us."

"Would you, though? "—brightening. "No, I can't go; though I would be glad to go with you anywhere. "

CHAPTER XX.

WHAT THE GIRLS SAID.

Kate's little party, out on the dry, bright yellow leaves, gay with early flowers, under the grand old maples, elms and beeches, in the warm sun, came and went, with laughter and light hearts. If it could be reproduced with its lights, and colors, and voices, what a bright little picture and resting-place it would be, in this sombre-colored annal! I am sad for poor Bart, and I cannot sketch it.

The young lawyers had been there, seen, talked to, got acquainted with, were looked up to, deferred to, admired and flirted with, and had gone, leaving themselves to be talked about.

Two young girls, amid the fading light, with the rich warm blood of young womanhood in their cheeks, and its latent emotions sending a softened light into their eyes, with their arms about each other's waists, were pensively walking out of the dusky woods to the open fields, with a little ripple and murmur of voices, like the liquid pearls of a brook.

They had been speaking of the young lawyers. "And these two, " said Julia, "are some of those who are to go out and shape and mould and govern. I am glad to have seen them, and hear them talk."

"Do you think these are to be leading men? " asked Flora Walters.

"I presume so. It is generally conceded that Henry Ridgeley is a young man of ability; and I don't think any one could be long in the company of Mr. Ranney without feeling that he is no ordinary man. Indeed, Henry said that he was destined to a distinguished career. "

"Well, now to me they were both a little heavy and commonplace. Mr. Ridgeley was easy and gentlemanly; Mr. Ranney a little shy and awkward. I've no doubt one would come to like either of them, when one came to know him. "

"Oh, Flora! the beauty of a man is strength and courage, and power and will and ability. When one comes to see these, the outside passes out of sight. "

"Do you think that absolute ugliness could be overcome in that way?"

"Yes, even deformity. I should be taken even by beauty, in a man, and should expect conforming beauty of heart and soul. Do you know, I sometimes half feel that I would like to be a man? "

"You, Julia! with your wealth, beauty and friends, who may, where you will, look and choose? "

"Yes, I, as much as you flatter me. I can feel the ambition of a young man; and were I one, how gladly would I put the world and its emptiness from me, and nurse and feed my soul and brain with the thoughts and souls of other men, till I was strong and great; and then, from my obscurity, I would come forth and take my place in the lead; " and her great eyes flashed.

"If you are ambitious, you have but to wait until the leading spirit comes. What a help you would be to him! "

"He might never come, or I might not know him when—"

"Or you would not love him, if you did know him. "

"He might not love me; or, if he did, I might drive him away. But that is not what was in my mind, although a woman must be ambitious through another. To be one of these young men, to know their minds, to feel their hopes and ambitions, and struggle with and against them, for the places, the honors and leaderships! "

"And would you never love and wed, woo and marry? "

"Yes; and I would like to see the woman who would scorn me. I would take her as mine, and she should not choose but love me! "

"Why, Julia! who would think that you, sweet and deep as you are, could say such things! Would you like to be wooed in that way? "

"I never came to that. I am only a woman without aim in life. I am only to float along between flowery banks, until somebody fishes me out, I suppose! "

"I am sure, were I you, I could well float on until the right man came; and you, Julia, it is your own fault if you do not marry for love. You will not be obliged to consult anything else. "

"And you? " said Julia, laughing.

"I? oh! I am dependent on my brother, you know. "

"Yes, and there comes in the hardship; were you a man, you could go out and make and choose. Now, a daughter remains where her father and mother leave her. The sons may rise, the daughters stay below, and if sought for, it is usually in the same channels in which the parents move, and that is the hardship of those who, unlike you, are on a lower plane, or who, like you, have no father and mother to sustain them in their proper place. If you could win wealth, you would only marry for love; and I am sure you will do so now. "

"A woman who wins fortune usually loses the capacity to win love, I fear, " said Flora.

"And the woman who wins nothing deserves nothing, " said Julia. "I am a little like my mother, I presume; but who would win you, and how, I wonder? "

"Oh, " answered Flora, "I suppose the man who really and truly loved me. I would like to have him come, as the breeze comes, with the odor of flowers, as the spring comes, with music and song, with all sweet and gentle influences, with beauty and grace; but he must not be effeminate. "

"He would have to be a good waltzer, I presume? "

"Would that be an objection? " asked Flora.

"No; but a man who excels in these light accomplishments may fail in the stronger qualities. I admit that beauty and grace would go a great way, if one could have them also. "

"Julia, were I you, I would have them all. "

"Girls, what are you loitering along there for? Talking over the young lawyers, I'll bet; who takes which? " called back Kate, impetuously; "I don't want either. "

* * * * *

All the afternoon long, Bart was sad and silent, and spite of himself, his thoughts would hover about that bright place in the maple woods, sweet with one face of indescribable beauty; one form, one low, many-toned voice which haunted — would haunt him.

He came in to a latish supper, with a grave face. The spring was not in his step; the ring was not in his voice, or the sparkle in his words.

The two guests were in high spirits, and talked gushingly of the young ladies they had met, and they wondered that it did not provoke even a sarcasm from him.

"It would compensate you for not going, " said Ranney, kindly, "if we were to tell you what was said of you in your absence. "

"And who said it, " added Henry. Not a word, nor a look even.

"One might be willing to be called a genius, for such words, and from such a young lady, " ventured Ranney.

"I am not sure but that I would even venture upon poetry, under such inspiration, " said Henry.

To the youth these remarks sounded like sarcasm, and he felt too poor even to retort.

"Oh, boys! " finally said Bart, "it is good exercise for us all; *persiflage* is not your 'best holt, ' as the wrestlers would say, and you need practice, while I want to accustom myself to irony and sarcasm without replying. If by any possibility you can, between you, get off a good thing at my expense, it would confer a lasting obligation; but I don't expect it. "

116

"Upon my word—" began Ranney.

"We all speak kindly of our own dead, " said Bart, "and should hardly expect the dead to hear what we said. Mother said you had determined to leave us in the morning; " to Ranney—"Our brother the Major will be home in the morning, and would be glad to make your acquaintance, and show you some attention. " And so he escaped.

When Ranney took leave the next morning, he kindly remarked to Bart that he would at any time find a place in his office, and should have his best endeavor to advance his studies. It was sincere, and that was one of the charms of his character. Bart was pleased with it, and it almost compensated for the unintentional wounds of the night before.

CHAPTER XXI.

A DEPARTURE.

Morris came, and the brothers were together, and the two elder went around to many of their old acquaintance—many not named here, as not necessary to the incidents of this story. For some reason Barton did not accompany them. If anything was said between them about him, no mention of it was made to him. Henry came to regard him with more interest, and to treat him with marked tenderness and consideration, which Bart took as a kindly effort to efface from his mind the pain that he supposed Henry must be aware he had given him. Had he supposed that it arose from an impression that he was suffering from any other cause, he would have coldly shrunk from it.

* * * * *

At the end of ten days, Henry's baggage was sent out to Hiccox's for the stage, and he took leave of his mother, Morris, Edward, and George, and, accompanied by Bart, walked out to the State road, to take the stage for Painesville, where his work was to begin. He was in bright spirits; his hopes were high; he was much nearer home; his communication was easier, and his absences would be shorter.

Bart, for some reason, was more depressed than usual. On their way down, Henry asked him about a Mr. Greer whom he first saw at the sugar party, and afterwards at Parker's, and who had seemed to take much interest in Bart. Bart had met him only once or twice, and was not favorably impressed by him. Henry said that he had talked of seeing Bart, and that he (Henry) rather liked him.

It had been already talked over and understood that Bart should go to Painesville in the Fall, and enter fully upon the study of the law. As they reached the stage-road, Bart's depression had been remarked by Henry, who made an ineffectual effort to arouse him. Finally the stage came rattling down the hill, and drew up. The brothers shook hands. Henry got in, and the stage was about to move away, when Bart sprang upon the step, and called out "Henry! " who leaned his face forward, and received Barton's lips fully on his mouth. Men of the Yankee nation never kiss each other, and the impression produced upon Henry was great. Tears fell upon his face as their lips met, and from his eyes, as the heavy coach rolled into the darkness of the night.

Are there really such things as actual presentiments? God alone knows. Is the subtle soul-atmosphere capable of a vibration at the approach and in advance of an event? And are some spirits so acutely attuned as to be over-sensible of this vibration? God knows. Or was the act of Bart, like many of his, due to sudden impulse? Perhaps he could not tell. If the faculty was his, don't envy him.

Barton had already resumed his connection with Gen. Ford's office. The General had returned full of his winter's labors, and found an intelligent and sympathizing listener in Bart, who had a relish for politics and the excitements of political life, although he was resolved to owe no consideration that he might ever win to political position.

Under the stimulus from his intercourse with his brother and Ranney, and profiting by their hints and suggestions, he plunged more eagerly into law-books than ever. He constructed a light boat, with a pair of sculls, and rigged also with a spar and sail, with which to traverse the pond, with places to secure it on the opposite shores; and early passers along the State road, that overlooked the placid waters, often marked a solitary boatman pulling a little skiff towards the eastern shore.

And once, a belated picnic party, returning from Barker's landing, discovered a phantom sail flitting slowly in the night breeze over the dark waters to the west. They lingered on the brow of the hill, until it disappeared under the shadow of the western wooded shore, wondering and questioning much as to who and what it was. One, the loveliest, knew, but said nothing.

The Markhams, one day, in their carriage, passed Bart with his books toiling up Oak Hill. He removed his hat as they passed, without other recognition. All of them felt the invisible wall between them, and two, at least, silently regretted that they might not invite him to an unoccupied seat. They were at the Fords' to dinner that day, and Bart, being invited to join them by the General, politely declined.

The General was a little grave at the table, while Mrs. Ford was decided and marked in her commendation of the young student, and described, with great animation, a little excursion they had made over to the pond, and the skill with which Bart had managed his little sail-boat.

CHAPTER XXII.

A SHATTERED COLUMN.

In mid June came the blow. George brought up from the post-office, one evening, the following letter:

"PAINESVILLE, June 18, 1837. BARTON RIDGELEY, ESQ. :

"*Dear Sir,* —I write at the request of my sister, Mrs. Hitchcock. Your brother is very ill. Wanders in his mind, and we are uneasy about him. He has been sick about a week. Mr. Hitchcock is absent at court. Sincerely yours,

Edward Marshall. "

"Henry is ill, " said Barton, very quietly, after reading it. "This letter is from Mrs. Hitchcock. He has been poorly for a week. I think I had better go to him. "

"He did not write himself, it seems, " said his mother.

"He probably doesn't regard himself as very sick, and did not want us sent for, " said Bart, "and they may have written without his knowledge. I will take Arab, and ride in the cool of the night. "

"You are alarmed, Barton, and don't tell me all. Read me the letter. " And he read it. "I will go with you, Barton, " very quietly, but decidedly.

"How can you go, mother? "

"As you do, " firmly.

"You cannot ride thirty miles on horseback, mother, even if we had a horse you could ride at all. "

"I shall go with you, " was her only answer.

121

An hour later, with a horse and light buggy, procured from a neighbor, they drove out into the warm, sweet June night. At Chardon, they paused for half an hour, to breathe the horse, and went on. Bart was a good horseman, from loving and knowing horses, and drove with skill and judgment. They talked little on the road, and at about two in the morning they drove up to the old American House in Painesville, and, with his mother on his arm, Barton started out on River Street, to the residence of Mr. Hitchcock.

How silent the streets! and how ghostly the white houses stood, in the stillness of the night! and how like a dream it all seemed! They had no difficulty in finding the house, with its ominous lights, that had all night long burned out dim into the darkness.

The door was open, and the bell brought a sweet, matronly woman to receive them.

"We are Henry Ridgeley's mother and brother, " said Barton. "Is he still alive? "

The question indicated his utter hopelessness of his brother's condition.

"Come in this way, into the parlor, " said the lady; and stepping out, "Mother, " she called, "Mr. Ridgeley's mother has come. Please step this way. "

A moment later, a tall, elderly lady, sad-faced as was her daughter, and much agitated, entered the room.

"My mother, " said the younger lady. "I am Mrs. Hitchcock. "

"Your son—" said the elder lady.

"Take me to him at once, I pray you! Let me see him! I am his mother! Who shall keep me from him? "

"Mother, " said Barton, stepping up and placing his hands about her, "don't you feel it? Henry is dead. I knew it ere we stepped in. "

"Dead! who says he is dead? He is not dead! "

"Tell her, " said Barton; "she is heroic: let her know the worst. "

"Take me to him! " she said, as they remained silent.

Up the stairs, in a dimly-lighted room, past two or three young men, and a kind neighbor or two, they conducted her; and there, composed as if in slumber, with his grand head thrown back, and his fine strong face fully upward, she found her third-born, growing chill in death. She sprang forward—arrested herself when within a step of him, and gazed. The light passed from her own eye, and the warmth from her face; a spasm shook her, and nothing more.

She did not shriek; she did not faint; she made no outcry, —scarcely a visible sign; but steadily and almost stonily she gazed on her dead, until the idea of the awful change came fully to her. The chill passed from her face and manner; and seating herself on the bed, —"You won't mind me, ladies. You can do no more for him. Leave him to me for a little; " and she bent over and kissed his pallid lips, and laid her face tenderly to his, and lifted with her thin fingers the damp masses of his hair, brown and splendid, like Bart's, but darker, and without the wave.

"What a grand and splendid man you had become, Henry! and I may toy with and caress you now, as when you were a soft and beautiful baby, and you will permit me! " and lifting herself up, she steadfastly gazed at his emaciated face and shrunken temples, and opening his bosom, and baring its broad and finely-formed contour, she scanned it closely.

"Oh, why could not I see and know, and be warned! I thought he could not die! Oh, I thought that all I had would remain! that in their father God had taken all he would reclaim from me! that I should go, and together we should adorn a place where they should come to us! Oh, Merciful Father! " and the storm of agony, such as uproots and sweeps away weak natures, came upon her.

As for Barton, his sensibilities were stunned and paralyzed, while his mind was left to work free and clear. All his anguish was for his mother; for himself, the moment had not come. He was appalled to feel the almost indifference with which he looked upon the remains of his manly and high-souled brother, and he repeated over and over to himself: "Henry is dead! he is dead! Don't you hear? don't you know? He is dead! Why don't you mourn? "

An hour later, came a gentle tap at the door. Barton went to find Mrs. Hitchcock standing there.

"Your mother must be aroused and taken away. My mother and I will take you to her house. She must be cared for now. "

"Mother, " said Bart, taking her lightly in his arms, "these dear good ladies must care for you. Let me take you out; and our dear Henry must be cared for, too. "

How unnatural his voice sounded to him! Had he slain his brother, that he should care so little? —that his voice should sound so hoarse and hollow?

His mother was passive in his hands, —wearied, broken, and overwhelmed. He carried her across a small open space, and into a large house, where her kind hostess received and cherished her as only women experienced and chastened by sorrow can.

Barton was conducted to a spacious, cool room, luxurious to his eyes; yet he felt no weariness, but somehow supernaturally strained up to an awful tension.

"Why don't I shriek, and tear my hair, and make some fitting moan over this awful loss? Why can't I feel it? O God! am I a wretch without nature, or heart, or soul? He is dead! Why should he die, and now, plucked and torn up by the root, just at flowering? What a vile economy is this! what a waste and incompleteness! and the world full of drivellers and dotards, that it would gladly be quit of. Wasn't there space and breath for him? Why should such qualities be so bestowed, to be so wasted? Why kindle such a light, to quench it so soon in the dark river? What a blunder! Why was not I taken? "

Why? Oh, weak, vain questioner!

He threw off part of his clothing, and lay down on the bed and slept. He awoke, offended and grieved that the sun should shine. Why was it not hidden by thick clouds, and why should they not weep? But why should they, if he did not? And what business had the birds to be glad and joyous, and the perfume of flowers to steal out on the bright air?

He knew he was wrong. He was no longer angry and defiant, but his grief was dry and harsh, and his sensibilities creaked like a dry axle.

He found his mother tender, calm, and pitying him. Awful as was the bereavement to her, she felt that the loss was, after all, to him. Her strong nature, quivering and bleeding under the blow, had righted itself, and the sweet influence of faith and hope was coming up in her heart. She saw Barton with his pallid face, and steady but bright eyes. She knew that she never quite understood, had never quite fathomed, his nature.

Gentle voices, assuaging hands, and sweet charities were about the stricken ones; and pious hands, with all Christian observances, ministered to their beautiful dead. Nothing more could be done; and before mid-day Barton, with his mother, started on their return, to be followed at evening by the remains of the loved one, arrayed for sepulture.

Barton, with every faculty of mind intensely strong and clear, and weighted with the great calamity to absolute gravity, had struck those he met as a marvel of clear apprehension and perception of all the surroundings and proprieties of his painful position. The younger members of the Painesville Bar, who had begun to know and love their young brother, had gathered about him in his illness, and now came forward to take charge of and prepare his remains for final rest, and to render to his friends the kindness of refined charity. Barton knew that somehow they looked curiously at him, as he introduced himself to them, and fancied that his dazed and dreamy manner was singular; but knew that such considerate and kind, such brotherly young men, would make allowances for him.

When they gathered silently to take leave, he turned: "Gentlemen, you know our obligations to you. Think of the most grateful expression of them, and think I would so express them if I could. Some day I may more fittingly thank you. "

They thought he never could. He remembered the fitting words to Mrs. Hitchcock and her mother, Mrs. Marshall, and drove away, with his pale, silent mother.

All the way home in a dream. Something awful had happened, and it was not always clear what it was, or how it had been brought about.

CHAPTER XXIII.

THE STORM.

About midnight the Painesville hearse drove up, accompanied by the four young pall-bearers, of the Painesville Bar, who attended the remains of their young brother. The coffin was deposited in the little parlor, and the carriages drove to Parker's for the night.

The stricken and lonely mother was in the sanctity of her own room. The children had cried themselves to sleep and forgetfulness. The brother, who had been sent for, could not reach home until the next morning.

Barton had declined the offers of kind friends to remain, and was alone with his dead. The coffin-lid had been removed, and he lifted the dead-cloth from the face. He could not endure the sharp angle of the nose, that so stabbed up into the dim night, unrelieved by the other features.

The wrath of a strong, deep nature, thoroughly aroused, is sublime; its grief, when stirred to its depths, is awful. Barton knew now what had happened and what he had lost. The acuteness of his fine organization had recovered its sharpest edge. The heavens had been darkened for him nearly a year before, but now the solid earth had been rent and one-half cloven away, and that was the half that held the only hopes he had. He didn't calculate this now. Genius, intellect, imagination, courage, pride, scorn, all the intensities of his nature, all that he supposed he possessed, all that lay hidden and unsuspected, arose in their might to overcome him now. He did not think, he did not aspire, or hope, or fear, or dream, or remember: he only felt, and bled, and moaned low, hopeless, helpless moans. If it is given to some natures to enjoy intensely, so such correspondingly suffer; and Bart, alone with his pale, cold, dead brother, through this deep, silent night, abandoned himself utterly to the first anguish at his loss, and it was wise. As it is healthful and needful for young children to cry away their pains and aches, so the stricken and pained soul finds relief in pouring itself out in oversweeping grief.

The storm swept by and subsided, and Bart, kneeling by the coffin of his brother, in the simple humility of a child, opened his heart to the pitying eye of the Great Father. His lips did not move, but steadily and reverently he turned to that sweet nearness of love and compassion. Finally he asked that every unworthy thought, passion, folly, or pride, might be exorcised from his heart and nature; and then, holding himself in this steady and now sweet contemplation and silent communion, a great calm came into his uplifted soul, and he slept. And, as he passed from first slumber to oblivious and profound sleep, there floated, through a celestial atmosphere, a radiant cloud, on which was reclining a form of light and beauty. He thought it must be his departed brother, but it turned fully towards him, and the face was the face of Julia, with sweetest and tenderest compassion and love in her eyes; and he slept profoundly.

In the full light of the early morning, the elder brother stole into the room, to be startled and awed by the pale faces of his dead and his sleeping brothers, now so near each other, and never before so much alike. How kingly the one in death! How beautiful the other in sleep! And while he held his tears in the marvellous presence, his pale, sweet mother came in, and placed her hand silently in his, and gazed; and then the young boys, with their bare feet; and so the silent, the sleeping, and the dead, were once more together.

* * * * *

At mid-day, those who had heard of the event gathered at the Ridgeley house, sad-faced and sorrow-stricken. The family had always been much esteemed, and Henry had been nearly as great a favorite as was Morris, and all shared in the hope and expectation of his future success and eminence. Uncle Aleck came, feeble and heart-stricken. A sweet prayer, a few loving words, a simple hymn, and the young pall-bearers carried out their pale brother, and, preceding the hearse in their carriage, followed by the stricken ones and the rest in carriages and on foot, the little procession went sadly to the burying-ground. There a numerous company, attracted from various parts where the news had reached, were assembled and awaiting the interment. The idle and curious were rewarded by the sight of a hearse, and the presence of the deputation of the Painesville Bar, and impressed with a sense of the importance and consideration of the young man in whose honor such attentions were bestowed.

The ceremony of interment was short, and of the simplest. The committing of the dead to final rest in the earth, is always impressive. Man's innate egotism always invests the final hiding away of the remains of one of his race in perpetual oblivion, with solemnity and awe. One of the lords has departed; let man and nature observe and be impressed.

Uncle Aleck was too feeble to go to the grave.

The mourners—the mother sustained by Barton, and Morris, attended by his promised bride, a sweet and beautiful girl, and the two young boys so interesting in their childish sorrow, so few in number, and unsupported by uncles, aunts or cousins—were objects of unusual interest and commiseration. But now, when the last act was performed for them, and the burial hymn had been sung, there was no one to speak for them the usual thanks for these kindnesses, and just as this came painfully to the sensibilities of the thoughtful, Barton uncovered his head and said the few needed words in a clear, steady voice, with such grace, that matronly women would gladly have kissed him; and young maidens noticed, what they had observed before, that there was something of nameless attraction in his face and manner.

Kind hands and sympathizing hearts were about the Ridgeleys, to solace, cheer and help; but the great void in their circle and hearts, only God and time could fill. The heart, when it loses out of it one object of tenderness and love, only contracts the closer and more tenderly about what it has left.

* * * * *

Time elapses. It kindly goes forward and takes us with it. No matter how resolutely we cling to darkness and sorrow, time loosens our hearts, dries our tears, and while we declare we will not be comforted, and reproach ourselves, as the first poignancy of grief consciously fades, yet we are comforted. The world will not wait for us to mourn. The objects of love and of hate we may bear along with us, but distance will intervene between us and the sources of deep sorrow.

So far as Bart was concerned, his nature was in the main healthy, with only morbid tendencies, and the great blow of his brother's death seemed in some way to restore the equilibrium of his mind, and leave it to act more freely, under guidance of the strong common sense inherited from his mother. He knew he must not linger about his brother's grave and weep.

He knew now that he was entirely upon his own resources. His brother Morris's speculations, and dashing system of doing things, had already hopelessly involved him, and Bart knew that no aid could be expected from him. He had returned to Painesville, and closed up the few matters of his brother Henry; had written to Ranney, at Jefferson, and already had resumed his books with a saddened and sobered determination. He supposed that Henry had died in consequence of a too close and long-continued application to his studies; and while this admonished him, he still believed that his own elasticity and power of endurance would carry him forward and through, unscathed.

He began also to mingle a little with others, and to take an interest in their daily affairs. People affected to find him changed, and vastly for the better. "He's had enough to sober him. " "It is well he has been warned, and heeds it. " "God will visit with judgments, until the thoughtless forbear, " and other profound and Christian remarks were made concerning him. As if Providence would cut off the best and most promising, for such indirect and uncertain good as might, or might not be produced in another less worthy!

CHAPTER XXIV.

A LAW-SUIT (TO BE SKIPPED).

A young lover's first kiss, a young hunter's first deer, and a young lawyer's first case, doubtless linger in their several memories, as events of moment.

Bart had tried his first case before a justice of the peace, been beaten, and was duly mortified. It is very likely he was on the wrong side, but he did not think so; and if he had thought so, he would not have been fully consoled. A poorer advocate than he could have convinced himself that he was right, and fail, as he did, to convince the court. It was a case of little importance to any but the parties. To them, every case is of the gravest moment. He acquitted himself creditably: showed that he understood the case, examined his witnesses, and presented it clearly.

Others came to him, and he advised with caution and prudence; and as Fall approached, he was in request in various small matters; men were surprised at the modesty of his deportment, and the gentleness of his speech. Instead of provoking his opponents, and answering back, as was to be expected of him, he was conciliating and forbearing.

A case finally arose, of unusual importance in the domestic tribunals; it attracted much attention, helped to bring him forward in a small way, and gained him much reputation among some persons whose esteem was enviable.

Old man Cole, "Old King Cole, " as the boys derisively called him, an inoffensive little man, with a weak, limp woman for a wife, and three or four weaker and limper children, had for many years vegetated on one corner of an hundred-and-sixty acres of woods, having made but a small clearing, and managed in some unknown way to live on it. His feeble condition exposed him to imposition, and he was the butt for the unthinking, and victim of the unscrupulous and unruly. For some years his land, a valuable tract, had been coveted by several greedy men, and especially by one Sam Ward. Failing to induce Cole to sell what right it was admitted he had, Ward, as was supposed, attempted to intimidate, and finally to annoy Cole to such an extent, that for peace and safety he would willingly part with his possession. He was one of the earliest settlers, had become attached to his land, and declined to be driven off.

A lawless set of young men and boys were Ward's agents, although his connection with them was never made very apparent, and had committed various depredations upon the old man; until one night they made a raid upon his premises, cut down several fruit-trees, filled up his spring, tore down his old barn, and committed various acts of trespass of a grave character. It would seem as if some intelligence controlled their movements; no act criminal by the statutes of Ohio had been committed, and, so far as was suspected, none but those under age had been concerned in the affair.

Poor old Cole, an object of derision, was barely within common sympathy; and living remote, few knew of, and fewer cared for his misfortunes. He applied for advice to Bart, who was indignant at the recital, and entered upon an investigation of the outrage with great energy. He was satisfied that the fathers of the trespassers could not be held for their acts, that no breach of the criminal laws had been committed; but that the boys themselves could be made liable in an action, and that on failure to pay the judgment, they could themselves be taken in execution and committed to jail. He at once commenced a suit for the trespass before a magistrate, against all whom he suspected.

The commencement of the suit caused greater excitement then the perpetration of the outrage. Many of the young men belonged to respectable families, while many were old offenders, who had been permitted to escape for fear of provoking graver misdemeanors. It was known that Bart had taken up the case, and there was a feeling that he had at least the courage to encounter the dangerous wrath of the young scamps; the only ground of apprehension was that he had mistaken the law. The popular impression was that an action could not be maintained against minors.

On the return-day of the summons Barton appeared, and demanded a jury, then allowable, and the time for trial was fixed for the fifth day afterwards.

In that day, with the exception of one or two small lawyers at Chardon, and Ford at Burton, there were none within twenty-five miles of Newbury, and the legal field was gleaned in the magistrates' courts, as in all new countries, by pettifoggers, of whom nearly every township was made luminous with one. Of these, the acknowledged head was Brace. In ordinary life he was a very good sort of a man, not without capacity, but conceited, obstinate, and opinionated; he never had any law learning. In his career before justices of the peace, he was bold, adroit, unscrupulous, coarse, browbeating, and sometimes brutal; anything that occurred to his not uninventive mind, as likely in any way to help him on or out, he resorted to without hesitation. At this time he was in full career, and was constantly employed, going into two or three counties, occasionally meeting members of the profession, who held him in detestation, and whom he was as likely to drive out of court as he was to be worsted by them.

He had been employed by the young scamps to defend them. He and Bart had already met, and the latter was worsted in the case, and had received from Brace the usual Billingsgate. He was on hand well charged on the day for the appearance of the defendants, and was at no pains to conceal the contempt he felt for his young opponent.

Bart said no more than the occasion demanded, and seemingly paid no attention to Brace.

The magistrate, a man of plain, hard sense, adjourned the case to a large school-house, and invited Judge Markham to sit in, and preside at the trial, to which the Judge consented, which secured a decorous and fair hearing.

On the day, parties, witnesses, court, jury, and counsel, were on hand—a larger crowd than Newbury had seen for years. The case was called and the jury sworn, when Brace arose, and with a loud nourish demanded that the plaintiff be nonsuited, on the ground of the nonage of the defendants, and concluded by expressing his surprise at the ignorance of the plaintiff's counsel: everybody knew that a minor could not be sued; he even went so far as to express his pity for the plaintiff. Bart answered that it did not appear that any of the defendants were under age. If they were infants, and wanted to escape on the cry of baby, they must plead it, if their counsel knew what that meant; so that the plaintiff might take issue upon it, and the court be informed of the facts. The court held this to be the law, and Brace filed his plea of infancy. Bart then read from the Ohio statutes that when a minor was sued in an action of tort, as in this case, the court should appoint a guardian *ad litem*, and the *parol* should not *demur*; and he moved the court to appoint guardians *ad litem*, for the defendants.

Brace's eyes sparkled; and springing to his feet, he thundered out: "The parol shall not demur—the parol shall not demur. I have got this simpleton where I wanted him! I didn't 'spose he was fool enough to run into this trap; I set it on purpose for him: anybody else would have seen it; anything will catch him. The case can go no farther; the phrase, may it please the court, is Latin, and means that the case shall be dismissed. The *parol*, the plaintiff shall not *demur*, shall not have his suit. Why didn't Ford explain this matter to this green bumpkin, and save his client the costs? "

Barton reminded the court that the statute made it the duty of the court to appoint guardians *ad litem*, which was a declaration that the case was to go on; if it was to stop, no guardians were needed. Brace had said the terms were Latin; he presumed that his Latin was like his law; he thought it was old law French. He produced a law—dictionary, from which it appeared that the meaning was, the case should not be delayed, till the defendants were of age. Guardians should be appointed for them, and the case proceed, and so the court ruled.

Bart went up immensely in popular estimation. Any man who knew a word of Latin was a prodigy. Bart not only knew Latin, but the difference between that and old law French. Who ever heard of that before? and he had lived among them from babyhood, and they now looked upon him in astonishment. "It does beat hell, amazingly! " said Uncle Josh, aside.

After brief consultation the court appointed the fathers of the defendants their guardians, when Bart remarked that his learned and very polite opponent having found nurses for his babies, he would proceed with the case, and called his witnesses.

Against two or three of the ringleaders, the evidence was doubtful. When Bart moved to discharge three of the younger of the defendants, Brace opposed this. Bart asked him if he was there to oppose a judgment in favor of his own clients? The court granted his motion; when Bart put the young men on the stand as witnesses, and proved his case conclusively against all the rest.

What wonderful strategy this all seemed to be to the gaping crowd; and all in spite of Brace, whom they had supposed to be the most adroit and skilful man in the world; and who, although he objected, and blustered, and blowed, really appeared to be a man without resources of any sort.

Barton rested his case.

Brace called his witnesses, made ready to meet a case not made by the plaintiff, and Bart quietly dissmissed them one after the other without a word. Then Ward, who had kept in the background, was called, in the hope to save one of the defendants. Him Bart cross-examined, and it was observed that after a question or two he arose and turned upon him, and plied him with questions rapid and unexpected, until he was embarrassed and confused. Brace, by objections and argument, intended as instructions to the witness, only increased his perplexity, and he finally sat down with the impression that he had made a bad exhibition of himself, and had damaged the case.

It was now midnight, when the evidence was closed, and Barton proposed to submit the case without argument. Brace objected. He wanted to explain the case, and clear up the mistakes, and expose the rascalities of the plaintiff's witnesses; and the trial was adjourned until the next morning.

When the case was resumed the following day, Bart, in a clear, simple way, stated his case, and the evidence in support of it, making two or three playful allusions to his profound and accomplished opponent.

Brace followed on full preparation for the defence. Of course it was obvious, even to him, that he was hopelessly beaten; and mortified and enraged, he emptied all the vials of his wrath and vituperation upon the head of Bart, his client and witnesses, and sat down, at the end of an hour, exhausted.

When Bart arose to reply, he seemed to stand a foot taller than he ever appeared before. Calmly and in a suppressed voice he restated his case, and, with a few well—directed blows, demolished the legal aspects of the defence. He then turned upon his opponent; no restraint was on him now. He did not descend to his level, but cut and thrust and flayed him from above. Even the Newbury mob could now see the difference between wit and vulgarity, and were made to understand that coarseness and abuse were not strength. His address to the court was superb; and when he finally turned to the jury, with a touching sketch of the helplessness of the plaintiff, and of the lawless violence of the defendants, who had long been a nuisance, and had now become dangerous to peace and good order, and submitted the case, the crowd looked and heard with open-mouthed wonder. Had a little summer cloud come down, with thunder, lightning and tempest, they would not have been more amazed. When he ceased, a murmur, which ran into applause, broke from the cool, acute, observing and thinking New Englanders and their children, who were present.

Judge Markham promptly repressed the disorder, and in a few words gave the case to the jury, who at once returned a verdict for the largest amount within the court's jurisdiction; judgment was promptly rendered, execution for the bodies of the defendants issued, and they were arrested.

The excitement had now become intense. Here were half a score of young men in the hands of the law, under orders to be committed to jail. No one remembered such a case in Newbury. Breaches of the law, in that usually orderly community, were unknown, until the acts which gave rise to this suit, and some fainter demonstrations of the same character. The poor youths and their friends gathered helpless and anxious about Brace, who could suggest nothing. Finally, Barton came forward, and offered to take the promissory notes of the parties and their fathers, for the amount of the judgment and costs, and release them from arrest, which offer they gladly accepted, with many thanks to their prosecutor; and the blow which he thus dealt was the end of disorder in Newbury.

For the time being Cole was left at peace, and enjoyed more consideration than had ever been conceded to him before. He was destined, however, not long after, to appear in the higher court, to defend the doubtful title of his property, as will appear in the progress of this narrative.

As a general rule, the people of new communities are more curious and interested in law—suits, and trials, and lawyers, than in almost anything else to which their attention can be called. Lawyers, especially, are the objects of their admiration and astonishment.

Unaccustomed to mental labor, conscious of an inability to perform it, and justly regarding it as holding the first place in human effort, the power and skill to conduct and maintain a long-continued mental conflict, to pursue and examine witnesses, answer questions as well as ask them, make and meet objections, make impromptu speeches and argue difficult propositions, and, finally, to deliver off-hand, an address of hours in length, full of argument, illustration, sometimes interspersed with humor, wit, and pathos, and sometimes really eloquent, is by them always regarded, and not without reason, as a marvel that cannot be witnessed without astonishment.

And here was this young Bart Ridgeley, who had been nowhere, had read next to nothing, whom they had esteemed a lazy, shiftless fellow, without capability for useful and thrifty pursuits, and who had in their presence, for the last two days, taken up a hopeless case, and conducted it against a man who, in their hearts, they had supposed was more than a match for Joshua R. Giddings or Chief Justice Hitchcock, beaten and baffled him, and finally thrashed him out of all semblance of an advocate.

When the case was over, and he came out, how quickly they made way for him, and eagerly closed in behind and followed him out, and looked, and watched, and waited for a word or a look from him. "What did I tell you? " "What do you say now? " "I allus knew it was in 'im. " "He'll do, " etc., rained about him as he went into the open air.

Greer had attended the trial, and was one of the warmest admirers of Bart's performance. Nobody knew much about this man, except that he was often on hand, well dressed, drove good horses, was open, free and pleasant, with plenty of leisure and money, always well received, and often sought after. He had, at the first, taken a real liking to Bart; and now, when the latter came out, he pleasantly approached him, and offered to carry him home in his carriage, an offer the tired youth was glad to accept.

On their way, he mentioned to Bart something about a very profitable and pleasant business, conducted by a few high-minded and honorable gentlemen, without noise or excitement, which consisted in the sale of very valuable commodities. They employed agents—young, active, and accomplished men, and on terms very remunerative, and he thought it very likely that if Bart would enter their service, it could be made much for his advantage to do so; he would call again after Bart had thought it over.

His remarks made an impression on Bart's mind, and excited his curiosity, and he remembered what Henry had said about Greer when at home.

Judge Markham had been very much impressed by Bart's management of his case; perhaps to say that he was very much astonished, would better express its effect upon him. He had always given him credit for a great deal of light, ready, dashing talent, but was wholly unprepared for the exhibition of thought, reflection, and logical power which he had witnessed; the young man's grave, cautious and dignified manner won much upon him, and he was surprised when he reflected how slender was the ground of his dislike, and how that dislike had somehow disappeared. Then he recalled the favorable estimate which his wife had always put upon the qualities of Bart, and that he had usually found her opinions of persons accurate. The frank appeal of Bart to him was manly, and almost called for some acknowledgment; and he felt that the invisible barrier between them was unpleasant. After all, was not this young man one of the few destined to distinction, and on all accounts would it not be well to give him countenance? And in this the Judge was not wholly politic. He felt that it would be a good thing to do, to serve this struggling young man, and he came out of the crowded room with the settled purpose of taking Bart home to his mother's, if he would ride with him, let what would come of it. He would frankly tell him what he thought of his conduct of his case, and at least open the way to renewed intercourse.

He was detained for a moment, to answer questions, and got out just in time to see Bart, apparently pleased, get into Greer's carriage and ride away. The Judge looked thoughtful at this; and a close observer would have noticed a serious change in the expression of his face.

Of course he was well and intimately known to all parties present, and his frank and cordial manners left him always open to the first approach. He listened to the comments upon the trial, which all turned upon Bart's efforts, and the Judge could easily see that the young advocate had at once become the popular idol. He was asked what he thought of Bart's speech, and replied that one could hardly judge of a single effort, but that the same speech in the higher courts would undoubtedly have gained for its author much reputation, and that if Bart kept on, and did himself justice, he was certainly destined to high distinction. It was kind, judicious, and all that was deserved, but it was not up to the popular estimate, and one remarked that "the Judge never did like him"; another, "that the Judge was afraid that Julia would take a liking to Bart, and he hoped she would"; and a third, "that Bart was good enough for her, but he never did care for girls, who were all after him. "

How freely the speech of the common people runs!

CHAPTER XXV.

THE WARNING.

Two or three things occurred during the Autumn which had some influence upon the fortunes of Barton.

Five or six days after the trial, he received a letter, postmarked Auburn, which read as follows:

"Beware of Greer.
Don't listen to him.
Be careful of your associations."

Only three lines, with the fewest words: not another word, line, mark, or figure on any side of it. The hand was bold and free, and entirely unknown to him. The paper was fine-tinted note, and Bart seemed to catch a faint odor of violets as he opened it; a circumstance which reminded him that a few days before he had found on the grave of his brother, a faded bouquet of flowers. There was perhaps, no connection between them, but they associated themselves in his mind. Some maiden, unknown to him, had cherished the memory of his brother, may have loved him; and had secretly laid this offering on his resting-place. How sweet was the thought to him! Who was she? Would he ever know? She had heard something of this Greer—there was something bad or wrong about him; Henry may have spoken to her about the man; and she may have seen or known of Greer's taking him home, and had written him this note of warning. The hand was like that of a man, but no man in Ohio would use such paper, scented with violets. How queer and strange it was! and how the mind of the imaginative youth worked and worried, but not unpleasantly, over it! Of course, if the note was from a woman, she must have written because he was Henry's brother; and it was, in a way, from him, and to be heeded, although Henry had himself been favorably impressed by Greer. The warning was not lost upon him, although it may not have been necessary.

A few days later, the elegant and leisurely Greer made his appearance; and after complimenting Bart upon his success in an easy, roundabout way, approached the subject of his call; and Bart was duly impressed that it arose from considerations of favor and regard to him, that Greer now sought him. The visitor referred to the rule among gentlemen, which Bart must understand, of course, that what he might communicate, as well as their whole interview, must be purely confidential. The agents, he said, were selected with the utmost care, and were usually asked to subscribe articles, and sworn to secrecy; but that he had so much confidence in Bart, that this would not be necessary. Bart, who listened impassively, said that he understood the rule of implied confidence extended only to communications in themselves right and honorable; and that of course Mr. Greer could have no other to make to him. Greer inquired what he meant. Bart said that if a man approached, with or without exacting a pledge of confidence, and made him a proposition strictly honorable, he should of course regard it as sacred; but if he proposed to him to unite in a robbery, house-burning, or to pass counterfeit money, or commit any breach of morality, he should certainly hold himself at liberty to disclose it, if he deemed it necessary. "If I am, in advance, asked to regard a proposed communication as confidential, I should understand, of course, that the proposer impliedly pledged that it should be of a character that a man of honor could listen to and entertain; of course, Mr. Greer, you can have no other to make to me, and you know I would not listen to any other. "

During this statement, made with the utmost courtesy, Bart looked Greer steadily in the face, and received a calm, full, unwinking look in return. Greer assured him that his notions of the ethics of honor, while they were nice, were his own, and he was glad to act upon them; that he was not on that day fully authorized to open up the matter, but should doubtless receive full instructions in a day or two; and he had called to-day more to keep his word with Bart than to enter upon an actual business transaction. Nothing could be franker and more open than his way and manner in saying this; and as he was trained to keenness of observation, he may have detected the flitting smile that just hovered on Bart's lips. After a little pleasant commonplace talk of common things, the leisurely Greer took a cordial leave, and never approached Bart but once again.

At the Whig nominating convention, for the county of Geanga, that Fall, Major Ridgeley, who had, by a vote of the officers of his regiment, become its Colonel, was a candidate for the office of sheriff. He was popular, well-known, and his prospects fair. The office was attractive, its emoluments good, and it was generally sought after by the best class of ambitious men in the counties.

He was defeated in the convention through a defection of his supposed friends, which he charged, justly or otherwise, upon Judge Markham. The disappointment was bitter, and he was indignant, of course. Like Bart, when he thought a mishap was without remedy, he neither complained nor asked explanations. When he and the Judge next met, it was with cool contempt on his side, and with surprise, and then coldness, on the part of Markham. Their words were few and courteous, but for the next eighteen months they avoided each other. Of course, Bart sympathized with his brother Morris; although he did not suppose the Judge was ever committed, still he felt that he and all his friends should have stood by his brother, and apprehended that the Judge's dislike to him may have influenced his course. However that may have been, Judge Markham never approached Bart, who continued to act upon his old determination to avoid the whole Markham family.

His engagements took the Judge to the State capital for the winter, where, with his wife and Julia, he remained until the early spring, following; as did also General and Mrs. Ford.

Barton undertook the school in his mother's neighborhood for the winter, with the understanding that he might attend to calls in the line of his proposed profession, which grew upon his hands. He pushed his studies with unremitting ardor; he had already made arrangements with Mr. Ranney to enter his office on the first of the April following, and hoped to secure an admission in the next September, when he should seek a point for business, to which he proposed to remove his mother and younger brothers, as soon afterwards as his means would warrant.

His friend Theodore had gone away permanently, from Newbury, and the winter passed slowly and monotonously to Bart. He knew, although he would not admit to himself, that the principal reason of his discontent was the absence of Julia. What was she to him? What could she ever be? and yet, how dreary was Newbury—the only place he had ever loved—-when she was away. Of course she would wed, some time, and was undoubtedly much admired, and sought, and courted, by elegant and accomplished men, this winter, upon whom she smiled, and to whom she gave her hand when she met them, and who were permitted to dance with her, and be near her at any time. And what was it all to him? How sore, after all, his heart was; and how he hated and cursed himself, that he must still think of her! He would go forever and ever away, and ever so far away, and would hear and think of her no more. But when she came back, with March, he somehow felt her return, and Spring seemed naturally to come with her; and bright thoughts, and beautiful and poetic figures and images, would arrange themselves in couplets and stanzas, with her in the centre, in spite of him.

Then came sugar making, with life and health of spirit, in the woods. His brother was arranging to dispose of his interests, and had gone further West, to look for a new point, for new enterprises.

CHAPTER XXVI.

LOST.

March and sugar making had gone, and Bart had completed his scanty arrangements to depart also; and no matter what the future might have for him, he knew that he was now leaving Newbury; that whatever might happen, his home would certainly be elsewhere; although it would forever remain the best, and perhaps sole home of his heart and memory.

What he could do for his mother he had done. His limited wardrobe was packed. He went to the pond, to all the dear and cherished places in the woods; and one night he was guilty of the folly, as he knew it was, of wandering up the State road, past Judge Markham's house. He did not pretend to himself that it was not with the hope of seeing Julia, but he only passed the darkened house where she lived, and went disappointed away. He would go on the morrow, and when it came, he sent his trunk up to Hiccox's, intending to walk down in the evening, and intercept the stage, as Henry had done.

He went again to his brother's grave, and there, on its head, was an almost fresh wreath of wild flowers! He was unmanned; and, kneeling, touched the dead children of the Spring with his lips, and dropped tears upon them. How grateful he was that a watchful love was there to care for this consecrated place, and he felt that he could not go that night. What mattered one day? He would wait till to-morrow, he thought, but was restless and undecided. George left him at the cemetery, and went to the post-office, and was to have gone with Edward to see him off, on the stage. As the time to leave approached, Bart found his disinclination to go even stronger; and he finally told his mother he would remain until the next day.

She, unwomanlike, did not like the idea of his yielding to this reluctance to go. "He was ready, nothing detained him, why not have the final pain of going over at once? "

He made no reply, but lounged restlessly about.

At about nine o'clock George came bursting in, with his eyes flashing, and his golden hair wet with perspiration; and catching his breath, and reducing and restraining his voice, cried out: "Julia Markham is lost in the woods, and they can't find her! " The words struck Bart like electricity, and at once made him his best self.

"Lost, George? " taking him by both hands, and speaking coolly, "tell me all about it. "

A few great gasps had relieved George, and the cool, firm hands of Bart had fully restored his quick wits.

"She and Nell Roberts had been to Coe's, and Orville started to go home with Julia, and he did go down to Judge Markham's fields, where he left her. "

"Well? "

"She did not go home, nor anywhere, and they have been looking for her, all through the woods, everywhere. "

"All through what woods, Georgie? "

"Down between Coe's and the State road. "

"They will never find her there; there is a new chopping, back of Judge Markham's fields, which she mistook for the fields, and when she found out the mistake she turned back to the old road, and I will wager the world that she went into 'the woods, ' confused and lost. " After a moment—"Mother, put some of your wine in my hunting-flask, and give me something that can be eaten. Edward, bring me two of those bundles of hickory; and George, let me have your hatchet and belt. "

He spoke in his ordinary voice, but he looked like one inspired. Throwing off his coat, and arraying himself in a red "wamus, " and replacing his boots with heavy, close-fitting brogans, he was ready.

"Boys, " said he, "go about and notify all in the neighborhood to meet at Markham's, at daylight; and tell them for God's sake, if she is not found, to form a line, and sweep through the west woods. If I am not back by daylight, push out and do all you can. Mother, don't be anxious for me. If it storms and grows cold, you know I am a born woodsman. I know now what kept me. "

"I am anxious, Barton, only that you may find her. God go with you!"

With the other things, Edward placed in his hands a long wax taper, made for the sugar camp, lighted, and with a kiss to his mother, and a cheery good-night to the boys, he sprang out.

As Julia did not return at dark, her father and mother supposed she had stopped with Nell Roberts. Mrs. Markham remembered the adventure which signalized her last walk from Coe's, and was anxious; and the Judge went down to Roberts's for her. Nell had been home one hour, and said Orville had gone home with Julia. A messenger was hurried off to Coe's, and word was sent through the neighborhood, to call out the men and boys. It had been years since an alarm and a hunt for the lost had occurred. The messenger returned with young Coe, who said that he went with Miss Markham to within sight of her father's fields, when she insisted that he should return, and he did.

Cool and collected, the Judge and his party, with lanterns and torches, accompanied by Coe, proceeded to the point where he parted with Julia, when it was discovered that what she had mistaken for her father's fields, was a new opening in the woods, a considerable distance back from them. It was supposed that in endeavoring to find a passage through, or around the fallen timber, she had lost her way. Obviously, if she went back towards the old road, which was a broad opening through the woods, she would in no event cross it, and must be somewhere within the forest, east of it, and between the State road and the one which led from it to Coe's. Through these woods, with flashing torch and gleaming lantern, with shout and loud halloa, the Judge and his now numerous party swept. As often as a dry tree or combustible matter was found, it was set on fire, there being no danger of burning over the forest, wet with the rains of Spring.

This forest covered hundreds of acres, traversed by streams and gullies, and rocky precipices, rendered difficult of passage by fallen trees, thickets, twining vines and briers.

The weather had been intensely hot for the season, ominously so, for the last two days, and on this day, the sun, after hanging like a fiery ball in the thickening heavens, disappeared at mid-afternoon, in the dark mass of vapor that gathered in the lower atmosphere. The night came on early, with a black darkness, and while there was no wind, there was a low, humming moan in the air, as if to warn of coming tempest, and the atmosphere was already chill with the approaching change.

CHAPTER XXVII.

THE BABES IN THE WOODS.

"There, Orville, here are our fields. I am almost home; now hurry back. It is late. I am obliged to you. " They had reached the opening, and the young man turned back, and the young girl tripped lightly and carelessly on; not to find the fence, as she expected, but an expanse of fallen timber, huge trunks, immense jams of tree-tops, and numerous piles of brush, under which the path was hidden. As she looked over and across, in the gloomy twilight, trees seemed to stand thick and high on the other side. Julia at once concluded that they had taken a wrong path; and she thought that she remembered to have seen one, which she and Barton passed, on the memorable night of their adventure; and without attempting to traverse the chopping, or go around it, she turned and hurried back to the old road. As she went, she thought of what had then happened, and how pleasant it would be if he were with her, and how bad it had all been since that time.

When she got back to the old road, it seemed very strange, and as if it had undergone some change; looking each way, for a moment, undecided, she finally walked rapidly to the north, until she came to a path leading to the left, which she entered, with a sense of relief, and hurried forward.

It was quite dark, silent, and gloomy in the woods, and she sped on—on past huge trees, through open glades, down through little sinks and swales, and up on high ground, until she came to an opening. "Thank God! thank God! " cried the relieved and grateful child; "I am out at last. How glad I am! " And she reached the margin of the woods, to be confronted with an interminable black jungle of fallen and decaying tree-trunks, limbs and thick standing brush, over which, and out of which, stood the dense tops of young trees. She paused for a moment, and turning to the left, thought to skirt about this obstruction, until she should reach the fence and field, which she was sure were now near her. On and on, and still on she went; over the trunks of fallen trees, through tangles of brush and pools of water, until, when she turned to look for the opening, she was alarmed and dismayed to find that it had disappeared. Her heart now for the first time sank within her. She listened, but no sound, save the ominous moan in the air, came to her ear. The solemn, still, black night was all about her. She looked up, and a cold, starless, dim blank was all over her; and all around, standing thick, were cold, dark, silent trees. She stood and tried to think back: where was she, and how came she there? She knew she had once turned back, from something to somewhere—to the old road, as she remembered; and it flashed across her, that in the strange appearance of things, and in her confusion, she had crossed it, and was in the awful, endless woods! How far had she gone? If lost, had she wandered round and round, as lost folks do? Then she thought of her dear, distracted mother, and of her brave and kind father. She had been missed, and they were looking for her. Everybody would hear of it, and would join in the hunt; and Barton might hear of it, and if he did, she knew he would come to find her. He was generous and heroic; and what a wonder and a talk it would all make, and she didn't care if it did. Then she wondered if she had not better stop and stand still, for fear she would go wrong. How awfully dark it was, and the air was chilly. Did she really know which way home was? And she strained her unseeing eyes intently for a moment, and then closed them, to let the way come into her mind. That must be the way, and she would go in that direction until she thought she could make them hear; and then she would call. And ere she started, amid the cold, unpitying trees, in her purity and innocence, that savage nature reveres and respects, she knelt and prayed; she asked for guidance and strength, and arose hopeful. But she found that she was very weary: her feet were wet and cold, and when she was to start, that she was confused and uncertain as to the direction. One more invocation, and she went forward. How far or how long she travelled, she had no idea. She paused to listen: no sound. Perhaps they would now hear her, and she raised her voice, and called her father's name, and again and again, with all her force, through the black, blank, earless night, she sent her cry.

As her voice went out, hope, and spirit, and strength went with it. She trembled and wept, and tried once again to pray. She clasped her hands; but suffocating darkness seemed to close over her, and she felt lost, utterly and hopelessly lost!

A sense of injustice, of ill-usage, came to her, and she dried her eyes; she was young, and brave, and strong; and must; and would care for herself. She should not perish; day would come some time, and she should get out. She found she was very cold, and must arouse and exert herself. Then came the thought and dread of wild animals; of that awful beast; and she listened, and could hear their stealthy steps in the dry leaves, and she shrunk from meeting the horrid glare of their eyes. Oh, if Barton were only with her, just to drive them away! God would protect him.

There—as she could not help but stare into the black darkness, there surely was the glare of their eyes, that horrid, yellowish-green, glassy glare! and with a shriek she fled—not far, for she fell, and a half swoon brought her a moment's oblivion; when the dead cold night, and the dumb trees came back about her again. With the reaction she arose, and found that she had lost her hood. She felt that a wild beast had torn it from her head; and that she had taken his hot, brute breath.

Weak, hardly with the power of motion, she supported herself by the trunk of a tree. "Father! Father God! a helpless, weak child calls to Thee; show me my sin, let me repent of it; weak and lost, and hopeless; sweet Saviour, with Thy loving sympathy, stay and help my fainting heart. If it be Thy will that I perish, receive my spirit, and let this weak, vain body, unmangled, be given back to my poor grief-stricken parents. God and Saviour, hear me! "

There now came to her ear the voice of running water. It had a sweet sound of companionship and hope, and she made towards it, and soon found herself on the banks of a wild and rapid stream. "Oh, thanks! thanks! " she murmured, "this runs from darkness out to human habitations, somewhere. It will lead out to daylight, and on its banks are human homes, somewhere. Oh, give me strength to follow it, it is so hard to perish here! "

The wind had long been blowing, and had now risen to a tempest, bitter and sharp from the north, and the trees were bending and breaking under its fury. Julia was thoroughly chilled, and her feet were benumbed with cold. She had been aware for some time that snow was sifting over her, and rattling on the dry leaves under her feet. She was dizzy, and almost overcome with sleep; and was conscious of strange visions and queer voices, that seemed to haunt her senses. Could she hold out till morning? She could not fix her wandering mind, even on this question. She occasionally heard her own voice in broken murmurs, but did not understand what she said. It was like the voice of another. She knew her mouth was dry and parched with thirst, but never thought of trying to drink from the stream, whose drowsy voice ran through her wandering consciousness. The impulse to move on remained long after all intelligent power of directing her movements had left her; and blindly and mechanically, she staggered and reeled about for a few or many minutes, until she sank to the earth unable and unwilling to struggle further. Her last act was with pure womanly instinct, to draw her torn and draggled skirts about her limbs and feet. The faces of her father and mother, warm and sweet, were with her for a moment, and she tried to think of her Heavenly Father; and another face was all the time present, full of tenderness and love; and then all faded into oblivion, blank and utter ...

What was it? something whispered, or seemed to whisper in her heart as vague consciousness returned, unutterably sweet; was it the voice of an angel coming to bear her hence? Once again! and now her ear caught—and still again—a voice of earth, clear; and it had power to start her up from under the snow, that was surely weaving and thickening her virgin winding-sheet. God in heaven! once again! Strong, clear and powerful, it pealed through the arches of the forest, overtopping the tempest. It was a voice she knew, and if aught might, it would have called her back from death; as now, from a deadly swoon.

And once again, and nearer, with a cadence of impatience, and almost doubt, a faint answer went back; and then a gleam of light; a broad, wavering circle of glory, and Barton, with his flashing eyes, and eager, flushed face, with his mass of damp curls filled with snow, and dashed back, sprang with a glad cry to her side!

"Barton! " she cried, trying to rise, and throwing out her hands to him.

"Oh, Julia! you are found! you are alive! Thank God! thank God! " Throwing himself on his knees by her, and, clasping her cold hands in his, and, in a paroxysm, pressing them to his lips and heart, and covering them with kisses and with tears.

"God sent you to me! God sent you to me! " murmured the poor, dear grateful girl.

Bart's self-command returned in a moment; he lifted her to her feet, and supported her. "You are nearly frozen, and the snow had already covered you. See what my mother sent to you, " filling the top of his flask and placing it to her lips. "It is nothing but old wine.

" How revivingly it seemed to run through her veins! "I am very thirsty, " she said, and he brought her a full draught from the running stream.

"Can you walk? let me carry you. We must get to some shelter. "

"I thought you would come. Where is my father? "

"I am alone—may I save you? "

"Oh, Barton! "

"I have not seen your father; they are looking for you, miles away. How under the heavens did you ever find your way here? How you must have suffered! See! here is your hood! " placing it over her tangled and dripping hair. "And let me put this on you. " Removing his "wamus, " and putting her arms through the sleeves, he tied the lower corners about her little waist, and buttoned the top over her bosom and about her neck. He gave her another draught of wine, and paused for a moment—"I must carry you. "

"Oh, I can walk! " said the revived girl, with vivacity.

He lifted his nearly consumed torch, and conducted her to the stream. "We must cross this, and find shelter on the other side. " He let himself at once from the abrupt bank, into the cold, swift water, that came to his middle. "I must carry you over; " unhesitatingly she stooped over to him, and was taken with one strong arm fully to himself, while he held his torch with the other. He turned with her then, and plunged across the creek, holding her above its waters. Its deepest part ran next the bank where he entered; fortunately it was not very wide, and he bore her safely to the opposite and lower bank.

The other side was protected from the tempest, which was at its greatest fury, by a high and perpendicular ledge of rocks which the course of the creek followed, but leaving a narrow space of hard land along the base. Under the shelter, Bart turned up stream with his charge, occasionally lifting his torch and inspecting the mossy ledge. Within a few feet of them the snow fell in wreaths and swirls, and sometimes little eddies of wind sifted it over them.

"Somewhere near here, is a place where they made shingles last summer, and there was a shed against the rocks, if we could only find it. " Finally they doubled an abrupt angle in the nearly smooth wall, which bent suddenly back from the stream, for many feet, making a semicircle of a little space, and in the back of which Bart discovered the anxiously looked-for shed; —a mere rude cover, on posts driven into the ground.

Under and about it were great quantities of dry shavings, and short bits of wood, the hearts and saps of shingle blocks. To place a pile of these on the margin of the creek, and apply his torch to them, took but a moment; and in an instant a bright, white flame flashed and lit up the little sheltered alcove. Another, and the almost overcome girl was placed on a seat of soft, dry shavings, against the moss-grown rock, under the rude roof, out of the reach of the snow or wind; and another fire was lit of the dry shingle blocks, at her feet, from which her saturated shoes were removed, and to which warmth was soon restored.

Barton now took from a pocket on the outside of the "wamus, " a small parcel, and produced some slices of tongue and bread, which the famished girl ate with the relish and eagerness of a hungry child. More wine, now mingled with water, completed her repast; and Bart made further preparations for her comfort and rest. A larger mass of the shavings so adjusted that she could recline upon them, was arranged for her, which made an easy, springy couch; and as she lay wearily back upon them, still others were placed about and over her, until, protected as she was, warmth and comfort came to her.

What a blessed sense of shelter, and safety, and peace, as from heaven, fell upon the rescued girl's heart! And how exquisitely delicious to be carried, and supported, and served by this beautiful and heroic youth, who hovered about her so tenderly, and kneeling at her feet, so gently and sweetly ministered to her! No thought of being compromised, none of impropriety in the atmosphere of absolute purity, came to cloud the stainless mind of the maiden. No memory of the past, no thought of the future, was near her. She was lost, exhausted, and dying, and God sent him to her; and she accepted him as from the hand of God. He had restored, warmed and cheered her. She was under shelter and protection, and now heavy with sleep, and still the storm raged all about and over their heads, and the snow still fell within a few feet of them, while in that little circle warmth and light pulsated, like a tender human heart.

When all was done that occurred to the tender, thoughtful youth, and the eyes of the maiden were dreamily closing: "Have you said your prayers? " asked Bart, who had spoken barely a word since lighting the fires.

"Not of thanks for my deliverance, " replied the girl. "Will you say a prayer for us? " in a low, sweet voice.

The youth knelt a little from her.

"Our Father, Whose Presence is Heaven, and Whose Presence is everywhere, let this weary, wandering one feel that Presence in Its sweetest power; let her repose in It; and through all time rest in It. Hush the storm, and make short the hours of darkness, and with the dawn give her back to her home of love. Impress her parents with a sense of her safety. Remember my widowed mother and young brothers. Be with all wanderers, all unsheltered birds, and lambs on bleak hill-sides, and with all helpless, hopeless things. "

He ceased.

"You ask nothing for yourself, Barton, " in her tenderest voice.

"Have I not been permitted to save you? What remains for me to ask? "

How these words came to her afterwards! She turned, moved a little, as if to make room, and slept.

Barton shall at some time, in his own way, tell of his experiences of that strange night.

It had never come near him—the thought of seeking and saving her for himself—-and when he found her perishing, and bore her over the water, and found shelter, and cheered and restored her, and as he now sat to protect her, the idea that she was or could be more to him, or different from what she had been, never approached him. It had been an inspiration to seek her, and a great possession to find her. It had brought back to him his self-respect, and had perhaps redeemed him, in her eyes, from the scorn and contempt with which she had regarded him, and in his heart he gratefully thanked God for it. Now his path was open and serene, although unwarmed and unlighted with this precious love, and so, in the heart of the forest, in the soul of the night, in the bosom of the tempest, he had brought life and hope and peace and rest to her, and an angel could not have done it with a purer self-abnegation.

He sat near her, at the foot of an old hemlock, waiting for the dawn. The forest and night and storm thus held in their arms these two young, strong, brave, sweet, and rich natures, so tender, and so estranged, till the morning light brightened and flashed up in the serene sky, and sent a new day over the snow-wreathed earth. The tempest subsided, the snow ceased, the wind sunk to whispers, and the young morning was rosy in the east.

Barton had kept the fire burning near Julia, and when the new light became decided, approached her, and not without some anxiety: "Miss Markham—Miss Markham—Miss Markham! " raising his voice at each repetition. She did not hear. "Julia! " in a low voice, bending over her. Her eyes opened to the rude roof over her, and she started, turned to him, flushed, and smiled: "Oh, we are still here in the woods! Is it day? "

"Yes; how do you feel? Can you walk? " cheerily.

"Oh yes, I haven't suffered much! " rising from the woody coverings, which she gayly shook from her.

"Excuse me, while you make your toilet in this extensive dressing-room, and I will look about. I will not go far, or be gone long. " Going still further up the stream, he found the end of the ledge of rocks, with a steepish hill sloping down to the creek, down which, under the snow, appeared to wind a road, which crossed the creek when the water was low. He turned into this road, and went up to the top of the hill, from which he could see an opening in the otherwise unbroken woods, and a little farther on he was gladdened with the sight of a smoke, rising like a cloud-column, above the trees.

He hastened back to find Julia equipped, and busy placing new fuel to the crackling fire. "There is a cabin not more than half a mile away, and the snow is not more than two or three inches deep; we can easily reach it, " he said, brightly.

"Oh, Barton! " said the girl, with a deep rich voice, coming to him, "how can we ever—how can my father and mother ever—how can I repay"—and her voice broke and faltered with emotion, and tears fell from her wondrous eyes.

"Perhaps, " said Bart, off his guard, "perhaps you may be willing to forget the past! "

"The past—forget the past? "

"Pardon me, it was unfortunate! Let us go. "

"Barton! "

"Not a word now, " said Bart, gayly. "I am the doctor, you are terribly shaken up, and not yourself. I shall not let you say a word of thanks. Why, we are not out of the woods yet! "—this last laughingly. "When you are all your old self, and in your pleasant home, everything of this night and morning will come to you. "

"What do you mean, Mr. Ridgeley? " a little coolly.

"Nothing, " in a sad, low voice. They had gained the road. "See, " said he, "here is somebody's road, from some place to somewhere; we will follow it up to the some place. There! I hear an axe. I hope he is cutting wood; and there—you can see the smoke of his cabin.

'I knew by the smoke that so gracefully curled. '

Oh, I hope he will have a rousing fire. "

Julia walked rapidly and silently by his side, hardly hearing his last words; she was thinking why he would not permit her to thank him—and that it would all be recalled in her home—finally, his meaning came to her. He would seek and save her from death, and even from the memory of an unconsidered word, which might possibly be misconstrued; and she clung more closely to the arm which had borne her over the flood.

"I am hurrying you, I fear. "

"No, not a bit. Oh, now I can see the cabin; and there is the man, right by the side of it. "

"It must be Wilder's, " said Bart. "He moved into the woods here somewhere. "

As they approached, the chopper stopped abruptly, and gazed on them in blank wonder. The dishevelled girl, with hanging hair, and red "wamus, " and the wild, haggard-looking, coatless youth, with belt and hatchet, were as strange apparitions, coming up out of the interminable woods, as could well meet the gaze of a rustic wood-chopper of an early morning.

"Can you give this young lady shelter and food? " asked Bart, gravely.

"I guess so, " said the man; "been out all night? " and he hurried them into a warm and cheerful room, bright with a blazing fire, where was a comely, busy matron, who turned to them in speechless surprise.

"This is Judge Markham's daughter, " said Bart, as Julia sank into a chair, strongly inclined to break down completely; "she got lost, last night, near her father's, and wandered all night alone, and I found her just beyond the creek, not more than two hours ago. I must place her in your hands, my good woman. "

"Poor, precious thing! " cried the woman, kneeling and pulling off her shoes, and placing her chilled feet to the fire. "What a blessed mercy you did not perish, you darling. "

"I should, if it had not been for him, " now giving way. Mrs. Wilder stepped a moment into the other of the two rooms, into which the lower floor of the cabin was divided, and spoke to some one in it; and giving Julia a bowl of hot milk and tea, led her to the inner apartment.

"Take care of him; " were her words, as she left, nodding her head towards Barton.

"How far is it to Markham's? " asked Bart.

"'Bout seven mile round, an' five 'cross. "

"Have you a horse? "

"Fust rate! "

"Saddle him, and go to Markham's at once. The father and mother of this girl are frantic: a thousand men are hunting for her; you'll be paid. "

"I don't want no pay, " said Wilder, hurrying out. Five minutes later, sitting on his saddle, he received a slip of paper from Bart.

"Who shall I say? " said Wilder, not without curiosity on his own account.

"That will tell the Judge all he'll want to know. He will hear my name as soon as he will care to. "

Wilder dashed off down the forest-road by which Bart and Julia had approached his house.

Bart went listlessly into the house. His energy and excitement had suddenly died out, with the exigency which called them forth; his mental glow and physical effort, both wonderful and long-continued to an intense strain, left him, and in the reaction he almost collapsed. Mrs. Wilder offered him one of her husband's coats. He was not cold. She placed a smoking breakfast before him. He loathed its sight and fragrance, and drank a little milk.

She knew he was a hero; so young and so handsome, yet a mere boy; his sad, grave face had a wonderful beauty to her, and his manners were so high, and like a gentleman born. She asked him some questions about his finding Julia, and he answered dreamily, and in few words, and seemed hardly to know what he said.

"Is Miss Markham asleep? —is she quiet? "

Mrs. Wilder stepped to the inner room. "She is, " she answered; "nothing seems to ail her but weariness and exhaustion. She will not suffer from it. "

"Is she alone? "

"She is in bed with my daughter Rose. "

"May I just look at her one moment? "

"Certainly. "

One look from the door at the sweetly-sleeping face, and without a word he hurried from the house. He had felt a great heart-throb when he came upon her in the woods, and now, when all was over, and no further call for action or invention was on him, the strong, wild rush of the old love for a moment overwhelmed him. It would assert itself, and was his momentary master. But presently he turned away, with an unspoken and final adieu.

Two hours later the Judge, on his smoking steed, dashed up to the cabin, followed by the Doctor and two or three others. As he touched the ground, Julia, with a cry of joy, sprang into his arms.

She had murmured in her sleep, awoke, and would get up and dress. She laughed, and said funny little things at her looks and dress, and examined the "wamus" with great interest, with a blush put it on, and tied it coquettishly about her waist, then seemed to think, and took it off gravely. Next she ran eagerly out to the other room, and asked for Bart, and looked grave, and wondered, when Mrs. Wilder told her he had gone, and she wondered that Mrs. Wilder would let him go.

She kissed that good woman when she first got up, and was already in love with sweet, shy, tall, comely Rose, who was seventeen, and had made fast friends with Ann and George, the younger ones. Then she ran out into the melting snow and bright soft air. How serene it all was, and how tall and silent stood the trees, in the bright sun! How calm and innocent it all was, and looked as if nothing dreadful had ever happened in it, and a robin came and sang from an old tree, near by.

And she talked, and wondered about her mother and father, and, by little bits, told much of what happened the night before; and wondered—this time to herself—why Bart went off; and she looked sad over it.

159

Mrs. Wilder looked at her, and listened to her, and in her woman's heart she pondered of these two, and wished she had kept Bart; she was sad and sorry for them, and most for him, for she saw his soul die in his eyes as he turned from Julia's sleeping face.

Then came the tramp of horses, and Julia sprang out, and into her father's arms.

One hour after came Julia's mother and Nell, in the light carriage; and kisses, and tears, and little laughy sobs, and words that ran out with little freshets of tears, and unanswered questions, and unasked answers, broken and incoherent; yet all were happy, and all thankful and grateful to their Father in Heaven; and blessings and thanks — many of them unsaid — to the absent one.

And so the lost one was restored, and soon they started back.

CHAPTER XXVIII.

AT JUDGE MARKHAM'S.

When Mrs. Markham at last realized that Julia was lost, she hastily arrayed herself and went out with the others to search for her, calmly, hopefully, and persistently. She went, and clambered, and looked, and called, and when she could look and go no further, as woman may, she waited, and watched, and prayed, and the night grew cold, and the wind and snow came, and as trumpets were blown and guns discharged, and fires lighted in the woods, and torches flashed and lanterns gleamed through the trees, she still watched, and hoped, and prayed.

When at last the storm and exhaustion drove men in, she was very calm and pale, said little, and went about with chilled tears in her eyes.

Judge Markham was a strong, brave, sagacious man, and struggled and fought to the last, but finally in silence he rejoined his silent wife. At about three in the morning, and while the storm was at its height, she turned from the blank window where she stood, with a softened look in her eyes, from which full tides were now for the first time falling; and approaching her husband, who man-like, when nothing more could be done by courage and strength, sat with his face downward on his arms, resting on the table, and breathing great dry gasps, and sobs of agony.

"Edward, " said she, stooping over him, "it comes to me somehow that Julia is safe; that she has somewhere found shelter, and we shall find her. "

And now she murmured, and whispered, and talked, as the impression seemed to deepen in her own heart, and she knelt, and once more a fervent prayer of hope and faith went up. The man came and knelt by her, and joined in her prayer, and grew calm.

"Julia, " said he, "we have at least God, and with Him is all. "

When the morning came, five hundred anxious and determined men, oppressed with sad forebodings, had gathered from all that region for the search.

Persistently they adhered to the idea that the missing girl was in the lower woods.

A regular organized search by men and boys, in a continuous line, was resolved upon. Marshals were appointed, signals agreed upon, and appliances and restoratives provided; and the men were hastening to their places. A little knot near the Judge's house were still discussing the matter, as in doubt about the expediency of further search in that locality.

George was in this group, and had, as directed, given Barton's opinion. Judge Markham, who was giving some last directions joined these men, and listened while Uncle Jonah, in a few words, explained Bart's theory—that the girl would turn back from the chopping to the old road, and if there confused, would be likely to go into the woods, and directly away from her home.

"And where is Bart? " asked the Judge.

"He started at about nine last night, with two big bundles of hickory, " said George, "to look for her, and had not returned half an hour ago. "

"Where did he go? " asked the Judge eagerly.

"Into the woods. "

"And has not returned? "

"No. "

"Your girl is safe, " said Uncle Jonah. "The boy has found her, I'll bet my soul! "

While the Judge stood, struck and a little startled, by this information, and Jonah's positive assurance, a man on a foaming steed came plunging down the hill, just south of the house, and pulling up, called out, "Where is Judge Markham? "

"I am he. "

"Oh! Good-morning, Judge! This is for you. Your girl is safe. "

The Judge eagerly took the paper, gazed at it, and at the man, speechless.

"She's at my house, Judge, safe and sound. "

And then the group of men gave a shout; a cheer; and then another, and another—and the men forming in the near-line heard it and took it up, and repeated it, and it ran and rang miles away; and all knew that the lost one was found, and safe.

No man who has not felt the lifting up of such an awful pressure, can estimate the rush of escaped feeling and emotion that follows it; and none who have not witnessed its sudden effect upon a crowd of eager, joyous men, shouting, cheering, crying, weeping, scrambling and laughing, can comprehend it, and none can describe it. All hurried eagerly back to the Judge's, gathered about the happy, wondering Wilder, and patted and caressed his smoking horse.

Mrs. Markham knew it, and with radiant face and eyes came out with her grateful husband, when the bright sky again rang with the cheers of the assembled multitude. After quiet came, the Judge read to them the paper he had received from Wilder:

"JUDGE MARKHAM:

"Your daughter was found this morning, on the banks of the creek, a mile from Wilder's, overcome and much exhausted. She rallied, got into Wilder's, and appears strong and well. Wilder will take you to her. "

"Whose name is to it, Judge? "

"There is none—who gave it to you? "

"The young man who found the young lady, and he didn't give his name, said the Judge would hear it as soon as he would want to, " was the answer; "he didn't talk much. "

"It was Barton Ridgeley, " said Jonah. And the name of Barton went up with new cheers, and louder than any.

Soon away went the Judge, on a splendid chestnut, with the Doctor, and two or three others, on horseback, followed by Mrs. Markham and Nell Roberts in a carriage. The sun mounted up, the snow melted away, and so did the crowd. Some returned home, and many gathered in little knots to talk up the exciting event. The absurdest speculations were indulged in, as to how Bart found Julia, and what would come out of it. There was an obvious element of romance in the affair that appealed to the sensibilities of the rudest. And then, would Bart come back with Julia?

As the day advanced, the neighboring women and children gathered at Judge Markham's, all glad and happy, and a little teary over the exciting incidents, and all impatient for the return of Julia.

At a little past two the party returned—the Judge, Mrs. Markham, Julia, and Nell, in the carriage—Julia on the front seat with her father, a little pale, but with sparkling eyes, radiant, and never so lovely. As the carriage drove up, a noisy welcome saluted her. As she arose to alight, and again as she was about to enter the house, her mother observed her cast her eyes eagerly over the crowd, as if in search of some face, and she knew by her look that she did not find it. What a gathering about her, and kissing and clinging and crying of women and girls! Then followed, "ohs! " and "ahs! " and "wonders! " and "did you evers! " and "never in my born days! " "and did Barton really find you? " and "where is he? " etc.

Every one noticed that he did not come with them, and wondered, and demanded to know where he was, and doubted if he had had anything to do with it, after all.

The Judge told them, that by some means not yet explained, Barton had found her, overcome, chilled, exhausted and in a swoon, and had carried and conducted her out to Wilder's; that when she was restored, he sent Wilder off with the news, and then went home, and that the Doctor and Roberts had gone around to his mother's to see him. Beyond doubt he had saved his daughter's life. He spoke with an honest, manly warmth, and the people were satisfied, and lingeringly and reluctantly dispersed to talk and wonder over the affair, and especially the part Barton had performed.

Toward sunset, Julia, in her luxurious chamber and night-robes, seemed anxious and restless. Her mother was with her, and tried to soothe her. Her father entered with a cheery face.

"Roberts has just returned, " he said. "Barton got home in the morning, very much exhausted, of course. He seems not to have told his mother much, and went to his room, and had not been out. His mother would not permit him to be disturbed, and said he would be out all right in the morning. "

"Did the Doctor see him? " asked Julia.

"I suppose not; I will go and bring him around in the morning myself, " said the Judge.

"Thank you, Papa; I would so like to see him, and I want to know how he found me, " said Julia.

"I wonder he did not tell you, " said the Judge.

"He hardly spoke, " said Julia, "unless compelled to, and told me I was too broken down to say anything. I tried to thank him, and he said I was not myself, and stopped me. "

CHAPTER XXIX.

AFTER.

Toward noon of the next day, the Judge drove up to his own gate, alone, and not a little troubled. His wife and daughter were evidently expecting him. They seemed disappointed.

"Wouldn't he come? " asked his wife.

"He was not there to come. "

"Not there! " from both.

"No; he went off in the stage last night to Jefferson. "

"Went off! Why, father! "

"Well, it seems that he had arranged to leave on Tuesday, and sent his trunk out to Hiccox's, but didn't go; and all day Wednesday he wandered about, his mother said, seeming reluctant to start. At evening she said he appeared much depressed, and said he would not go until the next evening. "

"Thank God! " said the ladies.

"George, " continued the Judge, "who had been down to the Post-office, heard that you were lost, and hurried home, and told him all he had heard. His mother said when he heard it he asked a good many questions, and said, 'I know now why I stayed, ' and that in five minutes he was off to the woods. "

"Father, there was a special Providence in it all. "

"And did Providence send him off last night? "

"Perhaps so. "

"Did his mother tell how he came to think Julia had crossed the old road? "

"He didn't tell his mother much about it. She said he was more cheerful and lighter hearted than he had been for a year, but did not seem inclined to talk much; ate a very little breakfast, and went to bed, saying that he hoped she would not let anybody disturb him. He did not come down again until five, and then told her he should leave that evening. She tried to dissuade him, but he said he must go—that he was not wanted here any more—that he felt it was better for him to go at once. She said that she spoke to him of us, of Julia, saying that she thought he ought to remain and let us see him, if we wished. He answered that he had better go then, and that they would understand it. He said they might perhaps call and say some things to her; if they did, she should say to them that he could understand what their feelings might be, and appreciated them; that it was not necessary to say anything to him; that he wished all the past to be forgotten, and that nothing might be said or done to recall it; he had left Newbury forever as a home.

"I told her that I wanted to provide for his studies, and to start him in business—of course in as delicate a way as possible. She rather started up at that, and said she hoped I would never in any way make any offer of help to him. I asked who went with him to meet the stage, and his mother replied that he went alone—walked down just at dark, and wouldn't permit either of the boys to go with him. "

"Why Edward! how strange this is! "

"It isn't strange to me at all, " remarked Julia, in a low, depressed voice.

"Father, I've a little story to tell you. I should have told it last night, and then you would have better understood some things that have occurred. It was nothing that happened between us yesterday morning. I have told you every word and thing of that. "

Then she recited to the astonished Judge the incidents of her adventure in the woods with Bart and the wolverine.

"And I, " said the Judge, "have also a little incident to relate, " and he told of the occurrence on the river with which this tale began.

"Oh, father! " exclaimed Julia, "could you leave him, away there, weary and alone? "

"I did not mean to do that; I stopped, and lingered and looked back, and waited and thought he would ask or call to me, " said the humiliated Judge: "and now he has repaid me by saving your life. "

"Father! father, dear! " going and laying her arm around his neck, and her cheek against his, "You are my own dear papa, and could never purposely harm a living thing. It was all to be, I suppose. Mamma, do you remember the night of Snow's ball, when you playfully complained of his inattention to you? and he said he would atone for all offences, —

> 'In that blissful never,
> When the Sundays come together,
> And the sun and glorious weather,
> Wrapped the earth in spring forever?'

and he has. "

"I remember, but I could not recall the words. "

"I can repeat the very words of the beautiful prayer that he made in the woods, " said the young girl.

"And which I seemed to hear, " said her mother.

"And that 'blissful never' came, mother, and all its good was for me—for us. "

"Not wholly, I trust. This young man's mind and nature are their own law. His mother said he was lighter-hearted and more like himself than for a long time. He has suffered much. He mourned more for his brother than most could. He had lost his own self-respect somehow, and now he has regained it, and will come to take right views of things, and a blissful ever may come for him. "

"And he wanted all the past forgotten, " said the girl.

"Of all that happened between you before he has only remembered what you said to him, " said her mother. "And you possibly remember what he said to you. "

"I remember his generosity and bravery, mother, " replied Julia.

The Judge remained thoughtful. Turning to his wife, "Would you have me follow him to Jefferson? "

"No. He went away in part to avoid us; he will be sensitive, and I would not go to him at present. Write to him; write what you really feel, a warm and manly letter like your own true self. I am not certain, though, how he will receive it. "

A silence followed which was broken by Julia.

"Father, do you know this Mr. Wade with whom Barton has gone to study? "

"Yes; I have met him several times and like him very much. He was our senator, and made that awful speech against slavery last winter. He is a frank, manly, straightforward man. "

"How old is he? "

"Thirty-five, perhaps; why? "

"Nothing. Is he married? "

"He is an old bachelor; but I heard some one joking him about a young lady, to whom it is said he is engaged. Why do you inquire about him? "

"Oh! I wanted to know something of the man with whom he is. I met Mr. Ranney a year ago, you know. "

That night the fair girl remained long in a serious and thoughtful attitude.

* * * * *

In the afternoon of the next day, the ladies drove to Mrs. Ridgeley's. The elders embraced cordially. One was thinking of the boy who had died, and of him who had gone so sadly away; the other of her agony at a supposed loss, and her great joy at the recovery. Julia took one of Mrs. Ridgeley's thin, toil-hardened hands in her two, rosy and dimpled, and kissed it, and shed tears over it. Then they sat down, and Mrs. Markham, in her woman's direct natural way, poured out the gratitude they both felt; Julia, with simple frankness, told the happenings of the night, and both were surprised to learn that Bart had told her so little.

Mrs. Ridgeley described his going out, and coming back next morning, and going again at evening. It was his way, his mother said. She was proud of Barton, and wondered that this sweet girl should not love him, and actually pitied her that she did not. She would not betray his weakness; but when she came to speak of his final going, the forlorn figure of the depressed boy walking out into the darkness, alone, came before her, and she wept. Then Julia knelt by her, and again taking her hand, said "Let me love you, while he is gone; I want to care for all that are dear to him; " and the poor mother thought that it was in part as a recompense for not loving Barton. There was another thing that Julia came to say, and opening her satchel, she pointed to something red and coarse, and putting her hand on it, she said, "This was Bart's. He took it off himself, and put it on me; and went cold and exposed. I did not think to restore it, and I want very much to keep it—may I? " The poor mother raised her eyes to the warm face of the girl, yet saw nothing. "Yes. " And the pleased child replaced it and closed her satchel.

Then Mrs. Markham said their friends and neighbors were coming in on the Tuesday evening following, to congratulate them, and would Mrs. Ridgeley let them send for her? The gathering would be informal and neighborly. But Mrs. Ridgeley begged to be excused. Julia wanted to see the boys, and they came in from the garden—Ed shy, quiet and reserved; George, dashing, sparkling and bashful. Julia went up and shook them by their brown hands, and acted as if she would kiss George if he did look very much like Bart. She talked with them in her frank girl's way, and took them captive, and then mother and daughter drove away.

* * * * *

The gathering at the Judge's was spontaneous almost, and cordial. The whole family were popular individually, and the young girls especially gathered about Julia, who was a real heroine and had been rescued by a brave, handsome young man; —the affair was so romantic!

They wondered why Bart should go away; and wouldn't he be there that night? They seemed to assume that everything would be a matter of course, only he behaved very badly in going off when he must know he was most wanted. Of course he would come back, and Julia would forgive him; and something they hinted of this. Kate and Ann, and sweet Pearly Burnett, who had just come home from school, and was entitled to rank next after Julia, with Nell and Kate, were very gushing on the subject.

Others took Bart to account. His sudden and mysterious flight was very much against him, and his reputation was at a sudden ebb. Why did he go? Then Greer's name was mentioned, and Brown, and New Orleans; and it was talked over that night at Markham's with ominous mystery, and one wouldn't wonder if Bart had not gone to Jefferson, at all—that was a dodge; and another said that at Painesville he stopped and went west to Cleveland; or to Fairport, and took a steamer; and Greer went off about the same time.

Julia caught these whispers and pondered them, and the Judge looked grave over them.

In the morning Julia asked him what it all meant. She remembered that he had spoken of Bart in connection with Greer, when he came home from the Cole trial, which made her uneasy; she now wanted to know what it meant.

The Judge replied that there was a rumor that Bart was an associate of Greer, and engaged with him. "In what? " He didn't know; he was a supposed agent of Brown's, and a company. "What were they doing? " Nobody knew; but it was grossly unlawful and immoral. "Did anybody believe this of Bart? " He didn't know; things looked suspicious. "Do you suspect Bart of anything wrong? " He did not; but people talked and men must be prudent. "Be prudent, when his name is assailed, and he absent, and no brother to defend him? " "Why did he go? " asked the Judge, "and where did he go? "

"Father! "

"I don't suspect anything wrong of him, and yet the temptation to this thing might be great. "

Julia asked no more.

171

The next morning she said that she had long promised Sarah King to pay her a visit, and she thought she would go for two or three days. Sarah had just been to Pittsburg, and had seen Miss Walters, and she wanted so much to hear from her. This announcement quite settled it. She had recently taken the possession of herself, in a certain sweet determined way, and was inclined to act on her own judgment, or caprice. She would go down in the stage; she could go alone—and she went.

The morning after, the elegant and leisurely Mr. Greer, at the Prentiss House, Ravenna, received a dainty little note, saying that Miss Markham was at Mr. King's, and would be glad to see him at his early leisure. He pulled his whiskers down, and his collar up, and called. He found Miss Markham in the parlor, who received him graciously.

What commands had she for him?

"Mr. Greer, I want to ask you a question, if you will permit me. "

Anything he would answer cheerfully.

"You know Barton Ridgeley? "

"Yes, without being much acquainted with him. I like him. "

"Have you now, or have you ever had any business connection with him? "

"I have not, and I never had. "

"Will you say this in writing? "

"Cheerfully, if you wish it. "

"I do. "

Greer sat down to the desk in the library adjoining.

"Address my father, please. "

He wrote and handed her the following:

"Hon. E. MARKHAM:

"*Dear Sir*, —I am asked if I have now, or have ever had any business relations of any kind with Barton Ridgeley. I have not, and never had, directly or indirectly, on my own, or on account of others.

"Very respectfully,

"THOS. J. GREER.

"RAVENNA, April 1838. "

"May I know why you wish this? " a little gravely; "you've heard something said about something and somebody, by other somebodys or nobodys, perhaps. "

"I have. Mr. Ridgeley is away. You have heard of our obligations to him, and I have taken it upon myself to ask you. "

"You are a noble girl, Miss Markham. A man might go through fire for you; " enthusiastically.

"Thank you. "

"And now I hope your little heart is at rest. "

"It was quite at rest before. I am much obliged, Mr. Greer; and it may not be in my power to make other returns. "

"Good morning, Miss Markham. "

"Good morning, Mr. Greer. "

In the afternoon, as the Judge was in his office, a little springy step came clipping in. "Good afternoon! Papa Judge, " and two wonderful arms went about his neck, and two lips to his own.

"Why Julia! you back! How is Sarah? "

"Splendid! "

"Your friend Miss Walters? "

"Oh, she is well. See here, Papa Judge, " holding out the Greer note.

The Judge looked at and read it over in amazement.

"Where under the heavens did you get this? "

"Mr. Greer wrote it for me. "

"Mr. Greer wrote it for you? I am amazed! no man could have dared to ask him for it! What put this into your head? "

"You almost suspected Bart"—with decidedly damp eyes—"and others did quite, and while in Ravenna I wrote a note to Mr. Greer, who called, and I asked the direct question, and he answered. I asked him to write it and he did, and paid me a handsome compliment besides. Papa Judge, when you want a thing done send me. "

"Well, my noble girl, you deserve a compliment. A girl that can do that can, of course, have a man go through night and storm and flood for her, " said the Judge with enthusiasm.

"Mr. Greer said a man should go through fire, " said Julia, as if a little hurt.

"And so he may, " said the Judge, improving.

"That is for you, " said Julia, more gravely, and gave him the note.

CHAPTER XXX.

JEFFERSON.

Bart has come well nigh breaking down on my hands two or three times. I find him unmanageable. He is pitched too high and tuned too nicely for common life; and I am only too glad to get him off out of Newbury, to care much how he went. To say, however, that he went off cheerful and happy, would do the poor fellow injustice. He did his best to show himself that it was all right. But something arose and whispered that it was all wrong. Of course Julia and her love were not for him, and yet in his heart a cry for her would make itself heard.

Didn't he go voluntarily, because he would? Who was to blame? Yet he despised himself as a huge baby, because there was a half conscious feeling of self-pity, a consciousness of injustice, of being beaten. Then he was lame from, over-exertion, and his heart was sore, and he had to leave his mother and Ed and George. Would it have been better to remain a day or two and meet Julia? He felt that he would certainly break down in her presence, and he had started, and shut her forever out. If she did not stay shut out it would be her own fault. And that was logical.

He got into the stage, and had the front seat, with wide soft cushions, to himself, and drawing his large camlet cloak about him, he would rest and sleep.

Not a bit of it. On the back seat was an old lady and a young one with her; and a man on the middle seat. At Parkers, where they changed horses, they had heard all about it, and had it all delightfully jumbled up. Barton Markham had rescued Miss Ridgeley from a gang of wolves, which had driven her into the Chagrin River, which froze over, etc., but it had all ended happily, and the wedding-day was fixed.

Miss Ridgeley was a lovely girl, but poor; and Bart was a hero, whom the ladies would be glad to see.

The old lady asked Bart if he knew the parties.

175

"Yes. " And he straightened out the tangle of names.

"Was Julia a beauty? "

"Decidedly. "

"And Bart? "

Well, he didn't think much of Bart and didn't want to speak of him. He thought the performance no great shakes, etc. The ladies were offended.

"No matter, Julia would marry him? "

"She would never think of it. "

At Hiccox's somebody recognized Bart and told the old lady who he was.

"Oh, dear! " He wished he had walked to Jefferson and had a good mind to get out.

A few years ago, when Jefferson had become famous throughout the United States as the residence of two men, a stranger, who met Senator Wade, "old Ben, " somewhere East, asked him what were the special advantages of Jefferson. "Political, " was the dry response.

Those privileges were not apparent to Bart, as he looked over the little mud-beleaguered town of two or three hundred inhabitants, with its two taverns, Court House, two or three churches, and half a dozen stores and shops, and the high, narrow wooden sidewalks, mere foot bridges, rising high above the quaggy, tenacious mud, that would otherwise have forbidden all communication. The town was built on a low level plain, every part of which, to Bart's eye, seemed a foot or two lower and more depressed than every other.

In fact, his two days and two nights wallow in the mud, from Newbury to Jefferson, had a rather depressing effect on a mind a little below par when he started; and he was inclined to depressing views.

Bart was not one to be easily beaten, or stay beaten, unless when he abandoned the field; and the battle at Jefferson was to be fought out. Lord! how far away were Newbury and all the events of three days ago. There was one that was not inclined to vacate, but Bart was resolute. It was dark, and he would shut his eyes and push straight forward till light came.

This, then, was the place where Henry had lived, and which he had learned to like. He would like it too. He inquired the way, and soon stood in front of a one-story wooden building, painted white, lettered "Wade & Ranney, Attorneys at Law. " The door was a little ajar and Bart pushed it open and entered a largeish, dingy, soiled room, filled with book-cases, tables and chairs, with a generally crumpled and disarranged appearance; in the rear of which was its counterpart. A slender, white-haired, very young looking man, and another of large and heavy mould occupied the front room, while in the rear sat a third, with his feet on the table. Bart looked around and bowing to each: "I see Mr. Ranney is not in; " and with another glance around, "I presume Mr. Wade is not? "

"No. Both would be in during the evening. "

"I am Bart Ridgeley, " he said. "You may remember my brother Henry? "

"How are you, Bart? We know you, but did not at first recognize you, " said white-hair frankly. "My name is Case, —this is Ransom, and there is Kennedy. We all knew your brother and liked him. "

Bart shook hands with, and looked at, each. Case had small but marked features—was too light, but his eyes redeemed his face; and his features improved on acquaintance. Ransom was twenty-seven or twenty-eight, of heavy build, dark, and with a quick, sharp eye, and jerky positive way. Kennedy was sandy—hair, face, eyebrows and skin, with good eyes.

"I think we shall like you, Bart, " said Case, who had examined him.

"I hope you will; it must be very pleasant to be liked, " said Bart vivaciously. "I've never tried it much. "

"There is one thing I observe, " continued Case, "that won't suit Ransom—that way of taking off your hat when you came in. "

"Oh! " said Bart, laughing, "I'm imitative, with a tendency to improve; and shall doubtless find good models. "

"Don't mind Case, " said Ransom; "he's of no account. Just come in?"

"Yes. "

"How do you like our town? "

"Very well. There seems to be a little confusion of dry land and sea. "

"You see, Mr. Ridgeley, " said Case, "that the dry land and sea never were separated here. The man that had the job failed, and nobody else would ever undertake it. I think, Mr. Ridgeley, " after a pause, "I had better tell who and what we are, as we shall be together for some time. This is Ransom—B. Ransom. His temperament is intellectual—I may say, brainy. That B. stands for brains emphatically, being the whole of them. He is rather a matter of fact than a conclusion of law, and were you to apply a rule of law to him, although matter of fact, he would be found to be immaterial, and might be wholly rejected as surplusage. He's rather scriptural, also, and takes mostly to the prophets, Jonadab, Meshac, and those revered worthies. He's highly moral, and goes for light reading to the elder Scriptures, drawing largely upon Tamar and Rachel and Leah, and the pure young daughters of Lot. Ruth is too tame for him. He was the inventor of our 'moral reform' sidewalks, on which, as you see, no young man can walk beside a maiden. The effect on morals is salubrious. "

"Case! Case! " protested Ransom.

"As for law, he goes into a law book as a mite goes through a cheese, head on, and with about—"

"Case! Case! Case! " broke in Ransom again, "hold up your infernal gabble. "

"I know the importance of first impressions, " said Case, with gravity, "and I want you should start favorably; and if you don't come up to my eulogium, something will be pardoned to the partiality of friendship. "

"Yes, yes! partiality of friendship! " said Ransom, excitedly; and turning to Bart, "he is a Case, as you see; but if a man should go into Court with such a Case, he would be non-suited; he isn't even *prima facie. "*

"Good! " exclaimed Kennedy.

"Ransom, you are inspired; flattery does you good. "

"Go on! " said Case; "don't interrupt him, he'll never get such another start. "

"He's a poetic cuss, " continued Ransom, "and writes verses for the Painesville papers, and signs them "C., " though I've never been able to see anything in them. He's strong on Byron, and though he's— he's—" and he stopped in excessive excitement.

"There you're out, Ransom, " said Case, "and that is by far the ablest as well as the longest speech you ever made. If you had let me go on and fully open out your excellencies, you might have completed the last sentence. Now, Kennedy here—" resumed Case.

"Spare me! " said Kennedy, laughing; "give Ridgeley a chance to find out my strong points, if you please. "

"Now, Case, " said Ransom, reflectively, "Case is not a bad fellow, considering that he is good for nothing, and a smart fellow for one who knows nothing, and you will like him. He's a little stiffish, and devotes himself mostly to young ladies. "

"Thank you, " said Case.

Bart was amused at these free sketches, especially as none but good feeling prevailed, and remarked, "that it was fortunate for him that no acquaintance of his was present, who could do him justice. "

He walked up to the large and well-filled book-cases, and mused about. "My brother wrote and told me so much of all this that I thought I was familiar with it, " he said at last.

"He used to sit in that corner, by the table, with his back to the window, " said Kennedy, pointing to a place in the back room, which Bart approached. "He was usually the first here in the morning and the last to go at night, and then often took a book with him. "

"We liked him very much, " said Ransom, "and we forwarded to you a set of resolutions on hearing of his death. "

"I received them, " replied Bart, "and if I did not acknowledge it, I owe you an apology. "

"You did, to Ranney, " said Case.

The memory of his brother, who had read and worked, talked and laughed, mused and hoped in that little nook, came up very fresh to Barton.

Case proposed that they take a stroll, or a "string" as he called it, about the village, and as they walked in single file on the narrow sidewalks, the idea of "string" seemed to be realized. They went into the Court House and up into the court-room, and down into the Recorder's office, filled with books, and introduced Bart to Ben Graylord, the Recorder, who showed him a record-book written by his brother, every page of which sparkled with the beauty of the writing. Then they went to the clerk's office of Col. Hendry, with its stuffed pigeon-holes, and books, and into the sheriff's office, and to divers other places.

Jefferson was about eleven or twelve miles from the lake, south of Ashtabula. It was selected as the county seat, and at once became the residence of the county officers, and of many wealthy and influential citizens, but never became a place of much business, while Ashtabula and Conneaut were already busy towns. Each lay at the mouth of a considerable creek, whose names they respectively bore, and which formed harbors for the lake commerce, and were both visited daily by the steamers that run up and down Lake Erie. These facts were communicated to Bart, as they walked about, and the residences of Mr. Giddings, Judge Warren, Colonel Hendry, Mr. St. John, and others, were pointed out to him.

CHAPTER XXXI.

OLD BEN.

That evening, Case and Bart went in rather late to supper at the Jefferson House, and Case pointed out B. P. Wade sitting at the head of one of the tables. Bart studied him closely.

He was then about thirty-five or thirty-six years of age; of a fine, athletic, compact and vigorous frame, straight, round, and of full average height, with an upward cast of the head and face that made him look taller than he was. He had a remarkably fine head and a striking face—a high, narrow, retreating forehead, a little compressed at the temples, aquiline nose, firm, goodish mouth, and prominent chin, with a deep dark eye, and strongly marked brow, not handsome, but a strong, firm, noticeable face, which, with his frank, manly, decided manner and carriage, would at once arrest the eye of a stranger, as it did that of Bart, who knew that he saw a remarkable man. The head was turned, so that the light fell upon the face, giving it strong light and shadow in the Rembrandt style; and Bart studied and contemplated it at great advantage.

He tried to reproduce the recent scene in the Ohio Senate, in which Wade performed so conspicuous a part. It was in the worst of the bad days of Northern subserviency to slavery, which now seem almost phantasmagorical; when, at the command of the Kentucky State Commissioners, the grovelling majority of the Ohio Legislature prostrated the State abjectly in the dust beneath its feet, it was demanded that no man of African blood should be permitted to remain in the State unless some responsible white man should become bail for his good conduct, and that he should never become a public charge.

The bill was about to be put on its final passage in the Senate, by a majority made up of men so revoltingly servile, that even such infamy failed to preserve their names. "Tin Pan" had decreed that a vote should be taken before adjournment for the night, and the debate ran into the deep hours. Gregg Powers, a tall, dark-haired, black-eyed, black-browed young senator, from Akron, had just pronounced a fervent, indignant, sarcastic and bitter phillipic against it, when, after midnight, Wade arose, with angry brow and flashing eye. Argument and logic were out of place; appeals to honor could not be comprehended by men shameless by nature, abject by instinct, and infamous by habit, and who cared nothing for the fame of their common State. Wade, at white heat, turned on them a mingled torrent of sarcasm, scorn, contempt, irony, scoffing, and derision, hot, seething, hissing, blistering, and consuming. He then turned to the haughty and insolent Commissioners of slavery, who were present, that the abasement of the State might lack no mark or brand, and with an air haughtier and prouder than their own, defied them. He declared himself their mortal foe, and cast the gauntlet contemptuously into their faces. He told them they would meet him again in the coming bitter days, and with prodigious force, predicted the extirpation of slavery. Nobody called him to order; nobody interrupted him; and when he closed his awful phillipic, nobody tried to reply. The vote was taken, and the bill passed into a law. And as Bart called up the scene, and looked at the man taking his tea, and conversing carelessly, he thought that a life would be a cheap price for such an opportunity and effort.

Nature had been generous to Wade, and given him a fine, well-balanced, strong, clear intellect, of a manly, direct, and bold cast, as well of mind as temperament. He was not destitute of learning in his profession, but rather despised culture, and had a certain indolence of intellect, that arose in part from undervaluing books, and although later a great reader, he was never a learned man. His manners were rude though kind; he had wonderful personal popularity, and was the freest possible from cant, pretence, or any sort of demagogueism. He was as incapable of a mean thought as of uttering the slightest approach to an untruth, or practising a possible insincerity. He was a favorite with the young lawyers and students, who imitated his rude manner and strong language; was a dangerous advocate, and had much influence with courts. In all these early years he was known as Frank Wade; "Ben" and "old Ben" came to him years after at Washington.

When he left the supper room Case found an opportunity to introduce Bart to him. Wade received him very cordially, and spoke with great kindness of his brother Henry, and remarked that Bart did not much resemble him.

"So I am generally told, " said Bart; "and I fear that I am less like him in intellect than in person. "

"You may possibly not lose by that. Most persons would think you better looking, and you may have as good a mind—that we will find out for ourselves. "

Bart felt that this was kind. Wade then remarked that they would find time on Monday to overhaul his law. Later, Bart met Ranney, who, he thought, received him coolly.

The next day the young men went to church. Nothing in the way of heresy found foothold at Jefferson. It was wholly orthodox; although it was suspected that Wade and Ranney had notions of their own in religion; or rather the impression was that they had no religion of any kind. Not to have the one and true, was to have none according to the Jefferson platform.

Monday was an anxious day for Bart. He would now be put to a real test. He knew he had studied hard, but he remembered the air with which Henry and Ranney waived him off. Then he was so poor, and was so anxious to get through, and be admitted in September, that he was a little nervous when the lawyers found leisure in the afternoon to "overhaul his law, " as Wade had expressed it.

Ranney had no idea of letting him off on definitions and general rules, and he plunged at once into special pleading, as presented by Chitty, in his chapter on Replications. No severer test could have been applied, and the young men thought it a little rough. Bart answered the questions with some care, and gave the reason of the rules clearly. Ranney then proposed a case of a certain special plea, and asked Bart how he would reply. Bart enumerated all the various replies that might be made, and the method of setting each forth. Ranney then asked him to state an instance of new assignment, in a replication; and when Bart had stated its purpose and given an instance, he said he thought that a good pleader would always so state his case in his declaration as to render a new assignment unnecessary, perhaps impossible. He was then asked what defects in pleading would be cured by a general verdict? and gave the rules quite luminously.

Ranney then asked him what books he had read; and Bart named several. "What others? " and he named as many more. "Is that all? " laughing.

"Oh! " said Bart, "I remember what you and Henry said about my reading, and really I have dipped into a good many besides. "

"Well, Ranney, " said Wade, "what can we do for this young man? I think he will pass now, better than one in a hundred. "

"I think so too; still, I think we can help him, or help him to help himself. " And he finally named a work on commercial law, a book on medical jurisprudence, and a review of Kent. At leisure moments, he would have him practise in drawing bills in Chancery, declarations, pleas, etc.

Bart certainly might be pleased with this result, and it evidently advanced him very much in the estimation of all who had listened to his examination, although he felt that the work imposed upon him was rather slender, and just what he should do with the spare time this labor would leave him he would not then determine.

He liked his new position with these ambitious young men, engaged in intellectual pursuits, with whom he was to associate and live, and upon whom he felt that he had made a favorable impression. It did not occur to him that there might be society, save with these and his books; nor would it have occurred to him to enquire, or to seek entrance into it, if it existed; with a sort of intellectual hunger he rushed upon his books with a feeling that he had recently been dissipated, and misapplied his time and energies.

CHAPTER XXXII.

THE LETTERS.

Tuesday evening's mail brought him two letters, post-marked Newbury. The sight of them came with a sort of a heart-blow. They were not wholly expected, and he felt that there might still be a little struggle for him, although he was certain that this must be the last.

The well-known hand of Judge Markham addressed one of them. The writing of the other he did not recognize; only after he had lost its envelope, he remembered that it very much resembled the hand that wrote the Greer warning. He put the letters into an inside pocket, and tried to go on with his book; like a very young man he fancied that he was observed. So he took his hat and went to the room he occupied with Case. He pulled open the unknown, knew the hand, ran down and turned over to the second page, and found "Julia" at the bottom, and below, the words "with the profoundest gratitude. " It ran:

"NEWBURY, April 8, 1838.

"BARTON RIDGELEY:

"*Dear Sir*, —Is it characteristic of a brave and generous man to confer the greatest obligations upon another, and not permit that other the common privilege of expressing gratitude? Were I a man, I would follow and weary you with a vain effort to utter the thanks I owe you. But I can only say a few cold words on paper at the risk of being misunderstood. " ("Um-m, I don't see what danger she could apprehend on that score, " said Bart quite sharply.) "When I had wandered beyond the help of my father and friends, into danger, and, I think, to certain death, you were inspired with the heart, skill and strength, to find and save me. Next to God, who led you, I owe my life to you. When this is said, I cannot say more. I know of no earthly good that you do not deserve; I can think of no gift of Heaven, that I do not ask of It for you.

"You will not be offended that I should most anxiously insist that some little benefit should in some way come to you, from my father; and you will certainly, when you first return to Newbury, give me

186

an opportunity to say to you how much I owe you, and how heavy the obligation rests upon me. You promised me this and will fulfil it. My mother, who sees this note, wants you to realize her profound sense of your service to us, enhanced if possible by the noble and manly way in which you rendered it. She was always your discerning and discriminating friend. "

"Discriminating, "—Bart did not like that, but no matter. That was all.

"A very pretty letter, my lady Julia, " said Bart with a long breath. "Quite warm. I confess I don't care much for your gratitude—but very pretty and condescending. And it is kind to advise me that whatever may have been your estimate of me, your sweet lady mother 'discerned' differently. What you mean by discriminating is a very pretty little woman mystery, that I shall never know. "

"And now for my Lord Judge: "

"NEWBURY, April 8, 1838.

"BARTON RIDGELEY, ESQ. :

"*My Dear Sir*, —I was disappointed at not finding you at Wilder's, where your noble exertions had placed my daughter. I was more disappointed on calling at your mother's the following morning, hoping to carry you to my house. If anything in my conduct in the past contributed to these disappointments, I regret it. " ("Very manly, Judge Markham, " remarked Bart. "Don't feel uneasy, I should have acted all the same. ") "You saved to us, and to herself, our daughter, and can better understand our feelings for this great benefit than I can express them. " ("All right Judge, I would not try it further, if I were you. ") "Whoever confers such a benefaction, also confers the right upon the receiver, not only to express gratitude by words, but by acts, which shall avail in some substantial way. " ("Rather logical, Judge! ") "I shall insist that you permit me to place at your disposal means to launch you in your profession in a way commensurate with your talents and deservings. " ("Um-m-m. ") "I trust you will soon return to Newbury, or permit me to see you in Jefferson, and when the past may" ("I don't care about wading the Chagrin, Judge, and helping your daughter out of the woods was no more than leading out any other man's daughter, and I don't want to hear more of either. Just let me alone. ") "be atoned for. I need not say that my wife unites with me in gratitude, and a hearty wish to be permitted to aid you; nor how anxious we are to learn the details of your finding our daughter, all of which is a profound mystery to us.

"Sincerely yours,

"EDWARD MARKHAM. "

There was a postscript to the Judge's, instead of Julia's, and Bart looked at it two or three times with indifference, and walked up and down the room with a sore, angry feeling that he did not care to understand the source of, nor yet to control. "Very pretty letters! very well said! Why did they care to say anything to me? When I came away they might have known—but then, who and what am I? Why the devil shouldn't they snub me one day and pat me on the head the next? And I ought to be glad to be kicked, and glad to be thanked for being kicked—only I'm not—-though I don't know why! Well, this is the last of it; in my own good time—or somebody's time, good or bad—I will walk in upon my Lord Judge, my discriminating Lady the Mother, and the Lady Julia, and hear them say their pieces without danger of misapprehension. " And his eye fell again on the Judge's postscript. Reads:

"Before I called at your mother's on that morning, I set apart the chestnut 'Silver-tail, ' well caparisoned, as your property. I thought it a fitting way in which one gentleman might indicate his appreciation of another. I knew you would appreciate him; I hoped he would be useful to you. He is your property, whether you will or no, and will be held subject to your order, and the fact that he is yours will not diminish the care he will receive. May I know your pleasure in reference to him?

"E. M."

This found the weak place, or one of the weak places, in Bart's nature. The harshness and bitterness of his feelings melted out of his heart, and left him to answer his letters in a spirit quite changed from that which had just possessed him.

To Julia he wrote:

"JEFFERSON, April 11, 1838.

"Miss JULIA MARKHAM:

"Yours has just reached me. I am so little used to expressions of kindness that yours seem to mock me like irony. You did not choose to become involved in discomfort and danger, nor were you left to elect who should aid you, and I can endure the reflection that you might prefer to thank some other.

"If your sense of obligation is unpleasant, there is one consideration that may diminish it. A man of spirit, whose folly had placed him in the position I occupied towards you, would have eagerly sought an opportunity to render you any service, and would have done his poor best in your behalf. When it was accomplished he would not have been covetous of thanks, and might hope that it would be taken as some recompense for the past, and only ask to forget and be forgotten. No matter; so little that is pleasant has happened to me, that you surely can permit me to enjoy the full luxury of having saved you without having that diminished by the receipt of anything, in any form, from anybody, by reason of it. It is in your power to explain one thing to your father; by which he will see that I must be left to my own exertions so far as he is concerned. I do believe that your gracious mother was my one friend, who looked kindly upon my many faults, and who will rejoice if I ever escape from them.

"When in Newbury hereafter I shall feel at liberty to call at your father's house.

"With the sincerest wishes for your welfare, I remain

"Your obedient servant,

"A. B.E. "

To the Judge:

"Hon. EDWARD MARKHAM:

"*Dear Sir,* —I am in receipt of yours. It was, perhaps, necessary for you to say some words to me. I may not judge of what would be fitting; I feel that you have said more than was required. I had a boy's sincere liking for you; but when I failed to secure the good-will of anybody, it is certain that there were radical defects in my character, and you but entertained the common feeling towards me. It was an honest, hearty dislike, which I have accepted—as I accept other things—without complaint or appeal. There is one near you who can explain how impossible it is that I can become an object of your interest or care. I am poor; let me remain so; I like it. Let me alone to buffet and be buffetted. The atmosphere in which I live is cold and thin, and exercise is needful for me. I have not deserved well of the world, and the world has not been over kind to forget it. Leave me to wage the war with it in my own way. It was God's pleasure to remove from me those upon whom I had natural claims, and I do not murmur, nor do I allude to it only as an indication that I am to go on alone.

"I am aware that I do not meet you in the spirit which prompts your generous and manly kindness—no matter. Think that it proceeds from something ignoble in my nature, and be glad that you may in no way be involved in any failure that awaits me.

"I am sure Mrs. Markham has always been most kind to me, and if on the miserable night when I left my own mother I could have stolen to her somewhere, and have touched her robe with my lips, it would have been most grateful to me. We shall meet probably again, and I am sure our intercourse may be that at least of pleasant acquaintances.

"With the sincerest respect,

"A. B.E.

"P. S.—Your postscript takes me at disadvantage. What can I say? Its kindness is most unkind. The horse is a mount fit for a Prince. I wish he might be found useful to Miss Markham; if she will accept him, I would be glad that he might be devoted to her service. More than this I cannot say.

"B. "

I am inclined to follow these letters back to Newbury. It took a round week for a letter and its answer to pass between Newbury and Jefferson both ways. Somehow, it so happened that Julia, on the third day after mailing hers to Bart, was at the Post-office every day, on the arrival of the Northern mail, with the air of an unconcerned young woman who did not expect anything. On the seventh, two letters in a hand she knew were handed her by the clerk, who looked at the time as if he thought these were the letters, but said nothing.

On her way home she opened one of them and read it, and paused, and read, and studied as if the hand was illegible, and looked grave and hurt, and as if tears would start, and then calm and proud. "When she got home she silently handed the other to her father, and her own to her mother; then she went to her room. An hour later she came back, took her letter, and going into her father's office, laid it open before him, receiving his in return. This she read with a sad face; once or twice a moisture came into her eyes in spite of her, and then she sat and said nothing; and her mother came in and read her husband's letter also.

"Mother, " said Julia, "are all young men really like this proud, haughty, sensitive fellow? and yet he is so unhappy! Was father at all like him? "

"I don't know. You must remember that few at his age have been placed in such trying positions, and had he been less, or more, or different, we might have been without cause for gratitude to him. "

"Well, he graciously permits us to know that he may at least once again approach 'Your father's house! '"

"Julia! Could he have done it before? "

"Could he not, mother, when he saved my life? "

"Julia, was this poor youth more than human? "

"Mother, I have sometimes felt that he was, and that somehow more was to be required of him than of common men. "

The Judge sat in silence, with an expression that indicated that his reflections were not wholly cheerful. The frank words that this youth had always liked him, and that the Judge had cause for dislike, so generous, were like so many stabs.

"Papa Judge, " said Julia, suddenly springing to her father's side, "may I have him? "

"Have him! Who? "

"Why, Silver-tail, of course, " laughing. "There is nobody else I can have; " rather gravely.

"Will you accept him? "

"Of course I will, and ride him too. I've always coveted him. My old 'Twilight' has almost subsided into night, and is just fit for Nell and Pearly. They may ride her; and when this prince wants his charger, as he will, he must come to me for him—don't you see? "

An hour later a splendid dark chestnut, with silver mane and tail, round-limbed, with a high dainty head, small ears, and big nostrils, with a human eye, spirited and docile, was brought round, caparisoned for a lady, and Julia stood by him with his bridle in her hand, caressing and petting him, while waiting for something ere she mounted. "Your name shall not be 'Silver-tail' any longer; you are 'Prince'"—whispering something in his ear. "Do you hear, Prince? You shall be my good friend, and serve me until your own true lord and master comes for you. Do you hope it will be soon? " Prince slightly shook his head, as if the wish was not his, at any rate. "Well, soon or late, you naughty Prince, he alone shall take you from my hand. Do you hear? " and being mounted, she galloped away.

CHAPTER XXXIII.

AT WILDER'S.

April brightened out into May, and over all the beautiful fields, and woods, and hills of Newbury, came bright warm tints of the deepening season; and under the urgency of Julia, her mother and herself made their contemplated visit of thanks to the Wilders, who could at least be benefitted by their kindness to Julia, bearing a good many nice new things for Mrs. Wilder and Rose, and the two younger children. Julia, in her warmth, found everything about the neat log house and its surroundings quite attractive. The fields were new, but grass was fresh about the house, and shrubs and plants had been put out.

She had taken a strong liking to Rose, a tall, sweet, shy girl of seventeen, who had received her into her bed, and who now, in her bashful way, was more glad to see her than she could express. The house, in a lovely place, was sheltered by the near forest, and everything about it was as unlike what Julia remembered as could well be. It seemed to have changed its locality, and the one outside door opened on the opposite side. She went all about and around it; and out to the margin of the woods, gray and purple, and tenderest green, with bursting buds and foliage.

Her mother found Mrs. Wilder a comely, intelligent woman, who was immensely obliged by her visit, and thankful for her generous presents of dresses for herself, and Rose, and the children.

After dinner, Julia went with Rose out by the road into the woods, through which, a month ago, Bart had conducted her. She recognized nothing in the surroundings. How bright and sweet, with sun and flowers, the woods were, with great maple trees opening out their swollen buds into little points of leaves, like baby-fists into chubby fingers and thumbs. On they went down to the creek which flowed the other way. Julia remembered that they came up it to find the road, and they now turned down its bank. How sweet, and soft, and bright it looked, flecked with sunbeams, and giving out little gurgles of water-laughs, as if it recognized her—"Oh! it is you, is it, this bright day? Where is the handsome youth you clung to, on a winter morning, we know of? I know you! "—with its little ripples.

They soon came to where the rock cropped out from the sloping ground and formed a ledge along the margin of the diminished stream, and soon reached the little cove; there was the rude shelter which had covered Julia, and under it the couch of shavings on which she had rested, a little scattered and just as she had left it; and, near its foot, the still fresh brands that almost seemed to smoke. How strong and real it all came to the sensibilities of the girl! Nothing had been there but the tender silent fingers of nature. Yes, as she sat down on her old bed, and glanced up, she saw a bright-eyed Phoebe-bird who had built just over her head, and now was on her nest, while her mate poured out the cheery clang of his love song, on a limb near by. The little half circle of ground, walled in by the high mossy rocks, opened southerly, and received the full glow of the afternoon sun, while in front of it ran the laughing, gleeful creek. It was very bright, but to Julia very, very lonely. In a few words she pointed out to the sympathizing Bose the few localities, and mentioned the incidents of that awful morning, and then she turned very gravely and thoughtfully back.

Rose very, very much wanted to ask about Barton; her woman's instincts told her that here was a something sweet and yet mysterious, that made everything so dear to this beautiful and now pensive girl by her side. His name had not been mentioned, and Julia had only referred to him, as "he did this; " "he sat by that tree. " At last Rose ventured: "Where is he—this Mr. Ridgeley? Mother said he went away. "

"Yes; I never saw him after you took me into your bed, Rose, " said Julia.

"He saw you after that, Miss Markham. "

"What do you mean, Rose? "

"I am sure you would like to know, " said Rose. "I know I would. Mother said that after father had gone, and after we were asleep, he asked her if he might just look upon you for a moment; and she opened the door, and he stood in it, looked towards you for a second, and then turned and went out without a single word, seeming very much agitated. " Rose's voice was a little agitated too. Though she felt the arm that was twined tenderly about her waist, she did not dare to look in the face so near her own. "Mother says, " she continued, "that he was very handsome and very pale. I suppose he is very poor, but—"

"But what, Rose? "

"I am sure, " she said, hesitatingly, "that will make no difference. "

Julia only answered with a little caress.

"When he comes back, " said simple Rose, who was certain that it would all come right, "he will want to come and see that lovely little place, and you will want to come with him; I would like to see him. "

"When he comes back, " said Julia, brightly, "you shall see him, little Rose; you are a dear, good girl, and if you are ever in peril, I am sure some brave, handsome man will come to you. "

Rose hoped he would.

The older women had talked matters over also in their grave, prudent woman's way, and both learned from the brightness in Julia's face and eyes, that the ramble in the woods had been pleasant. On their way home Julia described it all to her mother.

They drove around by way of Mrs. Ridgeley's, and found her busy and cheerful. She had a letter from Bart full of cheerful encouragement, and the Colonel had returned, and would remain in Newbury for the present.

Julia caught George and this time actually kissed the blushing, half-angry, yet really pleased boy.

The next day Mrs. Ridgeley visited the graves of her husband and son, on her way from her friend Mrs. Punderson's, and was touched by the evidences of a watchful care that marked them. At the head of Henry's grave was planted a beautiful rose tree, full of buds, and a few wild flowers lay withered among the green grass springing so freshly over him. The mother wondered what hand performed this pious act. Like Bart, she supposed that some gentle maiden thus evinced her tenderness for his memory, and was very anxious to know who she was.

CHAPTER XXXIV.

ROUGH SKETCHES.

The sun drank up the waters out of Jefferson, and the almanac brought the day for the May term of the Court for Ashtabula county; came the Judge, the juries and unfortunate parties; came also some twenty lawyers, from the various points of North-eastern Ohio. It was to be a great time for our young students. Bart had seen the Court once or twice at Chardon, and had heard the advocates in the famous case of Ohio *vs.* Joe Smith, the Mormon Prophet, for conspiring to murder Newell, and came to know some of them by name and sight. The same judge presided on that trial as in the present court—Judge Humphrey. Bart was much interested of course in the proceedings, and observed them attentively from the opening proclamation, the calling and swearing of the grand jury, calling of the calendar of cases, etc. Much more interested was he in Case's graphic sketches of the members of the bar, who hit them off, well or ill, with a few words.

"That elderly man, shortish, with the soft, autumn-like face, is Elisha Whittlesey, sixteen years in Congress; where he never made a speech, but where he ranks with the most useful members: sober colors that wear. He was a good lawyer, and comes back to practice. The old men will employ him, and wonder why they get beaten. "

"That brisk, cheery, neat man by his side is Norton—lively, smirky and smiling—you see the hair leaves the top of his head, to lay the fact bare that there is not much there; and just why that snubby little nose should perk itself up, I can't tell, unless to find out whether there really is anything above it. He has quite a reputation with juries, and a tendency to bore, sometimes in very dry places, for water, and usually furnishes his own moisture. When he isn't damp he is funny. They both live in Canfield. "

"Who is that fine-looking, fine-featured, florid man? "

"That is Crowell, from Warren. Mark him and see how studied are all his motions. He tears up that paper with an air and grace only reached by long and intense practice and study. He is a little unpopular, but is a man of ability, and is often effective with a jury.

The trouble is, his shadow is immense, and falls all about him on every thing, and he sees every thing through it. "

"That young, dark-eyed handsome man is Labe Sherman, admitted last year. He and Ranney are the two young men of the democracy; but there is enough of Ranney to make two of him. He is a fine advocate. "

"Look at that tall, rather over-dressed, youngish man. "

"The one with weak, washed-out gray eyes? "

"Yes. "

"Does he know anything? "

"Not a devilish thing. His strong point, where he concentrates in force, is his collar and stock; from that he radiates into shirt bosom, and fades off into coat and pants. Law! He don't know the difference between a bill in Chancery and the Pope's Bull. Here's another knowledge-cuss. He's from Warren—McKnight. His great effort is to keep himself in—to hold himself from mischief, and working general ruin. He knows perfectly well that if he should let himself loose in a case, in open court, the other side would stand no chance at all; and his sense of right prevents his putting forth his real power. It would be equal to a denial of justice to the other side. "

"An instance where the severity of the law is tempered and modified by equity, " remarked Bart.

"Exactly. "

"Who is that man on the left of Bowen, and beyond, with that splendid head and face, and eyes like Juno, if a man can have such eyes? "

"That is Dave Tod, son of old Judge Tod, of Warren. Two things are in his way: he is a democrat, and lazy as thunder; otherwise he would be among the first—and it will do to keep him in mind anyway. There is some sort of a future for him. "

"Here's another minister of the law in the temple of justice—that man with the cape on. He always wears it, and the boys irreverently call him Cape Cod—Ward of Connaught. He puts a paper into the clerk's office and calls it commencing a suit. He puts in another and calls it a declaration. If anybody makes himself a party, and offers to go to trial with him, and nobody objects, he has a trial of something, at some time, and if he gets a verdict or gets licked it is equally incomprehensible to him, and to everybody else.

"There are Hitchcock and Perkins, of Painesville, whom you know. What great wide staring eyes Hitchcock has: but they look into things. And see how elegantly Perkins is dressed. I'd like to hear Frank Wade on that costume—but Perkins is a good lawyer, for all that. Look at that stout, broad, club-faced man—that's old Dick Matoon. You see the lower part of his face was made for larger upper works; and after puckering and drawing the under lip in all he can, he speaks in a grain whistle through an opening still left, around under one ear. He knows no more law than does necessity; but is cunning, and acts upon his one rule, 'that it is always safe to continue. '

"Here is a man you must get acquainted with; this dark swarthy man with the black eyes, black curling hair, and cast-iron face, sour and austere. That is Ned Wade, Frank's younger brother, and one of the pleasantest and best-hearted men alive. He has more book than Frank, and quite as much talent, and will hammer his way towards the front. "

"Who is that little, old, hump-backed, wry-necked chap hoisting his face up as if trying to look into a basket on his shoulder? "

"That? That is the immortal Brainard, of Unionville. He is the Atlas who has sustained the whole world of the law-on his back until he has grown hump-backed; and that attitude is the only way in which he can look into the law on his back, as you remark.

"And there is Steve Mathews, mostly legs. His face begins with his chin, and runs right up over the top of his head; that head has no more brains inside than hair out. You see that little knob there in front? Well, that was originally intended for a bump, and, as you see, just succeeded in becoming a wart. Ranney suggested to him at the last term that the books were all against his straddling about the bar, as he always does. "

"That smallish man with the prominent chin and retreating forehead, is Horace Wilder, one of the best men at the bar. You see he is pleasant and amiable. He is a good lawyer, and give him a case which involves a question of morals and he develops immense power. "

"Who is that dark, singular-looking young man, with full beard and open throat? Is he a lawyer? "

"That, " said Case, sadly, "is Sartliff, the most brilliant intellect our region has produced; full of learning, full of genius and strange new thoughts! He is a lawyer, and should equal Daniel Webster. "

"What is the matter with him? "

"God only knows! men call him crazy. If he is, the rest of us never had intellect enough to become crazy. Look at his dress; he wears a kind of frock, tied with a hay rope, and is barefoot, I presume. Some strange new or old idea has taken possession of him to get back to nature. If he keeps on he will become crazy. I must introduce you; he and you will like one another. "

"Because I am crazy, too? " laughing.

"Because you have some out-of-the-way notions, Bart, and I want you should hear him. He will make you feel as if you were in the visible presence of the forces of nature. He knew your brother well and liked him. "

"Where does he live? "

"Nowhere! He remains in the open air when he can, day and night; drinks water and eats roots and herbs; sometimes a little plain bread—never meat. He was formerly vigorous, as you see, he is now thin and drooping. "

"Has he had any unusual history, any heart agony? "

"None that I ever heard of; nor was he particularly poetic or imaginative. He does not attempt any business now; but goes and comes with lawyers, the most of whom now avoid him. He has brothers, able and accomplished men, and whom he usually avoids. He commenced business with Giddings, with a brilliant opening, ten years ago. "

The calendar was finished, a jury sworn in a case, and the court adjourned.

How closely the young men watched the proceedings of the court, all the trials and points made, and the rulings, and how stripped of mystery seemed the mere practice, as at that time in Ohio it really was. Wise men had taken the best of the old common law practice, and with the aid of judicious legislation and intelligent courts, had got about the best it was capable of.

Bart managed to make himself useful and do himself some good on one occasion. Ranney had taken a position in a case, on a trial of some importance, on which the court was apparently against him. Bart had just gone over with it, in a text-book, and in a moment brought it in, with the case referred to, and received, as men often do, more credit than he was entitled to, Ranney carried his point, and could afford to be generous.

CHAPTER XXXV.

SARTLIFF.

Bart had been introduced to Sartliff, who was an object of universal curiosity, even where he was best known, and coming out of the court-room one delicious afternoon, he asked the young students to walk away from the squabbles of men to more quiet and cleaner scenes. They took their way out of the town towards a beech forest, whose tender, orange-tinted, green young leaves were just shaping out, and relieving the hard skeleton lines of trunks and naked limbs. Passing the rude and rotting fences, by which rank herbage, young elders and briars were springing up:

"See, " said Sartliff, "how kindly nature comes to cover over the faults and failures of men. These rotting unsightly 'improvements, ' as we call them, will soon be covered over and hidden with beautiful foliage. "

"With weeds, and nettles, and elders, " said Case, contemptuously.

"Weeds and nettles! " repeated Sartliff; "and why weeds and nettles? Was there ever such arrogance! Man in his boundless conceit and ignorance, after having ruined his powers, snuffs and picks about, and finds the use of a few insignificant things, which he pronounces good; all the rest he pushes off in a mass as weeds and nettles. Thus the great bulk of the universe is to him useless or hurtful, because he will not, or cannot, learn its secrets. These unknown things are standing reproaches to his ignorance and sloth. "

"Poisons, for instance, might become sanitary, " said Case.

"If man lived in accord with nature, " said Sartliff, "she would not harm him. It is a baby's notion that everything is made to eat, and that all must go into the mouth. Men should have got beyond this universal alimentiveness, ere this. Find the uses of things, and poisons and nettles fall into their places in harmony, and are no longer poisons and nettles. "

"And accidents would help us on, instead of off, " suggested Case.

"They help as often one way as the other now, " replied Sartliff. "But there are really no accidents; everything is produced by law. "

"There must be two or three systems then, " suggested Case. "Things collide, while each obeys its law. Your systems clash. "

"Not a bit. This is apparent only; man acts abnormally under evil influences; he will not observe law; he turns upon nature and says he will subvert her laws, and compel her to obey his. Of course confusion, disorder, and death are the consequences, and always will be, till he puts himself in harmony with her. "

"It seems to me, Mr. Sartliff, that in your effort to get back individually, you have encountered more difficulties, collisions, and ills, than the most of us do, who keep on the old orthodox civilized way to the devil. "

"That may be; I am one, looking alone; nobody helps me. "

"And like the younger Mr. Weller, you find it a pursuit of knowledge under difficulties. "

"Precisely; I inherited an artificial constitution, and tastes, and needs. I began perverted and corrupted, and when I go back to Nature, she teaches me less than she does the beasts and birds. Before I can understand, or even hear her voice, I must recover the original purity and strength of organs and faculties which I might have had. I may perish in the attempt to reach a point at which I can learn. The earth chills and hurts my feet, the sun burns my skin, the winds shrivel me, and the snows and frosts would kill me, while many of the fruits good for food are indigestible to me. See to what the perversions of civilization have reduced me. "

"Do you propose in thus getting back to nature, to go back to what we call savagery? " asked Bart.

"Not a bit of it. It was the wants and needs of the race that whipped it into what we call civilization. When once men got a start they went, and went in one direction alone, and completely away from Nature, instead of keeping with her and with an unvarying result; an endless series of common catastrophes has overtaken all civilized nations alike, while the savage tribes have alone been perpetual. I don't say that savage life is at all preferable, only that it alone has been capable of perpetuating races. In going back to Nature, I propose to take what of good we have derived from civilization. "

"As historic verity, " said Bart, "I am not quite prepared to admit that savage races are perpetual. We know little of them, and what little we do know is that tribes appear and disappear. General savagery may reign, like perpetual night, over a given region, but who can say how many races of savages have destroyed and devoured each other in its darkness? "

They had reached the forest, and Sartliff placed himself in an easy position at the foot of an old beech, extending his limbs and bare feet over the dry leaves, in such a way as not to injure any springing herb. "Mr. Ridgeley, " said he, "I would like to know more of you. You young men are fresher, see, and what is better, feel quicker and clearer than the older and more hackneyed. Are you already shelled over with accepted dogmas, and without the power of receiving new ideas? "

"I hardly know; I fear I am not very reverent. I was born of a question-asking time, like that Galilean boy, whose, mother, after long search, found him in the Temple, disputing with the doctors, and asking them questions. "

"Good! good! that is it; my great mother will find me in her Temple, asking questions of her doctors and ministers! " exclaimed Sartliff.

"And what do you ask, and what response do you get? " asked Bart.

"I lay myself on the earth's bosom in holy solitudes, with fasting and great prayer, and send my soul forth in one great mute, hungry demand for light. I, a man, with some of the Father God stirring the awful mysteries of my nature, go yearningly naked, empty, and alone, and clamor to know the way. And sometimes deep, sweet, hollow voices answer in murmurs, which I feel rather than hear; but I cannot interpret them, I cannot compass their sounds. And sometimes gigantic formless shadows overcloud me. I know they have forms of wondrous symmetry and beauty, but they are so grand that my vision does not reach their outline, and I cannot comprehend them. I know that I am dominant of the physical creation on this earth, but at those times I feel that these great and mighty essences, whose world in which they live and move, envelopes ours and us, and to whom our matter is as impalpable air—I know that they and we, theirs and ours, are involved in higher and yet higher conditions and elements, that in some mysterious way we mutually and blindly contribute and minister to each other. "

"And what profit do you find in such communication? " asked Bart.

"It is but preparatory to try the powers, clear the vision and senses, train and discipline the essential faculties for a communion with this essence that may be fully revealed, and aid in the workings and immediate government of our gross material world, and the spirits that pertain to it more immediately, if such there are. "

"And you are in doubt about that? "

"Somewhat; and yet through some such agencies came the givings forth of the Prophets. "

"You believe in the Prophets? " asked Case.

"Assuredly. The many generations which inherited from each other the seer faculty, developed and improved, living the secluded, severe, and simple lives of the anchorite, amid the grand and solemn silence of mountain and desert, were enabled, by wondrous and protracted effort, to wear through the filament—impenetrable as adamant to common men—that screened from them the invisible future, and they told What they saw. "

"Yet they never told it so that any mortal ever understood what they said, or could apply their visions to any passing events, and the same givings out of these half-crazed old bards, for such they were, have been applied to fifty different things by as many different generations of men, " said Case.

"That may have arisen, in part, " said Bart, "from the dim sight of the seer, and the difficulty of clothing extraordinary visions in the garb of ordinary things. It is not easy, however, for the common mind to see why, if God had a special message for His children of such importance that He would provide a special messenger to communicate it, and had a choice of messengers, it should reach them finally, in a form that nobody could interpret. With God every thing is in the present, all that has happened, and all that will, is as the now is to us. If a man can reach the power or faculty of getting a glimpse of things as God sees them, he would make some utterance, if he survived, and it would be very incoherent. Besides, human events repeat themselves, and a good general description of great human calamities would truthfully apply to several, and so might be fulfilled your half hundred times, Mr. Case. "

"That isn't a bad theory of prophecy, " said Case approvingly; "but all these marvels were in the old time; how came the faculty to be lost? "

"Is it? " asked Bart. "Don't you hear of it in barbarous and savage conditions of men, now? Our friend Sartliff would say that the faculty was lost, through the corruptions and clogs of civilization; and he proposes to restore it. "

"No, I don't propose to restore that exactly. I want to find a way back to Nature for myself, and then teach it to others, when the power of prophecy will be restored. I want to see man restored to his rightful position, as the head of this lower universe. There are ills and powers of mischief now at large, and operative, that would find their master in a perfect man. One such, under favorable auspices, was once born into this world; and we know that it is possible. He took His natural place at the head; and all minor powers and agencies acknowledged Him at once. I have never been quite able to understand why He, with His power of clear discernment, should have precipitated Himself upon the Jewish and Roman power, and so perished, and at so early a day in His life. "

"So that the prophets might be fulfilled, " said Case.

"It may have been, " resumed Sartliff.

"Upon the merely human theory of the thing, " said Bart, "He could foresee that this was the only logical conclusion of his teachings, and best, perhaps only means of fixing his messages and doctrines in the hearts of men. I may not venture a suggestion, Mr. Sartliff, " Bart continued; "but it seems to me, that your search back will necessarily fail. In searching back, as you call it, for the happy point when the strength and purity and the inspiration of nature can be united with all that is good in Christian civilization, if your theory is correct, your civilized eyes will never discern the place. You will have passed it before you have re-acquired the power to find it, and your life will be spent in a vain running to and fro, in search of it. Miracles have ceased to be wonders, for we work them by ordinary means now-a-days, and we don't know them when we meet them. "

Sartliff arose; he had been for sometime silent. His face was sad.

"It may be. I like you, Barton; you have a good deal of your brother's common sense, uncommon as that is, and I shall come and see you often. "

And without another word he strode off deeper into the woods, and was lost to the eyes of the young men.

"Is it possible, " said Bart, "that this was an educated, strong, and brilliant mind, capable of dealing with difficult questions of law? I fear that he has worn or torn through the filament that divides the workings of the healthy mind from the visions of the dreamer— wrecked on the everlasting old rocks that jut out all about our shores, and always challenging us to dash upon them. Shall we know when we die? Shall we die when we know? After all, are not these things to be known? Why place them under our eyes so that a child of five years will ask questions that no mortal, or immortal, has yet solved? Have we lost the clue to this knowledge? Do we overlook it? Do we stumble over it, perish, wanting it, with it in our hands without the power to see or feel it? Has some rift opened to a hidden store of truth, and has a gleam of it come to the eyes of this man, filling him with a hunger of which he is to die? When the man arises to whom these mysteries shall reveal themselves, as he assuredly will, the old gospels will be supplemented. "

"Or superseded, " said Case. "And is it not about time? Have not the old done for us about all they can? Do we not need, as well as wish for, a new? "

"A man may doubtless so abuse and deprave his powers, that old healthy food ceases to be endurable, and yields to him no nutrition; of course he must perish, " answered Bart. "He will demand new food. "

CHAPTER XXXVI.

OLD GID.

Towards the close of the term, there came into the court-room, one day, a man of giant mould: standing head and shoulders above his fellows, broad shouldered, deep chested, with a short neck and large flat face, a regal brow, and large, roomy head in which to work out great problems. He had light grayish blue, or blueish gray eyes, and a scarlet mark disfiguring one side of his face. The proceedings paused, and men gathered about him. His manner was bland, his smile, that took up his whole face, very pleasant. Bart knew that this was J. R. Giddings, just home from Washington, where he had already overhauled the Seminole war, and begun that mining into the foundation of things that finally overthrew slavery.

During the term Bart heard him before the court and jury, and found him a dullish, heavy speaker, a little as he thought the indifferently good English parliamentary speaker might be. He often hesitated for a word, and usually waited for it; sometimes he would persist in having it at once, when he would close his eyes very tight, and compel it. His manner and gesture could not be called good, and yet Bart felt that he was in the presence of a formidable man.

His mind was one of a high order, without a scintilla of genius or any of its elements. He had a powerful grasp, and elude, as it might, he finally clutched the idea or principle sought it never escaped him: and he never rested until its soul and blood were his, or rejected as useless, after the application of every test. It was a bad day for slavery when Giddings determined to enter Congress. Cool, shrewd, adroit, wary and wily, never baffled, never off his guard and never bluffed; with a reserve of power and expedients always sufficient, with a courage that knew no blenching, he moved forward. He had more industry and patience, and was a better lawyer than Wade, but was his inferior as an advocate. They were opposed in the case in which Giddings appeared, and Bart already felt that in the atmosphere of the contest was the element of dislike on the part of Wade, and of cool, watchful care on the part of Giddings. Wade made two or three headlong onsets, which were received and parried with bland, smiling coolness. From his manner no one could tell what Giddings thought of his case or opponent.

Two or three evenings after, an informal "reception, " as it would now be called, was held at the Giddings residence, to which the students and nearly everybody else went. It was a pleasant greeting between friends and neighbors, and a valued citizen, just home after a half year's absence. Nothing could be more kind and natural than the manner of Mr. Giddings, supported by motherly Mrs. Giddings, and the accomplished Miss Giddings, who had spent the winter with her father at Washington. She was like her father, in mind and person, softened and sweetened and much more gracious by sex; tall, graceful, and with the easy presence and manner of society and cultivation.

Bart was taken to her, and taken by her at once. She seemed like an old acquaintance, and spoke in the kindest terms of his brother, told him of Washington, its society and customs, and called him Barton at once, as if they were to be on the best of terms. Bart could see that she was plain, but he forgot that in a moment, and it never occurred to him again.

In the course of the evening she returned to him, and said she wished to introduce him to a young lady friend, whom she was sure he would like on her own account, and on that of his brother, to whom she was to have been all that woman might be. It took Bart's breath away. He was unaware that his brother had ever been engaged, or wished to be, to any lady.

"She knows you are in Jefferson, " said Miss Giddings, "and has wanted very much to see you. "

She conducted him into a small sitting-room, and leading: him up to a young lady in black, introduced him to Miss Aikens—Ida Aikens. The young lady came forward, gave him her little hand, and looked him full and sadly in the face. "You are like him, " she said, "and I have much wanted to see you. "

"I received a letter from you, " said Bart, "and fear my answer was a poor one. Had I known you better, I could have written differently. My brother was more to me than most brothers can be, and all who were dear to him come at once into my tenderest regard. "

"You could not answer my letter better than you did. I never had a brother, and nothing can be more grateful to me than to meet you as we now meet. "

They sat, and he held the hand that belonged to his dead brother, and that the hand of lover was never again to clasp. Gentle in deeds of charity and tenderness, it would linger in its widowed whiteness until it signalled back to the hand that already beckoned over the dark waters.

Strangers who saw them would have taken them for lovers. They were of nearly the same age. She, with dark, luminous eyes, and hair colored like Haidee's, matched well with the dark gray and light brown. What a world of tender and mournful sweetness this interview opened up to the hungry heart of Bart—the love of a sweet, thoughtful, considerate, intellectual and cultivated sister, unselfish and pure, to which no touch or color of earth or passion could come. How fully and tenderly he wrote of her to his mother, and how the unbidden wish came to his heart to tell another of her, and as if he had the right to do so.

Miss Aikens was a young lady of high mental endowments, and great force of character, cultivated in the true sense of culture, and very accomplished. How sad and bitter seemed the untimely fate of his brother; and the meeting of this sweet and mourning girl lent another anguish to his heart, that was so slow in its recovery from that blow.

The court ran on, grew irksome, and passed. Bart saw something more of Sartliff, and felt a melancholy interest in him. He also saw much of Ida, whom he could not help liking, and something of Miss Giddings, whom he admired.

CHAPTER XXXVII.

THE OLD STORY.

On the morning after Wade's return from the Geauga Court, upon entering the office, where Bart found him and Ranney and Case, and one or two others, there was the sudden hush that advises a new arrival that he has been a subject of remark.

"Good morning, Mr. Wade. "

"Good morning, Ridgeley. "

"You returned earlier than you anticipated? "

"Yes. How do you come on? "

"About the old way. Did you see my old client, Cole, " the King? "

"Old King Cole? Yes, I saw that worthy, and they say on the other side that they can't try the case under a year, perhaps. "

"Well, we defend, and our defence will be as good then as ever, " said Bart.

"The suit was commenced to save the statute of limitations, " said Wade; "and if any defence exists I fear it will be in chancery. "

"My dear sir, we will make a defence at law, " was the decided answer.

"I saw some of your friends over there, " said Wade, "who made many enquiries about you. "

"They are kind. " said Bart.

"Of course you know Judge Markham? " said Wade.

Bart bowed. "He is a very honorable and high minded man! " Bart bowed again. "He spoke of you in the very highest terms, and I was very glad to hear him. "

"You are very kind, " said Bart.

"And by the way. " pursued Mr. Wade, "I heard a little story: the Judge has a very beautiful daughter, " looking directly at Bart, who bowed to this also. "It seems that the girl in going home from somewhere, got lost in the woods, and wandered off into a devil of a big forest there is down there, covering two or three townships. It was in the night of that awful storm in April, and she went miles away, and finally overcome, lay down to die, and was covered with the snow, when a young chap found her—God knows how—took her up, carried her across the Chagrin River, or one of its branches, in under some rocks, built a fire, and brought her to, and finally got her to a man's house in the woods, sent word to her father, and went off. Do you know anything about it? The story is, that you are the chap who did it. "

All eyes were on Bart.

"I heard something of it, " said he, smiling. "I came off the evening after this marvel; and in the stage two ladies were full of it. They made it a little stronger than your version. I think there were several wild animals in theirs. We stopped at a tavern two or three miles on, when somebody told the old lady that I was 'the chap that did it; ' but as I had told her that this Bart wasn't much of a fellow, she was inclined to doubt her informant. The old lady stopped in Chardon, and you must have heard her story. "

"The young lady herself said that you saved her, " said Wade, with his usual directness. "What do you say to that? "

"If the young lady was in a condition to know, " replied Bart, "I should take her word for it. " And passing into the back room he closed the door.

"What the devil is there in it? " said Wade. "It is just as I say. Has he ever said a word about it? "

"Not a word, " said the young men.

"I met Miss Markham a year ago, when I was in Newbury, at a sugar party, " said Ranney. "She is one of the most beautiful girls I ever saw, and superior in every way. Bart was not there—he wouldn't go; and I remember her talking about him, with Henry. When we got back we undertook to tell him what she said, and he wouldn't hear a word. "

"The fact is, " said Case, decidedly, "her father is rich, and she is proud and ambitious. Bart wasn't good enough for her, and he has taken his revenge by saving her life, and now he won't yield an inch."

"They say he came off and won't have anything to do with them, " said Wade.

"That's it, " said Case, "and I glory in his spunk. They have just found out their mistake. "

During the day Bart was asked by Wade if he had yet seen Mr. Windsor; and replied that he had not, but that he was anxious to do so, as his brother always spoke of him with gratitude, as one who had been very kind to him. Mr. Wade said that the day before he had seen Windsor, who expressed a wish to meet Henry's brother, and thought he would come to Jefferson in a day or two, when he would call on him. Bart was much gratified, and remarked that he was doing quite a business on his brother's popularity.

CHAPTER XXXVIII.

THE OLD STORY OVER AGAIN.

"Mr. Ridgeley, " asked Miss Giddings, "what is this delightful little romance about the rich Judge's beautiful daughter, and the chivalrous young law student? I declare, if it does not bring back the days of knight-errantry, and makes me believe in love and heroism. " It was one evening at her father's where Bart had called with his newly found sister Ida, to whom he was quite attentive.

The young man looked annoyed in spite of his good breeding. "Has he told you the story? " —to Miss Aikens.

"Not a word of it, " said the latter. "You know, " she then said to Miss Giddings, "that some things so pleasant to hear may not be pleasant for a party concerned to tell about. "

"Forgive me, Mr. Ridgeley. It never occurred to me that this could be of that sort, but as it was so delightful as told to me, I wanted to know if it was an actual occurrence, in this humdrum world. "

"I suppose, " said Ida, "that a great many beautiful and heroic events are very prosy and painful to the actors therein, and they never dream the world will give them the gloss of romance. "

"Ladies, " said the young man, with a gay and mocking air, "hear the romance of the Judge's daughter, and the poor student— certainly a *very* poor student. There was a rich, powerful and proud Judge; he had an only daughter, more beautiful than a painter's dream, and proud as a princess born. In the neighborhood was a poor and idle youth, who had been the Judge's secretary, and had been dismissed, and who loved the proud and beautiful maiden, as idle and foolish youths sometimes do. The beautiful maiden scorned him with a scorn that banished him from her sight, for he was prouder than Judge and daughter, both. While disporting with her damsels among the spring flowers in the forest, one day, the beautiful maiden wandered away and became lost in the heart of an interminable wood, more wild and lonely than that which swallowed up the babes of the old ballad. Day passed and night came, and in its bosom was hidden a fierce tempest of wind and hail and snow. The poor maiden wandered on, and on, and on, until she came upon the banks of a dart, cold river; wild and lost amid tempest and storm, she wandered down its banks, until, in despair, chilled and benumbed without heart or hope, she laid her down to die, and the pure snow covered her. Her father, the proud Judge, and his friends, were searching for her miles away.

"A little boy told the story to the poor student, who hurried into the forest, and under the inspiration of his scorned love, ran and ran until he found the swooning maiden under the snow, took her up in his arms, placed his garments upon her, and bore her through the cold and rapid stream, found a shelter under the rocks on the other side, kindled a fire, gave the maiden, proud no longer, a cordial, warmed and restored her, made her a couch of moss and dried leaves, and while she slept he watched over her until the day dawned. Then he conducted her to a wood-chopper's cabin in the forest, where she was tenderly cared for. The poor, proud youth would hear no thanks from the maiden. He sent a note, without his name, to the proud Judge, telling him where his daughter could be found; and never saw the beautiful maiden, or proud rich Judge afterwards. This, ladies, " with the same gay banter, "is the romance of the Judge's daughter and the poor student. "

"And I suspect, " said Miss Giddings, seriously, "that it is about the literal truth of the affair, and it is more romantic than I had thought."

* * * * *

"Barton has made the acquaintance of poor Sartliff, " said Ida, willing to introduce a new subject, "and was much struck by him. "

"Do you think he is actually shattered? " asked Miss Giddings.

"I really have no opinion. His mind moves in such unaccustomed channels: we find it in such unusual haunts, that nobody can tell whether it remains healthy or not. It works logically enough, granting his premises. Of course he is under delusions—we should call them mistakes merely, if they occurred in ordinary speculations; but with him, in his abnormal pursuits, they are to be expressed under the vapory forms of delusions. "

"Oh, it is the saddest sight to see this young man, with a nature so richly endowed, asking only for light, and the right way; to see him turning so blindly from the true given light, and searching with simple earnestness along sterile, rocky byways and thorny hedges, to find the path or opening that conducts back to a true starting place. He opens his bosom to sun and air, and bares his feet to the earth, thinking that inspiration will, through some avenue, reach his senses, and so inform him. It is the most pitiful spectacle that the eye can see, " said Ida, pathetically.

"Like a kind spirit sent from heaven to earth, " said Bart, "who, having forgotten his message, can never find his way back; but is doomed to wander up and down the uncongenial region, searching in vain for the star-beam by which he descended. "

"My father has quite given him up, " said Miss Giddings; "he says he passed long since the verge of healthy thought and speculation. I used to think that possibly some new and powerful stimulus, such as might spring from some new cause—"

"Love, for instance, " suggested Bart.

"Yes, love, for instance. I declare, Mr. Ridgeley, you think as a woman. "

"Do women really think? I thought their minds were so clear and strong that thought was unnecessary, and they were always blest with intuitions. "

"Well, sir, some of them are obliged to think—when they want to be understood by men, who don't have intuitions, and can't go at all without something to hold up by—and a woman would think, perhaps, that if Sartliff could fall in love—"

"And if he can't he isn't worth the saving, " interjected Bart.

"Exactly; and if he could, that through its medium he might be brought back to a healthy frame of mind, or a healthy walk of mind. There, Mr. Ridgeley, I have got out with that, though rather limpingly, after all. "

"And a forcible case you have made. Here is a man crazy about Nature; you propose as a cure for that, to make him mad about a woman. And what next? "

"Well, love is human—or inhuman, " said Miss Giddings; "if the former, marriage is the specific; if the latter, his lady-love might get lost in a wood, you know. "

"Yes, I see. Poor Sartliff had better remain where he is, winking and blinking for the lights of Nature, " said Bart.

"I remember, " interposed Ida, "that he and your brother, among the matters they used to discuss, disagreed in their estimate of authors. Sartliff could never endure N. P. Willis, for instance. "

"A sign, " said Miss Giddings, "that he was sane then, at least. Willis, in Europe, is called the poet's lap-dog, with his ringlets and Lady Blessingtons. "

"I believe he had the pluck to meet Captain Marryatt, " said Bart.

"Was that particularly creditable? " asked Miss Giddings.

"Well, poets' lap-dogs don't fight duels, much; and Miss Giddings, do you think a lap-dog could have written this? " And taking up a volume of Willis, he turned from them and read "Hagar. " As he read, he seemed possessed with the power and pathos of the piece, and his deep voice trembled under its burthen. At the end, he laid the book down, and walked to a window while his emotion subsided. His voice always had a strange power of exciting him. After a moment's silence, Miss Giddings said, with feeling:

"I never knew before that there was half that force and strength in Willis. As you render it, it is almost sublime. Will you read another?"

Taking up the book, he read "Jepthah's Daughter: " reading it with less feeling, perhaps, but in a better manner.

"I give it up, " said Miss Giddings, "though I am not certain whether it is not in you, rather than in Willis, after all. "

"Six or seven years ago, when my brother Henry came home and gathered us up, and rekindled the home fires on the old hearth, " said Bart, "he commenced taking the *New York Mirror*, just established by George P. Morris, assisted by Fay and Willis. Fay, you know, has recently published his novel, 'Norman Leslie, ' the second volume of which flats out so awfully. At that time these younger men were in Europe; and we took wonderfully to them, and particularly to Willis's 'First Impressions, ' and 'Pencillings by the Way. ' To me they were authentic, and opened the inside of English literary society and life, and I came to like him. The language has a wonderful flexile power and grace in his hands; and I think he has real poetry in his veins, much more than John Neal, or Dr. Drake, though certainly less than Bryant. Yet there is a kind of puppyism about the man that will probably prevent his ever achieving the highest place in our literature. "

"You are a poet yourself, Mr. Ridgeley, I understand, " said Miss Giddings.

"I like poetry, which is a totally different thing from the power to produce it; this I am sure I have not, " was the candid answer.

"You have tried? "

"Most young men with a lively fancy and fervid feelings, write verses, I believe. Here is Mr. Case, quite a verse writer, and some of his lines have a tone or tinge of poetry. "

"Would you like literature for a pursuit? "

"I like books, as I like art and music, but I somehow feel that our state of society at the West, and indeed our civilization, is not ripe enough to reach a first excellence in any of these high branches of achievement. Our hands are thick and hard from grappling with the rough savagery of our new rude continent. We can construct the strong works of utility, and shall meet the demands for the higher and better work when that demand actually exists. "

"But does not that demand exist? Hasn't there been a clamor for the American novel? A standing advertisement—'Wanted, the American Novel'—has been placarded ever since I can remember; and I must forget how long that is, " said Miss Giddings.

"Yes, I've heard of that; but that is not the demand that will compel what it asks for. It will be the craving of millions, stimulating millions of brains, and some man will arise superior to the herd, and his achievement will challenge every other man of conscious powers, and they will educate and ripen each other till the best, who is never the first, will appear and supply the need. No great man ever appeared alone. He is the greatest of a group of great men, many of whom preceded him, and without whom he would have been impossible. Homer, alone of his group, has reached us; Shakespeare will live alone of his age, four thousand years hence. "

"But, Mr. Ridgeley, our continent and our life, with our fresh, young, intense natures, seem to me to contain all the elements of poetry, and the highest drama, " said Miss Giddings.

"So they seem to us, and yet how much of that is due to our egotism—because it is ours—who can tell? Of course there is any amount of poetry in the raw, and so it will remain until somebody comes to work it up. There are plenty of things to inspire, but the man to be inspired is the thing most needed. "

"So that, Mr. Ridgeley, " said Ida, "we may not in our time hope for the American novel, the great American epic, or the great American drama? "

"Well, I don't know that these will ever be. That will depend upon our luck in acquiring a mode and style, and habit of thought, and power of expression of our own, which for many reasons we may never have. An American new writes as much like an Englishman as he can—and the more servile the imitation, the better we like him—as a woman writes like a man as nearly as she possibly can, for he is the standard. What is there in Irving, that is not wholly and purely English? And so of Cooper; his sturdiness and vigor are those of a genuine Englishman, and when they write of American subjects, they write as an Englishman would; and if better, it is because they are better informed. "

"Mr. Ridgeley, " said Miss Giddings, "can't you give us an American book? "

"'When the little fishes fly
Like swallows in the sky, '

An American will write an American book, " said Bart, laughing. "But your question is a good answer to my solemn twaddle on literature. "

"No, I don't quite rate it as twaddle, " said Ida.

"Don't you though? " asked Bart.

"No, " seriously. "Now what is the effect of our American literature upon the general character of English literature? We certainly add to its bulk. "

"And much to its value, I've no doubt, " said Bart. "Well, with increased strength and vigor, we shall begin by imperceptible degrees, to modify and change the whole, and the whole will ultimately become Americanized, till the English of this continent, partaking of its color and character, imparts its tone and flavor finally to the whole everywhere. I have not much faith in a purely American literature, notwithstanding Miss Giddings' advertisement."

"Mr. Ridgeley, " said Miss Giddings, "your notions are depressing. I don't believe in them, and will oppose my woman's intuitions to your man's argument. "

"My dear Miss Giddings, " said Bart, laughing, "you value my notions quite as highly as I do; and I wouldn't take the criticisms of a young man who ran away from the only college he ever saw, and who has only heard the names of a few authors. "

"I wont. They are not American; and yet there seems to be force in them. "

CHAPTER XXXIX.

ABOUT LAWYERS, AND DULL.

Mr. Giddings was always much interested in all young men, and put himself in their way and society, and while he affected nothing juvenile, no man could make himself more winning and attractive to them. It was said by his enemies, who were of his political household, that in this, as in all else, he was politic; that he sought out and cultivated every young man in the circle of his acquaintance; made himself familiar with his make-up; flattered and encouraged him with little attentions; sent him speeches and books, and occasional letters, and thus attached nearly all the rising young men of Northeastern Ohio to himself personally. This may have been one source of his great and long continued popularity and strength; he thoroughly educated at least one generation of voters.

However that may be, he was much in the old office where he had done so much effective work, and laid the foundations of his position at the bar, which was with those of the first in the State.

He associated on terms of the pleasantest intimacy with the young men, and early evinced a liking for Bart, who, poor fellow, was ready to like anybody who would permit him.

Mr. Giddings was at pains to impress them with the absolute impossibility of even moderate success at the bar, without industry, while with it, mediocrity of talents would insure that. "Of the whole number who were admitted, " he said, "about ten or fifteen per cent. succeeded; and one in a hundred became eminent. Undoubtedly the greatest lawyer in the world did not possess the greatest intellect; but he must have been among the most industrious. Brilliant parts may be useful; they are always dangerous. The man who trusts to the inspiration of genius, or his capacity to get advantage by ingenious management in court, will find himself passed by a patient dullard. The admiring world who witness some of the really fine intellectual performances that sometimes occur in court, haven't the faintest conception as to when the real work was done, nor at all what it consisted in; nor when and how the raw material was gathered and worked up. The soldier in war is enlisted to fight, but really a small part of his time is spent in battle; almost the whole of it

220

is in preparation, training, gathering material, manoeuvring, gaining strategic advantages, and once in a while producing a field day, which tests the thoroughness of the preparation. This illustrates the value of absolute thoroughness in the preparation of cases. A good case is often lost, and a bad one gained, wholly by the care or negligence in their preparation. You really try your cases out of court. "

Barton asked why it was that, while the world generally admired and respected the bar, there was a distrust of its honesty? —at which there was a general smile.

"Because, " said Mr. Giddings, "there really are unworthy members of it; and the bar, like the ministry and the medical faculty, being comparatively a small body, is tried by its failures. The whole is condemned in the person of a few; while a majority—the bulk of men—estimate themselves by their successes. One great man sheds glory on his race, while one villain is condemned alone. The popular judgment, that lawyers are insincere and dishonest, because they appear on both sides of a case, with equal zeal, when there can be but one right side, is not peculiar to the bar. It should be remembered that learned and pious divines take opposite sides of all doctrinal points of Scripture, and yet nobody thinks of questioning their honesty. "

"When both are wrong, " put in Wade.

"Now there are, nominally at least, two sides in a law suit—certainly two parties. One party goes to Frank, here, and tells his side, most favorably to himself, and gets an opinion in his favor, and a suit is commenced. The other tells his side to me, for instance, and on his statement I think he has a good defence. From that moment each looks for evidence and law to sustain his side, and to meet the case made by the other; and invariably we come to the final trial, each honestly thinking he is right. We try the case zealously and sincerely, and the one who is finally beaten, feels that injustice has been done. It is the first task of an advocate to convince himself, and unless he has already done that, he may not expect to convince court and jury; and a man must be a poor advocate, or have a very bad case, who fails to convince himself, however he may fare with a jury. You need never expect to convince your opponent; he is under a retainer not to agree with you. "

"There is another thing about it, " said Wade. "The bar and writers talk about the ethics of the bar, and legal morality, and all that nonsense, until there is an impression, both among lawyers and the public, that there is one rule for lawyers and another for the rest of mankind—that we are remitted to a lower standard of honesty. This is all bosh; there can be but one standard of right and wrong; and that which is wrong out of court, cannot be right in it. I'll have but one rule. A man who will lie to a court or a jury, will lie anywhere— he is a liar. "

"Will you submit to that rule? " asked Giddings, laughing.

"I always have, " said Wade, "and I wont have any other. Now of all men, a lawyer can the least afford to be dishonest; for a taint, a doubt of his honor, ruins him; and there cannot be a more honorable body of men in the world, and never was, than the fair majority of the bar. The habit of contesting in open court, in the face of the world, engenders an honorable, manly highmindedness, free from the underhanded jealousy and petty wars of the doctors. If a man lies, or is mean, he is pretty certain to be detected and exposed at once. A lawyer cannot afford to lie and be mean. And besides, I have observed that there is really no healthy, manly development of intellect, without a healthy, manly development of the moral nature."

"Now, Frank, " said Mr. Giddings, "why not go a step further, and perfect the man, and say that religion should add its strength and grace, as a crown? "

"Well, Gid, I've no objection to your religion—that is, I have no objection to religion—I don't know about yours—but I have known a good many religious men who were very bad men, and I have known a good many bad men to get religion, who did not mend their morals. If a man is a good man, it don't hurt him to join a church, as far as I know; and a bad man usually remains bad. "

"Well, Frank, leave these young men to form their own opinions. "

"Certainly; I did not broach the subject. "

"They ought to become better lawyers than we are, " said Mr. Giddings. "Their means of education are far in advance; the increase of new and valuable text-books, the great progress in the learning and competency of the courts, as well as the general rapid improvement of the people in intelligence, are all in their favor; they ought to be better lawyers and better Christians. "

"They couldn't well be worse, " was the bluff response of Wade.

The young men remained pondering the remarks of their seniors.

"Well, boys, " said Ranney, "you've heard the ideas of two observing men. They give you the result of their experience on two or three very important practical points; what do you think of it? "

"Ransom, " said the ready Case, "is thinking who and what must be the one hundred, of whom he is to be the one. They would be a sad sight. "

"And Case, " rejoined the ever irate Ransom, "that if John Doe and Richard Roe, with a declaration in ejectment, could only be turned into doggerel, he would be an eminent land lawyer. "

"What has happened to Ransom? " asked Kennedy.

"I don't know, " replied Case; "he has sparkled up in this same way, two or three times. Can it be that an idea has been committed to his skull, lately? If one has, a *habeas corpus* must be sued out for its delivery. Solitary confinement is forbidden by the statutes of Ohio. "

"Never you mind the idea, " said Ransom. "I mean to find a lawyer in good practice, and go into partnership with him at once. "

"Now, Ransom, " said Case, still gravely, "you are a very clever fellow, and devilish near half witted; and you would allow such a man, whom you thus permitted to take himself in with you, one third or one fourth of the proceeds of the first year. "

"I would have no trouble about that, " said Ransom, not quite feeling the force of Case's compliment.

"Well, " said Ranney, "I suspect that generally lawyers, desirable as partners, if they wish them, will be already supplied, and then, when one could secure an eligible connection of this kind, the danger is, that he would be overshadowed and dwarfed, and always relying on his senior, would never come to a robust maturity. Well, Kennedy, what do you say? "

"Not much; I hope to be able to work when admitted. I mean to find some good point further West, where there is an opening, and stop and wait. I don't mean to be a failure. "

"Ridgeley, what are your views? "

"Modest, as becomes me; I don't think I am to be counted in any hundred, and so I avoid unpleasant comparisons. I don't mean to look long for an opening, or an opportunity; I would prefer to make both. I would begin with the first thing, however small, and do my best with it, and so of every other thing that came, leaving the eminence and places to adjust themselves. I intend to practice law, and, like Kennedy, I don't mean to fail. "

"Mr. Ranney, " continued Bart, "what is the reason of this universal failure of law students? "

"I think the estimate of Giddings is large, " said Ranney. "but of all the young men who study law, about one half do it with no settled purpose of ever practising, and, of course, don't. Of those who do intend to practice, one half never really establish themselves in it. That leaves one fourth of the whole number, who make a serious and determined effort at the bar, and one half of these—one eighth of the whole—succeed; and that brings out about as Giddings estimated. "

"Well, on the whole, that is not a discouraging view, " said Bart, "and for one, I am obliged to you. "

Nevertheless, he pondered the whole matter, and turned to face calmly as he had before, the time when his novitiate should end, and he should actually enter upon his experiment.

"Now, Case, this is a serious matter. A young and utterly unknown man, without money, friends, acquaintances or books, and doubtful whether he has brains, learning and capacity, in some small or large town, attacks the world, throws down his gage—or rather nails it up, in the shape of a tin card, four by twelve inches, with his perfectly obscure name on it. Think of it! Just suppose you have a little back room, up stairs, with a table, two chairs, half a quire of paper, an inkstand, two steel pens, Swan's Treatise, and the twenty-ninth volume of Ohio Statutes. You would be very busy arranging all this array of things, and would whistle cheerfully till that was accomplished, and then you would grow sad, and sit down to wait and think—"

"Of the rich Judge's beautiful daughter, " broke in Case.

"And wait, " continued Bart.

"Oh, Bart! I glory in your pluck and spunk, " said Case, "and I think of your performance as Major Noah said of Adam and Eve: 'As touching that first kiss, ' said he, 'I have often thought I would like to have been the man who did it; but the chance was Adam's. '"

"Ridgeley seems to be taken in hand by Miss Giddings, " said Kennedy; "that would not be a bad opening for an ambitious man. "

"Of the ripe years of twenty-three, " put in Case. "The average age would be about right. She has led out one or two of each crop of law students since she was sixteen. "

"What has been the trouble? " asked Kennedy.

"I don't know. They came, and went—

> 'Their hold was frail, their stay was brief,
> Restless, and quick to pass away' —

while she remains, " replied Case. "Bart seems to be a new inspiration, and she is as gay and lively as a spring butterfly. "

"And worth forty young flirts, " observed Ransom.

"Oh, come, boys! " cried Bart, "hold up. Miss Giddings is an attractive woman, full of accomplishment and goodness—"

"And experience, " put in Case.

"Who permits me to enjoy her society sometimes, " continued Bart. "The benefit and pleasure are wholly mine, and I can't consent to hear her spoken of so lightly. "

"Bart is right, as usual, " said Case, gravely; "and I don't know of anything more unmanly than the way we young men habitually talk of women. "

"Except the way they talk of us, " said Kennedy.

"You would expect a lady to speak in an *un*manly way, " remarked Bart. "Of course, if we are ever spoken of by them, it is in our absence; but I'll venture that they seldom speak of us at all, and then in ignorance of our worst faults. We are not likely to receive injustice at their hands. "

"Bart, you must always have been lucky, " said Ransom.

"I am doing my best not to be conceited and vain, and find it confounded hard work, " was the frank, good-natured reply.

CHAPTER XL.

THE DISGUISE.

Mrs. Ridgeley received the following:

"JEFFERSON, June 8, 1838.

"*Dear Mother*: —A strange thing has happened to me, for which I am indebted to Henry; indeed, I am destined to trade upon his capital. You remember how kind he said a Mr. Windsor was to him, employing him to transact small business matters for him, and paying him largely, besides making him useful and valuable presents? He seems to have been dissatisfied with himself for not doing more, and I am to be the recipient of his bounty in full.

"He called to see me about a week ago; and then two or three days after, he sent a carriage for me, and I have just returned. He is very wealthy, an old bachelor, lives elegantly, is a thoroughly educated man, and not eccentric, except in his liking to Henry, which he transfers to me. He is without near relations, and has had a history. Now he insists on advancing to me enough to carry me through, clothing me, and starting me with a fine library. He says I must go East to a law school at least a year, and so start from a most favorable and advanced position.

"It took my breath away. It seems fairly wrong that I should permit myself to take this man's money, for whom I have done nothing, and to whom I can make no return, and whose money I might never repay. He laughed, and said I was very simple and romantic. Wasn't the money his? and couldn't he do what he pleased with it? and if he invested it in me, nobody was harmed by it. I told him I might be; I am not sure that I should be safe with the pressure and stimulus of poverty removed from me.

"Moreover he had purchased an elegant watch, to be given to Henry, on his marriage with poor Miss Aikens, of whom I told you; and this he insists on my taking and wearing, with a chain big and long enough to hang me in. I told him if he wanted to give it away, that it should, I thought, properly go to Miss A. —to whom, by the way, I gave that beautiful pin. I cannot wear anything that was Henry's, and this would be one objection to wearing this watch. Mr. Windsor said it certainly was never intended for Ida; that it had never been Henry's, that it was mine, and I had to bring it away. I feel guilty, and as if I had swindled or stolen, or committed some mean act; and as I hold it to my ear, its strong beat reproaches me like the throb of a guilty heart.

"What can I do? Your feelings are right, and your judgment is good. I can't afford to be killed with a weight of obligation, nor must I remit or relax a single effort. This may stimulate me more. If I were to relax and lie down now, and let another carry me, I should deserve the scorn and contempt I have received.

"Write me upon this, and don't mention it to the Colonel.

"I have made the acquaintance of Miss Giddings, who is very kind to me; and she and Ida furnish that essential element of ladies' society which you desired I should have. I confess I don't care much for men; but I have so little to give in return for the kindness of these noble, refined and intellectual ladies, that here again I am a receiver of alms. No matter; women never receive any proper return from men, any way.

"Ask Ed and George to write, and tell me all the little pleasant details of the farm life and home. How tender and sweet and dear it all is to me; and what a gulf seems to have opened between me and all the past!

"Ever with love, dear mother,

BART. "

Mrs. Ridgeley received and read the letter in the store. While she was absorbed in it. Mrs. Markham came in, and was struck by the expression of her face. As she finished the perusal, she discovered Mrs. Markham, and her look of recognition induced the latter to approach her. The incidents of the last few weeks had silently ripened the liking of the two women into a very warm and cordial feeling. As Mrs. Markham approached, the other gave her her hand, and held out Bart's letter. Mrs. Markham received it, and as her eye ran over it, Mrs. Ridgeley could easily see the look of pleasure and warmth that lit up her face.

"Oh, by all means, " she said, "tell him not hesitate a moment. Providence has sent him a friend, and means, and his pride should not be in the way of this offer. "

"He is proud, " said Mrs. Ridgeley, gravely; "but it is not wholly pride that makes him hesitate. "

"Pardon me, " said Mrs. Markham, "I don't mean to blame him; I sympathize with even his pride, and admire him for the very qualities that prevented his allowing us to aid him, and I hope those high qualities will never lose a proper influence over him. "

The mother was a little more than appeased.

"Am I to read the rest? "

"Certainly. "

And she resumed. A little graver she looked at one or two lines, and then the sweet smile and light came back to her face; and she handed back the letter.

"What a treasure to you this son must be, " she said; and she again urged her to write to Bart at once, and induce him to accept the kind offer made to him.

Mrs. Ridgeley explained who Miss Aikens was, and her relations to Henry; that Miss Giddings was the daughter of the member of Congress, &c. Mrs. Markham had noticed that Bart spoke of them as "ladies, " and not as young ladies, though what mental comment she made upon it was never known.

People in the country go by the almanac, instead of by events, as in cities; and May quickened into June, June warmed into July, and ran on to fervid August. Quiet ruled in the Ridgeley cottage, rarely broken, save when Julia galloped up and made a pleasant little call, had a game of romps with George, a few quick words with Edward; an enquiry, or adroit circumlocution, would bring out Bart's name, which the young lady would hear with the most innocent air in the world. She always had some excuse; she was going, returning to, or from some sick person, or on some kind errand. Once or twice later, young King, of Ravenna, accompanied her; and still later, Mr. Thorndyke was riding with her frequently.

It was observed that while her beauty had perfected, if possible, the character of her face had deepened, and a tenderer light was in her eyes. As the time came for Bart's examination, she carelessly remarked that he would be home soon, and was told that he had decided to take a short course in the Albany law-school, and would go directly from Jefferson; that when he left in the spring, he had determined not to return to Newbury until the end of a year; but that his mother might expect him certainly at that time. Julia was turning over a bound volume of the *New York Mirror*, and came upon a Bristol board, on which was a fine pen-and-ink outline head of Bart. She took it up and asked Mrs. Ridgeley if she might have it. "Certainly, " was the answer, "if you wish it, " and she carried it away. After leaving the house she discovered on the other side, a better finished and more artistic likeness of herself in crayon, with her hair falling about her neck and shoulders; and surrounding it, two or three outlines of her features in profile, which she recognized by the hair—one of poor Bart's "ships" that had escaped the general burning.

* * * * *

Barton decided to avail himself of the kindness of Mr. Windsor, and quietly made his arrangements accordingly. The summer was very pleasant to him. He devoted himself with his usual ardor to his books, but gave much of his leisure to Ida, who began to feel the approach of a calamity that gradually extinguished the light in her eyes. She was already suffering—although not anticipating a serious result—a pressure in the forehead, and a gradual impairing of vision, without pain. Under its shadow, that no medical art could dissipate, she found a wonderful solace in the tender devotion of her newly found brother, who read to her, walked with her, and occasionally rode with her, in all tender, manly ways surrounding her with an atmosphere of kind and loving observances, which she more than repaid, with the strong, healthy and pure womanly influence, which she exercised over him.

CHAPTER XLI.

THE INVITATION.

Late one wondrously beautiful August night, as Bart was returning from a solitary stroll, he was suddenly joined by Sartliff, bare-headed and bare-footed, who placed his hand within his arm, and turning him about, walked him back towards the wood. Bart had not seen him for weeks, and he thought his face was thinner and more haggard, and his eyes more cavernous than he had ever seen them.

"What progress are you making? " asked Bart, quietly.

"I am getting increase of power. I don't know that I need light; I think I want strength. I hear the voices oftener, and they are wonderfully sweeter; I find that they consist of marvelous musical sounds, and I can distinguish some notes; meanings are conveyed by them. If I could only comprehend and interpret them. I shall in time if I can hold out. I find as the flesh becomes more spirit-like, that this power increases. If I only had some fine-fibred soul who could take this up where I must leave it! Barton, you believe God communicates with men through other than his ordinary works? "

"I don't know; I see and hear God in the wondrous symbols of nature; when they say that he speaks directly, I don't feel so certain. I am so made up, that the very nature, the character and quality of the evidence, is unequal to the facts to be proven, and so to produce conviction. If a score of you were to say to me, that in the forest to-day, you saw a fallen and decayed tree arise and strike down new roots, and shoot out new branches, and unfold new foliage and flowers, I would not believe it: Nor, though five hundred men should swear that they saw a grave heave up, and its tenant come forth to life and beauty, would I believe. The quality of the evidence is not equal to sustain the burthen of the fact to be established, and it does not help the matter, that alleged proofs come to me through uncertain historical media. Yet I can't say that I disbelieve. Who can say that there is not within us a religious spiritual faculty, or a set of faculties, that take impressions, and receive communications, not through the ordinary perceptions and convictions of the mere mind—that sees and hears, retains and transmits, loves, hopes and worships, in a spiritual or religious atmosphere of its own; whose memories are superstitions, whose realizations are extatic visions, and whose hopes are the future of blessedness; and that it is through these faculties that religious sentiments are received, transmitted and propagated, and to which God speaks and acts, spirit to spirit, as matter to matter? Who can tell how many sets of faculties are possible to us? We may have developed only a few of the lowest. I sometimes fancy that I feel the rudiments of a higher and finer set within me. Who shall say that I have them not? "

"Go on, Barton; I like to hear you unfold yourself, " said Sartliff.

"I can't, " said Bart, "I can only vaguely talk about what I so vaguely feel. "

"Barton, " said Sartliff, "go with me; let me impart to you what I know; perhaps you have a finer and subtler sense than I had. At any rate I can help you. You can be warned by my failures and blunders, and possess yourself of my small gains. I know I have taken some steps. I shall last long enough to place you well on the road. You are silent. Do you think me crazy—mad? "

"No, not that, nor do I think that we have occupied all the fields of human knowledge. We are constantly acquiring a faculty to see new things and to take new meanings from the common and old. Nature has not yet delivered her full speech to man. She can communicate only as he acquires the power to receive. This idea of finding new pathways, and new regions and realms, with new powers, of finding an opening from our day into the more effulgent, with new strange and glorious creatures, with new voices and forms, with whom we may communicate, is alluring, and may all lay within the realm of possibility. I don't say that to dream of it, is to be mad. "

"It is possible, " said Sartliff with fervor. "I have seen the forms and heard the voices. "

"And to what purpose do you pursue these mystical studies and researches. "

"Partly for the extacy and glory of the present, mainly for the ultimate good to the races of men, when the new and powerful agencies that come of the wisdom and strength which will be thus acquired, the powers within and about us, are developed and employed for the common good; and man is emancipated from his sordid slavery to the gross and physical of his worst and lowest nature, and when woman through this emancipation takes her real position, glorified, by the side of her glorified companion; when she seeks to be wife and mother, with free choice to be other—what a race will spring from them! Strong, brave, beautiful men, great, radiant, beautiful women, like the first mothers of the race, bringing forth their young, with the same joy and gladness, as that with which they receive their young bridegrooms. "

"Go and help me find the way for our common race. "

He had turned, and stood with intent eyes burning into the soul of the young man. "I have faith in you. Of all the young men I have met, you have exhibited more capacity to comprehend me than any other, and I am beginning to feel the need of help, " said Sartliff, plaintively.

"God alone can help you, " said Bart, "I cannot. You believe in this; to me it is a dream, with which my fancy, when idle, willingly toys. I like to talk with you. I sympathise with you; I cannot go with you. I will not enter upon your speculations. Don't think me unkind. "

"I don't, " said Sartliff, "nor do I blame you. You are young and gifted, and opportunities will come to you; and distinction and fame, and some beautiful woman's love await you, and God bless you. " And he walked away.

There was always something about Sartliff that stimulated, but at the same time excited an apprehension in Bart, who regarded him as past recall to healthy life, and he felt a sense of relief when he was alone; but the old, melancholy chords continued to vibrate, and Bart returned to the village under a depression that lingered about him for days.

CHAPTER XLII.

ADMITTED.

At the September term of the Supreme Court, Mr. Ranney presented the certificates and applications for the admission of Case, Ransom, and Bart on the first day, and they were, as usual, referred to a Committee of the whole bar, for examination and report.

The Committee met that evening in the Court room, the Supreme Judges, Wood and Lane, being present.

Old Webb, of Warren, whom Case ought to have sketched in his rough outlines as the senior of the bar, turned suddenly to Bart, the youngest of the applicants, and asked him if a certain "estate could exist in Ohio? "

After a moment's reflection, Bart answered that it could not.

"Why? "

Bart explained the nature and conditions of the estate, and said that one of them was rendered impossible by a statute; and explained how. A good deal of surprise was expressed at this; the statute was called for, and on its being placed in his hands, Bart turned to it, read the law, and showed its application.

Wood said, "Judge Lane, I think this young man has decided your Hamilton Co. case for you. "

Some general conversation ensued, and when it subsided, old Webb said, "Well! well! young man, we may as well go home, when we get such things from a law student. " And they did not ask him another question.

The examination was over at last. Case had acquitted himself well, and Ransom tolerably. Bart was mortified and disgusted. This was the extent then of the ordeal; all his labor, hard study, and anxiety, ended in this!

The next morning, on the assembling of the Court, the three young men were admitted, sworn in, and became attorneys and counsellors at law, and solicitors in chancery, authorized to practise in all the courts of Ohio. All this was made to appear by the clerk's certificate, under the great seal of the Supreme Court of the State, tied with a blue ribbon, and presented to each of them.

It tended not much to relieve Bart, to know that the question he had so summarily disposed of had much excited and disturbed the legal world of Middle and Southern Ohio; that the best legal minds had been divided on it; and that a case had just been reserved for the court in bane, which turned on this very point.

It was over; he had his diploma, but he felt that in some way it was a swindle.

What a longing came to him to go to Newbury; and he was half mad and wholly sad to think that one face would come to him with the sweet, submissive, reproachful, arch expression, it wore when he forbid its owner to speak, one memorable morning, in the woods and snow; and he found himself wondering if what Ida told him might by any possibility be true; he knew it could not be, and so put it all away.

He took Ida over to Mr. Windsor's for a long day's visit, made a few calls, packed his trunk, bade Miss Giddings, who did not hesitate to express her sorrow at his departure, a regretful good-bye, and the next morning rode to Ashtabula, and there took a steamer down the lake.

I am glad to have him off my hands for six months; and when he falls under them next time, seriously, I will dispose of him.

CHAPTER XLIII.

JULIA.

It will be remembered that Greer was a somewhat ambiguous character, about whom and whose movements some suspicions were at times afloat; but these did not much disturb him or interrupt his pleasant relations with the pleasant part of the world.

He was at Jefferson during the first term of the Court while Bart was there, and it so happened that there was a prosecution pending against a party for passing counterfeit money; who finally gave bail and never returned to take his trial; but nobody connected Greer with that matter. He was also there after Bart was admitted, and had an interview with the young lawyer, professionally, which was followed by some consequences to both, hereafter to be mentioned.

Just before this last visit, a man by the name of Myers—Dr. Myers—a young man of fine address and of fair position, was arrested in Geauga for stealing a pair of valuable horses. The arrest created great astonishment, which was increased when it was known that in default of the heavy bail demanded he had been committed to the jail at Chardon. This was followed by the rumor of his confession, in which it was said that he implicated Jim Brown, of Akron, and various parties in other places, and also Greer, and, as some said, Bart Ridgeley, all of whom belonged to an association, many members of which had been arrested. The rumors produced much excitement everywhere, and especially in the south part of Geauga; and the impression was deepened and confirmed by an article in the *Geauga Gazette*, issued soon after Myers was committed. With staring head-lines and exclamation points, it stated that Dr. Myers, since his imprisonment, had made a full confession, which it gave in substance, as above. Bart was referred to as a young law student at Jefferson, and a resident of the south part of the county, who, as was said, had escaped, and it was supposed that he had gone East, where the officers had gone in pursuit. Most of the others had been arrested.

Mrs. Ridgeley had caught something of the first rumor in her far off quiet home; but nobody had told her of Barton's connection with it, nor did her neighbors seem inclined to talk with her about the general subject. As usual, one of the boys went to the Post Office on the day of the arrival of the Chardon paper; and brought in not only that journal, but the rumor in reference to Barton. His mother read and took it all in, and was standing in blank amazement and indignation, when Julia came flashing in, and found her still mutely staring at the article.

"Oh, Mrs. Ridgeley! Mrs. Ridgeley! " exclaimed the aroused girl, seizing her hands; "it is all false—every word of it—about Barton! Every single word is a lie! "

"I know it is; but how can that be made to appear? Men will believe it, if it is false! "

"Never! No one will ever believe evil of him. He is now surrounded by the best and truest of men; and when this wretched Myers is tried, everything will be made clear. I knew you would see this paper, and I came at once to tell you what I know of Barton's connection with Greer. Please listen; " and she told her of the old rumor about them, and of her journey to Ravenna, to see the latter, and showed her his note, addressed to her father.

The quick mind of the elder lady appreciated it as it was stated to her; and another thing, new and sudden as a revelation, came to her; and with tears in her eyes, and a softened and illuminated face, she turned to Julia, a moment since so proud and defiant, and now so humble and subdued, with averted eyes and crimsoned face: "Oh, Julia! " and passed one arm around the slender girl.

"Please! please! " cried her pleading voice, with her face still away. "This is my secret—you will not tell—let him find it out for himself—please! "

"Certainly; I will leave to him the joy of hearing it from you, " said the elder, in her inmost soul sympathizing with the younger.

What a deep and tranquil joy possessed the heart of the mother, and with what wonder she contemplated the now conscious maiden! and how she wondered at her own blindness! And so the threatening cloud broke for her: broke into not only a serene peace, but a heartfelt joy and gratitude; and she parted with Julia with the first kiss she had ever bestowed upon her.

At the ensuing fall term of the Geauga Common Pleas, Myers was indicted for horse-stealing. The prosecuting officer refused to make terms with him, and permit him to escape, on condition of furnishing evidence against others, as he had hoped when he made his confession; and when arraigned, he plead not guilty, and upon proper showing, his case was continued to the next term, in January.

A great crowd from all parts of the adjacent country, and many from a distance, had assembled to witness the trial of Myers. The region of Eastern Ohio had, like many new and exposed communities, suffered for years from the occasional depredations of horse thieves. It was supposed that an organization existed, extending into Pennsylvania. The horses taken were traced to the mountain region in that State, where they disappeared; and although Greer and Brown were never before connected with this branch of industry, it was thought that the horses in question, which had been intercepted, were in the regular channels of the trade, which it was hoped, would now be broken up. One noticeable thing at the court was the presence of Greer, who apparently came and went at pleasure. He was cool and elegant as usual, and seemingly unconcerned and a little more exclusive. His being at large was much at variance with the understood programme, and necessitated its reconstruction. Little was said about Bart, and it was apparent that the public mind had returned to a more favorable tone towards him.

CHAPTER XLIV.

FINDING THE WAY.

On an early December evening, in a bright, quiet room, at the Delavan House, in Albany, sat Bart Ridgeley alone, thoughtfully and sadly contemplating a manuscript, that lay before him, which ran as follows:

"UNIONVILLE, Nov. 27, 1838.

"*My Dear Bart*: —Poor Sartliff has, it seems, finally found the way. It was that short, direct, everlasting old way, so crowded, which everybody finds, and nobody loses or mistakes. You told me of your last interview with him, as did he, not long after you left. It seemed to have depressed him. He spoke of you as one who could have greatly aided him, but did not blame you.

"The next time I saw him, I found him much changed for the worse. He was thin and haggard—more so than I had ever seen him. His old hopefulness and buoyancy were gone, and he was given to very gloomy and depressing views of things. He thought he had made great progress, in fact had reached a new discovery, and it was not in the least encouraging.

"He finally concluded that the grand and wondrously beautiful spirits that he seemed to get glimpses of, and whose voices he used to hear, were really convict spirits, or angels, imprisoned on or banished to this earth, for a period of years, or for eternity, for crimes committed in the sun, or some less luminous abode; and I presume are cutting up here, much after their old way. Though it must be conceded that this world is a place of severe punishment.

"He went on to a more depressing view of us mortals, and said he had concluded that our souls were also the souls of beings who had inhabited some more favored region of the universe, also sent here for punishment; and that each was compelled to enter and inhabit a human body, for the lifetime of that body; and to suffer by partaking of all of its wretched, sensual, and degrading vicissitudes; and that whenever the soul is sufficiently punished, the body dies and permits it to escape.

"I suggested that it made no difference where the soul came from, if there was one, nor how many bodies it had inhabited; and that it made against his idea, that the soul was older than the body; for if it was, it would be conscious of that pre-existence. He said that every soul did at times have a consciousness of existence in another and older form, which was very dark from its transgressions. But he took the part of the native body against this alien soul, and felt hurt and grieved that our world was a mere penal colony—a penitentiary for all the scabbed and leprous souls and spirits of the rest of God's creation. It was bad economy; and he grieved over it as a deep and irreparable personal injury.

"This was a month ago; and I never saw him again. He wandered off down into the neighborhood of Erie, where he had many acquaintances, took less care of himself, went more scantily clad, was more abstemious in diet, and more and more disregarded the conditions of human existence. Finally, his mind became as wandering as his body.

"He wanted nothing, asked for nothing, rejected food, and refused shelter, and as often as taken in and cared for, he managed to escape, and wander away, feebly and helplessly, from human association and ministration. He complained to himself that his great mother, Nature, had deserted him, a helpless child, to wander and perish in the wilderness. He said he had gone after her, until weary, starving, and worn, he must lie down and die. He had called after her until his voice had sunk to a wail; and he finally died of a child's heart-broken sense of abandonment and desertion.

"He was found one day, nearly unconscious, with the tears frozen in his eyes, and on being cared for, wailed his life out in broken sobs.

"Let us not grieve that he has found rest.

"I am too sad to write of other things, and you will be melancholy over this for a month.

"CASE. "

CHAPTER XLV.

SOME THINGS PUT AT REST.

At the January term of the Court, the case of Ohio *vs.* Myers, came up; and the defendant failing on his motion to continue, the case was brought on for trial, and a jury was sworn. His principal counsel was Bissell, of Painesville, a man of great native force and talent, and who in a desperate stand-up fight, had no superior at that time in Northern Ohio. He expected to exclude the confession, on the ground that Myers had been induced to make it upon representations that it would be for his advantage to do so; and if this could be got out of the way, he was not without the hope of finding the other evidence of the State too weak to work a conviction.

The interest in the case had not abated, and a great throng of people were in attendance.

Hitchcock, with whom Henry Ridgeley was in company at the time of his death, then an able lawyer, was the prosecuting officer, aided by the younger Wilder, who had succeeded Henry as his partner.

Wilder was a young lawyer of great promise, and was the active man in the criminal cases.

He stated the case to the court and jury, saying among other things, that he would not only prove the larceny by ordinary evidence, but by the confession of the prisoner himself. Bissell dropped his heavy brows, and remarked in his seat, "that he would have a good time doing that. "

Wilder called one of the officers who made the arrest, proved that fact, and then asked him the plump question, in a way to avoid a leading form, whether the prisoner made a confession? Bissell objected, on the ground that before he could answer, the defendant had a right to know whether he was induced to make it, by any representations from the witness or others.

Wilder answered, that it did not yet appear that a confession had been made. If it should be shown that one had, it would be then time

241

to discuss its admissibility; and so the court ruled; and the witness answered that Myers did make a full confession. Wilder directed him to state it, Bissell again objected, and although Wilder urged that he had a right to go through with his witness, and leave the other side to call out the inducement, if any, on cross-examination, the court ruled that the circumstances under which the confession was made was a preliminary matter that the defendant had a right to show. When the witness answered to Bissell, that he told Myers after his arrest that they knew all about the larceny, but did not know who his accomplices were, and that if he would tell all about them he would undoubtedly be favored; and that then the defendant told his story. Upon this statement, Wilder cross-examined the witness, and managed to extract several items of the confession, when the court held that the confession was inadmissible.

Myers drew a breath of relief, but Bissell's brow did not clear. He knew that the State had gained all it expected to; it had proved that a confession was made, which was about as bad as the confession itself. Under this cloud, Wilder called his other evidence, which of itself, was very inconclusive, and which, with the added weight that a confession had been made, left much uncertainty as to the result, and Bissell was girding himself for the final struggle. Wilder then called the name of John T. Greer—when the head of Myers dropped, and midnight fell upon the brow of Bissell.

Placidly and serenely, that gentleman answered the call, and took the stand—seemingly the only unconcerned gentleman present. He said that he knew Myers well—had known him for years; that on the morning after the larceny, he saw him and another man, at McMillan's, near Youngstown; that they brought with them a pair of horses, which he described exactly as the stolen horses, and that Myers told him they got them the night before, at Conant's barn in Troy; that he denounced Myers to his face as a horse thief, and threatened to expose him.

This evidence produced a prodigious sensation. Bissell put the witness through a savage cross-examination. In answer to the questions, he said that Myers and himself, and others, belonged to an association, of which Jim Brown was the head, for manufacturing paper currency and coin, and supplying it at various points; had never passed a dollar himself; that he broke with Myers because he was a thief, and no gentleman; that the association had never had any connection with running off horses, &c.

"To whom did you first disclose this act of Myers? "

"To a young lawyer at Jefferson, in his private room. "

"Who was he? "

"Barton Ridgeley. " Great sensation, and men looked at one another.

"Did he belong to your financial association? "

"Never! " Sensation.

"Why did you go to him? "

"I had a little acquaintance with him, and had great confidence in him. I wanted to consult somebody, and I went to him. " He went on to say that he consulted him as a lawyer and not as a friend; that when he told Ridgeley of the association, which was drawn out of him by a cross-examination, Ridgeley told him at once, that while he would not use this against the witness, he certainly would against his associates. That soon after Mr. Wade came in, and he found out that Ridgeley had managed to send for him. That Ridgeley then insisted that he should tell the whole story to Mr. Wade, and he did. That Wade called in a United States Deputy Marshal, and induced the witness to make an affidavit, when the Marshal went to Columbus, got warrants, and arrested Brown and others.

He was asked what fee he paid young Ridgeley, and he answered, nothing. He offered him a liberal fee, and he refused it. He understood Ridgeley had gone East, but did not know; nor who furnished him with money.

The prosecution rested.

Wade was present, and Bissell called him; and in answer to Wilder, said he proposed to contradict Greer. Wilder replied, that although he was not entitled to such a privilege, yet he had no objection; and Wade, in the most emphatic way, corroborated Greer throughout. He said that Ridgeley was at that time at the Albany law-school, and would soon be back to answer for himself; and when asked if he was not poor, answered, that friends always came to such young men, with a glance at the bench, where Markham sat with Humphrey. The perfect desperation of his case alone warranted Bissell in calling Wade, with whose testimony the trial closed; and on the verdict of guilty, Myers was sentenced to the Penitentiary for ten years. And for the third or fourth time Barton's acquaintances were disposed to regard him as a hero.

Bart Ridgeley: A Story of Northern Ohio

CHAPTER XLVI.

PRINCE ARTHUR.

It was not in nature, particularly in young man-nature, that such a creature as Julia should ripen into womanhood without lovers. In her little circle of Newbury, boys and girls loved her much alike, and with few shades of difference on account of sex. No youth of them dreamed of becoming her suitor; not even Barton, whom I have sketched in vain, if it is not apparent that it would not have been over presumption in him, to dream of anything.

Of the numerous, and more or less accomplished young men from other places, who had met and admired her, two had somewhat singled themselves out, as her admirers, both of whom, I fear, had a good way passed the pleasant, though dangerous, line of admiration.

Young King, of Ravenna, a frank, handsome, high-spirited youth, had for a long time been at no pains to conceal his partiality; so far from that, he had sought many occasions to evince in a modest, manly way, his devotion. His observing sister, Julia's warm and admiring friend, had in vain looked wise, lifted her finger, and shaken her warning head at him. He would inevitably have committed himself, had not the high-souled and generous Julia, by her frank, ingenuous woman's way with him, made him see and feel in time the uselessness of a more ardent pursuit; and so content himself with the real luxury of her friendship. The peril to him was great, and if for a time he was not unhappy, he had a grave and serious mood, that lasted many months. She had a real woman's warm, unselfish friendship for him, which has much of the sweetness and all the purity and unselfishness of a sister's love; and all unconscious as she seemed, that he could wish for more or other, she succeeded in placing him in the position of a devoted and trusted friend.

Thorndyke, the fourth or fifth of aristocratic generations, of a good old colonial strain, elegant to a fault, and refined to uselessness, of tastes and pursuits that took him out of the ordinary atmosphere; languid more for the want of a spur, than from lack of nerve and ability; and unambitious for want of an object, rather than from want of power to climb, was really smothered by the softness and luxury of his surroundings, rather than reduced by the poverty and feebleness of his nature; had really the elements of manly strength and elevation, and had misfortune or poverty fallen upon him, early, he would undoubtedly have developed into a man of the higher type, like the first generations of his family.

Like every man he was struck as much as he could be, with Julia, and when he saw her in the rudeness of pioneer surroundings, he began by pitying her, and finally ended by pitying himself. When it first occurred to him to carry her out of the woods, to the actual world, and real human life, he was not a little surprised. She was not born in Boston, nor did her father's family date back to the flood, but her mother's did. Indeed, that came over with it.

In revolving this grave matter, the only factors to be considered, were Mr. Thorndyke's own judgment, taste and inclinations, and Julia has matured in these pages, to a small purpose, or Mr. T. was much less a man than I have supposed, if these parties should not finally unite in consenting to the alliance. Of course, Miss Julia could be had, both of herself and parents, for the asking. But his fastidious notions could alone be satisfied with a gentlemanly course of gradually warming and more devoted attentions, with all the forms and observances, so far as the disadvantages of her surroundings would permit. It was some time in the last summer, that he had made up a definite judgment in the premises under which he commenced his lambent action. During the autumn he often met King at her father's, and the young men occasionally made up small parties with Julia and Nell or some other young ladies for rides and excursions. Towards winter, King was less at Newbury; and as winter approached, Mr. Thorndyke seemed left to monopolize the time and society of Julia. So gracious, frank and open was her invariable manner to him, that he could not for a moment doubt that after a gentlemanly lapse of time, and a course of rides, calls, walks and teas, he might in his own way dispose of the matter.

His splendid gray, "West Wind, " was no mean companion for Prince, and many a gallop they had together, and Thorndyke was a gentlemanly rider and drove well, and during the winter he often drove Julia out in a single sleigh.

In a moment of weakness it occurred to him that West Wind and Prince would go well in double harness, and he proposed to Julia to match them for a drive.

"What! " exclaimed that young lady, "put Prince in harness? make a draught horse of him? "

"With West Wind — certainly. Why not? "

"Because I don't choose it. There is but one man in the world who shall drive Prince, and I am sure he will not want to. "

"I presume Judge Markham don't care to drive him? "

"I presume he don't; " laughing and blushing.

That was the end of that, and not overly pleasing to the gentleman. It was apparent, that she was disinclined to match the horses.

And March was coming, and Julia was sweet and arch and gracious, and at times as he came to know her better, he thought a little grave and pensive. This was certainly a good sign; and somehow, he found himself now often watching and calculating the signs, and somehow again they did not seem to deepen or change, or indicate much. He could not on the whole convince himself that he had made much progress, except that he should ask her at some time and she would accept him, and he was certainly approaching that time. The matter in hand had become absorbing — very: and he knew he was very much interested in it; and the laugh of the beautiful girl was as rich, musical and gay as ever, though he some how fancied, that it was a little less frequent; and once or twice something had been dropped about some day early in April, at which there was a little flutter in Julia. What could it be? did she think he was slow? He would speak, and put an end to it. But he didn't, and somehow he could not. He might do it any day; but did not. At any event, before that April, something should be asked and answered — but how answered?

The sleigh was left under cover, the roads hardened in the March sun and wind, and several horseback excursions had been made. Toward the close of the month, on their return one day, Thorndyke, who had been unusually silent, suddenly asked Julia if she would be at leisure that evening, at about eight; and might he call? She answered that she would be at home, and as he knew, he was quite at liberty to call. He said that he had something quite particular which he wished to say to her, and that of course she must know what it was.

"Indeed! If I must know what it is, you must, by the same rule, know what I will say in reply. Let us consider the thing said and answered, and then your business call can be one of pleasure. "

"I had hoped that it might possibly be one of pleasure. "

The girl, looked grave for a moment, and then turning in her best manner to her escort—

"Mr. Thorndyke, I think I had better tell you the little story of my horse. If we ride slow, I will have time before we reach the gate. " With a little increase of color, "It is not much of a story, but you may see a little moral in it. "

"Certainly, I shall be glad to hear it. No doubt it will interest me. "

"You see his name is Prince. "

"I hear that is his name. "

"You will see presently that is not his whole name. "

"Silvertail? "

"Silver-sticks! Please attend, sir. His name is Prince Arthur. "

"Named after a gentleman who lived a few years ago; who dined off 'a table round, ' and who was thought to be unfortunate in his lady. "

"No, sir. He was named for a man who may have been called after that personage; and whose life shows that the old legend may have been true, and this Arthur is not unfortunate in his lady, " with a softening voice, and deepening blush on her averted face.

"Have you never heard the story of the lost girl? who less than a year ago, bewildered and distracted, wandered away into the endless woods, in the night, mid darkness and storm; and who, o'ercome with fright and weariness and cold, lay down to die, and was covered over with snow; and that a young man with strength and courage, was conducted by God to her rescue, and carried her over an icy stream, and revived and restored her to her father and mother. Did you ever hear of that? " Her voice was low, deep, and earnest. He bowed.

"My father gave him this horse, and he gave him to me, and I gave him that young man's name. Prince is a prince among horses, and that youth is a prince among men, " proudly, and with increasing color.

"I thought that young man's name was Bart Ridgeley, " very much disgusted.

"Arthur Barton Ridgeley. Prince bears his first name, and he bears me; " lowering her voice and turning away.

"A very pleasant arrangement, no doubt, " querulously.

"Very pleasant to me, " very sweetly.

"It seems to me I have heard something else about this Arthur Barton Ridgeley, Esq. ; and not quite so much to his credit. " Oh dear! But then he was hardly responsible.

"I presume you have. And you heard it with the same ears with which you hear everything disconnected with your precious self. Were their acuteness equal to their length, you would also have heard, that in this, as in everything else, he was true and noble. " The voice was shaken a little by two or three emotions, and tears sprang to her eyes and dried there.

When Thorndyke recovered, they had reached Judge Markham's gate; and springing unaided from her saddle, Julia turned to him with all her grace and graciousness fully restored.

"Many thanks for your escort, Mr. Thorndyke. I shall expect you at eight. "

At about that hour, a boy from Parker's brought her the following note:

"THURSDAY EVENING.

"*Miss Markham*: —Pardon, if you can, my rudeness of this afternoon. Kindly remember the severity of my punishment. Believe me capable of appreciating a heroic act; and the womanly devotion that can alone reward it. From my heart, I congratulate you.

"With the profoundest respect.

"W. THORNDYKE. "

As she read, a softer light, almost a mist, came into the eyes of the young girl.

"I fear I have done this man a real injustice. "

CHAPTER XLVII.

THE TRIAL

The March term of the Court at Chardon was at the beginning of its third and last week. The important case in ejectment of Fisk *vs.* Cole, was reached at the commencement of the second, and laid over for the absence of defendant's counsel. This directly involved the title of Cole to his land; a title that had been loosely talked about, and generally supposed to be bad.

In the fall of 1837, a stranger by the name of Fisk appeared in the country, placed a deed of the land in question on record; gave Cole notice to quit, commenced his suit, and leisurely proceeded to take his evidence in Conn, and Mass., and get ready for the trial. Bart's trial of Coles's first case had rendered the latter an object of interest; and it was generally felt that the new case was one of great oppression and hardship; and popular opinion and sympathy were wholly with Cole, and all the more so, as the impression was that he would lose his land.

The people of Newbury, however, really believed that if Bart would return and take the case in hand, in some way, he would win it; but the Court had commenced, the case was called, and he still lingered in the East. In the spring before he left Newbury, he had spent much time in examining the case, looking up the witnesses, and with such aid as his brother, the Colonel, could give, their names had been obtained and they were all subpoenaed to attend. Among them were two or three old hunters and soldiers, on the Western frontier.

Ford was in the case, and had made up the issue, and at the trial, Bart had intended to secure the aid of Wade or Hitchcock. Except himself, no one knew much of the case, and none had confidence that Cole would prevail in the trial, and a general feeling of despondency prevailed as to his prospect. On the afternoon of the third Monday, Bart reached Chardon, from Albany, secured a room, assembled his witnesses, talked up the matter with the old hunters, and by his quiet, modest confidence, and quick, ready knowledge of all the details, he at once put a new aspect upon the defence. Wade was also in Chardon, and on that evening, Bart laid his programme before him and Ford, who were not more than half convinced, and it was arranged that Bart should go forward with the case, to be backed and sustained by his seniors.

On the next morning he made his first appearance in Court, and in person, air and manner, he had become one to arrest attention, in a crowd, such as thronged the court room; and when his name transpired, he was at once identified as a prominent person in the detection and arrest of Brown & Co., whose name had become widely known; and men scanned him with unusual interest. Some noticed and commented upon the brown moustache, that shaded the rather too soft and bland mouth; and observed the elegant tone of his dress, which, when it was examined, resolved itself rather into the way his clothes were worn. Ford introduced him to the lawyers present, with whom his quiet, modest manner deepened the impression made by his person. As he took his seat, his eye fully met the eager gaze of Judge Markham, from the bench. Bart felt the earnest, anxious look of the Judge, and the Judge thought he saw a shadow of sadness in the frank eyes of Bart.

A case on trial ran until late in the afternoon, when Fisk *vs.* Cole was called, was ready, and a jury sworn. Mr. Kelly, of Cleveland, appeared for the plaintiff, a very accomplished lawyer and a courteous gentleman. He produced the record of the old Conn. Land Co., an allotment and map of the lands showing that the tract in dispute was originally the property of one John Williams. He then made proof of the death of Williams, and that certain parties were his heirs-at-law; and produced and proved a deed from these to the plaintiff. This made what lawyers call a paper title, when the plaintiff rested his case.

For the defendant, Barton said he would produce and prove a deed from John Williams, junior, only child of Williams, mentioned by the plaintiff, to the defendant, directly, dated January, 1816, under which he took possession of the land in January, 1817; and that he also found a man in possession of the premises, who had possessed and claimed the land for years, and whose right he purchased. It would thus appear, whatever might be said of his written title, that he had complete right by possession, adverse to the plaintiff, for twenty years.

"You will do well if you sustain that claim, " said Kelly, incredulously.

"I shall labor for your commendation, " was Bart's pleasant reply.

The deed was proven, as well as the relationship of John and John, Jr. Bart also produced a book of the Probate records of Geauga County, which he said contained a record of the administration of one Hiram Fowler, which he might want to refer to, for a date, thereafter, and if the Court would permit, he would refer to, if it became necessary. He wished the record to be considered in evidence, for what it was competent to prove.

"Certainly, " from the Court, who made a note of it.

He then proved that Cole left Massachusetts early in the spring of 1817, but failed to show when he reached Ohio, whether in 1817, or 1818. One man remembered to have seen Hiram Fowler at work for him on a tree fence, along the back line of it, during the summer of his arrival on the land. He also made proof, that at a very early day, tree fences were about at least three sides of the land, thus forming a cattle range, and evidencing possession and occupancy. He then called McConough, of Bainbridge, and men bent eagerly forward to gaze at the old Indian hunter, who had been a sharp-shooter on the ill-fated "Lawrence, " in Perry's sea fight, off Put-in-Bay, and who was also with Gen. Harrison at the Thames; a quiet, compact, athletic, swarthy man, a little dull and taciturn. He said he was first on the ground in 1810 or 1811, and found a man by the name of Basil Windsor, who lived in a small cabin by the spring, near which he had then two small apple trees. He was there again, with John Harrington, in 1816. They drove a herd of elk through an opening, into and through Basil's yard, at the south side, and back into the woods north, until they came to a tree fence, when they turned east, and were headed off by another hedge, and the elk were too tired to get over; and there in the angle they killed two or three, when it came on dark. That Harrington lit a fire, staid by the slaughtered elk through the night, to keep the wolves from devouring them, and that he, McConough, went and staid with Basil. That Basil was a sort of hermit, who lived in the woods and kept two or three cows. That on their way to Court a few days ago, he and Harrington went to the premises of Cole, and found his house near the old Basil spring, and that one of the apple trees was still standing there. The other had been recently cut down.

Harrington, a still more celebrated hunter and pioneer, and who furnished a good idea of old Leatherstocking, and who was with

Winchester at the battle of River Raisin, from which he escaped, and was one of Harrison's scouts, had been often at Basil Windsor's. Hunters often found shelter there. He was there both before and after the war; and he fully corroborated McConough.

Old Bullock was then called, a heavy-framed, sluggish giant, of that strong, old-fashioned type of head and face, now nearly out of date. He, too, had served in the army, and was a famous hunter and trapper.

He knew Basil, a man who avoided others, and who had met with misfortunes "down country. " "He had hunted and trapped all through the woods about him, and knew of his having had fences to confine his cows. Knew Cole; he came in in 1817, 18 or 19, couldn't tell which. Cole showed him his deed; went with him to find his land, and found it was the same on which Basil was living. Went with him to see Basil, who thought it was hard. He said that the land was his'n. He had a hundred and sixty acres; showed no deed or writin's. Cole finally bought him out—his right, and 'betterments; ' and gave him a horse and harness, and we went down to Square Punderson's, to git writin's made, and he wa'n't to home, and none was made. Basil took the horse and left, and Cole moved into the old cabin. I knew about the slash fences, and ketched a spotted fawn once, hid in one on 'em. I used to cross over by the big maples, by the spring run, where Coles's two children were buried, to go to my traps. "

Bullock was put under a sharp cross-examination, but his story was not shaken. He had a plenty of good-natured, lazy force, and took care of himself. A witness brought in a short section of one of the apple trees, which had twenty-nine rings showing its age, which made a sensation.

Several other witnesses swore that when they were boys, they used to hunt for cattle, on the bottoms, to the north of Cole's land, and often got on to the old tree fences, to listen for the cow-bells. And Bart rested his case.

One branch of this defence looked ugly. The defendant had not clearly proven that he in person took possession of the land in time to perfect his title by adverse possession. But he had shown another man in possession, of some of the property, at least, and claiming it, and he had purchased this right, whatever it was, had gone in under him, and so succeeded to his possession, and right, if he had any.

This took the plaintiff by surprise, and when the defendant rested, he and his counsel were on the alert to meet it. A note came in from the outside, and the plaintiff and his counsel retired under leave of the Court, for consultation. Meanwhile Judge Markham and the President, who had taken much interest in the case, engaged in an earnest conversation. Then Judge Markham came down from the bench, and calling Bart to him, shook him warmly by the hand, and introduced him to Judge Humphrey, and his associates. All of which the jury observed.

Upon resuming the case, the plaintiff produced his depositions, and proved that the defendant's grantor, John Williams, Junior, was the reputed natural son of Williams, of the Land Company, &c. ; also called witnesses to show that Cole came into the county in 1818. An attempt was then made to impeach Bullock, which failed. Ward was then put on the stand, and swore that he met Basil Hall, on a certain time, who told him that he had no claim, right or title to the land whatever. He also swore that he saw Hiram Fowler at work, mending the tree fence, on the north, the summer that Cole came in.

Bart, who had evinced rare skill in the examination of his own witnesses—a more difficult thing, by the way, than to cross-examine those of an adversary—put him through a sharp and stinging cross-examination. Under pretence of testing his memory, and of showing bias, he took him over the whole course, and it appeared that if he ever had the conversation he claimed with Basil, it must have been after his sale to Cole; and got from him such damaging statements, that it could be fairly claimed to the jury that the whole case was prosecuted in the interest of Ward. If so, this would exclude his testimony wholly. This was in the dark legal days, when not only were parties excluded from giving evidence, but a pecuniary interest in the result of the suit to the value of one mill, would render a man incompetent as a witness.

Ward had not expected to appear as a witness at all, and though a shrewd man, he came upon the stand not well knowing the legal ground he was upon; and the questions came so thick upon each other, that they fairly took his breath. If plaintiff objected to a question, it was at once withdrawn, and another instantly put, so that he was rather confused, than aided, by his counsel's interference.

It was certainly a relief to both Kelly and Ward, when the latter, tattered and battered, was permitted, with the ironical thanks of Bart, to retire; and the plaintiff's rebutting evidence closed. Bart called two or three to sustain Bullock, and rested also. This was near the close of Wednesday.

Mr. Kelly then arose, and delivered the opening of the final argument to the jury, contenting himself with presenting his own case. He only glanced at the case of defense, and said he would reserve full argument on this, as he might, until he had heard from the other side. As Bart arose to commence, the Court said:

"Mr. Ridgeley, we will hear you in the morning. Mr. Sheriff, adjourn the Court until to-morrow morning. "

CHAPTER XLVIII.

THE ADVOCATE.

At the opening of the Court on Thursday, the court room was crowded. The interest in the case was general, and the character of the facts, and principal witnesses for the defense, was such as appealed powerfully to the memories and early associations of the people, and there was an earnest desire to hear the speech of the young advocate, whose management of the case had so far, won for him the heartiest admiration.

When the jury had answered to their names, "Mr. Ridgeley, proceed with your argument, " said Judge Humphrey. The young man rose, bowed to the Court and jury, and stood silent a moment, with his eyes cast down, and it was at first thought on his rising for his speech, that he was laboring under embarrassment. When he raised his eyes, however, embarrassed as he certainly was, and commenced with a low sweet voice, it was discovered that his faltering was due mainly to the emotions of sensibility. Nature had been liberal in bestowing many of the qualifications of a great advocate upon him. He had a strong compelling will, when he chose to exercise it, which in the conflicts of the bar often prevails, and courage of a chivalrous cast, which throws a man impetuously and audaciously upon strong points, and enables him to gain a footing by the boldness and force of his onset. Barton was one to lead a forlorn hope, or defend a pass single handed, against a host. Without something of this quality, a great advocate is impossible.

With a warm, poetic imagination, Nature had given him quick perceptive powers, and the faculty of expressing his thoughts without apparent effort, in simple, strong language, as well defined, and sharply cut as a cameo. Beyond this, and better than all, was a tender, sympathetic sensibility; which, if it sometimes overmastered him, made him the master of others. The commonest things in his hands took the motion and color of living things. It was not the mere sensuous magnetism of powerful physical nature; but it excited the higher intellectual sympathies, which in turn awoke and captivated the reasoning and reflective organs, that found themselves delightfully conducted along a natural and logical course, that led them unconsciously to inevitable conclusions and convictions, ere the danger was perceived, or an alarm was sounded.

On the present occasion, he had not been on his feet five minutes ere it was felt that a real power, of an unusual order, was manifesting itself.

The case was not one framed or arranged with any vulgar reference to a forensic display. Cases never will get themselves up for any such occasion; and if the lawyer waits for such a case, he will die unknown. Cases spring out of dry, hard contentions, with nothing but vulgar surroundings; and it is to these, that the real advocate applies himself, breathes upon them the breath of genius and creative power, and clothes them with life, and interest, and beauty, endows them with his own soul and imagination, and lifts them from the level of the common to the height of the remarkable, the unusual, and sometimes of the wonderful; and endeavors to establish between them, and a jury and himself, the bonds of intense sympathy, upon which their emotions and sensibilities will come and go, as did the angels on the dream-ladder of the patriarch.

In the advocate's hour of strength and glory, the formulas of the law burst their mouldy cerements and leap forth into life, tender and beautiful to protect, or awful to warn or punish. Mysteries are unfolded, secrets reveal themselves, hidden things are proclaimed, and courts and juries, awed and abashed, yet elevated and inspired, accept and act upon his conclusions as infallible. For one hour he touches the pinnacle of human achievement.

After all, the effectiveness of the advocate is not so much in what he says, as in the way he says it. One man with real strength arises outside, and batters and bangs with real power, deals forcible blows, and yet does not carry his point; while another, with less intellect, gets up within the charmed circle of the sympathies, by the warm, human side of a jury, whom they don't think of resisting, and could not if they tried.

The speaker usually rises a little outside of the subject, on a sort of neutral ground, and Bart made the transit of this, naturally and simply. He graphically explained to the jury those legal phantoms, John Doe and Richard Roe; how Richard was always maltreating and dispossessing John, and how John was always going to law with Dick, and was hence an immense favorite with lawyers; and how, when Dick is sued, he always, having got up a muss, notifies the actual party in possession, and who ought to have been sued; tells him he must look out for himself, and hurries off to find where John has squat himself into other property; and thereupon he thrusts him out again, and so on. It was a fiction invented by the English lawyers to try the right of two parties to the possession of real estate; because they could do it in no other way, and the 4th of July had not freed us from this relic of antiquity. The issue here was, whether Fisk had a better right to the possession of this land, than had Cole; and whatever did not in some way help to enlighten them on that issue, had no business to be said at all.

In a few happy strokes, he sketched the defendant buying this land, packing up, bidding adieu to the dear down-country home, and his toilsome journey into the woods, arrival, and purchase, and poor, hard life of toil and deprivation: here was his all. He sketched the plaintiff as a well or ill-to-do gentleman, of a speculative turn of mind, whose eye coveted the rich bottom-lands of the defendant; and finding him helpless and poor, searched out the weak place in his title, hunted up obscure relatives, and procured for a song sung by themselves, their signatures to a deed of property of which they had never heard; he had proven that John Williams, Junior, son of John Williams, Senior, was born out of wedlock, had gone grubbing back into forgotten burying-places, and disinterred the dead, searched out the weakness of their lives; had raked out a forgotten scandal, carefully gathered it up in its rottenness, and had poured it out, before the jury; and the frailty and infamy of an unhappy woman, and the crime of one wretched man, were the sole virtue and strength of his case—sole source of his title to the land in dispute. And the plaintiff demanded that the law in its honor should now rob poor Cole of his homestead, and of the graves of his children, that John Fisk—or rather, Sam Ward—might possess that to which he had just the same moral right, that Dr. Myers had to the horses he stole. And this learned Court, and gentlemen of the jury, pioneers in these receding woods, are to be the instruments of this transfer.

The language was simple and plain, the imagery bold and striking, and the closing sentences were pronounced with great fervor. The jury shrank from the issue, which might have a possible conclusion, and looked eagerly for any escape, as jurors will.

The young advocate clearly opened out the nature of the defence of adverse possession, and the philosophy upon which it rested; and explained that the defendant, to meet the plaintiff's paper case, must show that he and those under whom he claimed, had been in the open, continued, and notorious possession of the property for twenty years, before suit was brought, claiming to be the owners. This the defendant was to show, at the peril of destruction; and in a few happy sentences he brought the jury to feel an intense anxiety that he should succeed.

Then he turned back the years, blotted out the highways, re-planted the forests, till the court house dissolved, and a wondrous maple wood crowned the hill on which it stood. And so back, till the Indians returned, and elk and panthers roamed at will. Then he pointed out a sorrow-stricken, moody, brooding man, seeking a "lodge in the vast wilderness, " hunting the spring, and building his shanty, making his clearing, and planting a few apple seeds, brought from his old home; and picking up the section of the tree trunk, he read off from its end, "twenty-nine years ago! "

He sketched in rapid, natural lines, the life of the recluse, the necessities of his situation, his keeping cows, and the means of restricting their range; dwelt upon the evidence of the tree fences, and argued that the fact that two of them were used for that purpose, was conclusive that the other sides were also fenced, for without them no enclosure could exist. And he referred to the well known universal custom of that early day.

Lord! how those old and somewhat mythical tree fences grew, and came out under his hands! The hunters had herded elk in their angles; bears had been trapped in their jungles; the doe hid her fawn in their recesses; wolves and foxes had found lairs in them; birds had built nests in them; men in search of strayed cattle had climbed upon them to listen for the tinkling bell; balm and thyme, wild sun-flowers and celandine had made them fragrant with perfume, and bright with color.

Basil Hall went to that spring, and built and occupied, because he owned it. His very settlement and occupancy was a proclamation of ownership—an assertion of right—the most satisfactory, and so the Court would say. Here he read from the Ohio Reports, to show that a parol claim, without any written color of title, was sufficient to make the claim. He then referred to the evidence of Bullock, that Hall did by word claim such right; that the claim was acknowledged by Cole, who bought and paid for it. If Hall had been without claim of right, Cole would have turned him out; but he acknowledged it, bought, got it, and held it. The word of Ward could not be taken; he was interested; if taken, it could not be believed; if believed, it proved nothing, for the admission of Hall to him, that he had no right, was made after Hall had sold out, and hence not evidence against the purchaser, all of which he forcibly illustrated; and the proposition was conceded to be law. He claimed that this defence under the purchase from Hall, was perfect in itself.

His defence of Bullock from the attack on him, was forcible and beautiful. The old man was a hunter, had been a soldier, etc., and the unforgotten Indian battles of the recent war flashed before the jury, and all the sylvan romance of a hunter's life was reproduced as by magic.

In the second place he contended that Cole made an absolute defense on his claim of title under his deed; no matter though John Williams, Junior, was the bastard of a bastard; his deed was good to make a claim of title under, by the common law of England, and that of every State of the United States; and he read authorities to the Court.

He then showed pretty conclusively that Cole left Connecticut in the spring of 1817, and was not a year and two months on the road; that he came in in 1817, and not in 1818; and this, he said he would demonstrate. John Fowler, Hiram Fowler's son, had sworn positively that his father worked for Cole, repairing the fence on the north. Ward swore to the same; he had told this one bit of truth by some unaccountable accident; so that the plaintiff had also proven that Hiram Fowler had worked for Cole on this land, and hence Cole was in possession of it in the lifetime of Fowler. When did Fowler die?

"Now, " said Bart, "I will read from this probate record, already put in evidence, but not read, " and he opened and read from the record of the Court, begun and held in the court house at Chardon, for the county of Geauga, commencing April 17, 1818, the appointment of an administrator on the estate of "Hiram Fowler, late deceased, of the township of Newbury, in said county, " and closed the book with a clap. "Thus this record of absolute verity declares that Hiram Fowler had died before April, 1818, and the plaintiff and defendant both prove that he was alive, after Cole came into this State. Beyond the possibility of doubt then, Cole came to the possession of this land in 1817, and his title is perfect in law, equity and morality. "

When he closed this part of his case, a murmur almost of open applause ran through the densely packed house. Here he rested the argument.

In a rapid *resume* of the case, he seemed to have stumbled upon the two little grass-grown graves of Cole's children, up under the old maples. He paused, hesitated, faltered, and stopped, tears came to his eyes, and his lips quivered. No art could have produced this effect, and a sob broke from many in the court room. Suddenly resuming, he finished his grouping in a saddened voice, and paused for a moment, sending his eager glance through the court room, till it finally rested on the face of Sam Ward. Looking at him, in half a dozen sentences, he pilloried him for the scorn and derision of the jury; and then turning to them, in a voice of wonderful sweetness, half sad and regretful, he committed the case to them, and sat down.

A great hum like that of swarming bees, ran through the court house, and men who had looked often into each other's eyes, looked again, with a joyous sense of relief.

During some parts of his speech, which occupied an hour and a half, men at times leaned from all parts of the room towards him, open-eyed and open-mouthed. At others they swayed gently to and fro, like tree tops in a breeze; and when he sat down, the oldest at the bar—the President on the bench—felt that it was among the best speeches they had ever heard, if not the best. The youthfulness of the orator of course enhanced its effect. It had some faults of redundancy, both of words and imagery, but its tone and manner were admirable. At times his delivery was very rapid and vehement, but his voice, always rich and full, never broke, or seemed strained; while in the moments of excitement, every nerve and fibre of his form quivered with the intensity of his emotion. His form was lithe and elastic, and admitted of easy, rapid and forcible action, which was never more than was allowable to one of his passionate temperament.

When he closed, almost everybody supposed the case was ended. Wade arose with a radiant face, and said the defense rested the argument on that which had just been delivered.

Kelly was taken by surprise again, both by the quality and force of Bart's speech, and the submission of the case. The first carried him off his feet, and he hoped to recover during the delivery of another on the same side. He was a good chancery and real estate lawyer, but he was not the man to reply to Barton's argument. He followed him, however—that is, he spoke after him, and on the other side, for a half hour, and submitted the case.

The Court gave the case to the jury on the law, as the defense claimed it. Indeed there was no dispute about the law. He explained fully and clearly the case, which arose on the defense; and saying, in a very graceful and gracious way, that the merits of the case had been presented with a force and beauty rarely equalled, and which might tend to aid the jury in coming to their conclusion, he submitted it to them, and took a recess for dinner.

At the recess, the lawyers crowded about Bart to congratulate him for his defense, among whom Kelly was the foremost. Judge Markham came up, and with moisture in his eyes, took him by both hands and drew him away to Judge Humphrey, who complimented him in the highest terms, and insisted upon his dining with him, which invitation Bart accepted. The Judge was as much taken with his modest, quiet, gentlemanly manners, and quick, happy wit, as with his splendid speech in the court room. The fact was, his exertions had fully awakened his intellectual forces, and they were all in the field, armed and with blades drawn. He could not eat, and never drank, save water or milk; and now between the two Judges, and surrounded by lawyers, with a glass of milk and a plate of honey, petted and lionized for the moment, he gave himself up to sparkling and brilliant answers to the numerous questions and remarks addressed to him, and showed that, whatever draft had been made upon him, he had plenty of resources in reserve.

Upon a return to the court house, at half past one, the jury, who had made up and sealed their verdict, were called; it was opened and read, and as anticipated, was for the defendant. This announcement was received with scarcely suppressed applause. The verdict was recorded by the clerk, and in due time followed by the judgment of the Court, and so ended Fisk *vs.* Cole. Cole went out of the court room, with one exception, the most observed man in the crowd.

Very naturally Barton and his last performance was the common theme of conversation in the region round about for many days. All over Newbury, as witnesses and other spectators returned, the whole thing was talked over, with such various eulogies as suited the exaggerated estimate his various admirers put upon his merits.

"What do you say now? " said Uncle Jonah to Uncle Josh, as the two had just listened to an account of the trial, in Parker's bar room.

"It does beat hell amazingly! " answered that accomplished rhetorician.

"What did I tell you? " said Jo, at Jugville, to Uncle Cal, and that set.

"Oh, I was there, " said Uncle Cal. "I always said, ever since the trial here, that he had the stuff in him. But he went beyond anything I ever hearn, " and Uncle Cal relapsed into admiring silence.

CHAPTER XLIX.

WAITING.

Julia sat alone that evening in an elegantly, and, for that day, luxuriously furnished room, around which she had many times glanced, and in which her own hands had several times arranged and re-arranged the various articles. There was a bed in the room, which was large and airy, a vase filled with wild and hot-house flowers; yet it was evidently not a lady's room, and unoccupied save at this moment by the fair Julia, who with an abundance of color in her cheeks and lips, and a liquid light in her eyes, was nevertheless pensive and seemingly not quite at ease. She held two letters in her hands, which she many times re-read. They ran as follows:

"CHARDON, Wednesday P. M.

"*My Dear Wife*: —Barton reached here on Monday P. M. I did not think it best to call upon him, and did not see him till yesterday morning in the court room, when, without looking me in the face save for a second, he bowed to me. He had so changed that I did not at first recognize him, and did not acknowledge his bow as I would. Later, when his case was called and he came to make a remark to the court, he looked me in the eye, calmly and steadily, and I thought I could see in his face regret, the shadow of suffering, and a very kindly, but sad expression, which seemed almost like a revelation.

"He is much changed and improved. The old boyish recklessness and dash is gone. His face is thinner, has much character, and is disfigured, as I think, with a moustache, which gives him the look of a foreigner. He is, of course, well dressed, and has the quiet, high-bred air of a thorough gentleman.

"Judge Humphrey is immensely taken with him, and he has so far managed his case admirably, and like an experienced lawyer. We cannot keep our eyes from him, but watch every word and movement with great interest. Though Wade and Ford are with him, he tries the case alone, thus far.

"I shall see him—if he will see me—as of course he will, the moment he is free from his case.

"Of course you will show this to Julia.

"Ever yours, EDWARD. "

"CHARDON, Thursday P. M.

"*My Dear Wife:* —I cannot in sober language express my astonishment and admiration for Barton's masterly speech this forenoon. As much as I expected from him, I was completely taken by surprise. Judge Humphrey is unbounded in his praises of him; but I will tell you about all this when I return.

"At the recess, among others I went to congratulate him, which was the second time I had been where I could give him my hand. He held out both of his, and seemed unable to speak. As soon as he could extricate himself from the ovation, he went with me to Judge Humphrey, who took him to dine with us. His conversation at the dinner table was more brilliant than his speech. He ate nothing but a little honey, and drank a glass of milk. I confess I was a little alarmed at some of his sallies.

"On our way back to court, I observed he began to grow serious, and I arranged to see him as soon as his case was at an end. The jury returned a verdict for Cole, on the coming in after dinner, and that case, thanks to Bart, is finally ended.

"After this, I left the bench and was joined by Bart. It was difficult for him to escape from the crowd who followed him out; when he did, he joined me, and we walked off down the hill toward Newbury. Bart was evidently depressed. The re-action had come; the great strain of the last three days was removed, and the poor boy was sad and melancholy.

"We went on in silence, I not knowing just how to commence.

"' Judge Markham, ' said he, turning frankly to me, 'you know I am a born fool, and just now I feel like breaking entirely down, and crying like a woman. For these last four years I have lived utterly alone, confiding nothing to any one, and I am too weak to go so, always. '

"Oh, how I wished you had been there, with your sweet woman's heart, and voice, and tact.

"'My dear boy, ' said I, 'if there is anything in the wide world that I can say and do *only let me know what it is. I am more anxious to help you, than you are to be helped, if I only may.* '

"'I don't know how I ought to meet you, Judge Markham. You wrote me a manly letter, full of kindness, and I answered—God knows what—I was so wretched. '

"'I could not blame you, 'I said, 'I am much in fault towards you, but it was from my not knowing you. I regret it very much. '

"'I don't know, ' he answered, 'that you should say that to me. I feel sorry and hurt that anybody should make apologies to me. Why should you have known me"? I did not not know myself, and don't now. I know I can not hate or even dislike anybody, and I always liked you, and I do now. '

"'Barton, ' said I, 'God bless you! you never can have cause of complaint against me or mine again: only give us your confidence, and trust us. '

"'I am sure you are very kind, ' said he, 'and it is very pleasant to hear it said. I want to see Mrs. Markham, and in some way say how grateful I am for her kind expressions towards me, and she and — and you all, have been very kind to my poor dear mother for the past year. '

"'You would not let us be kind to you, ' said I.

"'No. How could I? ' he answered.

"'I don't know, 'said I. 'I only hope now that there may be no more misunderstandings; that you will now let us—will give Julia an opportunity, at least to express her gratitude to you, and that we may all unite in so doing. '

"He was silent a moment, and then went on as if thinking aloud:

267

"'Julia! Good Heavens! how can I ever meet her! —Pardon me; I mean Miss Markham. I shall certainly call upon the ladies at a very early day, ' he said, coldly. 'The fact is, Judge Markham, ' continued he, 'I have been under a little strain, and I am not used to it. I come back here near home, and see so many old Newbury people, who make me forget how they used to dislike me, and all the old, and all the more recent things, come back upon me so strongly, and I find I am as weak and boyish and foolish as ever. '

"He did not say much more—he finally asked about you, and after much hesitation, about Julia. It is so easy to see that his heart is full of her, that I could not help feeling almost wretched for him. I then asked him when he was going to Newbury. He thought of going to-morrow in the stage, but said some parties wanted to see him Friday evening. He has finally consented to wait and ride down with us on Saturday, after the term closes.

"Now, my dear wife, come and bring Julia, if you think it best. I confess I wish that they might meet at an early day—but be governed by your better judgment in this—and you will show her this letter of course.

"Ever, with love and kisses to you both,

EDWARD. "

"Mother, " she said afterwards, "let me suggest that you send up a carriage to-morrow evening, which Papa Judge may take as an invitation to come early on Saturday morning. If Mr. Ridgeley sees me, had he not better find me in my mother's and father's house? "

"*If* he sees you, Julia? "

"Of course if he wishes to, he will. "

And she was not conversational, and wandered about, and if possible would have been a little pettish.

"Are you not glad, Julia, that he has acquitted himself so well? He seems to have carried the Court and jury and all by storm. "

"Of course he did. Does that surprise you? But it is all so stupid, staying there to try that pokey old case. "

"Julia, what under the sun is the matter? " looking at her in surprise.

The girl turned and knelt by her mother, and laid her face down in her lap, and burst into violent sobbings.

On the morrow Julia arose, sweet and composed, with the old light in her eyes, and her wonted color coming and going with the mysterious emotions within. She was almost gay and joyous at breakfast, and then grew fitful and restless, and then became pensive again.

The day was a marvel of the forward spring, and the sun filled the whole heavens with its wondrous light. The blue bird called down in his flight, with his trill of gladness, and the robins flooded the leafless trees and the lawn with gushes of purest melody. Julia could not remain in the house; she could not remain anywhere; and as the morning deepened, she took a sudden resolution and ordered Prince to be saddled at once.

"Mother, " said she, "I have the whole of this long, long day. I must gallop off through the woods, around to Wilder's. I haven't been there since last fall; and then I will come around by Mrs. Ridgeley's and tell her, and so home. Don't gay a word, mother; I must go. I cannot stay here. I'll be back in good time. "

So mounting Prince she bounded off. When she felt herself going with the springy, elastic leap of her splendid steed, she thought she had found what she most wanted—to go to that little blessed nook of shelter and repose under the rocks by the running stream, in the sun. Something seemed to call her, and the day, the rapid motion, the exhilaration of the atmosphere, as she dashed through it, softened her excitement, and a calm, elevated, half-religious extasy possessed her; and the sky and air, and brown, desolate earth, just warming with the April sun, all glowed with hope. How near to her seemed Heaven and all holy, sweet influences; and the centre of it all was one radiant, beautiful face, looking with sad, wistful eyes to her for love and life which she so wanted to give. She felt and knew that to this one in some way, she would be fully revealed, and misconception and absence and doubt would vanish. She should meet him, but just how he would look, or what he would say, or how she should or could answer him, she could not shadow out, and would not try. All that, she was sure, would take care of itself, and he would know and understand her finally.

Prince seemed fully to appreciate the day, and to be inspired with its subtle and exhilarating elixir; but after a mile or two of over-spirit, he sobered down into his long, easy, springy, untiring gallop. They passed the fields and went along the hard and dry highway, till she reached the diverging trail that struck off through the woods toward the settlement on the other side, the nearest house of which was Wilder's.

On she went among the trees, past recently deserted sugar camps, away from human habitations, into and through the heart of the forest, joyous and glad in her beauty and young life and hope, and happy thoughts; and finally she came to the creek; here she drew up her still fresh horse, and rode slowly through its clear, rapid waters, and turned down on its other bank. How glad it seemed, gurgling and rippling, and swirling, with liquid music and motion! Slowly she rode down and with a half timid feeling, as somehow doubting if she would not return. But it was all silent and quiet; the sunshine and the voice of the stream seemed to re-assure her, and the strange feeling passed away, as she entered the little nook so dear to her memory. How silent and empty it was, in the rich, bright light of the mid-forenoon! She dismounted, and taking her skirt upon her arm, was about to step under the rude shed, with the thought of the birds who had reared their young there the year before, when Prince lifted his head with a forward movement of his ears, and turning her eyes down the stream, they fell upon Barton, who had just passed around the lower angle of the rocks, and paused in speechless surprise, within a few feet of her.

With a little cry of joy, she threw out her hands and sprang towards him. Her forgotten skirt tripped her, and she would have fallen, but the quick arms of Barton were about her, and for an exquisite moment she abandoned herself fully to him.

"Oh, Arthur, you have come to me! "

Their lips found each other, the great mass of dark brown hair almost overflowed the light brown curls, and their glad tears mingled.

"Julia! I am alive—awake! and you are in my arms! Your kiss has been on my lips! You love me! "

"With my whole heart and soul! "

"Oh, how blessed to die at this moment! " murmured Bart.

"Would it not be more blessed to live, love? " she whispered.

"And you have always loved me? "

"Always—there—there! " with a touch of her lips at each word.

"I thought—"

"I know you did. You shall never, never think again—there! "

She withdrew from his arms, and adjusted her skirt, and stood by him in her wondrous beauty, radiant with the great happiness that filled her heart.

Barton was still confused, and looked with eyes wide open with amazement, partly at seeing her at all, partly at her marvellous beauty, which to him was seraphic, and more and most of all, at the revelation of her great love.

"Oh Julia! How was this? how is this—this coming of Heaven to me; this marvel of your love? "

"Did you really think, Arthur, that I had no eyes; that I had no ears; that I had no woman's heart? How could you think so meanly of me, and so meanly of yourself? "

"But you so scorned me. "

"Hush! that was your word: it was not true; you were even then in my foolish girl's heart. Don't speak of that to me now; surely you must have known that that was all a mistake. "

"And you always loved me? How wonderful that we should meet here and to-day! " he said, unable to take his eyes from her.

"You know the place and remember the day? Is it more marvellous, than that we should have been here before? I never knew how you found me then, and I am as much puzzled about your being here now. Father wrote us that you would come down with him to-morrow. "

"Tell me how *you* come to be here, to-day, of all the things in the world? " said Bart.

"Am I to tell first? Well, you see, I wanted to see Mrs. Wilder and Rose; I have not been to their house since last fall, and so, having nothing else to do, I rode over, and just thought we would come down here—didn't we, Prince? "

"And so you call him Prince? " said Bart, who had recognized the horse.

"Yes, and I will sometime tell you why, if you will tell me how you came here to-day. "

"I came on purpose, because I wanted to. Because you had hallowed the place, I knew that I should find your haunting presence in it. Oh, when that case was over, and I got out, all the old dreams, and visions, and memories, and voices came to me. And your face never absent, not with the old look of scorn that it seemed to wear, but sweet, and half reproachful, haunted me, and made me half believe what poor Henry's smitten love said to me of you, when I told her my story. "

"Bless her, " murmured Julia.

"And I walked, and mused, and dreamed all the night; and this morning I sent your kind, good father a note, and came off. I came as directly here as I could, and now indeed I believe God sent me. "

His arm was about her, and he held both her hands. The frank confession, so sweet to her, had its immediate reward from her lips.

"Arthur, " she said, "I, too, came to see this place, with its sweet and sacred memories. I have been here three times before. You may know every thought and feeling of my heart. I could not have got through the day without coming: and how blessed I am for coming. Do you remember, when you had done all you could for my rest and comfort, how, on that awful yet precious night, you asked me if I had said a prayer, and I asked you to pray? Do you know that my mother and I both believe that that prayer was answered, and that she was impressed with my safety in answer to it? Oh, how grateful to our Father for his goodness to us we should be. Arthur, can you thank Him for us, now? " And they knelt in the forest solitude, with God and his blessed sun and blue sky, and their two young, pure, loving hearts joined in a fervent outpouring of gratitude.

"Our Father, for the precious and blessed revelation of our hearts, each to the other, we thank Thee. Let this love be as pure, and sacred, and holy, and eternal, as we now feel it to be. Grant, dear Father, that it may be sanctified by holy marriage; and that through Thy gracious providence, this union of hearts and souls may ever be ours. Hear us, thy young, helpless, yet trusting, believing, and loving children. "

And she: "Sweet and blessed Saviour; let Thy precious love and presence be also about us, to keep us, help us, and bless us; and Father, let the maiden's voice also join in the prayer that Thou wilt bless us, as one. "

They arose, and turned to each other, with sweet, calm, restful, happy faces; with souls full of trust and confidence, that was to know no change or diminution.

CHAPTER L.

THE GOSPEL OF LOVE.

Julia pointed out the bird's nest under the roof, and to a faded garland of flowers, hung upon the rough bark of the old hemlock, against which Barton had reclined, and another upon the rock just over where she had rested. In some way these brought to Bart's mind the flowers on Henry's grave; and in a moment he felt that her hand had placed them there; the precious little hand that lay so willingly in his own. Raising it to his lips, he said: "Julia, this same blessed hand has strewn my poor dear brother's grave with flowers."

"Are you glad, Arthur? "

"Oh, so glad, and grateful! And the same hand wrote me the generous warning against that wretched Greer? "

"Yes, Arthur. Father came home from that first trial distressed about you, and I wrote it. I thought you would not know the hand. "

"I did not—though when your letter came to me in Jefferson, the address reminded me of it. But I did not think you wrote it. And when rumors were abroad of my connection with these men, after I went to Albany, who was it who sent somebody to Ravenna, to get a contradiction from Greer, himself? "

"No one sent anybody: some one went, " in the lowest little voice.

"Oh, Julia! did you go, yourself? "

"Yes. "

"With the love of such a woman, what may not a man do? " cried Bart, with enthusiasm. "Julia, I suspect more—that I owe all and everything to you. "

"You saved my life, Arthur, and will you not take little things from me? "

"I owe you for all the love and happiness of all my future, Julia, and for the stimulus that has made me work these three years. You love me; and love takes from love, and gives all it can and has, and is content. "

"Bless you, Arthur! " and affecting to notice the passage of the sun towards the meridian—she turned to him a little anxiously—"What time is it, Arthur? "—as if she cared! He told her, and she extended her hand and took the watch, and toyed with it a moment; "it is a pretty watch, open it, please, " which he did. Looking at it intently, with heightened color, she pointed with the rosy tip of a finger, to an almost hidden inscription, which Bart had never seen before, and which he saw were letters spelling "Julia. " He started up amazed, and for the moment trembled.

"Oh, Julia! all that I have and am, the food I have eaten, the clothes I wear, all came from you! Old Windsor is a fraud—an instrument—and I have carried your blessed name these long months, not knowing it. "

"Arthur, 'you love me, and love takes from love. It gives all it has and can, and is content. ' It is a blessed gospel, Arthur. Think how much I owe you—gladly owe you; —the obligation was not a burthen; but you would not even let me express my gratitude. Think of your dreadful letter. When you knelt and prayed for me, I would have put my lips to yours, had you been near me. I let you see my very heart in every line I wrote you, and you turned from me so coldly, and proudly, and blindly, and I could see you were so unhappy. Oh, I would not have been worthy to be carried a step in your arms, if I had not done the last thing in my power. I went and saw Mr. Wade, and father promised me the money, and Mr. Wade arranged it all for me; and dear, blessed Mr. Windsor is not a fraud; he loves you himself, and loved your brother. "

"Forgive me, forgive me, Julia, " said Bart, who had sunk on the leaves at her feet, and was resting his head against her bosom, with one arm of hers about his neck; "and this watch? "

"That I purchased and had engraved, and perhaps—what would you have done had you seen my name? "

"Come straight to you at once. "

"And you are content? "

"Perfectly; you love me, and I accept the gospel of love, " and he looked up with his clear, open brow and honest, transparent eyes, and gazing down into them and into the depths of his soul, seeming to see great happiness, dimmed a little with regret, she bent her head and put her lips to his, and tears fell from her eyes once again upon his face.

"Arthur, " again lifting her head, "how glad I am that this is all told you now, when you are tenderest to me, and I have no secret to carry and fear, nothing to do now but to make you happy, and be so happy. Sometime, soon, you will tell me all your precious heart history, keeping nothing from me. "

"Everything, everything, Julia! and something I may say now —I don't want to leave this sweet, sacred place, without a word about my letter. It was written in utter hopelessness of your love. The occurrences of that strange night had replaced me within the reach of my own esteem. "

"How had you ever lost that, Arthur? "

"By my own folly. I loved you when I came back—before I went away—always. It was a dream, a sweet, delicious dream—that inspired poetry, and kindled ambition, but was purely unselfish. I had not a thought or a hope of a return. This passion came to possess me, to occupy my mind, and absorb my whole being. I knew it could not in the nature of things be returned. "

"Arthur! "

"And I rushed into your presence, and declared it, and received what I expected and needed—though it paralyzed me, but my pride came to my rescue, and what strength I had; I went away humiliated, and aroused myself and found places on which I could stand, and strength to work. So far as you were concerned, Julia, I only hoped that in the far future, if you ever recalled my mad words—"

"That did not fall in the dust under my feet, and were not forgotten, sir, " interrupted Julia.

"Thank you, dearest—but if they should come to you, you would feel that they had not insulted you. I avoided you, of course, and had to avoid your mother. I would not see you, but you were ever about me, and became an inspiring power. I burned all the sketches I had made of you, but one, and that I mislaid. "

"I found it. I am glad you lost it, you naughty child. "

"Did you? Well, I went through the winter and spring, and the awful calamity of Henry's death, and the next fall and winter, and you wore away, and although I might not see you, your absence made Newbury a desert. And I felt it, when you came back. And when I got ready to go I could not. I set the time, sent off my trunk, and lingered. I even went one night past your father's house, only to see where you were, and yet I lingered; I found flowers on my brother's grave, and thought that some maiden loved him. "

"When she loved you. "

"That Wednesday night I would go, but couldn't. "

"Tell me all that happened to you that night; it is a mystery to us all; you did not even tell your mother. "

"It is not much. I had abandoned my intention of going that night, and was restless and uneasy, when George rushed in and told me you were lost. He had learned all that was known, and told it very clearly. I knew of the chopping, and where the path led up to it, and I thought you would tarn back to the old road, and might enter the woods, on the other side. Everything seemed wonderfully clear to me. My great love kindled and aroused every faculty, and strung every nerve. I was ready in a moment. George brought me two immense hickory torches, that together would burn out a winter night; and with one of our sugar camp tapers. I lighted one, as I went. I must have reached the point where you left the old road, in ten minutes. I was never so strong, I seemed to know that I would find you, and felt that it was for this I had staid, and blamed myself for the selfish joy I felt, that I could serve and perhaps save you.

"I examined the old road, and in one wet place, I found your track going north, and a little further was the old path, that led to the slashing. At the entrance to it, the leaves had been disturbed, as if by footsteps; I saw many of them, and thought you had become lost, and would follow the path; so I went on. When I reached the slashing, I knew you would not enter that, but supposed you would skirt around on the east and south side, as the path led southwesterly to it. Of course I looked and searched the ground, and could occasionally see where a footfall had disturbed the leaves.

"I concluded that sooner or later, you would realize that you were lost; and then—for I knew you were strong and brave—would undertake to strike off toward home, without reference to anything; and I knew, of course, that you would then go exactly the wrong way, because you were lost. After skirting about the slashing, I could find no foot-marks in the leaves; and I struck out southerly, and in a little thicket of young beeches and prickly ash, hanging to a thorn, I found your hood. Oh, God! what joy and thankfulness were mine; and there in the deep leaves, going westerly, was your trail. "

"I thought I saw that awful beast, just before I reached that place, and fled, not knowing where, " said Julia.

"Did you call, Julia? "

"I had called before that, many times. "

"You were too far to be heard by your father and friends; and I was too late to hear you. I called several times, when I found the hood. Of course no answer came, and following the trail where it could be seen, I went on. I missed it often, and circled about until I found it, or something like it, always bearing away deeper and deeper into the wood. Then the wind blew awfully, and the snow began to sift down. My first torch was well burned out, and I knew I had been out some hours. I lighted the other and went on; soon I struck this creek, and fancied that you, if you had reached it, would follow it down. "

"I did. "

"Soon after, at a soft place where a little branch came in, I found your tracks again, several of them; and I knew I was right, and was certain I should find you. In my great joy, I thanked God, with my whole heart. It was storming fearfully; and trees were cracking, and breaking, and falling, in the fury of the wind. I called, but I knew nobody could hear me a dozen rods away. It had become intensely cold, and I feared you would become exhausted and fall down, and perhaps perish ere I could reach you. I hurried on, looked by every tree and log, calling and searching. I don't know where I struck the creek, though I knew every rood of the woods: I am, as you know, a born woodsman, and know all wood craft. Although I was certain I would find you, I began to grow fearfully anxious, and almost to doubt. As I went I called your name, and listened. Finally a faint sound came back to me, and I sprang forward—when you rose partly up before me. Oh, God! oh, God! " and his voice was lost in emotion. "For one moment I was overcome, and did, I know not what, save that I knelt by you and kissed your hands. Their chilly touch recalled me. I felt that I had saved you not only for your father and mother, but for your pure self, and to be the bride of some unknown man; and I was resolved that no memory of yours, and no thought of his, should ever occasion a blush for what should occur between us. "

"How noble and heroic you were—"

"You know all that happened after. "

"And in your anxiety to save me from myself, you would not even let me thank you. And when I slept, you stole away. "

"What could I do. Julia? I had saved you, I had redeemed myself; and found a calm, cold peace and joy in which I could go. In view of what had happened between us before, how hard and embarrassing for you to meet and thank me, and I feared to meet you. It was better that I should go, and with one stolen look at your sweet, sleeping face, I went. "

"Arthur, my poor best will I do to repay you for all your pain and anguish. "

"Am I not more than repaid, proud and happy? It was for the best. I needed to suffer and work; and yet how blessed to have carried the knowledge of your love with me! "

"Oh, I wanted to whisper it to you, to have you know; and I was unhappy because I knew you were, " she murmured.

"My poor letter in answer to yours I fear was rude and proud and unmanly. What could I say? The possibility that I could be more than a friend to you never occurred to me, and when Ida tried to persuade me that you did love me, her efforts were vain; I could hardly induce her to abandon the idea of writing you. "

"There is a blessed Providence in it all, Arthur; and in nothing more blessed than in bringing us together here, where we could meet and speak, with only the sunshine and this bright stream for witnesses. "

"And what a sweet little story of love and hope and joy it carries murmuring along! " said Bart, struck with the poetry of her figure.

"But we must not always stay here, " said the practical woman. "We must go home, must not we, Prince? " addressing the horse, which had stood quietly watching the lovers, and occasionally looking about him.

"You have changed his name? " said Bart.

"Yes. You see he is your horse, and I called him Prince Arthur the very day I received him, which was the day your letter came. I call him Prince. He is a prince—and so is his namesake, " she added, playfully pulling his moustache. "You don't like that? " said Bart; "the moustache? I can cut it away in a moment. "

"I do like it, and you must not cut it away. Stand out there, and let me have a good look at you; please turn your eyes away from me—there so. "

"You find me changed, " he said, "and I find you more lovely than ever, " rushing back to her.

"You spoilt my view, sir. "

"You will see enough of me, " he said, gaily.

"You are changed, " she went on, "but I like you better. Now, sir, here is your horse. I deliver you, Prince, to your true lord and master; and you must love him, and serve him truly. "

"And I have already dedicated you to your lady and mistress, " said Bart, "and you must forever serve her. "

"And the first thing you do, will be to carry Wilder down to my dear mother, with a letter—how blessed and happy she will be! —asking her to send up a carriage—unless you have one somewhere? "

"Me? I haven't anything anywhere, but you. A carriage brought me into this region, and I sent it back. Keep and ride the Prince, as you call him; I can walk. I've done it before. "

"You shall never do it again; if you do I will walk with you. We will go to Wilder's, and see Mrs. Wilder, who is a blessed woman, and who knew your secret, and knows mine; and Rose, who took me into her bed; and we will have some dinner, unromantic ham and eggs; and when the carriage comes, I will drive you to your mother's, and then you shall drive me home—do you understand? "

"Perfectly; and shall implicitly obey. Do you know, I half suspect this is all a dream, and that I shall wake up in Albany, or Jefferson, or somewhere? I know I am not in Chardon, for I could not sleep long enough to dream there. "

"Why? "

"I was too near Newbury, and under the spell of old feelings and memories; and I don't care to sleep again. "

As they were about to leave the dear little nook, "Arthur, " said Julia, "let us buy a bit of this land, and keep this little romantic spot from destruction. " So they went out through the trees in the warm sun, Bart with Prince's bridle in his hand, and Julia with her skirt over one arm and the other in that of her lover.

"I hold tightly to your arm, " said Bart, laughing, "so that if you vanish, I may vanish with you. "

"And I will be careful and not go to sleep while we are at Wilder's, for fear you will steal away from me, you bad boy. If you knew how I felt when I woke and found you had gone—"

"I should not have gone, " interrupted Bart.

Thus all the little sweet nothings that would look merely silly on paper, and sound foolish to other ears, yet so precious to them, passed from one to the other as they went.

Wilder had eaten his dinner, and lounged out into the sun, with his pipe, as they walked up. He knew Julia, of course, and Prince, and looked hard at Bart, as they passed; when the comely wife came running out.

"Oh, " she exclaimed, taking Julia's hand, "and this—this is Mr. Ridgeley. "

"It is indeed, " said Bart, brightly.

"And you are not—not—Oh! your two hearts are happy I see it in both your faces. I am so glad. "

Julia bent and kissed her.

"Oh, I knew when he went off so heart-broken, that it wasn't your fault, and I always wished I had kept him. "

Sweet, shy, blushing Rose came forward, and Bart took her hands and hoped she would look upon him as an older brother long absent, and just returned. And little lisping George, staring at him curiously, "Are you Plinth Arthur? "

"Prince Arthur? " cried Bart, catching him up, "do I look like a prince? "

"Yeth. "

"Take that, " said Bart, laughing, giving him a gold coin.

"He is a prince, " said Julia, "and you see he gives like a prince. "

"Exactly, " answered Bart; "princes always give other peoples' gold for flattery. "

"And now, Mr. Wilder, I want you to put your saddle on Prince, and gallop straight to my mother, and drive back a carriage. I found this unhappy youth wandering about in these same woods, and I am going to take him with me this time. "

When Wilder was ready, she gave him the following note:

"*Dear Mother*: —I am so blessed and happy. Arthur and I met this morning in the dear old nook under the rocks, and we are the happiest two in the world.

"JULIA.

"P. S. I forgot. Send a carriage by Wilder. I don't want a driver. We will go round by Arthur's mother's, and be with you this evening. J.

"P. S. Send me a skirt. "

And whether the sun stood still or journeyed on, they did not note, nor could they remember what Mrs. Wilder gave them for dinner, or whether they tasted it. At last Wilder appeared with a light carriage and pair. Julia's saddle was put on board, and the lovers, Julia holding the reins, drove away.

CHAPTER LI.

THE RETURN.

Spring came with its new life and promise, sweetly and serenely to the home and heart of Barton's mother, who was looking and hoping for his return, with a strong, intense, but silent yearning. For herself, for his brothers, and more for Julia, whom she now understood, and tenderly loved, and whose secret was sacred to her woman's heart; and most of all for Barton's own sake; for she knew that when these two met, the shadow that had surrounded them would disappear. Some pang she felt that there should be to him a dearer one; but she knew that Julia did not come between them, and that nothing would chill that side of his heart—the child side—that was next her own.

On Wednesday morning Julia had galloped up and given her Bart's letter of Tuesday, so that she knew he was in Chardon, well and hopeful, and would return to her as soon as he escaped from his trial.

Thursday evening Dr. Lyman came all aglow from Chardon. He had seen Bart and heard his argument, and all the enthusiasm of his nature was fully excited.

Now on this long, warm Friday—the anniversary of his departure—he was to come; and naturally enough she looked to see him come the way he went—from the east. Often, even before noon, she turned her eyes wistfully down the road, and until it met the rise the other side of the little valley, so on up past the red school house, and was lost over the summit; but the road was empty and lonely.

As the afternoon ran toward evening, she began to grow anxious. Suddenly the sound of wheels caught her ear, and she turned as Judge Markham's grays headed up to her gate. She recognized Julia, who, without waiting to be helped, sprang lightly from the carriage, with her face radiant, and bounding to her threw her arms about her neck.

"Oh, mother—my mother now—he is here. I met him in those blessed woods and brought him to you. "

Then she made room for him, and for a moment the mother's arms encircled them both. How glad and happy she was, no man may know; as no man understands, and no woman can reveal, the depth and strength of mother love.

The three in happy tears—tears, that soon vanish, went into the dear old house, into whose every room Bart rushed in a moment, calling for the boys, and asking a thousand unanswered questions, and coming back, with a flood of words, half tears and half laughs.

"So, Bart, " said the proud and happy mother, "it is all right, " with a look towards Julia. "I knew it would be. "

"And, mother, you knew it, too? "

"A woman sees where a man is blind, sometimes, " she answered. "And boys must find these things out for themselves. Poor boy, I wanted somebody to whisper it to you. "

"Somebody has done so, mother, and I am now so glad that it was left for that one to tell me. "

The boys came in, and were a little overwhelmed, even George, with the warmth of their brother's reception. Julia went straight to George, saying, "Now, sir, you belong to me; you are to be my dear youngest brother! What a row of handsome brothers I shall have— there! —there! "—with a kiss for each word.

George at first did not quite comprehend: "Julia, are you going to be Bart's wife? "

"Yes, " with a richer color.

"When? "

"Hush! That isn't a question for you to ask. " And she bent over him with another low sweet "hush, " that he understood.

Soon the Colonel and his sweet young wife came in, and they all came to know that Julia was one of them; and she knew what warm, true hearts had come so suddenly about her with their strong, steady tenderness.

Then, as the sun fell among the western tree tops, Julia said to Mrs. Ridgeley, "Now Arthur must drive me home; his other mother has not seen him; and to-morrow I will bring him to you. He is to remain with us, and we will come and go between our two homes for, I don't know how long; until he grows stout and strong, and has run through all the woods, and visited all the dear old places, and grows weary of us, and sighs for Blackstone, and all those horrid books. "

She took her happy place by his side in the carriage, after kissing them all, including Ed, and they drove leisurely away.

As they went, he told her gaily of the lonely walk, in darkness, when he last went over this road. The sketch brought new tears to the tender eyes at his side.

"Oh, Arthur! if you could have only known! if you had come to me for one moment. "

"Today could never have come, " he interrupted. "I like it as it is. How could I ever have had the beautiful revelation of your high and heroic qualities, Julia? And we could not have met as we did this morning. The very memory of that meeting equals the hope and blessedness of Heaven. "

Down past the quiet houses they rode; through bits of woods that still fringed parts of the road; down past the old saw mill; up over the hill, where they paused to look over the beautiful pond, full to its high banks; then to the State road, and south over the high hills, overlooking the little cemetery, towards which Bart looked tenderly.

"Not to-night, love, " said Julia; "their beautiful spirits see and love, and go with us. "

So in the twilight, and with a pensive and serene happiness, they passed up through the straggling village, Julia and her lover, to her own home.

It had somehow been made known that Bart would that evening arrive. His trunk had been received by the stage, at the stage house, and a group of curious persons were on the look out in front of Parker's, as they drove past. When Bart lifted his hat, they recognized and greeted him with a hearty cheer; which was repeated when the carriage passed the store. Bart was deeply touched.

"You see, " said the happy Julia, "that everybody loves you. "

"You see they greet us on your account, " he answered.

A little group was also at her father's gate, and as Bart sprang out, Julia's mother took him by both hands.

"So you have come at last, and will be one of us. "

Just how he answered, or how Julia alighted, he could never tell. This was the final touch and test, and if the whole did not vanish, he should certainly accept it all as real.

"What a sweet and wonderful little romance it all is, " said the happy mother; "and to happen to us here, in this new, wild, humdrum region! Who shall say that God does not order, and that heroism does not exist; and that faithful love is not still rewarded. "

"Mrs. Markham" —

"Call me mother! " said that lady; "I have long loved you, and thought of you as my son. "

"And your husband? " said Bart.

"Is here to answer for himself, " said the Judge, entering. He came forward and greeted Bart warmly.

"Judge Markham, " said Bart, holding each parent by a hand; "Julia and I met by accident this morning, at the place where we were sheltered a year ago. We found that no explanation was needed, and we there asked God to bless our love and marriage. Of course we may have taken too much for granted. "

"No, no! " said the Judge, warmly, placing Julia's hand within his. "We will now, and always, and ever, ask God to bless your love, and crown it with a true and sacred marriage. Such as ours has been, my love, won't we? "

"Certainly, " answered Mrs. Markham. "And we take him to our home and hearts as our true son. "

Then all knelt, and the father's voice in reverent prayer and thanksgiving, was for a moment lifted to the Great Father.

Later, they were quiet and happy, around a tea, or rather a supper table. But Bart toyed with his fork, and sparkled with happy, brilliant sallies. Julia watched him with real concern.

"Arthur, " she said, "I am a woman; and a woman likes to see even her lover eat. It is the mother part, isn't it, mamma? " blushing and laughing, "that likes to see children feed. Now he has not eaten a mouthful to-day; and I shall be anxious. "

"For that matter he dined on a gill of milk, and one ounce of honey yesterday, " said the Judge, "Don't you ever eat? "

"And I shall shock him; " said Julia, "he will soon find that I am only common vulgar flesh and blood, to be fed and nourished. "

"Don't fear, " said Bart; "I like a strong, healthy, deep chested woman, who can live and endure. I am not the least bit of a Byron. And now let me get used to this new heaven, into which you have just taken me; let my heart get steady, if it will, in its great happiness. Let me have some good runs in the woods, some good rows on the ponds, some hard gallops. Let me get tired, and I'll astonish you with a famine. "

"I shall be glad to see it, " said Julia.

There came pleasant talk of trifles, that only lay about on the surface, and near the great joy of their new happiness; and little pleasantries of the Judge. He asked Julia, "how she liked the moustache, suggesting that it might be in the way.

"I like it, " said Julia, "and it isn't a bit in the way. "

Then he referred to a certain other grave matter, and wanted to know when?

"That isn't for you to ask, Papa Judge—is it, mamma? "

CHAPTER LII.

FINAL DREAM LAND.

Later still, when the elders had left the lovers to each other, Bart found himself reclining on the sofa, with his head in Julia's lap. And those little rosy tipped fingers toyed caressingly with that coveted moustache, and were kissed for it, and went and did it again, and so on; and then tenderly with the long light brown wavy curls.

"Julia, these blessed moments of love and rest, though they run into days or weeks, will end. "

"Arthur" —reproachfully.

"Time will not stand and leave us to float, and come and go on a sweet shaded river of delight; sometime I must go out to show that I am not unworthy of you, to find, and to make. You shall have your own sweet way, and will, and yet you will also—will you not? —tell me when this happiness shall be lost in the greater, merely that I may do my man's part. "

"Arthur, I take you at your word. My will is that for two blessed months, of which this shall not be counted as one day, for it must stand forever apart, you shall say nothing of books, or wanting them; or of business, or cases, or location, but shall stay with us, our mothers and father, with me, and run, and ride, and hunt, and fish, and grow strong, and eat, and I will let you go, and alone, when you wish; and at the end of two months, I will tell you when. "

"And Arthur, " stooping low over him, "a young girl's heart and ways are curious, and not worth a man's knowing, or thought, perhaps. Let me know you, let me be acquainted with you, and I would like you to know me also, though it may not repay you; and let me grow to be your wife. We have such funny notions, such weak girl ways and thoughts. I have not had my lover a full day yet. A young girl wishes to be courted and sought, and made believe that she is supreme; and she likes to have her lover come at a set time, and sit and wait and think the clock has been turned back, and that he won't come, and yet he must come, at the moment; and she will affect to have forgotten it. She likes to be wooed with music, and flowers, and poetry, and to remain coy and only yield when her full heart had gone long before; and then to be engaged, and wear her ring, and be proud of her affianced, and to be envied—oh, it is a thousand, thousand times more to us than to you. It is our all, and we can enjoy it but once, and think what is lost out of the life of the young girl who has not enjoyed it at all. See, Arthur, what poor, petty, weak things we are, not worth the understanding, and not worth the winning, as we would be won. "

Arthur had started up, and glided to the floor, on his knees, had clasped his hands about her slender waist, and was looking earnestly and tenderly into her coy, half-averted face, as, half seriously and half in badinage, she made her plaint.

"Oh, Julia! "

"Nay, Arthur, I like it as it is. It was in your nature to have known me, and to have courted me in the old way; but it would have been poor and tame, and made up of a few faded flowers and scraps of verses; and think what I have had—a daring hero between me and a wild beast—a brave, devoted and passionate lover, who, in spite of scorn and rejection, hunted for me through night and tempest, to rescue me from death, who takes me up in his strong arms, carries me over a flood, and nourishes me back to life, and goes proudly away, asking nothing but the great boon of serving me. Oh! I had a thousand times rather have this! It is now a beautiful romance. But I am to have my ring, and"—

"Be my sweet and blessed sovereign lady; to be served and worshipped, and to hear music and poetry; whose word and wish is to be law in all the realm of love. "

"From which you are not to depart for two full months of thirty-one days each. "

Then she conducted him to the apartment in which we beheld her the night before.

"This, " pushing open the door, into the room, warm and sweet with the odor of flowers, "is your own special room, to be yours, always."

"Always? " a little plaintively.

"Always—until—until—I—we give you another. "

"Good night, Arthur. "

"Good night, Julia. "

She tripped down the hall, and turned her bright face to catch a kiss, and throw it back.

With a sweet unrest in her full heart, the young maiden on her couch, set herself to count up the gathered treasures of the wonderful day.

How was it? Did her riding skirt really get under her feet? Would he have caught her in his arms if she had not fallen? She thought he would.

And so she mused; and at last in slumber dreamed sweet maiden's dreams of love and heaven.

And Bart found himself in a marvellous forest, wandering with Julia, wondrous in her fresh and tender beauty, on through endless glades, amid the gush of bird-songs, and the fragrance of flowers.

And there in the dream land whence I called them, I leave them. Why should I awake them again? For them can another day so bright and happy ever dawn? I who love them, could have kept them for a bright brief space longer. I could have heard the sparkling voice of Bart, and the answering laugh of Julia—and then I should listen and not hear—look anxiously around and not see!

I part in real sorrow with these bright children of my fancy, sweet awakeners of old time memories, placed amid far off scenes, to win from others, tenderness and love if they may. And may they be remembered as forever lingering in perennial youth and love, in the land of dreams.

Lightning Source UK Ltd.
Milton Keynes UK
UKHW010645160421
382097UK00001B/37